Praise for *December Park*

"A complex and chilling tale of friends, family and the often murderous secrets that hide in the dark." —Robert R. McCammon

"Malfi is a man of many voices, a sort of literary version of Mel Blanc (the 'man of a thousand voices'), but all of his voices are captivating, though none of them quite the same. Horror and crime fans will find much to like here." —*Booklist*

"A frightening, thoroughly engaging read with a deeply moving series of narrative motifs running throughout . . . A triumph of suspense, an affectionate ode to adolescence and by far Ronald Malfi's strongest effort to date." —*Horror Novel Reviews*

"Malfi is a master at horror, and his expertise shines through in this thriller set in the small town of Harting Farms. Skillfully plotted with carefully placed clues, the novel progresses like a map leading to the exhilarating ending." —*RT Book Reviews*

"*December Park* is one of those books you can't put down." —HorrorNews.net

DECEMBER
PARK

RONALD MALFI

OPEN ROAD

INTEGRATED MEDIA

NEW YORK

For Grandpa, who led the charge
And for Madison—my daughter, my student, my teacher

This edition published in 2021 by Open Road Integrated Media, Inc.
180 Maiden Lane
New York, NY 10038
www.openroadmedia.com

CONTENTS

DECEMBER
PARK

BOOK ONE

WELCOME TO HARTING FARMS
(OCTOBER 1993–JANUARY 1994)

In the fall of 1993, a dark shadow fell over Harting Farms. Newspapers called him the Piper, like the minstrel of Brothers Grimm lore who lured all the children away. There were other darker names, too—names kids whispered throughout the halls of Stanton School and carved in the wooden chairs of the library like dirty, fearful secrets. The cafeteria rumbled with talk of escaped mental patients from Sheppard Pratt and lunatic mariners, lustful for child blood, who ported in Baltimore and found their way to our sleepy bayside hamlet.

In homeroom, Michael Sugarland drew pictures of werewolves with dripping fangs and claws like bayonets until Mr. Johnson, shaking his head and looking terminally exhausted, told him it was disrespectful of the missing. No one referred to the children as dead because none of them were found—not at first, anyway. They were the Missing, the Disappeared. The first few were even thought to be runaways.

But all that changed soon enough, and my friends and I were there to see it happen.

CHAPTER ONE
WINTER CAME EARLY THAT YEAR

W e stood at the intersection of Point and Counterpoint, cigarettes dangling from our mouths like we were serious about something but too cool to show it, and shivered against the wind. Farther up Counterpoint Lane, the rack lights of police cars painted the trees with intermittent red and blue lights.

It was early October, but a premature cold spell had overtaken the city, coming in off the Chesapeake and freezing the water around the fishing boats down at the docks. The flower stands along the highway had traded in their potted plants and bristling ferns in favor of Indian corn and shiny orange pumpkins. Though it was still too early in the season for snow, the sky looked haunted by it.

It had been Peter's idea to skip out after lunch period, and we'd gone directly to Solomon's Field to smoke cigarettes and skim rocks across Drunkard's Pond. Neighborhood kids called it that due to the derelicts who drank whiskey beneath the overpass of Solomon's Bend Road. Its actual name was Deaver's Pond, named after a former constable from the 1970s, according to my father, who knew about such things.

Peter, Scott, and I watched the conga line of police cars that had sidled up Counterpoint Lane. On the other side of the guardrail, the embankment dropped into the swell of the woods that buffered the street from the vast park below. These woods were known as Satan's Forest, and some people said they were haunted. Most of the trees had already shed their leaves, though what foliage remained burned an almost iridescent orange, as if the tops of the trees were on fire.

An ambulance idled on the shoulder, too, its lights off. Twin sawhorses outfitted with flashing orange lights prevented traffic from turning onto Counterpoint Lane. A lone police officer stood behind the sawhorses, gazing at the detouring traffic, a look of abject boredom on his face.

"We shouldn't hang around," I said. "It looks like something important is going on." Which meant my dad might be here, and I didn't want him to catch me loitering on the sidewalk, smoking.

"Do you think another car went down there?" Peter said. He stared at the twisted remains of the guardrail and the deep grooves in the mud made by skidding tires.

Two days earlier, a college student named Audrey MacMillan, driving home drunk from Shooter's Galley on Center Street, went off the road, through the guardrail, and down into the woods. She was lucky to have come away with nothing more serious than a broken leg. Before a tow truck could hoist the shattered vehicle out of the woods, the county sent some guys down there to cut away a few of the bigger trees. It had been a fiasco.

"I don't know," I said, "but they've got the road closed for a reason."

"No chance another car went down," Peter said. "I mean, two in one week?"

"I don't see any new skid marks or tire tracks," I said.

"Check your underwear," Peter said, smirking. He was the oldest by just a few months, though the extra weight he carried afforded him a youthful, almost cherubic look. His pale green eyes were almost always alert, their color and intensity complemented by a shock of unruly red hair he kept too long in the back. He had been my best friend since we had unwittingly been dumped together in the same sandbox over in the Palisades all those years ago.

The tented black hats of two more uniformed officers materialized on the other side of the guardrail. A fourth officer stepped out from one of the cruisers and leaned against the vehicle's hood, appearing cold even in his fur-lined jacket.

Scott nodded in the direction of the police cars. "Come on. Let's check it out."

"They might grab us for truancy," I said. "I'm already in the doghouse with my dad over that whole Nozzle Neck thing."

Mr. Naczalnik, otherwise known as Nozzle Neck due to his faucet-shaped profile and a neck like Ichabod Crane's, was my English teacher at Stanton School. Last month, I had failed to turn in an assignment, and Nozzle Neck, forever at the ready to make some poor student's life miserable, had wasted no time telephoning my father. I had been grounded for a week.

Peter checked his Casio. "School's been out for twenty minutes already."

In tandem, we crossed the intersection and walked up the slight incline of Counterpoint Lane toward the police vehicles and the ambulance.

When we reached one of the flashing sawhorses, the bored-looking cop approached. "Sorry, fellas. Street's closed."

"What happened?" Peter asked, trying to peer around the cop.

"You boys need to get out of the street. You can watch from the other side."

"Did someone drive off the road again?" I asked.

"No." He was a young cop, almost familiar. I glanced at his nametag but didn't recognize his name. "Come on, guys. Shake a leg."

"It's a free country," Peter said but not with any force. He was still busy trying to look over the cop's shoulder.

The cop arched one of his eyebrows. "Yeah? Well, you can be as free as you want across the street."

"Can't we just take a quick peek?" Peter pushed.

The young cop's eyes settled on me. "Get your friends back across the street, Angelo."

His use of my name didn't surprise me. My father was a detective with the Harting Farms Police Department. Policemen frequently recognized me, even if I hadn't met them before. "Come on, guys," I said and stepped onto the sidewalk.

"Thanks." The police officer nodded at me, then glanced at my friends. "You boys are too young to smoke." Then he checked his watch, perhaps recognizing that it was maybe too early for us to be so far from school already, and strutted across the street.

There was increasing commotion over there now, although most of it was on the other side of the busted guardrail and farther down the embankment. Two men in white smocks milled about, smoking cigarettes and talking to each other while gazing at their shoes. At one point they spoke briefly with a uniformed officer. Their languid movements and casual air made me think that nothing too urgent was happening on the other side of the guardrail.

"You know that guy?" Scott whispered, even though the cop was too far away to hear him.

I shook my head.

"It's freezing out here." Peter zipped up his coat and blew into his hands. "What are they doing, anyway? What's going on over there?"

I shrugged. For the first time, I was aware of the faint, tinny sounds of Metallica spilling from the headphones Scott had hanging around his neck.

Loyal to his surname, Scott Steeple was tall and slender and possessed the coveted body of a natural athlete. His features were subtle, handsome, his eyes introspective and haunted. Having just turned fifteen one month earlier, Scott was the youngest of our group. He should have been in the grade below ours, but his academic prowess had enabled him to skip second grade. Thus, fate had dropped him in the empty desk beside me in Mrs. Brock's third grade class, consequently forging a friendship between us.

"You guys going down to the docks tonight?" Peter asked. He was pacing, his hands in his pockets, sometimes pausing to balance on one foot while the other hovered half an inch off the ground.

"I guess," Scott said.

"Angie?"

"I don't know, man," I said. "What time are you heading over?"

"Maybe around nine."

"I guess it depends if my dad's home or not. I've got that new curfew."

"But it's Friday," Peter said.

"You know how my dad is." Generally, I was allowed out until eleven o'clock on weekends, but since the disappearances, my father had cut my curfew back an hour. If everyone was getting together at nine, it left me precious little time to hang out. I wondered if it would be worth it.

Peter frowned. "Dude, you gotta come. Sugarland's gonna sink that stupid cow, remember?"

"Yeah, I know."

"Look," Scott said, taking a single step off the curb. "They're coming up."

More heads emerged from behind the slope of the embankment, rising like buoys on a gray sea, and I immediately felt both excited and dismayed. The officers leading the pack were the only ones conveying any sense of urgency; they moved quickly ahead of the rest and dispersed along Counterpoint Lane, presumably to make sure no vehicles disobeyed the roadblock. Two of them turned their heads in unison and looked straight at my friends and me. If they were considering shooing us away, these plans were aborted once the full surge of officers, so dense in their numbers that I couldn't count them all without losing my place, joined them.

A number of men wore monochromatic suits and thin black neckties. Detectives. Once again, I wondered with some trepidation if my father was among them. . . .

"What are. . . ?" Peter took another step in their direction, but we were still too far away to make out the important details. "What are they carrying? You see that, Angie?"

"Yeah," I said. "I see it."

It was long, white. It was a sheet. It was something wrapped in a sheet. My stomach dropped. I had watched enough TV to know what I was looking at.

"Oh, goddamn," Peter said, his voice quavering. "That's a person."

The body was carried on a steel gurney, the gurney's legs retracted, the whole thing covered by a plain white sheet. One of the uniformed officers walked with one hand pressed to the center of the sheet, keeping it from billowing in the wind, even though it was strapped down.

A body.

They brought the gurney around the opposite side of the ambulance, temporarily disappearing from our view. When they reappeared at the rear of the ambulance, they had rearranged their positions.

Unable to pry my eyes from the scene, I noticed the officer who had kept his hand pressed to the center of the sheet was no longer there. And as if my observation directly invoked the ire of fate, an icy slipstream of wind barreled across the escarpment, rattling the trees like party favors and kicking up whirlwinds of sand and dead leaves.

One corner of the sheet ballooned with wind like the sail of a great ship. Then the loose flap of sheet flipped over, exposing an emaciated, graying female profile, replete with the wet, matted net of black hair tangled with leaves, the hint of a bruised arm, the flank striated with ribs, and the swell of one tiny white breast.

It was the first dead body I'd ever seen, and it was strangely unreal. The mind-numbing barrage of fake blood and guts my friends and I digested each weekend watching horror movies at the Juniper somehow felt more authentic than this.

The head was turned slightly to the left, and I made out what could only be described as a bloodied dent on the right side of her scalp. That side of her head looked caved in, her right eye winking just below the unnatural concave of flesh.

"Holy shit," Scott uttered. Apparently, he had seen it, too.

The paramedics were clumsy covering the body back up. They rushed too quickly to do it and fumbled with the sheet. For a second there was a bit of tug-of-war before the sheet was replaced over the dead girl's head. One of the officers even tucked the sheet beneath her, securing it.

To my left, Scott stared across the road, his headphones providing a rather discordant soundtrack to the moment. Peter stood just slightly ahead of us, the wings of his coat beating in the gathering wind, his hands stuffed into the too-tight pockets of his jeans. He'd seen it, too.

No one said a word. We watched as they stowed the body into the back of the ambulance. Everyone moved with incredible slowness. It seemed inappropriate. The discovery of a dead body in the woods should not elicit such lethargy. It was fake, all of it.

"The Piper," Scott whispered.

"No." I still couldn't comprehend any of it. And I couldn't shake the dead girl's visage from my mind. I feared I would see it in my sleep tonight. "They've never found any of the Piper's victims. Anyway, there might not even be a Piper."

"There's a Piper," Scott said with unwavering certainty.

"Do you think it's anyone we know?" Peter asked. "You guys hear of anyone else gone missing?"

I shook my head. But of course he couldn't see me because he was watching the paramedics start up the ambulance.

A cloud of smoke belched from the ambulance's exhaust. I realized I was waiting for the sirens to come on, but they never did. Of course they didn't. Why would they? What was the hurry now? Yet for whatever reason, I wanted them to hurry. It seemed disrespectful to whoever was under that sheet for these policemen and paramedics to move so slowly.

"Did you guys get a good look?" Peter went on. "Did you recognize her, Angie?"

"I don't think so. It's hard to tell. Her face wasn't . . ." But I didn't need to finish the thought. Her face had been broken, and Peter and Scott had seen it just as clearly as I had.

"I wonder if it was someone from school," Peter said, finally turning around. His cheeks were rosy from the cold. His eyes gleamed. "You think she could be from Stanton?"

"I haven't heard of anyone else having gone missing," I told him.

"She was young," Scott said. I registered a twinge of disbelief in his voice. "Not a grown-up, I mean. Did you guys see her?"

"Yes," I said. "I saw her. I saw her."

"She could be from school," Peter said. "I didn't recognize her but she could have been . . ."

Too many cops were staring at us now. With all the commotion over, we were no longer curious onlookers. In our canvas army jackets with Nirvana and Metallica patches sewn on the sleeves, we were burgeoning troublemakers.

"Let's get out of here," I said.

We hoofed it down Counterpoint against the wind. Skipping out on tonight's get-together down at the docks suddenly didn't sound all that bad. Just imagining the freezing wind riding in off the black waters of the Chesapeake Bay caused something deep within the center of my body to clench up.

That caved-in side of the head, that unnatural creasing of the right side of her face. Did I really see what I thought I saw?

I trembled.

In collective silence, we sought refuge from the cold inside the bus stop portico at the end of the block. Scott changed tapes in his Walkman, and Peter distributed fresh cigarettes. Smoking, we watched the traffic on Governor Highway. Across the street, the two- and three-story concrete buildings looked like pencil drawings in the gray and fading afternoon. Multicolored vinyl flags fluttered above OK Used Kars, the half-empty car lot riddled with potholes.

Farther along the road, the lights of The Bagel Boutique abruptly went dark, their business done for the day. I'd worked there last summer, dragging myself from bed at four o'clock in the morning to twist dough into rings, dump the rings into a boiling vat, and slide the boiled rings into a six-hundred-degree oven. Even though I wore rubber gloves, the heat was intense enough to cause my fingernails to rise off my fingertips. It was an ungodly enterprise, particularly for a slacker like me.

"What do you think happened to her?" Scott said. "Someone did that to her. Someone killed her."

"Maybe Lucas Brisbee did it," Peter suggested.

"Who's that?" I said.

"You didn't hear about Lucas Brisbee?" Peter said. He held his cigarette, examining the ember while the wind coaxed water from his eyes.

"I heard," said Scott.

I leaned against the portico. "Who's Lucas Brisbee?" I repeated.

"Amanda Brisbee's older brother," Peter said. "He graduated like five years ago from Stanton. You know Amanda, right?"

"Sure," I said. Amanda Brisbee was a grade lower than us. She'd been on the girls' field hockey team her freshman year until she shaved the hair on one side of her head, started wearing black nail polish, and fell in with the wrong crowd. I knew her mostly through mutual acquaintances—I happened to be friends with the wrong crowd—though I'd never said a single word to her.

"Check this out," Peter said, and I could detect from his faint grin that he was happy to tell the story. "For the past month, Lucas had been coming to our American history class to talk about the Gulf War. He stopped in every Wednesday wearing his camouflage jumpsuit thingy to talk about what it was like over in Iraq."

"He spoke once in Mrs. Burstrom's class, too," Scott added. "It was bizarre. He wore one of those pith helmets, like they wear on *M*A*S*H*, and you could see he was sweating to death in the thing."

"Well," Peter continued, "he apparently showed up this Wednesday, right on schedule, walking across the football field from the senior parking lot, done up in his whole uniform. Only this time he had his rifle slung over his shoulder."

"Get the hell out of here," I said.

"I'm dead serious."

"Swear to God," Scott chimed in.

"Mr. Gregg was out with a gym class when it happened," Peter said. "He told everyone to go back inside, then went up to talk with Lucas. They argued for a bit, and Mr. Gregg actually had to wrestle him to the ground. Some cops showed up, and they took the dude away."

"Who told you this?" I asked.

"Jen and Michelle Wyatt. They were in the gym class and saw Lucas walking down the football field before Gregg told them to get inside. They said they could see the rifle on his back and that he marched toward them like a Nazi."

"That can't be true," I said, looking out across the highway. A cool darkness had settled over the city. Lampposts came on. Shopwindows on the opposite side of the highway glowed like tiny electric rectangles. At the next intersection, I watched the taillights of automobiles simmering at the foot of a traffic light.

"Like hell it isn't," Peter said.

"I would have heard about it on the news," I said. "Or at least from my dad."

Peter shrugged. "Does your dad tell you everything? And besides, maybe Brisbee hasn't, like, been charged with anything yet."

"Maybe the gun wasn't loaded," Scott suggested.

"Weirdest part is he apparently never went to Iraq," Peter said. "The dude never even enlisted in the frigging military. He worked as a mechanic rotating tires and changing oil and shit over in Woodlawn since graduation. The son of a bitch made the whole thing up."

"Come on," I said.

"It's true," Scott added, nodding. "I heard it, too."

"Can you believe that shit?" Peter said, turning away. He'd smoked his cigarette down to the filter. "Guy was nuts, and he's been giving lectures at our high school for the past month."

A car sped by and honked at us. I didn't recognize the driver.

"Maybe nobody killed her. Maybe she died from an accident." Yet even as I spoke those words I didn't believe them. I kept seeing the way her head had been smashed and the sallow fish-belly hue of her skin.

"I guess so," Peter said, but he didn't sound convinced, either.

Scott glanced at his watch. "It's getting late."

"Yeah," Peter said, tossing his cigarette butt on the ground.

I flipped my jacket collar up around my neck. "I'll catch you guys later. I gotta stop by the deli for my grandmother."

"You want us to come with?"

"Nah, I'm cool. Thanks, though."

"Hey." Peter thumped me on the forearm. "Come out tonight, all right?"

I sighed.

"Maybe your dad will give you an extension on your curfew," Peter said. "It's not like we're gonna stay out all night."

"It'll be fun," Scott added.

Stuffing my hands into my pockets, I said, "I'll see."

"Cool." Peter grinned at me. Then he turned and shoved Scott out onto the sidewalk. They waited for a break in traffic before hurrying across Governor Highway. I lost sight of them as they disappeared among the shadows of an unlit parking lot.

I walked parallel to the highway until I hit the crosswalk, then waited for the traffic lights to change. Pastore's Deli was a small family-run shop at the end of a strip mall. It stood across the street from the Generous Superstore, the grandiose supermarket whose slogan was *Convenience is King!* Even so, my grandmother had been patronizing Pastore's since I was a little boy, and I maintained fond memories of Mr. Pastore feeding me slices of Boar's Head bologna and wedges of stinky cheese as my grandmother did her shopping.

The store was usually empty, but on this evening, I noted a bit of a commotion outside. Several adults loitered by their cars in the parking lot, talking animatedly. My head down, I shuffled past them and entered the deli.

"Hello, Angelo." Mr. Pastore peered at me over the bifocals perched on the edge of his nose. He was a dark-skinned old man with tufts of white hair over his ears. A man I did not recognize stood in front of the counter, and it seemed that my arrival had interrupted their conversation.

"Hi, Mr. Pastore," I said, unzipping my coat. The little shop was sweltering, due to an overworked space heater mounted above the doorway.

At the back of the store, I grabbed a loaf of sliced Italian bread, then surveyed the rack of candy that lined the wall. Pastore's always had the good candy, the stuff that was generally difficult to find: Astro Pops, giant Sugar Daddies, shoelace licorice and black licorice buttons, Jujubes, candy dots on rolls of white paper, wax lips, wax bottles filled with syrupy liquid, candy whistles, peanut brittle, Ocean City taffy, exotic jelly beans. After some deliberation, I selected a giant Sugar Daddy and a pack of Trident gum to mask the smell of cigarettes on my breath.

I walked to the counter, where I knew Mr. Pastore would have the rest of my grandmother's order waiting for me.

Mr. Pastore talked in a low voice to the man I did not know. At one point, he glanced at me from over the man's shoulder and forced a smile.

The man, who was dressed in a navy-blue sweater and chinos, stepped aside so I could put the bread and candy on the counter.

Mr. Pastore winked at me, then fished around beneath the counter until he produced several packages of cold colds, already sliced and wrapped up in wax paper. "I read in the *Caller* that you won first place in their creative writing competition," he said as he rang up the items. "That's wonderful, Angelo. Congratulations."

"Thanks."

"Will they be publishing the winning story?"

"Well, they were supposed to, but they said it was too long," I said. "But they mailed me a check for fifty bucks."

"Fantastic!" Mr. Pastore pushed his bifocals up the bridge of his nose, then read the totaled amount on the cash register.

I handed over a twenty and waited for my change.

Beside me, the man in the navy-blue sweater tapped his foot nervously. I turned and looked at him. Our eyes locked. He had small, dark eyes that appeared equally as nervous as his tapping foot sounded. A second later, he looked away.

Undoubtedly sensing my unease, Mr. Pastore smiled wearily at me. "There's been some commotion down by the park tonight. They've got the intersection of Counterpoint shut down. Maybe you've seen the police cars."

"Well, yeah," I said, my mouth suddenly dry. The image of the dead girl with her head staved in flew in front of my eyes again. I couldn't shake it. All of a sudden, I could feel nothing but the volcanic heat radiating out of the space heater above the shop's door.

"People are worried something might have happened to someone," Mr. Pastore continued. That false smile was still firmly rooted to his face, yet the tone of his voice was grave. "People are worried it might be one of the . . . well, you know . . ."

I opened my mouth to say that I had seen the police carry a dead girl out of the woods on a gurney, but then I shut it. I looked at the man in the navy-blue sweater. What if he was the father of the dead girl? The notion struck me like a zap from an electrical outlet. Did I really want to be the one to break the news to him?

Mr. Pastore handed me my change, which I stuffed into the pocket of my coat. I snatched the bag of groceries off the counter and thanked him as I moved quickly to the door.

"Angelo?" Mr. Pastore said. When I turned around to face him, he said, "Maybe it's best you hurry straight home tonight, yeah? No dillydallying."

Temporarily unable to speak, I nodded.

"Good boy," he said.

I opened the door and ditched out into the encroaching darkness.

CHAPTER TWO
THE SHALLOWS

It was dark by the time I arrived home. There were lights on in the old Dunbar house next door and a car parked in the driveway. The new neighbors had arrived a few days ago, but I'd yet to lay eyes on them. There hadn't been a moving truck at the house yet, so I assumed they still hadn't fully moved in.

It was supposed to be my father's night off, but his unmarked police car wasn't parked in the driveway, and I wondered if he'd been called out to work because of the dead girl. Before going inside, I stomped mud from my sneakers against the doorjamb of the Cape Cod I'd lived in all my life.

Inside, I was greeted by a blast of hot air and the welcoming aroma of my grandmother's pasta fagioli simmering on the stove. There was something eternally comforting about entering a house infused with the aroma of Italian cooking. Kicking off my sneakers in the foyer, I felt my lips and the tips of my fingers tingling as they warmed up.

I went down the hall and poked my head into the den to observe my grandfather, engulfed in the flickering blue light of the television, snoring in his Barcalounger.

In the kitchen, I dumped the groceries onto the table, then shrugged off my jacket and folded it over a chair. My grandmother stood before the stove, conducting an orchestra of steaming, bubbling pots and pans, looking like wallpaper in her floral housedress, her silver hair petrified into that steel-colored dome fashionable among women over sixty-five.

"Where's Dad?" I said.

"Well," said my grandmother, "that's a fine how-do-you-do."

"Sorry." I kissed her cheek on my way to the refrigerator. "Smells good."

"Is your grandfather asleep?"

"He's watching TV," I lied.

"Asleep," she muttered. "So then he'll be up tossing and turning all night in bed."

I popped the tab on a can of Pepsi, eliciting a look of disapproval from my grandmother. For whatever reason and with no documentation to back up her hypothesis, she firmly believed all sodas caused cancer. "So where's Dad?"

"He got a call."

"Was it about a girl?"

"A girl?"

"Like, for work."

"He doesn't tell me anything, that son of mine. And I don't ask about his work, Lord knows." She stirred the pasta fagioli with a big wooden spoon. The pot was as big as a cauldron. Beside it, chicken cutlets spat and sizzled in a pan of vegetable oil. "What girl are you talking about?"

"Cops found some girl in the woods behind Counterpoint Lane. Me and the guys saw it on our way back from school."

"She was lost?"

"She was dead."

"Oh, Madonn'!" She set her spoon down on an oven mitt. "What happened?"

"I don't know. Maybe some kind of accident." But I knew it wasn't an accident, not the way she'd been naked and sour-looking beneath that sheet. Not the way her head had been smashed in. For the first time, I wondered how long she'd been in those woods before the police found her.

"Was she from around here?" my grandmother asked.

"I don't know who she is. Or was," I corrected.

"What a horrible thing."

"Did Dad say what time he'd be home tonight?"

"I told you, he doesn't tell me anything, that man. Now go wash up for supper, will you? And wake your grandfather. He fell asleep in front of the television again. I know he did. Don't lie for him."

We ate, accompanied by the lament of my grandfather who, for as long as I could remember, found fault with just about everyone and everything on the face of the planet. Recently, it had gotten so bad that my grandmother forbade him to watch the television news or read a newspaper, as the injustices depicted therein were enough to send the old man on a rambling monologue of such creative profanity, it would have inspired an entire regiment of longshoremen to take notes.

In August of 1990, after President Bush dispatched American troops into Saudi Arabia—my older brother, Charles, among them—my grandfather sifted through his own memorabilia from the Second World War. Our family made nervous jokes about his determination, at the age of seventy-eight, to reenlist alongside my brother. Yet my grandfather, as steadfast as he was old, was disillusioned in an altogether different fashion.

The collected relics from his time served in the South Pacific consisted of, among other things, several boxes of medals, an ashtray made of ammunition shells of varying sizes assembled to suggest a miniature B-29 Superfortress, and, perhaps most impressive, a samurai sword appropriated by my grandfather from the dead body of a Japanese soldier killed in New Guinea.

"I shot him dead right out of a tree," my grandfather had told me on more than one occasion, "and this sword fell with him. In fact, it stuck in the dirt, blade-first, and quivered there like a tuning fork."

The sword was impressive, shiny and handsome with colorful jewels embedded in the hilt, complete with an intricate foreign insignia of a dragon with the head of a tiger etched into the scabbard.

For a number of years after the war, my grandfather had received a barrage of letters from an attorney in New York—whom my grandfather was quick to deem a "shyster sympathizer"—representing the Takahashi family making request after request for the return of the sword to the family of the dead Japanese soldier. It was a family heirloom, and the Takahashis would gladly pay any asking price for its safe return. I'd seen the letters, typed on fancy law-office stationery with a Manhattan return address, and they were polite and sympathetic toward my grandfather. Yet my grandfather refused to even entertain their offers.

Finally, having resigned to the fact that my grandfather was a stubborn old mule of a man, the Takahashi family delivered one final letter to him. I'd seen this letter as well. All it contained were the directions for the appropriate cleaning, storage, and maintenance of the samurai sword. If they couldn't have it back, at least they could ensure that it would be properly taken care of.

However, it was not the sword or the other items of similar interest my grandfather dug out of the garage on that day in August. What he produced was a worn photo album with a leather cover, held together by rubber bands. It was filled with black-and-white photographs from the war and the year he spent as a lifeguard in Australia. He took the album to the yard and tore up the photographs and spread them like confetti into one of the metal trash cans.

At the time and in my naïveté, I attempted to ascribe some symbolic meaning to this humble act but could not, for the life of me, understand what it could be. I had no other choice but to ask my grandfather why he'd destroyed his photographs. With the practicality of a mathematician, he responded that the nightly recaps of the rising tension in the Middle East on the news merely reminded him that he had old junk stowed away in the garage and he was well overdue in getting rid of it all. It was nothing more symbolic than spring cleaning.

Seated around the dinner table, we ate while the television droned on in the den. My grandmother had parted the curtains over the kitchen windows in case my father returned home from work. As was the pattern, upon seeing the headlights of his sedan turn in to the driveway, my grandmother would rise and fill my father's plate, timing its placement on the table perfectly with the sound of the front door opening in the foyer. On these nights my father would wash his hands in the kitchen sink, then join us for dinner, still in his shirtsleeves and necktie.

Since my father rarely returned home before dawn on the evenings when he was called out, he would not be coming home in time for dinner this evening, yet the curtains remained parted and my grandmother remained vigilant, as she was not one to break tradition.

"How was school?" my grandmother asked.

"It was okay."

"Anything interesting happen?"

Since nothing interesting ever happened, I relayed the story Peter had told me about Lucas Brisbee coming to school wearing fatigues and carrying a rifle, only to be tackled in the school parking lot by the gym teacher.

My grandmother shook her head. "Why would someone do such a thing?"

"It happens all the time, Flo," said my grandfather. "It's nothing new. All you hear about is kids taking guns to school, shooting up classrooms, and building bombs in their garages."

"It wasn't like that," I said.

"Probably saying he was shell-shocked from the war," my grandfather went on.

"But he wasn't in the war. That's part of the story. He was living over in Woodlawn the whole time." Despite my incredulity while listening to Peter tell the tale, I found I had not only relayed the story with as much excitement and authenticity as I could muster, but I suddenly believed it wholeheartedly.

"Like in Vietnam," my grandfather continued, not hearing me. "That whole Agent Orange fiasco. Everybody's always looking for an out, looking to blame someone else for their problems. Don't you think there was enough to complain about in the South Pacific? But you don't hear me complaining, do you? And if you can't blame the war, you blame your parents, your upbringing. Or the music you listen to."

"But he wasn't in the war," I reiterated. "He—"

"Who?" My grandfather drew his wiry eyebrows together. He looked like someone suddenly asked to solve a complex math problem. "Who's that?"

"The guy who came to my school."

"What guy is this?" he said, though the corner of his mouth curled into a smile. He had been playing with me after all.

I laughed and said, "Forget about it."

Headlights rolled down Worth Street, which prompted my grandmother to spring up from her chair and stare out the window. She continued to watch even after it was evident it was not my father.

"I'm going out tonight," I said finally.

"Oh? Where's that?" asked my grandmother.

"Peter's house." It was a lie. I didn't like lying to my grandparents, but I couldn't tell them that we were all going down to the docks to watch Michael Sugarland sink the homecoming cow.

"You want me to give you a ride?" my grandfather offered. He was always concerned about me walking around at night, even before the disappearances.

"That's okay. I'll take my bike."

Despite the fact that I was fifteen and a half, which meant I was old enough to have my learner's permit, my father had made the executive decision that I was still too irresponsible to have anything of the sort. I knew I faced a whole new battle once I turned sixteen and was legally eligible for my driver's license.

My grandmother retrieved the pot of coffee that had been percolating for some time now. She set about filling two mugs while I carried my plate to the sink and washed my hands.

"Dress warm," she said. "It's cold out tonight."

"I will."

"And please," she said, the tone of her voice slightly different, "don't forget your curfew."

"I won't."

I showered and dressed hastily in jeans, a Nirvana T-shirt, and a hooded pullover. I was of less-than-average height and possessed the body of a runner, though I was not a natural athlete. My features were dark and classically Mediterranean, not in a movie star way but in the contemplative, brooding fashion one typically associates with the juvenile delinquents in movies from the 1950s.

Adults regarded me as rigidly courteous, well-meaning, and considerate yet slacking on my potential. These adults were always calling me handsome, but I was never able to see it. My nose was too big, my hair stiff and wavy when short but greasy and disobedient when long, as it was now. My hands were small, and I'd once had a doctor who'd seemed surprised when I told him I could play the guitar.

Despite my awareness of having descended from a line of full-blooded Italian Americans, it never occurred to me that I was any different than the majority of the kids at Stanton School or in all of Harting Farms until last year. This realization struck me just before school let out for the summer as I went around to a number of the local businesses filling out applications for a summer job.

At a frame shop on Canal Street, Mr. Berke, the potbellied proprietor with a deeply grooved face, had told me to sit in his office with him while he reviewed my application. He grumbled to himself the entire time, and at one point I even saw his eyebrows creep toward his hairline.

"Is there something wrong?" I had asked, sweating in my nervousness.

"Yeah." He set the application down on his desk, which sat between us in the cramped little office. He pointed to the nationality section. "You checked the box for Caucasian."

"Doesn't that mean white?"

"Yeah. But you're Italian, ain't you?"

"Well, yeah . . ." My gaze flitted down to the application. Perhaps there was a box for Italian American I had missed? But no, there was no such option. When I looked up at Mr. Berke, I couldn't read his expression.

"This would be you here," he said, jabbing a finger on the box beside the word *Other*. "See, you're an Other." His smile was humorless and caused the grooves in his face to deepen. "See that? See how we cleared that up?"

"Oh," I said.

When I had gone back to the frame store a week later to check on the status of my application, Mr. Berke gave me that same humorless smile and informed me that he had decided he wouldn't be hiring any summer help this year after all. Of course, I took him at his word, which was why I was confused when, weeks later, I learned that Billy Meyers, who sat next to me in homeroom, was working there.

Briefly, I had considered telling my dad what had happened. But then I thought I would be more uncomfortable relaying the story to my father than I had been sitting across from Mr. Berke in his stuffy little office, so I let the issue drop.

I dug my Nikes out of the closet and laced them up while I sat on my bed. All around me, my bedroom was devoted to my passions, the walls sheeted in posters of old Universal movie monsters and the more modern psychopaths such as Jason Voorhees and Freddy Krueger. A glow-in-the-dark bust of the Creature from the Black Lagoon stood atop my dresser, surrounded by *Star Wars* figures that appeared to be protecting it as if it were some holy idol.

There were a few videocassettes piled underneath my nightstand, movies like *Jaws*, *Gremlins*, and *Raiders of the Lost Ark*, along with some old Springsteen record albums and cassette tapes. A Fender acoustic guitar leaned against the wall in one corner beside a poster of John Lennon wearing his signature circular glasses.

But mostly my bedroom was a shrine to books. There were lots of Stephen King, Dean Koontz, Robert McCammon, Peter Straub, and Ray Bradbury, since horror stories were my favorite. Yet there were more than just a few classics among the pulp, like Daniel Defoe's *Robinson Crusoe*, Victor Hugo's *The Hunchback of Notre-Dame*, Stoker's *Dracula* alongside Shelley's *Frankenstein*, and a handsome collection of Robert Louis Stevenson novels in hardcover.

On my desk sat an old Olympia De Luxe typewriter, its sea-foam green and ecru metal body like the two-tone chassis of a 1950s Chevrolet. A few of the keys stuck from time to time, and the letter *O* had a tendency to punch holes in the paper if struck too hard, but the De Luxe was my most prized possession. I loved it more than my bike.

Set neatly beside the typewriter was the recent article from the Harting Farms *Caller*, the local paper, where my name was printed in stark bold font as the winner of the newspaper's creative writing contest. Paper-clipped to the article was a manila envelope addressed to me, and inside the envelope was a check for fifty bucks. Next to the newspaper article was the thirteen-page single-spaced winning story titled "Fishing for Chessie." It concerned two brothers living along the Chesapeake Bay who decide to try and catch Chessie, the Chesapeake's version of the Loch Ness Monster. The boys never catch the beast, though at the end of the story, they see its giant gray humps rise out of the water.

It was a simple enough story and was apparently just what the *Caller* had been hoping to read, but the one I'd wanted to submit was a horror story called "Fear." It was about a boy who learns an alternate reality exists between the first and second floors of his house. The entrance to this alternate realm is accessible through a linen closet, and the boy, who is the hero of the story, learns that there is a monster who occupies this realm and feeds on young children from his neighborhood. Eventually, the boy confronts and destroys the monster.

I had thought it was perfect and had handed it off to my grandmother with a sense of real pride and achievement.

While she had proclaimed that it was very well written, she opined that the *Caller* was probably hoping to receive submissions of a more palatable nature. "No dead children, in other words," she'd said but not unkindly.

My desk drawers were filled with such stories about werewolves and vampires, ghosts and goblins. Some were shameless rip-offs of other stories I'd read, though I emulated the plot and style in order to learn how the author had been so effective in transporting the reader. Other stories were wholly mine, salvaged from the depths of my own creativity. Last spring, I had purchased the newest edition of the *Writer's Market,* and only recently had I begun sticking Post-it notes on some of the pages, where the entries detailed the submission guidelines for various genre magazines.

I wanted more than anything to be a writer.

By the time I was ready to leave the house, my grandparents had retired to the den to watch television. I kissed them both on the tops of their heads before slipping out into the night. I had a cigarette between my lips before I reached the end of the flagstone walk. I fished my dirt bike out from the dense wall of ivy that clung to the side of our house and hopped on, my feet quick to pedal, my backside never touching the seat.

It was jarringly cold. The residential streets were dark and poorly lit, and there were hardly any cars on the road. Deciding to take the shortcut instead of sticking to the main roads, I rolled up the Mathersons' driveway, cut across their lawn, and whipped through a stand of hemlock trees that loomed tall and dark against the backdrop of night.

A moment later, I was thudding along a dirt path through the woods, my bike rattling while my teeth chattered. The woods here weren't too dense, letting the occasional porch lights shine through the thicket so that I felt like Magellan being guided by stars. I'd used this shortcut an inexhaustible number of times in the past, typically at night, but it was never the same. The woods were always moving, always shifting.

I cleared the trees at a fine pace, bursting out onto an open field. It was mostly scrubland and unkempt bluegrass, but it made for tough negotiation on a weary, tire-bald dirt bike. To the east, the field sloped gradually down into a small valley surrounded by more woods. A small white farmhouse, abandoned for as long as I'd known it, sat in the center of this valley, obscured on this night by a heavy veil of mist. All I could make out was the light of the solitary streetlamp on the edge of the property, boring an eerie pinpoint of yellow illumination through the fog.

My friends and I called it the Werewolf House, because it looked just like the run-down cottage in a werewolf movie we'd seen a few years ago at the Juniper.

Beyond the Werewolf House was the Butterfield homestead. After a heavy snowfall, the Butterfield family farm accommodated countless neighborhood children hefting colorful plastic sleds and chucking snowballs packed frozen with ice at one another. But it was fall now, and that meant the farm would be crowded with pumpkins, squash, Indian corn, cider in unlabeled plastic jugs, and a grand assortment of fruits and vegetables.

There were Holsteins, massive lazy things, at the far end of the property, and if your fists were packed with reeds, you could approach them and feed them through the slats in their pens, their purple mucus-coated tongues lolling from their steaming mouths to wrap around the reeds like the tentacle of an octopus. While they ate, you could put your palms against their smooth-haired flanks and feel the heat radiating from them.

I pumped my legs harder, the reeds whipping against my shins, my face down against the freezing wind. The cold caused tears to burst from my eyes, and wind shear caused them to stream along my temples where they froze. Once I cleared the thickest of the reeds and could see the dim sodium glimmer of the streetlamps up ahead through the thinning fog, I knew I could let up on the pedaling without fear that my tires and chain would catch in the tall grass and jerk me to a sudden halt.

A pair of headlights appeared off to my left, maybe one hundred yards away. An instant later I heard the coughing growl of the vehicle as it sped toward me. At first I thought nothing of it. It wasn't unusual for people to come off-roading in this field, particularly at night. Instead, I focused my attention on the glowing specks of the streetlamps along the road ahead of me. The reeds receded, giving way to frozen, ribbed dirt. It was like riding over a giant rib cage.

The pickup swerved, and I lost sight of its headlamps in my peripheral vision. Yet I still heard its engine, a bit louder than it had been a moment before. I didn't realize that the vehicle was closing in on me until its headlights forced my shadow to stretch out on the cold black earth ahead of me. I thought I could feel the heat from the headlights across my back.

I chanced a glance over my shoulder. It was a pickup all right, and its driver was not concerned with spinning donuts in the field. The truck was directly behind me about twenty yards away and quickly closing the distance. Crazily, I heard Mr. Pastore, telling me to head straight home and no dillydallying.

I faced forward again, my legs pumping like machinery, my breath wheezing up my throat. I swore I could hear, even over the growl of the truck's engine, the reeds whipping against the massive front grille and the tires biting into the solid, frozen earth, crushing stones into powder.

I was nearly to the street. For some ridiculous reason, I associated reaching the street with home base in a game of tag, until it occurred to me with a pang of hopelessness that pickups went faster on paved roads.

The driver of the pickup revved the engine. Despite the cold, I felt sweat bead my forehead and immediately freeze.

The streetlamps grew closer. Through the fog, I made out the cantilevered peaks of the nearest houses, pointed and triangular like the silhouette of a distant mountain range.

I was certain of it now: I could feel the heat of the truck breathing down my neck, could see the particles of dust and debris the tires kicked up floating in the headlights' illumination. I thought, too, that I could feel the bits and pieces of tiny stones flung at the backs of my legs.

Then a blast from the horn sent me reeling. I jerked the handlebars, and my front tire thumped over a groove in the packed earth. Before I knew what had happened, I was thrown from my bike and rolling in the dirt.

The pickup shuddered to a stop no more than five feet from me. I saw steam rising from the grille, smelled the burning rubber of the tires. Something hissed, simmered, clicked. Frozen with fear, I only stared up at the vehicle as the driver opened the door and the dome light brought into relief the impression of my best friend, Peter Galloway, hysterical with laughter.

"That," he said, hanging from the cab of the truck, "was priceless. Holy shit. I didn't know you could ride that fast. I bet you thought I was some lunatic, huh?"

"Would I have been wrong?" I said, standing up and slapping the filth from my pants. There was a tear in the left knee. "Jerk-off. What the fuck are you doing, anyway? Is that your stepdad's truck?"

Still chuckling, he climbed down from the cab and went over to my bike. With the toe of one sneaker, he lifted the handlebars out of the dirt until he was able to grab them without bending over. "Surprise, surprise. Got my license yesterday after school."

"No shit? That's awesome."

Together we hoisted my bike into the bed of his stepfather's pickup, then climbed into the cab, slamming the doors in unison. He had the heat blasting and Temple of the Dog playing low on the tape deck.

I wasted no time pressing my palms against the vents to resurrect the feeling in my numbed fingers. I was still out of breath, my heart still racing. "I can't believe you're driving," I said. Then added, "I can't believe your stepdad let you have the truck."

"I know, right?" Peter turned the truck onto the street. We were the only set of headlights in the thickening fog. "I was going to call and tell you. I figured I'd pick you up."

"Ah, but then you thought it would be more fun to scare the shit out of me and practically run me over in the process."

Peter laughed.

"Besides," I said, "I wasn't sure I was gonna come. But my dad got called out to work."

"Because of that girl?" he said.

"I don't know. Maybe. Probably."

"Well, don't worry. I can get you home before curfew."

"Whatever," I said.

"My stepdad asked me point-blank if your dad cut back your curfew," Peter said. "He figured your dad must have a good idea what's been going on with those missing kids, so if he cut back your curfew he probably had a good reason."

"What'd you tell him?"

"I told him your curfew hadn't changed. I hope you don't mind that I lied."

"Doesn't matter to me."

"Goddamn Ed the Jew," Peter said, adjusting his position in the driver's seat. He looked completely out of place behind the wheel, and I wondered if I was dreaming. "He's always getting in my face about shit."

Peter continually referred to his stepfather as Ed the Jew, but he never called him that to his face. Even though Peter was constantly bad-mouthing his stepfather, I didn't think Peter truly disliked him. I knew Mr. Blum pretty well and thought he was a decent enough guy. Peter's real father had stuck around till his son was almost three years old. Neither Peter nor his mother had heard from the man since. Peter didn't even know if he was still alive.

Thinking about Peter's stepdad made me think of my own father. I remembered how he had poured gasoline on a hornets' nest last summer and set it on fire. I had watched him do it through the kitchen windows. Tiny fiery sparks spiraled up into the air, and although I supposed they might have been bits of burning leaves or cinders, I thought they could have just as easily been the burning hornets themselves, desperate to escape the conflagration.

I thought, too, of the way I felt coming home from school on certain days to find my father's shit-brown sedan in the driveway and to know that we would share a few uncomfortable hours in the house together before he left for the night shift. Funny, the things the mind summons at the strangest times and for no reason at all.

"He's not so bad," I said, meaning Peter's stepdad. "He let you take the truck."

Peter shrugged. "Yeah, I guess."

There stood a stretch of white dunes overridden by sea grass between the beach road and the Shallows. As we approached, I spotted a number of cars partially hidden beneath the blackened loom of trees on the other side of the dunes. There was hardly any moonlight and the fog was too dense, so the world around us remained pitch-black.

Peter turned the headlights off and slowed the pickup to a loping ten miles an hour. We parked at the end of the queue of cars beneath the sweeping black fans of pine branches tumored with pinecones. Outside, the thin autumn air carried the strong and acerbic scent of the bay.

"You know," Peter said, climbing out of the truck, "I like this place best in the fall when it starts getting cold."

While the Shallows was certainly at its most beautiful in the autumn months, this was also where we gathered to watch the celebratory fireworks from Annapolis over the water every Fourth of July and swim in the sweltering heat of an August afternoon.

We walked down the slope of the dunes toward the beachfront. I noticed a milky funnel of light rising off one of the many docks and, closer to us, the flickering of a single tiki torch, the flame almost lifelike in the way it danced from the torch's crown. Along the beachfront, a cream-colored glow could be seen in the windows of the clapboard shanties. The occasional silhouette passed before these windows, though the occupants never paid us any attention. At that moment, a lone dog howled from somewhere across the beach.

Something like three thousand miles away, the Seattle grunge scene had managed to penetrate my group of friends; there was a conference of plaid flannel shirts and canvas army jackets arranged in a semicircle in the wet sand near the foot of the water. Some of my friends even wore scuffed jackboots mined from their fathers' old wardrobes.

As Peter and I approached, they were attempting to coax a bonfire to life with little success. While I considered these fifteen or so acquaintances to be my friends, I had never hung out with them on a one-on-one, day-to-day basis as I did with Peter Galloway, Scott Steeple, and Michael Sugarland. The others were good for filling in the background at parties and sharing beers in someone's garage, but they were not my close friends. I was fine with that. I preferred my small circle of intimates.

"Galloway! Mazzone!" someone boomed from the crowd of fire starters.

A can of Mountain Dew catapulted toward my head. I managed to catch it, more out of startled reflex than skill.

"You guys look like a bunch of cavemen," Peter said, selecting a can of soda from a cooler that was wedged in the sand. "Those logs are too wet to light."

I glanced around. "Where's Michael?"

"He's out on the dock," Brian Dassick said, jerking his chin in the direction of the rickety old dock that extended into the water. He was sitting on his knees, poking the damp logs with a long stick. "I heard you got into some deep shit with Nozzle Neck, Mazzone."

I said, "Yeah?"

"I heard you threw him over a desk when he went to collect an assignment."

"Who told you that?"

"Does it matter? It's true, isn't it?"

"Not exactly."

Brian frowned. "What's that mean? Either it happened or it didn't."

I watched him poke at the mound of logs with nothing to show for it but a few streamers of smoke. "It didn't. People like to exaggerate. I just didn't do the assignment, that's all."

"And you got kicked out of his class for that?"

Following the altercation, my guidance counselor, the principal, and my father decided that I would be transferred from Naczalnik's class to Mr. Mattingly's class. Mattingly was new to Stanton, and I had yet to earn a reputation with him. "What makes you say I got kicked out? Maybe I wanted a change of scenery."

Brian snickered. "Yeah, right."

Peter kicked some sand over the struggling bonfire. "I told you, Brian, those logs are too wet."

Popping the tab of my soda, I wandered down to the water. The black sheen of the bay unfolded before me. Fog had settled on the water, making it impossible to see the lights of the watermen's lighthouse and beyond that the blinking lights of the Chesapeake Bay Bridge far off in the distance.

I recalled two summers ago when a small fixed-wing plane tried to avoid striking the bridge and plummeted to the water below. Miraculously, all on board survived. It was on the TV news, and there had been a write-up in the *Caller*. In the photographs it looked like a partially submerged seesaw, one wing, shiny and white in the sun, jutting at an angle out of the water. The metal gleam of a propeller blade poked from the surface of the water like the dorsal fin of a mechanical shark.

I'd wanted my father to take me over the bridge before the water was dredged and the airplane was removed, so I could see it down there in the water firsthand. He didn't take me, though, and I resorted to the memory of the photos in the news to quench the thirst of my curiosity of the matter.

Peter came up beside me. "Hey, you okay?"

"Sure. Why?"

"I don't know. You seem messed up about something."

I was still thinking of the dead girl. The sight of her had troubled me more than I would have thought. Looking at Peter, I could tell it didn't weigh as heavily on him. "I'm cool," I said, wondering if he could see through my lie.

Peter turned and gazed down the length of the beach.

I looked, too. Floating ghostlike in the sheen of fog, a cone of light shifted around at the end of one of the docks. Something splashed in the water. There were people moving out there, and the fog made their laughter seem closer than it actually was. Faintly, I heard music drifting down the beach to us, although I couldn't recognize it. It was hollow and unsettling. A loon cried out.

Peter took a swig of his soda. When he cleared his throat, he said, "Okay, I've got a good one. How do you catch an elephant?"

I groaned and rolled my eyes. A few months ago, he had checked out a book called *101 Elephant Jokes* from the public library. These jokes were so bad, they couldn't properly be called jokes, yet Peter thought they were just about the funniest things ever committed to paper. He never passed up an opportunity to spout one of these pearls of comedy.

"Please," I said, though I couldn't help but grin, too. "Please don't . . ."

"Hide in the grass and make a noise like a peanut."

"Brilliant," I said.

Peter laughed.

"You're a rhino rod chomper," I told him.

"Just once," he said, and we were both laughing now. "I needed the money."

"All right, all right," I said.

"Chomp." He glanced over his shoulder at the distant boat dock and said, "Come on, Angie. Let's head over there. I don't wanna miss Sugar sinking the cow."

Together we trampled the reeds on our way across the snowy white dunes. As we closed the distance, the dock materialized through the diminishing fog. I recognized Michael Sugarland's voice issuing down the beach, and I heard more laughter. The sounds of the music grew louder, too: what I'd initially thought was a tape or CD was actually Sasha Tamblin playing an acoustic guitar on one of the dock pilings.

Peter and I mounted the dock and crossed the weather-warped and moss-slickened planks.

"Intruders," crooned Michael from the far end of the dock. For the sake of the moment, he'd adopted a very thick and very bad German accent. "Zee fog is great. Identify yourselves!"

"Immigration," Peter shouted.

Michael responded with a series of yelps, whoops, and catcalls in his bad German drawl.

Scott Steeple stood with the Lambeth twins midway down the length of the dock. They watched Sasha Tamblin strum a Pearl Jam song on his guitar.

Sasha was dark-skinned, with a low brow and tight black curls. His profile was severe and hawkish, and his eyes were small, black, deeply recessed. He played and sang well, much better than I could play. Jonathan Lambeth said something to him and Sasha laughed, exposing perfectly white teeth.

Sasha nodded at Peter and me as we paused beside Scott. "Hey," he said, stunting his final strum with his hand.

"Hey, Sasha," I said.

Sasha glanced down at his fingers, which were splayed along the fretboard. He arranged them in a C major chord and strummed it once. Then he fingered a hard G chord and picked the strings while sliding his pinky on the high E higher up on the fretboard. He played a few bars in this style, bending in a unique fashion a deep note on the G.

"That's pretty cool," I said. "Did you write that?"

"It's Dave Matthews," Sasha said.

"Who's that?"

"You haven't heard of the Dave Matthews Band? It's good stuff. Folkie but . . . modern, I guess. Original. They got a horn player and a violin." He played a bit more without looking at his hands. "Who do you listen to?"

I shrugged. "Nirvana, Pearl Jam, Stone Temple Pilots, Soundgarden." I was also into Metallica, U2, Nine Inch Nails, Jesus Jones, Van Halen, and the Talking Heads, with a mix of Springsteen and Mellencamp thrown in for good measure. I also maintained a secret love affair with Jerry Lee Lewis, Buddy Holly, Creedence Clearwater Revival, John Lennon's solo recordings, and, like a dirty little secret, ABBA.

"Cool." Sasha proceeded to strum with ease the opening chords of Metallica's "Nothing Else Matters."

Michael Sugarland stood at the edge of the dock, his birdlike chest, pale and hairless, puffed out in bravado, his miniscule nipples like twin bug bites. In all the years I'd known him, which had been the majority of my life, he'd maintained the unimposing physique of a sapling. His ribs protruded beneath the taut flesh of his chest cavity, and his belly button poked out from his abdomen like the thumb of a hitchhiker. His sandy hair was always trimmed and meticulously combed and parted to the right.

Michael rested one elbow on the head of the enormous ceramic bovine beside him. The life-sized cow was painted in alternating stripes of blue and gold. He'd busted off the shiny pink bulb of the cow's udder and cupped it now in both hands like Oliver Twist asking for more porridge. As Peter and I approached, he placed the udder on his head and grinned at us like a jack-o'-lantern.

"Mr. Sugar the Cosmic Booger," Peter said. "You're going to catch pneumonia dressed like that, you moron."

Michael wore a pair of floral Jams and a Swatch watch and nothing else. To the best of my knowledge, Michael Sugarland did not own a single article of clothing that hadn't ceased being fashionable at least a decade earlier.

Peter motioned to the ceramic cow. "And how the hell did you get this thing out here?"

Michael saluted us, then stood rigidly at attention. His teeth were vibrating in his skull from the cold. "Can't t-t-tell you that, s-s-sir. Top s-s-secret information, s-s-sir."

Peter waved him off. I could tell he was fighting more laughter. So was I. "Very well, soldier. Go about your business."

"Check it out," Michael said, reverting to his own naturally squeaky voice. He bent and gripped the lip of the gaping hole at the bottom of the ceramic cow where its udder had once been. "It'll fill up with water and sink like a stone."

"Buried treasure," Jonathan Lambeth added from his seat on the piling beside Sasha.

"Oh holiest of ceramic cows," Michael intoned. "Oh giver of blue and gold milk and creator of papier-mâché cow pies. How selfless of you to sacrifice yourself on this wondrous of nights, to sustain the idle youth of this sad little beach community . . ."

Had Michael Sugarland not maintained an unsurpassable disdain for Stanton School's student body, the ceramic cow would have appeared in the homecoming float in Monday's parade, just before the Stanton varsity football team took the field. However, Michael had used his charm to hasten a friendship with members of the homecoming committee, enabling him to secure a key to the garage where the float was stored. He'd enlisted the assistance of the Lambeth twins to break into the garage and kidnap the Stanton School cow. They'd strapped the giant ceramic bovine to the roof of Mrs. Lambeth's minivan with bungee cords and driven around the back roads of Harting Farms, the windows down, hooting and hollering, and blasting Led Zeppelin on the tape deck.

"So here's the deal," Michael said, turning to the ugly ceramic cow. His lips were turning purple, and knobs of gooseflesh had broken out on his forearms. "I woke up this morning realizing that my moment of greatness has yet to arrive. I'm nothing more than your average miserable teenage fuckup."

"I could have told you that and saved you the headache," said Peter.

"I mean," Michael went on, not missing a beat, "I nearly wept into my bowl of Count Chocula. But then it occurred to me—my purpose, my lot in life, is not to achieve greatness but to make the arrogant bastards around me equally as miserable."

Jason Lambeth stepped up beside us and distributed fresh beers.

Michael didn't take one. He didn't drink, didn't smoke, didn't try to finagle misguided coeds out of their bras. He was what we all aspired to be, although none of us were willing to condemn booze and girls in an effort to reach it. We admired him for his convictions, even if we could not fully commit to them.

Instead, we took enjoyment in his mischievous plots against a community that did not accept any of us because we liked music and not football and played guitars and not sports. That was what made him Sugarland the Answer Man: his ability to provide for all of us a sense of alleviation from our otherwise tepid lives. That was why we were here tonight to sink the homecoming cow.

By this time, the flannel-clad gang from down the beach joined us. They gathered around Sasha while he played his acoustic guitar, the few girls among the crowd meandering over to the edge of the dock, examining the ceramic cow and whispering to each other.

"Oh," one of the girls said, "it's too cute!"

"Is it a bull?" said another girl.

Michael clapped, then waved Peter and me over. Scott was already beside him. He wanted the three of us, his best friends, to help him push the cow into the water.

I placed one hand against the fake cow's flank and recalled the autumns when I'd fed the real cows at the Butterfield farm, feeling their body heat radiate through my palms and inhaling the sharply fetid stink of cow shit.

From his perch on the dock piling, Sasha reeled off a Mexican standoff progression—an alternating E major/F major progression.

A number of us laughed.

Michael squeezed between Peter and me, placing his hands against the flank of the ceramic cow. He thumped the side of his head against Peter's shoulder, then turned his gaze on me. His smile was as bright as the moon. For a moment he looked absolutely insane. "I want you to remember this, Mazzone. I want you to think back on this as one of the best times of your life. Promise me."

"I promise," I said.

Sasha began down strumming an E chord.

The rest of us stomped our feet in time with the beat.

"One!" Michael shouted, and the crowd repeated it. "Two!" I felt my toes curl in the tips of my sneakers. "Three!"

And we shoved, sending the ceramic cow tipping over the end of the dock. It struck the water on its side, creating a splash much larger and louder than I had expected.

The two girls beside me clapped and cheered.

"Yeah!" Michael bellowed, thrusting a fist into the air. He gripped one of the pilings with both hands and swung himself around the lip of the dock. One of his feet dangled precipitously in the air, and for a split second, I feared he would plummet into the water. "Yeah! Yeah! Yeah!"

Peering over the side of the dock, I watched the enormous ceramic cow suck water in through the gaping wound where its udder had been. It grew heavy and tipped on its back, causing its shiny plastic legs to stand straight up out of the water. This procured more laughter and applause from the crowd.

Michael dipped his dangling foot toward the cow's belly and stepped down on it, sending it bobbing in the water like a giant cork. "Cold," he shouted, laughing. "That water is fucking cold."

Peter and Scott hoisted him over the side of the dock while the rest of us watched the cow slowly sink beneath the surface of the Chesapeake Bay. It seemed to take forever for it to disappear from view and become fully submerged. Once it did, everyone cheered again, and someone sprayed beer into the air.

One of the girls grabbed me and hugged me tightly, and I smelled a mixture of cigarette smoke and cinnamon in her hair. I didn't know who she was.

Still perched on the piling, Sasha began playing "All Along the Watchtower." The few who knew the words chimed in.

I watched him from the edge of the dock, suddenly cold and damp and slightly winded from the excitement. My heart was pounding.

Michael slung an arm over my shoulder, and for one crazy moment, I thought he was going to plant a kiss on my cheek. It wouldn't have been unlike him. Instead, he looked at me with his startling and somewhat insane blue eyes. "You know, Angelo, someday I'm going to fall in love."

"Never. Don't ever fall in love, you son of a bitch. Please. Spare us all."

We were buzzed on adrenaline, we were loud and happy, and no one knew what it was all about until the evening ended. Less than an hour later, after the rest of our friends left, the four of us sat on the edge of the dock, our feet dangling mere inches above the coal-black water, and passed around a can of root beer.

Peter filled Michael in about the dead girl and how we'd watched the cops carry her body out of the woods. Michael listened with uncharacteristic solemnity, nodding when it seemed appropriate.

"This changes everything," Michael said once Peter had finished the story. "Now that they've found a body, they'll be looking for a killer. It's not just about kids who've gone missing anymore."

"The body might not have anything to do with those kids who've gone missing," I said. I found I very much wanted to believe this.

Michael nodded, then shrugged.

It occurred to me that we had all kept quiet about the dead girl until it was just the four of us, as if to speak about it around anyone else would be to corrupt what we had seen.

Michael took the can of root beer from Scott, downed the last of it, and unleashed an impressive belch. "I'm freezing my balls off out here," he commented, climbing to his feet.

Ten minutes later, Peter and I coasted back through town in Ed the Jew's pickup, simultaneously laughing and groaning at Peter's stupid elephant jokes while playing cassette tapes too loud.

When we pulled up to my house, I saw my father's unmarked police car in the driveway.

"Shit. I thought he'd be out all night," I said, turning down the tape deck and glancing at the digital clock on the dashboard. It read 11:36, which meant I was an hour and a half past my curfew. "Lights."

Peter snapped off the truck's headlights. He shut the engine down, too, and allowed us to coast up to the curb. If my father was asleep, I didn't want to wake him.

"Are you gonna be in trouble?" Peter asked.

"Probably."

"Want to stay at my place?"

My gaze scaled the house, observing the darkened windows and simmering silence in which it sat. Was it possible he had come home and gone to sleep? I felt more equipped to deal with any chastisement in the morning as opposed to right now. "No," I said finally, knowing from past experience that it would do more harm than good to avoid coming home altogether.

"You sure?"

I nodded.

"Okay. Take care, man. Glad you came out."

"Yeah," I said and hopped out of the truck. I made my way to the rear, popped the tailgate, and took out my bike.

Seconds later, I nodded to Peter as he turned over the ignition and spun the pickup around, the headlights still off, and sped down the street.

Shivering against the cold, I rolled my bike to the side of our house where I buried it within the wall of lush ivy, then decided to enter through the rear porch instead of the front door. It would be quieter. I'd done this before and knew the ropes.

I crept around back and mounted the porch steps. They creaked just slightly beneath my weight, as I'd expected them to—I had braced myself by wincing as I stepped on each one—but their protestations weren't loud enough to rouse anyone within the house. I fumbled for my keys, and, as I slipped the appropriate key into the dead bolt on the back door, I heard my father clear his throat.

Startled, I nearly dropped my keys. I took an instinctive step backward as my breath caught in my throat. Then I froze beneath the darkness of the porch awning, trying to adjust my eyes to the shapes all around me. I noticed my father sitting in one of the wicker chairs, so silent he could have been nothing more than part of my imagination.

"Dad," I uttered, my voice pathetic, "I didn't see you there."

He didn't say anything.

For one split second I almost convinced myself that I was out here alone talking to shadows and that it had been nothing but my imagination playing tricks on me after all. But then I saw him shift position in the wicker chair and heard him sigh in his exhausted, meditative way.

"Grandma said you were called out tonight," I continued, mostly because I couldn't think of anything else to say. Also, I couldn't bear the silence. But then I realized it sounded like a confession, and I immediately clamped my mouth shut before I could dig my grave any deeper.

"Where were you?"

"Just out with the guys," I said, desperate to sound casual. I smelled cigarette smoke on me—in fact, I smelled nothing but cigarette smoke. Surely my father could, too. "Peter got his driver's license so he drove me home in his stepdad's truck."

My father made a quick humming sound.

"I'm sorry I'm late," I blurted. "I lost track of time."

"Sit down for a minute," he said.

I moved across the porch toward him, all too aware and terrified of the odor of smoke wafting off my skin and my clothes, and sat directly in front of him in one of the other wicker chairs. I could see by the bluish light of the moon the weathered and hardened features that melded together to comprise the face of my father. It was a patchwork of lines, the dual pits beneath his formidable brow only hinting at the place where his eyes were. I was shocked by how old he looked.

He still wore his dress shirt and necktie from work, as the moonlight reflected off the tie clip and the gold badge at his hip, and this caused me to hang my head and fold my hands between my knees, shamed. I never felt more childish than when I was confronted by my father.

"Where've you been?" he said casually, evenly.

"Out with the guys. Just like I said."

"Specifically," he said.

"The Shallows." It came out before I could come up with a suitable lie. My dad didn't like me going down there at night since he knew that was where kids often got drunk, smoked dope, and had sex.

"I heard you and your friends were there when they took that girl out of the woods today."

"Yes," I said, wondering if my grandmother or one of the cops had said something to him. Either way and for whatever reason, I felt guilty.

"I'm sorry you had to see it," he said.

"Has she been . . . identified yet? Like, do you know who she . . . she is?"

"Courtney Cole," he said.

I didn't recognize the name. Nonetheless, having a name to go along with the body I'd seen only deepened the reality of it. I had been picturing her broken face and dented head ever since this afternoon. "Did she go to Stanton?"

"No, she was from the Palisades. She went to Girls' Holy Cross. She was fifteen. I guess you probably wouldn't have known her."

The Palisades was the southernmost part of Harting Farms. My grandmother had taken me there as a child to play, and my limited memory resurrected an image of a glistening field of grass and stately tamaracks, where swans carved paths through the mirrored surface of a beautiful man-made lake. To think of someone from the Palisades—someone my age, no less—having been murdered was almost beyond my ability to comprehend.

I just sat there, trying not to let my leg tap, trying not to pick at my fingernails. "Do her parents know? I mean . . . well, you found her parents?" I wasn't sure why this question jumped into my head, though I wondered if it had something to do with the man in the navy-blue sweater who had been talking to Mr. Pastore at the deli.

"Yes." Again my father shifted in the darkness.

"So . . . what happened to her?" This was what I really wanted to know. And for a moment I actually thought he was going to tell me. But I should have known better.

"Someone did something horrible to her," he replied, his voice low. "It's a sick and terrible thing. You don't need to know the details."

"Oh. Okay."

"When you go out," my father said, "you're always with your friends, right?"

"Yes."

"Good. That's good. You should stay with your friends."

"Dad," I began, and my voice cracked. "Does this have anything to do with those other kids who went missing? The person everybody's calling the Piper."

"It's too early to tell. But you're old enough to know the facts. I don't have to sugarcoat anything for you anymore, do I?"

"No, sir," I said, my voice terribly weak.

"There's something going on around here. Something bad. When you go out, stay with your friends in populated areas, preferably at their houses. Do you understand?"

"Yes."

"You stay away from remote places—the woods, the locks down at the poorer end of town, the bike path, and all the parks after dark. Stay away from those empty cabins along the Cape and the Shallows and the old railway station at the end of Farrington Road. And that bridge by Deaver's Pond where the homeless go in the winter. I don't want you hanging around by that underpass, not with your friends and certainly not alone. You understand me?"

"Yes, I understand."

"I'm being serious, Angelo. I want you to understand."

"I understand," I told him. "I promise."

"I'm telling you this because I want you to be careful and be aware."

"I know," I said.

His nod was almost imperceptible in the darkness. "Good. Now get up to bed."

For a second I thought it was a trick. I had anticipated a shouting match or at the very least a stern reprimand about breaking curfew.

My father must have registered my uncertainty; when I didn't immediately get out of the chair, he pointed at me and swiped his finger toward the door, as though I were a dog in need of specific instruction.

I stood and went to the door, turned the knob carefully. My grandparents' bedroom was on the ground floor, and my frequent nighttime escapes from the house over the years had schooled me in the proper technique to avoid the moaning hinges: turn the knob and pull up, lifting the door in its frame, then push inward. Silent as a nun's prayer.

"And don't think I'm letting you slide on breaking curfew," my father called after me.

"Yeah, I know. I'm sorry for coming home late."

"No, you're not," he said. Then he sighed again. He sounded ancient. "We'll talk about that tomorrow."

"Okay," I said. I couldn't move, couldn't take my eyes from his darkened, hunched shape across the porch. "You coming in, too?"

"In a bit."

"Good night," I said, and crept inside.

Later in bed, despite the heaviness of sleep pressing down on me in the dark, I forced myself to stay awake until I heard my father's leaden footfalls thumping down the hallway. When I heard his bedroom door creaking at the opposite end of the hall, I finally shut my eyes. Hot and gummy tears slid away from them, coursing down my temples. Their arrival shocked me.

I replayed the scenario from earlier that day—the cops carrying the stretcher out of the woods, the girl's body covered in a white sheet until a gust of wind lifted it and exposed her broken face to me. That face.

I tried to distract my mind with a myriad of safer things—music and girls and horror movies—but, like a hungry wolf, the visage of that broken and bloodied face pursued me into my dreams. Only in my dreams, it was the face of my brother.

CHAPTER THREE
MISCHIEF NIGHT

Daughter of Byron and Sarah Beth Cole, older sister of seven-year-old Margaret, Courtney Cole had been an attractive fifteen-year-old soccer player at Girls' Holy Cross in the Palisades. In the newspaper picture, which appeared to be a yearbook photo, she had thick black hair, stunning eyes that were surprisingly seductive for a girl her age, and the sort of half-crooked, memorable smile that resonated behind your eyelids like the afterimage of a flashbulb.

The account of her death in the *Caller* was cursory at best. Courtney had been visiting friends in a neighborhood near Stanton School, then walked home with Megan Meeks sometime in the late afternoon. According to Megan, they had split up just as they reached December Park. Megan turned down Solomon's Bend Road, and Courtney, who lived in the Palisades, cut through the park.

But Courtney Cole had never made it home. She'd had her head staved in by an unknown assailant, and two days after her parents had reported her missing, her body was found by two county workers who had been in the woods cleaning up after Audrey MacMillan's automobile accident.

Prior to the discovery of Courtney's body, there was speculation as to what had become of the three other Harting Farms children who had simply vanished over the past two months—thirteen-year-old William Demorest in late August and sixteen-year-old Jeffrey Connor and thirteen-year-old Bethany Frost in September. Without evidence of foul play—and without actual bodies—the police seemed most confident that they were a series of unrelated runaways. Of course, the parents of the missing children wanted the police to consider the prospect of abduction.

Before Courtney Cole's disappearance, Chief of Police Harold Barber was quoted in several papers, stating, "What is more probable? That some nameless, faceless Pied Piper has come to our town to systematically lead our unwitting children off into the sunset, or that we are looking at a few unrelated instances of kids running away from home?"

Thus, Chief Barber gave a name to the faceless monster, and that seemed to make the menace all the more real. The *Caller* adopted the name and ran with it. Soon thereafter, the television news reported on the existence of a possible child abductor known as the Piper stalking the residents of Harting Farms.

Nevertheless, it wasn't until Courtney Cole's body was discovered that the people of Harting Farms began to truly panic. The newspapers and TV news suggested that the Cole girl's death was related to the three disappearances over the past two months, and all four incidents may in fact be the work of a single individual.

"Are they talking about a serial killer?" I asked my grandfather.

"It's sensationalism," my grandfather advised me, looking somewhat agitated in his recliner. The television cast an eerie blue light over us both. "Yellow journalism and scare tactics to rile the public. It's nothing you need to worry about. Sells newspapers and brings up the television ratings. That's all it is."

While the nightly news was ordinarily saturated with shootings and murders in Baltimore and D.C., Harting Farms was a quiet middle-class suburb where the weekly crime blotter generally consisted of graffiti on the side of the local Generous Superstore or the occasional bout of mailbox baseball. Murder was something our community was unaccustomed to, and there were a multitude of reactions.

For starters, the community initiated the Courtney Cole Memorial Charity and elected a chairman. However, no one seemed to know the purpose of the charity aside from using donations to pay for the girl's funeral, and it wasn't long before my grandfather chastised the organization for defrauding the good and grieving people of our community.

The Elks, of which Courtney's parents and grandparents were members, planted a blue spruce in her memory on the lawn of their chapter house. Similarly, a bronze plaque engraved with her name and some quote from a semi-famous local poet was affixed to the wall outside the confessionals of St. Nonnatus.

Although Courtney had never set foot in our hallways, Stanton School erected a memorial bulletin board secured behind a glass enclosure in the main lobby. The memorial consisted of numerous pictures of the girl, mostly clipped from various newspapers, as well as the articles recounting her death. The whole thing was in poor taste, somehow made worse by the garland of pink and white flowers that hung beneath the largest of the photos, giving it a wholly incongruous Hawaiian flair.

Our school published a monthly newsletter of poetry and short fiction, spearheaded by Miss McGruder's creative writing class. That year, the Halloween issue detoured from its usual assemblage of ghost stories and poems concerning decapitated heads and button-eyed zombies returning from the grave. Instead, its pages were filled with overindulgent sentimentality about flowers wilting in the winter air and butterflies bursting forth from cocoons in a dazzling exhibition of colored wings.

Of course, a bout of gallows humor followed the tragedy. The most tasteless yet inventive one came in the form of a limerick on the wall of one of the bathroom stalls:

There once was a man called the Piper
Who'd see a nice girl and he'd swipe her
The girl was found dead
With a hole in her head
As though she'd been shot by a sniper

Perhaps the most disturbing thing was the circulation of an alleged love letter Courtney had given to a boy who attended Stanton School. According to the date scrawled in the upper margin of the first page, it was written roughly one week before her death. Whether or not the letter was authentic did not lessen the impact of seeing it, holding it.

In science class, I was tapped on the shoulder and handed the folded sheaves of ruled notebook paper like someone being presented with the Dead Sea Scrolls. I read the first few lines and realized, with a rising sense of unease, that it must have been real, because it was too unimpressive, too mundane, to be a forgery. Had it been a fake, the author would have included some less-than-subtle foreshadowing of Courtney's death or the irony of a profession of true love mere days before her life was snuffed out. The handwriting was bubbly and looping, the tone simple and without pretense. I couldn't finish reading it and passed it along to pimple-faced Mark Browmer who sat beside me, hoping someone more virtuous than me might dump it in the trash before the day was through.

The Harting Farms Police Department felt the impact, too. Chief Barber went on TV and said there was no evidence to show that Courtney's murder had anything to do with the disappearances of the three other kids. Unhappy with Barber's statement, the other kids' parents were often seen on the television news, giving their own opinions.

I registered this tension mostly from afar, just like any bystander, but it soon came home to me. On the nights my father made it home in time for dinner, he sat mostly in silence and would only speak when spoken to. And even then, it was in some foreign and guttural tongue, hardly intelligible. In the evenings, he sat on the back porch, sometimes with a glass of wine or a cup of coffee, and smoked countless cigarettes.

My father stayed up late and wore out the floorboards of the upstairs hallway like a ghost sentenced to haunt for eternity. I never slept on these nights, and I frequently heard his creaking footfalls pause outside my bedroom door. I remained silent in bed, staring at the ceiling, holding my breath as I waited for him to start walking again.

Once, I heard the shower come on, and I was reminded of how he had frequently gotten up in the middle of the night to shower in the months after we had learned that my brother, Charles, had been killed in combat in Iraq. It didn't take me long to figure out that the running water was really just noise to cover up the sounds of my father's grief in a house with thin walls.

That night, I realized this wasn't just about the dead girl. This wasn't about the Piper, or whoever was out there, and all the stress of my father's job. Not to him. Not to me, either.

My father had become a different person after my brother's death. Everything about him seemed to fade into a variant of semiexistence. His bedroom resembled a room you might get at a roadside motel. The items in it were purely functional: a bed, a dresser, a bedside lamp on a nightstand, an alarm clock, a closet full of dark suits, a mirror, and some toiletries on a bureau. He kept his shoes lined up at the foot of the bed, often with his socks still balled up inside them. Sometimes he left a tattered paperback mystery with a sensationalist cover and a gaudy foil-stamped title on the nightstand. There was always a stale quality to the air, as if the windows and door had been hermetically sealed off from the rest of the world.

The only sentimental items were the two framed photographs on the nightstand beside his bed, one of my mother, who had died when I was three. The few memories I had of her were muzzy and undependable, like looking at someone's shape behind a plastic shower curtain. The other photograph was of Charles in his military uniform. He appeared frighteningly young, and if you looked close enough, you could see the places on his chin where he'd cut himself shaving.

I kept my own photographs of Charles in a scrapbook on the top shelf of my bedroom closet, tucked beneath a stack of comic books and issues of *Mad* magazine. I used to look at the scrapbook a lot in the months following Charles's death, but I never took it out anymore. I'd stopped going in his room, too. It stood untouched at the end of the hall, the door shut but unlocked. Charles's football and track trophies were on his shelves, his record albums and tapes meticulously filed away in an old steamer trunk at the foot of his bed. His varsity jackets and Windbreakers with his name embroidered over the breast, his jeans and slacks and shirts and jerseys, his football gear and track shoes were still there, too.

Most days, I managed to get by without thinking of Charles. Maybe that sounds cold. I don't know if it is or not, but that's the truth of it. Yet ever since I saw Courtney Cole being hoisted out of the woods, it was Charles's face that haunted me at night, Charles's caved-in head beneath the white sheet on the gurney.

After a while, nighttime began to terrify me. And it didn't help that my friends couldn't let it go, either.

"I've been thinking about it nonstop," Scott said out of nowhere one afternoon as the two of us sucked on cigarettes outside the Quickman, our favorite burger joint. "I keep seeing the way she looked when that sheet blew off her."

"Yeah," I confessed, "I think about her, too. Sometimes. Mostly at night."

"Perv."

"You know what I mean."

"Do you think much about the killer?"

No, I didn't. It seemed implausible that there was actually a living, breathing human being responsible for the whole thing. It was easier to see the missing children and what Courtney Cole had looked like beneath that white sheet than to consider what type of animal could be behind such things.

"A cousin of mine sat next to Ted Bundy on a bus in Florida," Scott said before I could answer his question. "He was wearing a fake cast on his arm, too, like they say he used to so he could get his victims to help him carry stuff to his car. My cousin said she recognized him when he was arrested and they showed pictures of him all over the news. I always thought it was weird that she recognized him—I mean, how closely do you look at people on a city bus, right?—but I guess people like that stick with you in some caveman part of your brain that tells you something's just not right. Like a flashing neon sign that says *stay away*."

I gazed out across the parking lot, beyond the trees and toward St. Nonnatus. Cars scuttled along the highway like shiny beetles. The sky was the saturated monochromatic yellow of an old photograph.

"They say he drilled holes in girls' heads and poured boiling water into their skulls while they were still alive. That psycho tortured the shit out of them. Can you fucking imagine?"

"Who did?" My mind was wandering.

"Ted Bundy."

"It's not like that here," I said. "She just had her skull crushed."

"Yeah, but you don't know what kind of twisted things the Piper might have done to her before she died." After a moment of consideration, Scott added, "Or even after she died."

"You're sick."

Scott rolled his shoulders. "It's a sick world."

"I guess anything's possible."

"So what about the others?" he said. "The ones they haven't found yet?"

"I don't know. You think they'll find them eventually?"

"I would think so. I mean, they gotta be somewhere, don't they? People don't just disappear."

Even though I knew that people disappeared without a trace every year, I sucked at my cigarette and said, "I guess so."

"Doesn't your dad tell you anything?"

"About the missing kids? About the Cole girl's murder?"

"About anything," said Scott. "About his job. About being a cop."

"Not really. Besides, I don't think the cops know any more than anyone else. And if they do, they're not gonna tell me about it."

"Have you ever seen his gun?" Scott asked. He put one hand in the pocket of his coat, digging around for something.

"Well, sure," I said. I saw my father's issued firearm in its holster every night when he came home from work and took his coat off. I also knew he kept it in his sock drawer when he wasn't wearing it—the top drawer of his bedroom bureau. He also kept a six-shot revolver under his bed in an old cigar box.

The truth was that my father had carried a gun for as long as I'd been alive. It was as commonplace to me as if he'd been a salesman hauling around a brief-case full of encyclopedias. To my friends, however, the prospect of having a gun in the house was both foreign and tantalizing, so they professed an inordinate amount of interest in the weapon.

"He ever let you shoot it?"

"Nope," I said.

Scott produced a dangerous-looking butterfly knife from his pocket. With a magician's flourish, he flipped it open and held it out away from his body. The blade was shiny, a good five inches. He turned it over slowly in his hand. "I wonder how it happened."

Behind us, a mother and her two young children bounded out of the Quickman, and I caught a whiff of the deep fryer.

"I wonder how the Piper got to her."

"There is no Piper," I said, more out of habit than anything else. I was instantly reminded of what my father had told me the night he'd sat on the back porch, waiting for me to come home. *When you go out, stay with your friends in populated areas, preferably at their houses.*

So Harting Farms mourned the death of one of their own and feared that a similar fate might have already befallen the three children who had previously disappeared from its streets.

Mischief Night, the night before Halloween, saw a sky that trembled with snow. It seemed to swirl and hover above the streets and the low gabled peaks of the neighborhood houses without ever touching the ground. Halloween had always been my favorite holiday, but Mischief Night carried with it the sense of jittery anticipation of things to come, like Christmas Eve.

Before heading out for the evening, I helped my grandmother put up decorations on the front porch—rubber skeletons dangling from invisible wire, an electric cauldron that spewed dry ice smoke, a ceramic black cat whose eyes glowed a feral green. I filled a bowl with candy and left it on the kitchen counter in anticipation of the little kids who would come knocking on the door tomorrow.

In the den, while *It's the Great Pumpkin, Charlie Brown* played for perhaps the fiftieth time on TV, my grandfather grumbled about the shaving cream and toilet paper he would undoubtedly have to clean up in the morning.

An old box filled with Halloween costumes was tucked away at the far end of the basement, up against the hot water heater and suitably ghostlike beneath the drape of a paint-splattered white sheet. Inside were a number of masks, including one of Lon Chaney from *The Phantom of the Opera* that my father had donned a few years back just prior to waking me up for school, intent on—and successful in—scaring the shit out of me.

There were also rubber gloves whose fingers concluded in hooked claws; a set of glow-in-the-dark plastic vampire teeth; a large plastic cauldron; latex bats that tittered when jostled; a variety of wooden pitchforks; capes; furry hoods, some adorned with horns; oversized clown shoes; a Superman T-shirt; my old remote-controlled race car (I had no idea why this had been stored in the Halloween box); a rhinestone-infested bikini top and hula sarong; and various other things.

I spent nearly twenty minutes digging through the box before closing it back up with nothing to show for my efforts. Instead, a tin of shoe polish on a shelf caught my attention, and I absconded with it.

In my room, I dropped a Springsteen cassette into the tape deck and cranked "Born to Run" while I dressed in a black hooded sweatshirt, dark jeans, and my fastest sneakers. Standing before the mirror that hung on the inside door of my closet, I painted my cheeks, my forehead, and underneath my eyes with the black shoe polish.

Downstairs, my grandmother snagged a fistful of my sweatshirt and commented, "Black on black is a particularly bad idea for nighttime, don't you think? You'll get hit by a car."

I groaned. My grandmother was always telling me I'd get hit by a car. "I won't get hit. I'm always careful."

"Yes, well, be particularly careful tonight." She didn't have to explain what she meant. "And please don't forget your curfew."

"I won't," I said, though I knew it was a promise I might not be able to keep. My father worked every Mischief Night, and he wouldn't be home until dawn.

"Stay safe," she said and kissed me on the cheek.

On a normal night I would have taken my bike, but my friends and I would be weaving stealthily between the shadows on foot tonight, so I walked through the neighborhood, passing hordes of similarly dressed teenagers with backpacks on their shoulders and mischievous glints in their eyes. A few recognized me and raised their hands at me or tossed rocks and, in one case, an egg at my head. I dodged the rocks and the egg and picked up my pace.

When I hit the rear parking lot of the Generous Superstore, there was spooky music crackling from the public address speakers affixed to the brick columns outside the loading docks. A lone security guard wielding a flashlight eyed me with suspicion as I cut around the side of the building and hopped the curb. There was a brick alcove here, outfitted with a bank of pay phones, a wooden bench, and a single floodlight whose bulb had been busted for as long as I could remember. My friends were there in the shadows waiting for me.

"Hey," I said, joining them.

"Man," said Michael. "Are you ever on time?"

"I'll work on being more punctual if you work on being less ugly."

"Ha. You're a riot." He swung an overstuffed knapsack off his shoulder and set it down at his feet. He wore jeans and a dark sweatshirt with a hood, similar to mine, but had an old pith helmet cocked back on his head. "What'd you do to your face?"

"It's shoe polish," I said, taking the tin of polish out of the kangaroo pocket of my sweatshirt. I handed it to Scott.

Scott popped the lid off, then examined the contents. He brought it to his nose and sniffed it, pulling a face.

"It washes right off," I promised him, though I didn't know this to be true.

Scott shrugged, scooped a bunch of the tarry gunk out of the tin, then smeared it across his face. He wore plastic vampire teeth, which bulged out his lips, and a Dracula cape tied around his neck.

I peered over Michael's shoulder as he unzipped the knapsack and opened it wide so that we could all see what was inside: rolls of toilet paper, two full cartons of eggs, several cans of shaving cream, a large screwdriver and wrench he'd shoplifted a few days earlier from Second Avenue Hardware, and some other junk that promised to make the evening memorable.

"That toilet paper's not used, I hope," Peter commented.

Michael slugged him on the forearm.

"Here," Scott said, passing the shoe polish to Peter.

It looked like an old Buick had backfired in Scott's face. I tried to stifle a laugh.

"Hey," Scott groused, spitting out the plastic vampire teeth into his hand. "This was your idea."

"No, no, it looks cool. Trust me." Then I brayed laughter.

"Sweet," said Peter, streaking his own face in shoe polish. He dragged his fingers down his cheeks, leaving vertical black lines that resembled war paint. He was dressed in a tight-fitting navy-blue sweater that looked black in the dark and bright white sneakers. He had a plastic dime-store Batman mask propped on the top of his head, the elastic band cutting into the flesh under his chin.

"You should do your shoes with that polish, too," Scott suggested. "They're so white they're blinding."

"They're brand-new," Peter retorted. "I'm not gunkin' them up."

"Yeah, but they look like they glow in the dark. We're supposed to be incognito."

"Christ." Peter squatted and sighed, examining his new white sneakers . . . and then proceeded to smear them with shoe polish. He paused halfway through coating the second one to regard his work. "My mom's gonna shit birds."

Michael produced a map from within his knapsack, unfolded it, and splayed it out on the nearby bench. It was a map of Harting Farms, and even in the poor lighting I could see that Michael had marked a number of locations in either bright red or green marker. There were too many to count.

"Jesus, that's a lot of stops," I said.

"At least twice as many as last year," Scott added.

"I'm feeling particularly vindictive this year," Michael said.

He took the holiday seriously, and if you dissed him at one point during the year, he would remember. It wouldn't have surprised me if he actually kept a journal of all these betrayals.

Peter gazed down at the map as he gave the shoe polish to Michael. "Red and green," Peter commented, snatching a roll of toilet paper from the knapsack so he and Scott could clean the shoe polish off their hands. "This is Halloween, not Christmas."

Michael gave himself a Hitler moustache with the shoe polish before handing me the canister. "Mischief Night," he corrected. "It's better than Halloween."

"Why the different colors?" Scott asked.

"They're color coded in order of importance," said Michael. "The red are the hot spots, the priority. Like, we gotta hit those. If we have time, we hit the green."

"You've got my house on there, you dick," Peter said.

Michael nodded. "I was gonna tell you about that. I've had a few issues with you this past year. Sorry."

"I'll give you issues." Peter licked his thumb, then rubbed it against one of the red marks on the map.

"Okay, then. So we got one less house to hit this year." Michael zipped up the knapsack and gave it to Scott. "Hide it beneath your cape."

Scott swung the knapsack onto his back while I held his Dracula cape out of the way. Once he'd situated it on his shoulders, I draped the cape over it. "Does it look stupid?" Scott asked, craning his neck to see the large black lump on his back.

"Well, it's not inconspicuous," I said.

"Don't worry about it," Michael interjected. "You just look like a hunchback."

"But I'm Dracula, you idiot."

"Okay, so you're Dracula. With a hunchback."

I joined Peter, who was still examining the map, and said, "Okay. So where do we start?"

Michael slapped Peter's hand away and ran his finger down the grouping of red X's along Cypress Avenue. It was the residential neighborhood behind the Generous Superstore plaza. "We'll start here and work our way north so that we loop back around this way and end the night heading south toward the city limits." His finger stopped at the edge of Harting Farms, where on the map our city was separated from Glenrock by a swath of undeveloped land. "Sound good?"

"It's a lot of ground to cover," I said. "Maybe we should take our bikes."

"No way," Michael admonished. "No bikes on Mischief Night. We go on foot. We've always gone on foot. It's tradition. Besides, the time it would take to go back home and get our bikes—"

"Okay, okay," I said. "But we should get going."

"Yeah," said Peter, dropping his Batman mask over his face.

Michael clapped and gave us his grandest smile. "Okay, then! Let's move out, boys!"

Like ninjas, the four of us crept into the darkness of the nearest neighborhood.

* * *

That night, my friends and I toilet papered all the houses designated red and even a few marked green on Michael's map, egged some of the cars that sped along the streets, and dropped water balloons on unsuspecting perambulators from the bridge on Solomon's Bend Road.

A few entrepreneurial adults staged their traditional counterattacks. Teddy Boru's dad threw eggs at young trespassers from his bedroom window. Old Mr. Vandenberg, the hermetic desperado who lived in one of the dilapidated duplexes along Shore Acre Road, sprung out from behind a holly bush, wrapped in a white bedsheet and donning a rubber Frankenstein mask.

"If it wasn't so far out of the way, I'd love to hit the Keener farm tonight," Michael said as he chucked an egg over the hedgerow that lined the property in front of the McGee house on Prosper Street. The McGee girls were pudgy and freckle-faced with piercing green cat's eyes and mouths crowded and gleaming with braces. All three had turned down Michael's invitation to the homecoming dance, thus making the list.

"Old man Keener catches you on his property, he'll blow you off it with a shotgun," Scott said.

"And his son's even crazier," added Peter.

Nathan Keener was the youngest of three boys and undoubtedly the craziest. His family lived along the Cape on a tract of farmland that overlooked the Magothy River. It was a shitty-looking house with rusted cars up on blocks on the weedy front lawn. There were scarecrows posted along the long driveway, their clothing and potato-sack faces riddled with buckshot.

There was nothing in particular Nathan Keener had done to Michael this year, aside from simply making all our lives miserable every time we had the misfortune to run into him. And it wasn't just us—the son of a bitch tormented every kid he came into contact with. Every town has its bully, and Nathan Keener was ours. And while he had no goodwill for any of my friends, I knew he hated me a little bit more than the rest because my father was a cop. People like the Keeners grow up with an ingrained distrust of law enforcement, the way some breeds of dogs, after generations of abuse, will distrust people.

"Besides," Peter continued, "you don't have the balls to go after Keener."

Michael scowled, then chucked another egg at the McGee house; it shattered against the aluminum siding. "I've got balls like cantaloupes, asshole."

Both Peter and Scott laughed just as the porch lights came on. We all dropped down behind the hedgerow. Through the branches, I saw someone peering out of a lighted doorway, examining the detritus on the porch.

A man called out, "I see you kids."

But we knew this was a lie. It was what all the adults said, presuming they could fool us into revealing ourselves. We never fell for it.

After a moment, the door shut again.

We remained secreted behind the hedgerow, none of us making a sound. It was cold enough that our respiration fogged the air. Somewhere off in the distance, a lone dog howled despondently.

"Okay," Michael whispered after enough time had passed. He dug around in the knapsack on Scott's back, produced some more eggs, then handed them out to the rest of us. "Let's do the egg cream," he said, fishing one of the cans of shaving cream out from the knapsack.

We covered our eggs with shaving cream, and on Michael's three-count, we all sprung up simultaneously and launched our projectiles at the McGee house. Four distinct explosions—*flump! flump! flump! flump!*—resounded through the night as great foamy clouds appeared on the siding of the house.

This time, less than two seconds passed before Mr. McGee, massive and black and silhouetted, bolted out the door and down the porch steps.

None of us said a word; we all took off, laughing.

"You little bastards!" Mr. McGee shouted after us. "I know where you live! I know your parents!"

We didn't slow down until Scott, who'd chanced a glance over his shoulder, informed us that we were no longer being pursued. Still giggling, we continued down the street while attempting to catch our breath. Michael held his pith helmet as he tipped his head back and howled into the night.

At the end of the block, another group of kids returned the howl, followed by some derogatory catcalls. They chucked small twists of white paper at our feet, which popped with little explosions as they struck the pavement.

Scott, who still had an egg in his hand, skidded to a stop. He wound his arm back and tossed the egg, which exploded on the shirt of the nearest boy.

"Bull's-eye," Peter crowed, and we sprinted into the trees before the other kids could give chase.

We burst onto McKinsey Street, our hearts racing. With our laughter dying off in shuddery increments, we staggered over to the curb and sat down. A small A-frame house, nestled among heavy black spruce and about as dark as the interior of a coffin, stood at our backs. The name on the mailbox caught my attention.

"Shit," I said. "It's Nozzle Neck's house."

Still somewhat out of breath, Michael spread his map across his lap and examined it. "You know, I forgot to put old Nozzle Neck on the map."

"Why?" asked Scott. "What'd he do to you?"

"Not to me," Michael said, jerking a thumb in my direction. "To Angie."

"Oh," Scott said and looked at me.

I waved a hand at them. "Forget it. Doesn't matter."

"No way, man." Michael motioned for Scott to slide the knapsack over to him. "He got you in trouble with your pops. He got you grounded. He has to pay, just like everyone else."

"No one has to pay for anything," I said.

Ignoring me, Michael peered into the knapsack. "We got four eggs left."

"It's kismet," Scott said, his eyes brightening in the mask of black shoe polish he wore.

Michael removed the eggs from the knapsack and handed them out to each of us. Then he stood, anxiously rolling his egg back and forth between his palms as he surveyed Mr. Naczalnik's house.

"Shit," Scott said. "I think I saw someone in that window."

Peter looked at the house. "Which one?"

Scott pointed to one of the first-floor windows. The whole house was dark, and it was impossible to see anything. "Right there. Someone was looking out from the curtains."

"You're imagining things," Michael said. "No one's home. There's not even a car in the driveway."

In my hand, the egg felt cold and heavy, somehow more substantial than the others I'd chucked all evening. On the next block over, the disembodied whoops and hollers of children could be heard.

"Bombs away," Michael said, and pitched his egg at Naczalnik's house. It smashed against the siding of the front porch, a sound like a small firecracker.

Scott threw his egg next, and his aim was more precise than Michael's: it hit the front door dead center and shattered, the stringy goop seeming to glisten in the moonlight. Then Peter threw his egg in a high, lazy arc; the egg exploded against one of the porch balusters with a sound like a frog's croak.

A light winked on in one of the downstairs windows.

"I told you I saw someone," Scott said.

"Let's beat it." Michael backed away from the edge of the property.

I didn't move. I felt Peter whoosh by me and snag a fistful of my sweat-shirt, but I jerked myself free. Just as Naczalnik's front door opened, spilling a sliver of yellowish light onto the porch, I hurled my egg. But not just at the house—at him.

My aim was poor: the egg detonated against one of the front windows, causing the pinch-faced silhouette of Mr. Naczalnik to swing in that direction. A set of carriage lights on either side of the door blinked on. Then his voice boomed out, a sonorous bassoon, but I was already fleeing down the street with my friends, my heart thudding loudly in my ears, and I made out none of what Mr. Naczalnik said.

*   *   *

Gradually, we made our way back across town toward the evening's final destination—what Michael promised would be the pièce de résistance. The air was crisp and smoky with the distant scent of fireplaces. Cigarettes jouncing from our lips as we slunk through the shadows, we catcalled after some of the girls we recognized from school.

When one of the girls separated herself from the crowd and came over to us, I was surprised at her brazenness. But as she passed beneath the glow of a streetlamp, I recognized her.

Rachel Lowrey was the first girl I'd ever kissed. We'd been eleven or twelve, so it wasn't like a real openmouthed, fencing-tongues scenario, though it had been pretty intense at the time. The kiss came not because she liked me but because of the Kiss War.

The Kiss War started when a group of neighborhood girls ambushed Michael one summer and peppered him with kisses. Before the summer was over, all of us were casualties of the war. Rachel Lowrey had been my attacker. She had tackled me to the ground as I'd crested the dunes of the Shallows where I'd spent the afternoon swimming with my friends. Startled, the wind knocked out of me, I attempted to roll over and push myself to my feet but wound up only breading myself in the sand like a cutlet. Immediately, she dropped on top of me, straddling my waist, her knees driving divots into the sand on either side of my hips. Then her face was against mine, her lips on me. To my surprise, I didn't shove her off, and maybe that's why she stopped.

When she pulled away, there was a questioning look on her face. Before it could get too awkward, I bucked my hips and knocked her to the sand. Laughing, she scrambled to her feet, but by that time I was already tearing across the dunes, my bare feet punching boomerang shapes in the sand.

"I should have known it was you guys." Rachel materialized out of the darkness like a ghost taking form. She was dressed minimally in a red cloak, her face powdered white. Her dark curls were fashioned into pigtails. Fake blood on the left side of her neck gave the appearance of a gaping wound. She looked at each one of us, her gaze finally resting on me. "Why do you hang out with these creepazoids?"

Michael tittered. "What are you supposed to be, anyway?"

"I'm Little Red Riding Hood. Only I wasn't lucky enough to get away from the Big Bad Wolf. See?" She tilted her head to show off her glistening neck wound.

"Awesome," Scott said.

"You guys think you're so cool, standing around smoking," Rachel said. "Those things cause cancer, you know, in case you haven't read a newspaper or anything."

"She's like a goddamn public service announcement," Peter said.

Scott and I laughed.

Rachel reached into her cloak and pulled out a Krackel bar. She smiled sideways at me, then extended the candy bar to Michael, the only one of us without a cigarette. "Here. For not smoking."

"Sweet!" Michael snatched up the candy bar and unwrapped it. "Thanks."

"So, anyway, it looks like you guys are up to no good. I thought I'd warn you that there's a ton of cops out tonight. It's because of that girl they found. And the other kids, too, I guess. The missing kids. They're not messing around. We've already been stopped twice."

"We're not up to nothing," Peter said. "But thanks."

"Yeah," I said. "Thanks, Rachel."

Across the street, Rachel's friends shouted after her.

"Listen, I gotta go. Sasha Tamblin's having some people over. You guys want to come?"

I shrugged. So did my friends. Michael grunted something unintelligible around his candy bar. We had heard about the party but had more important plans for the evening. Yet I suddenly found myself wondering what it would be like to attend a party with Rachel . . .

"You guys." She looked like she wanted to shake her head at our hopelessness. "It must be exhausting having to look so tough all the time."

"Quit flirting," Michael said.

She smiled. "So what are you guys supposed to be?"

"We're ghosts. We're the disappeared." Michael waved a hand in front of her face, Jedi-style. "You never even saw us."

"I wish," she said, and laughed. Then she spun on her heels and hurried across the street to join her friends. A few of them shouted nonsense at us and made kissing noises before disappearing around the darkening bend in the road.

The streets were suspiciously silent. Aside from the occasional police cruiser tucked into a darkened alley, we were utterly alone. Even the older kids who usually meandered around town, laughing too loudly and talking in raised voices, or perched on the hoods of their cars, passing around bottles of beer—my grandmother referred to these troublemakers as neighborhood-lums—were noticeably absent. I didn't know if it was the presence of police patrolling the neighborhood or the whispers about the Piper that kept people inside.

"What did the elephant say to the naked man?" Peter said as we crossed Tarmouth Road. A blackened hillside of farmland rose to our right, studded with a few ramshackle farmhouses with tallow lights on in the windows. We were on the outskirts of Harting Farms.

"Oh, please," Michael groaned.

"How do you breathe with that thing?" Peter said, springing the punch line on us.

The rest of us lowed like pained cattle.

Then Scott shouted, "Car!"

We all rushed onto the shoulder of the road and ducked behind the overgrown grass of the embankment.

A station wagon with a headlamp out rolled past, its muffler rattling like a party favor.

After it had gone, we stood and swatted the dirt off our clothes. I glanced back and saw all the lights gathered in the distance. It looked like I could scoop up the whole town in my hands and carry it with me.

"Come on," Michael urged, climbing back up the embankment.

This part of town was nearly desolate. The premature winter had stripped the trees naked, and the wind, strong and unforgiving, came in off the bay. The sky was clear and unending, speckled with a thousand stars of varying brilliance, and the air was thin enough to make our footfalls on the pavement echo down the well of streets at every intersection. There was sustained electricity in the air, too, which usually preceded a summer thunderstorm, building all around us an awareness of impending calamity. As we walked I was alerted to the instinctual way each of my friends glanced skyward at different times, as if expecting to witness some rare celestial event.

Peter began singing a John Mellencamp song, his voice hollow and offkey. One by one, we all chimed in—even Scott, who had no interest in the down-home rockabilly anthems of Mellencamp.

A black Cadillac eased past us, its headlamps cleaving through the darkness. It seemed to slow as it went by, but then it kept going and turned at the next stop sign.

We crossed the street and continued north, the streetlights dotting Point Lane up ahead like Chinese lanterns. In this part of town the houses were spaced farther apart. We took Point to Counterpoint and headed for the edge of town.

To our right, the dark screen of woods rose over the embankment like a black shroud that separated us from the sloping moonlit field of December Park. It was a large swath of land flanked by Satan's Forest, which was nearly as expansive as an actual forest, and the imposing, medieval remains of the Patapsco School for Girls.

Back in the 1890s, L. John Stanton, an illustrious entrepreneur, erected two schools—the Patapsco School for Girls, named for the river it overlooked from its perch atop a wooded bluff, and the Stanton School for Boys, named after Stanton himself—at opposite ends of the town. This was an act of sheer immodesty on Stanton's part, as the then unincorporated wilds of Harting Farms did not boast enough of a head count to validate two monstrous, castle-like high schools, let alone segregate its population by gender. Moreover, half the city's adolescent population did not advance beyond ninth grade back then.

So the Stanton School for Boys became Stanton School, and it eventually incorporated the remaining student body from Patapsco. The girls' school was shut down and not reopened until after World War II when it became a convalescent home for soldiers returning from overseas with severe mental and physical handicaps. Despite the burgeoning city's displeasure at having mentally unstable war veterans housed adjacent to a neighborhood park, the school turned hospital remained open and functional for a number of years until faulty wiring caused a devastating fire in 1958. The inferno left nothing behind but the hollow stone shell that remained to this day, a miniature version of the Colosseum.

Several people had been killed in that fire, the story went, and their ghosts not only haunted the remnants of the former girls' school but the park and surrounding woods, too. There were many other ghosts that were said to haunt the park, those of children who had accidentally died when falling out of trees or drowned in one of the many rivers and tributaries that veined the land on the outskirts of the city. (The stories sounded mostly fake to me.)

I had never witnessed anything unusual in the park or the neighboring woods firsthand, though on occasion, after the day had grown old and the sky had begun to darken, there was an undeniable sense of apprehension that would overtake me. It seemed to emanate straight up out of the land itself. This feeling may have been only in my head, fueled by the power of suggestion from all the stories I had heard, but when it grabbed me, its grip was indeed strong and its fingers dug in deep.

Also, the fact that they had found Courtney Cole's body down there didn't help settle my nerves any. I supposed she would become yet another bit of the folklore surrounding December Park and the nearby woods, another ghost story to tell on chilly autumn nights as the wind moaned through the trees and dead leaves scraped along the asphalt.

"Christ," Peter huffed beside me. I had slowed my walk to accommodate his pace. "We should have taken our bikes."

"There is no bike riding on Mischief Night," Michael chided from the front of the line. "How many times do I gotta say it?"

"Where'd that stupid rule come from?" Peter said.

"Not sure," said Michael. "It's in the Bible, I think."

"And what if we need to make a quick getaway?"

"From what?"

"From . . . whatever," Peter said, though he no doubt got us all thinking now.

"I've got my butterfly knife," Scott suggested.

Peter seemed to consider this for a moment before saying, "Okay."

While Scott's butterfly knife had always impressed me with how deadly it looked, it suddenly seemed inconsequential now in light of all that had been going on in our hometown. But I said nothing.

At the top of the hill we crossed the intersection and continued north. Here, only a few clapboard houses dotted the landscape, which was pretty much farmland straight out to the main highway that led out of town.

A water tower appeared from behind a stand of leafless trees, looking like one of the giant alien fighting machines in *The War of the Worlds.* Just beyond the water tower was our destination—the Harting Farms town sign that stood at the southernmost border of our town. It had once proclaimed, Welcome to Harting Farms, before a wicked storm in the early eighties eradicated the first two words, leaving only the city's name on the sign.

The four of us approached the large hand-carved sign and stared up at it. This close, it was higher off the ground than any of us had originally thought—perhaps fifteen feet. It was spotlighted from beneath by two halogen bulbs that cast stark shadows around the three-dimensional wooden letters screwed into the wooden plank.

"Fuck, that's high up," Michael marveled. "Doesn't look so high when you drive past it, huh?"

"It's more lit up than I thought, too," Peter added. He was still trying to catch his breath. "Those lights are seriously bright."

"You changing your mind?" I asked Michael. I had forgotten about the halogen bulbs, too; it seemed foolish to climb up there while they burned so brightly. If a car happened along this stretch of road, we would be spotlighted like inmates escaping a prison yard.

"Heck no." Michael walked around the base of one of the two thick posts that held the sign up off the ground. "I'm just recalculating."

"Wonderful," Peter muttered under his breath.

Scott swiped at the air with his butterfly knife, feigning an attack on an invisible assailant. When he caught my eye, he looked briefly embarrassed, but then he smiled and shrugged, as if to say, *Eh, what can you do?*

"Here," Michael said. He was on the other side of the sign now, standing in the tall weeds. "Come take a look at this."

We all went around to the rear of the sign. Huge bolts had been drilled into the rear of the posts and into the back of the sign. Each bolt head looked nearly the size of a child's fist. Michael pointed them out to us even though they were perfectly evident.

"We can use them as handholds, like rungs in a ladder, and climb up," he said. "When we get to the top of the post, we can stand on it and lean over the top of the sign. This way we're partially shielded from cars, and we can duck behind it quickly if we have to."

"What's all this 'we' business?" I said.

"You're such a pussy, Mazzone," he countered. "You don't have to do a single thing, okay? How's that sound?"

"Sounds pretty good actually."

Hands on his narrow hips and his oversized pith helmet crooked on his head, Michael took a few steps backward while keeping his gaze trained on the rear of the sign and the twin posts. He chewed on his lower lip and looked lost in his own unique brand of mischievous contemplation.

"Anyway," he said after a moment, "we only really need one of us to do it."

"Not it," Peter barked.

"Not it," I shouted.

"Not it," Scott said just as Michael unhinged his jaw to perhaps disqualify himself from his own plan.

Peter laughed and pointed at Michael.

"Yeah, yeah," Michael said, dropping his pith helmet to the ground and motioning for Scott to hand over the knapsack. "I was gonna do it anyway. Couldn't leave something as important as this to one of you goofballs." He took a screwdriver out of the knapsack.

It looked huge and ridiculous in the garish light from the halogen lamps, like a rubber horror movie prop. If we were attacked by a faceless child killer tonight, I'd sooner take the screwdriver as protection than Scott's butterfly knife.

Michael stepped over to one of the posts and propped his sneaker on the lowest of the bolt heads. "You guys hoist me up."

Peter and I came up behind him and pushed against his bony ass. Michael pulled himself up, using the bolt heads as handholds. Without warning, he released a meaty and powerful fart.

"Oh, you shit head!" I cried, staggering backward and wrinkling up my face.

Peter, who'd burst out laughing the second we heard the trumpet call, waved a hand before his nose and tried to speak but couldn't. Tears streamed down his cheeks.

Scott poked his head up underneath the sign and laughed at us, then looked at Michael who was scaling the ledge along the back of the sign.

I hurried around to the front of the sign just as Michael's head appeared over the top.

He grinned like a Cheshire cat. In the light of the halogen lamps, he had the wild-eyed countenance of the devil himself. He brought his arms down and felt around for the letters below him. "They're bigger than they look. The letters, I mean."

"Just hurry." I felt naked out here in the open. If a car drove by we were screwed.

Still laughing, Peter came around the sign to stand beside me. He pawed tears from his eyes and gazed up at Michael with a look of amazement on his face. "He's gonna break his neck if he falls," he said low enough so Michael wouldn't hear him.

Scott stepped around to the rear of the sign. "I'll stay back here and try to catch him if he falls."

"Great," I said. "Then you'll both be killed."

"Probably," Scott said, then vanished behind the sign.

The whole thing didn't take longer than three minutes, though it seemed an eternity. Thankfully, no cars passed as Michael worked, but twice we thought we heard one approaching and Michael had ducked behind the sign while Peter and I ditched into the overgrown shrubbery at the shoulder of the road.

Once he finished, Michael climbed down, and then he and Scott joined us on the front side of the sign, where our quartet admired his work like appraisers at an art show.

He had switched the first letter of each word so that the sign now read, Farting Harms.

It was brilliant—a Michael Sugarland original.

The sound of a vehicle startled us. I turned and saw headlights coming down the road toward us. The four of us crouched in the heavy weeds and bushes as a rusted pickup whooshed by.

"Welcome to immortality, good buddy," Michael intoned and clapped me on the back.

We reached the intersection of Haven and McKinsey and waited as two cars rolled slowly beneath the traffic lights. A sharp wind rustled Scott's cape. I hugged myself, suddenly cold. This was where we departed.

Scott handed the knapsack to Michael, pulled the pointy collar of his Dracula cape around his neck, waved, and crossed the intersection. He disappeared around the bend of Haven Street.

Michael strapped the knapsack onto his back. The pith helmet was on his head again, his shoe-polish moustache smeared halfway across his left cheek. "Good night, punkos." He went straight, cutting through a darkened yard between two houses, a satisfied bounce to his gait.

Peter fished two smokes from his pocket and handed one to me.

"Thanks."

It was tough lighting the cigarettes in the relentless wind, but we managed.

"Your pops ain't home yet, is he?"

"No," I said. "Not till morning. Just like every year."

"You wanna get something to eat at the diner?"

"Not tonight. I should get home."

"Yeah," he said, "me, too."

"What?" I could tell there was something on his mind.

"It's nothing. It's just . . . I saw your face when we were trashing Naczalnik's house. I mean, you were really . . ." He frowned. "I don't know."

I hadn't told anyone, not even my father after he'd grounded me for a week, the real reason I didn't turn in that report to Naczalnik. Peter was my best friend and I considered telling him now. But in the end, I decided against it. Not because I didn't trust Peter with the information, but I didn't think I could bring myself to talk about it.

"Nozzle Neck's a jerk," I said, taking the easy route. "That's all."

Peter nodded and looked down at his new sneakers, which were still greased in black shoe polish. His lower lip quivered in the cold, and a plume of smoke wafted about his head until it was dispersed by the wind. "Seriously. My mom's gonna have me for breakfast over these stupid shoes."

"It might wash off," I suggested, though I didn't think it would.

"Yeah. Maybe." He grinned wearily at me. "All right. Later, skater."

"After a while, pedophile."

He crushed his cigarette out beneath one ruined sneaker, then stuffed his hands into the pockets of his jeans, his broad shoulders hunched and his plastic Batman mask hanging over the nape of his neck. He sauntered across the intersection. The green glow of the traffic light cast an eerie bluish radiance on him. He looked like one of the ghosts straight out of December Park folklore.

I stood on the corner and watched him go until the darkness swallowed him up whole.

As I continued along Haven Street toward home, I replayed the incident with Mr. Naczalnik. Had I been paying more attention to my surroundings, I might have noticed the vehicle hiding in darkness ahead of me. As it was, I nearly jumped out of my skin when the engine abruptly roared to life. Just as the headlights flashed on, the vehicle lurched forward, and I heard the chain saw shudder of grinding gears as it advanced toward me.

The suddenness of it all frightened me into temporary immobility; I merely stood in the center of the street, my hair bullied by the wind and blowing across my forehead and down into my eyes. I brought one arm up to shield my eyes and stepped over to the curb as the headlights roared toward me.

The notion to run, to dash over the curb and through the flanking woods, occurred to me right away, but I was powerless to move. I watched the headlights barrel down on me until the vehicle screeched to a sliding halt no more than ten yards away. It was a pickup, and the force of the stop caused it to fishtail across the center of the street. The tires smoked. I felt the heat of the truck even at this distance. I heard the muffled sound of the radio blasting in the cab and saw darkened, swarthy shapes spilling over the side of the truck's bed. In a flash, I caught the gleam of metal belt buckles.

Disembodied, someone's voice floated out to me. "Mazzone, you asshole, I've been looking all over town for you."

They moved around the truck, circling me like hyenas. The cab's dome light came on as the door opened, illuminating the driver.

Nathan Keener.

I sidestepped off the road and halfway into a row of thick shrubs. This new angle removed the glare of the truck's headlights from my eyes, enabling me to fully view my predators. Nathan Keener and four or five of his lackeys had spilled from the truck and now hovered around me, their white, skeletal faces seeming to float unanchored in the darkness. Cadaverous grins radiated all around me.

Keener paused alongside the front of his pickup and leaned against the hood, his body stiff. He poked a cigarette into his mouth and lit it with a Zippo. The Zippo gleamed in the moonlight. He inhaled, the cigarette's ember blazing red, his arms folded.

Nathan Keener was eighteen and a recent graduate of Stanton's vocational school, although just barely, from what I'd heard. He and his assemblage of like-minded cohorts looked wholly out of place in this section of Harting Farms. They haunted the alleys of the boulevards, the run-down brick-fronted establishments that flanked the industrial park, and desiccated bulwark of the fishing piers. They all lived out on the Cape and rarely came to this part of town, which made me suddenly very, very concerned.

"What's the matter with you, Mazzone?" Keener said. "How come you look so shaken up, man? You surprised to see me? You shouldn't be."

"The fucker's in blackface," said one of Keener's friends, and for a moment I forgot I had shoe polish smeared across my face.

"What do you want?" I tried to sound tough, but I couldn't muster the right tone.

Two of Keener's goons approached me from either side. They moved slowly at first, as if they were just shifting their positions. The glare of the truck's headlights, so strategically placed, made it impossible to see their faces until they were right up on me. Then they jumped at me, grabbing and squeezing my forearms and jerking me backward until I lost my balance and hung like a drying T-shirt on a clothesline between them.

The one on my left was Denny Sallis, his freckle-spattered moon face so close to my own I could smell his rancid breath. His eyes were sloppy, wet, and red-rimmed—the eyes of an ancient hound dog. When I turned away from him, he exhaled in my face, causing me to shudder at the toxic aroma of marijuana, beef jerky, and boiled cabbage.

To my right, clinging to my other forearm with both of his squirrelly claws, Carl Nance grinned like a lunatic, his deep-set eyes like two pits that had been drilled straight through to the back of his skull.

Keener took another drag on his cigarette, then tossed it to the ground. When he stepped toward me, I couldn't help but think I was about to be killed by a bad cliché. Two more of his lackeys, their hands in the pockets of their dark coats, their heads partially down as if they were ashamed of what they were about to do, approached me as well. I couldn't make out their faces, but I knew from past experiences they were probably Eric Falconette and Kenneth Ottawa.

I struggled against the two guys holding my arms.

Their grips tightened and Carl Nance muttered, "Cool it, fuck stick," into my ear.

I was accosted by a right hook to the jaw. I never saw it coming. Flash-bulbs went off beneath my eyelids, and a cold numbness pervaded the left side of my jawbone. A moment after that, a white-hot needling surged across the lower half of my face in concert with a high-pitched ringing in my left ear. It felt like the left side of my jaw had come unhinged. When I opened my eyes, Nathan Keener's face was mere inches from my own.

"One hundred hours of community service." Keener narrowed his eyes to slits and clenched his teeth. I swore I could hear him grinding his molars to powder. "You listening, Mazzone, you little faggot? One hundred hours."

"I don't know what you're talking about," I managed through my pained jaw.

"Your fucking father," said Keener. He jabbed a finger at my face. "Your fucking father, you faggot narc."

And then I remembered. Days ago, I had gone to the Generous Superstore for my grandmother, and as I biked around the back of the store on my way home, I saw Keener and his pals spray-painting the rear of the store. I had put my head down and pedaled faster, though Keener had caught me staring at him. Sometime later, Keener and his buddies were arrested for vandalism. I had nothing to do with his arrest, but I knew now that he believed otherwise.

"Hey, man, if this is about you guys tagging the Superstore, I never said shit." It was all I could say, since it felt like someone was trying to unhinge the jaw from my face with a screwdriver.

Keener lunged forward and administered an uppercut to my stomach. I buckled forward as far as Denny's and Carl's grasps would allow. Gasping for air, I felt my legs go rubbery. After a moment, Keener's friends hoisted me to my feet where I wavered like a drunkard between them. Someone tittered.

"You think I'm some kind of asshole?" Keener said, taking a step back from me. He was fuming, his chest heaving, both his fists clenched. I could almost see steam spewing from his nostrils.

"Is this a trick question?" I responded. It was a stupid thing to say, no doubt the result of spending too much time with bigmouthed Michael Sugarland, but I just couldn't help myself.

Keener kicked my legs out from under me. At the same instant, both Nance and Sallis let me go.

I dropped to the pavement like a sack of wet laundry, a stunning bright pain bolting through my hip. It took a second or two for the world to shift back into focus. Just as Keener's Doc Martens advanced toward me, Sallis and Nance yanked me to my feet, but this time my legs had difficulty cooperating.

"I'm not a fucking imbecile. We know you ratted us out to your old man," Keener said. Behind him, Ottawa looked like he wanted to leapfrog over Keener and tear me apart. "There's no way the cops could've known it was us unless you told them." His eyes gleamed. They were the eyes of a hungry wolf. "None of the cops saw us do it. But I know *you* saw us, you little rat fuck."

"You ever scrub paint off walls, cocksucker?" Sallis barked too close to my ear, shaking me in his grasp.

"Should make him scrape it off with his face," Ottawa said. "Should take him there tonight, watch him work it off for you, Nate. Use his teeth on it."

"Not a bad idea," Keener said. "But first, I'm gonna play cop, just like you and your old man. See, I got your community service right here, Mazzone. I got it for you good, bro."

I turned my head, and the punch caught me behind my right ear: the heat-filled sting of a giant wasp. A great bell began to ring in the center of my head.

"Hold his face up," Keener said calmly.

"Dude," Nance whined through the tolling of the bell as he gripped my chin and turned my face, "just watch where you're swinging."

I buried my chin against my collarbone like a frightened turtle.

"Hold him," Keener shouted.

"Hurry up," Nance protested while trying to pry my chin off my collarbone. "Just punch him in the face so we can get the fuck out of here."

"Yeah, man," Sallis added. "Push his teeth up into his gums so we can bolt."

Keener hit me again. I saw the swing come through blurry eyes. Again I managed to turn my head away, but he caught me high on the cheekbone. Pain exploded. It felt like the bones in my skull were about to shake apart.

Keener laughed maniacally.

I opened my eyes. The world swam in and out of focus. Tears froze to my face. Or it could have been blood.

"How's that feel, you stool pigeon faggot?" Keener said. "How's that community service working out for you?"

"Coward bitch," I spat.

The smile on Keener's face vanished. "You don't know when to shut the fuck up, do you, asshole?"

Headlights appeared around the bend at the intersection of Haven and Worth. All of them except for Ottawa, who seemed powerless to remove his eyes from mine, turned in the direction of the headlights.

I saw my opportunity and took it, bringing up one knee and swinging it forward, then swinging it back.

"He's—"Ottawa started but it was too late.

I planted my sneaker squarely against Nance's kneecap and felt something pop. A sound like someone snapping an elastic band rang through the sudden stillness. Nance's hands dropped from my forearm. Then an agonized howl burst from his lips as he collapsed in a messy heap to the pavement.

I wasted no time gathering my own feet beneath me. I headed straight for the woods but only managed about two strides until I was jerked backward and dragged to the ground. Something tightened around my neck. I heard something tear—it turned out to be the hood of my sweatshirt—and saw Sallis stumble to the ground beside me, a look of stunned agony on his pale face. He went down hard, his chin rebounding off the pavement. Then his body went limp.

I hopped to my feet and tore through the blinding darkness of the woods. My exhalations were a rhythmic, abrasive rattle in my throat. I heard Keener and his friends shouting at each other, trying to regroup. Sheer seconds later, their thundering footfalls crashed through the underbrush behind me.

Reinvigorated by their pursuit, I pushed myself harder through the trees. I found the dirt path that I had taken my bike down the night I rode to the Shallows and ran for all I was worth. But as the shouts and footfalls of my pursuers grew louder and louder, I knew I was an easy target on the dirt path, so I ditched into the woods.

"There!" someone shouted behind me. "He cut into the trees!"

I kept going and didn't look back. Through the tangled network of tree limbs I spotted the filaments of yellow light dancing in the windows of the houses on the next street over, which was Worth Street, where I lived. I could even hear the wind chimes that hung from the Mathersons' back porch tinkling in the wind.

Something hard struck the small of my back. Something else banged into my left elbow and jostled the nerves straight up through my forearm. A third object whizzed past my head, and even in the sightlessness of the woods I could see it was a large stone. The bastards were throwing rocks at me.

Keener's friends shouted, their heavy feet crashing through the underbrush. They made the brusque and confused noises of big, dumb mammals. On the far end of the street, I heard Keener's pickup growl to life and squeal as it shuddered into drive. I made out the truck's headlights streaming down the street, running parallel to me. He was planning to beat me to Worth Street and grab me when I came out of the woods behind the Mathersons' house.

I cut sharply to the right and vaulted over a fallen tree. The lights at the rear of the Mathersons' house were abruptly blotted out by a stand of pines.

"There! There!" someone yelled, and the voice was close enough behind me to trigger a perceptible twinge at the base of my spine.

For one moment, I considered bolting out onto Worth Street and making a mad dash for my house. There was a good chance I'd get to my porch before they grabbed me. But then for whatever reason, I threw myself forward through the wall of pine trees at the last second.

The trees swallowed me up. Blindly, I propelled myself forward, my hands swatting pine boughs out of my face. I struck a tree trunk and landed hard on my side in the dirt, temporarily liberating all wind from my lungs, and rolled until I came to rest in the approximation of a sitting position.

My eyes still closed, I felt the prickle of pine branches closing in on my head. I brushed them away, opened my eyes, and found myself corralled within a cover of dense and shaggy firs. I pulled my legs up to my chest and remained sitting, breathing harshly into the pit between my knees. I couldn't see my pursuers, couldn't see the lights of the Mathersons' house, couldn't even see the moon. My face stung and my eyes were blurry with tears.

I heard them, though: their shouts, their fury, calling out to one another as they got separated. They were all around me, yet they couldn't find me in my perfect hiding spot. Keener's truck, its exact location impossible to pinpoint, growled somewhere close by. Holding my breath, I listened to feet crunching through the woods. They were moving much more slowly now. Lost. Looking for me. I caught nonsensical snippets of disembodied voices.

"Come on," someone said. The voice was impossibly close, and I could not fathom how I hadn't heard the speaker's footsteps upon the carpet of crunchy dead leaves.

I pressed my face into my knees, wishing I could shrink to the point of disappearing.

The footsteps retreated. Their voices gradually grew more and more distant as they retreated toward the street. I heard Keener's truck roll coolly down Worth Street, then waited until the simmering sound of its engine was heard only in my memory.

Still, I did not move right away. It wasn't that they were clever enough to trick me into giving away my position by feigning retreat, because they weren't. They were morons. No, it was merely that I needed a moment to catch my breath and realign myself. The anger had not yet set in, temporarily bullied into submission by the stronger, innate sense of self-preservation. But it would strike soon enough. I knew it would.

I touched my face. My fingers came away wet with blood. Or mud. I couldn't tell for sure in the dark, but judging by how my face felt, I had a pretty good idea what it was.

I sat until my overheated body was once again aware of the cold. Turning over on my side, I crawled forward through the veil of trees, much more aware this time of the pricking and prodding and scratching of limbs. Then I paused. Listened. Because for a second, I had been certain . . . had been *certain . . .*

I risked it: "Who's there?" Then winced, bracing myself.

Someone was right beside me, hidden just beyond the trees. I was suddenly sure of it.

"Who's there?" I said again, my voice trembling.

Still, I received no answer. And I could no longer hear that whistling rasp of someone else's respiration.

I stared at the darkened curtain of pines, expecting at any moment to see a figure emerge. Those spiny black boughs would part like curtains, and a white face would appear from the depths, eyes rimmed in silver, a gaping mouth lined with razor-sharp teeth . . .

I turned and bolted out of the woods.

There were no lights on at my house when I arrived, and my father's car was gone from the driveway. Quiet as a baby's whimper, I stripped out of my clothes in the upstairs bathroom, only to feel a cold resignation wash over me at the sight of my mud-ruined jeans. Balling up the jeans, I buried them at the bottom of the laundry hamper.

Then I examined my face in the bathroom mirror. My lip was split, and there was dried blood smeared across my face. Also, it looked like I would have one hell of a shiner when I woke up tomorrow morning. I tried to convince myself that much of the bruising was really just shoe polish, even though I knew it wasn't. I washed up at the sink, then dabbed a swab of cotton doused in rubbing alcohol to the split in my lip.

The anger and humiliation struck me later as I struggled to find sleep in my bed, my face burning but only partially due to the rubbing alcohol and my injuries. I thought I would stay awake all night—that I would hear the shudder of my father's unmarked sedan coming to rest in the driveway at dawn, would smell coffee brewing on the stove . . .

Thinking all this, I fell quickly asleep.

CHAPTER FOUR
THE NEW KID

I awoke the next morning, Sunday, feeling bruised and sore all over. My ribs hurt, my face hurt, and there was an aggressive headache drilling through the center of my brain. I saw bright orange leaves float by my bedroom window and remembered that today was Halloween.

I got up, went into the bathroom, and spent the next few minutes gazing into the mirror, trying to convince myself that the wounds on my face incurred from last night's run-in with the Keener Gang didn't look as bad as I'd feared. But they did. My lip was puffy and the split at its center had dried to a brownish-purple scab, and the skin around my left eye was swollen and bruised.

Thankfully, it was early and everyone else in the house was still asleep, so I dressed and slipped out the back door before anyone could see me.

I trotted across the street to the edge of the woods behind the Mathersons' house. I noticed black tire marks on the pavement where Keener's pickup had burned rubber and peeled out. I hurried onto the Mathersons' lawn and headed toward the pine trees where I had hid from Keener and his gang. On my mind was the gut feeling that there had been someone else hidden among those trees with me last night. It hadn't been one of Keener's buddies—they would have snatched me and dragged me out—but it had been someone.

Now I attempted to locate the exact spot where I had crouched and hidden the night before. My gaze fell on broken limbs and crushed pinecones, so I assumed I was in the vicinity. I wasn't exactly sure what I was looking for, but I felt a compulsion to see if there had been any clue left behind. A shoe print, perhaps.

But I found no shoe print. I found no evidence of any kind. I continued to wend through the trees for several minutes, swatting at bristling boughs and crunching on brown pine needles, but the only shoe prints I discovered were the big sloppy impressions left behind by the Keener Gang's shit-kicker boots. Had I imagined someone else here? Had it all been in my head? I finally surrendered to defeat and gave up.

On my bike, I sped through the sleepy streets of the city while passing only the occasional neighbor shuffling to the edge of their driveway to retrieve their morning newspaper. Some looked dismayed at the dried egg yolk shellacked to the sides of their cars, a casualty of Mischief Night. Later the streets would be teeming with trick-or-treaters, and before the night was over there would be more cars to clean and fistfuls of candy corn chucked in the gutters, looking like busted teeth.

Cold air whipped in off the bay, smelling strongly of wood smoke and cedar and vaguely of impending snow. They were calling for a harsh winter this year. Already the Generous Superstore had its shelves stocked for the predicted snowstorms.

I rode my bike parallel to the highway and eventually turned in to the plaza where I chained my bike up outside the Quickman. Inside, rubbing the feeling back into my hands, I ordered pancakes, sausage links, bacon, and scrambled eggs. The Quickman made the best scrambled eggs, moist without being too runny, saturated in cheddar cheese, and drizzled with bacon bits.

I went over to the bank of pay phones at the rear of the eatery and dialed Peter's number.

"Hello?"

"Hi, Mrs. Blum. Is Peter up?"

"I think so. Hold on, Angie." She leaned away from the phone and called for Peter. I could hear a TV or a radio in the background. When she came back on the line, she said, "He's grabbing the upstairs extension."

"Thanks."

"How's your dad?"

"Oh, he's okay. I haven't seen him much lately. He's been busy with work."

She sighed. "I guess it's a hectic time for him, all right," she said and sounded glad to be rid of me when Peter picked up the extension.

"Hey," I said. "Get your butt down to the Quickman."

"What are you doing out so early?"

"I needed to leave before my dad got up."

"Jesus, man, what'd you do now? Are you in trouble again?"

"Just get down here, will you?"

He groaned. "Give me fifteen minutes," he said, and hung up.

I dropped the phone back on its cradle, then sat at a window booth where I waited for my food. I was the only one in the place, and I found idle contentment in watching the lights of the shops along the plaza come on one by one as daylight broke across the sky. There were paper jack-o'-lanterns taped to the shopwindows. On the front door of Mr. Pastore's deli was a cutout of a black cat, its spine arched and spiky as if it had been zapped by a current of electricity. Spooky tapestries hung from the old-fashioned streetlamps that ran the length of the sidewalk. The entire parking lot looked like a charcoal etching.

When my food came, I sliced up my pancakes and drowned them in blueberry syrup. I nibbled at the strips of bacon, avoiding the earlobes of jiggling fat at the ends, and ate a single forkful of egg before I set my fork down and just stared out the window. As ridiculous as it was for Keener to hate me for what had happened to him, so was it equally ridiculous for me to hate my father for what Keener had done to me. But I did. I knew it was stupid. My eyes suddenly burned. At that moment, I was all too aware of my swollen lower lip and my purpling eye.

Something banged against the plate-glass window. The palm of Peter's hand was pressed against the glass, pulsing like one of those face huggers in *Alien*. Pleased to have startled me, he grinned. I shook my head and waved him in. He leaned his bike against the window and entered the Quickman on a gust of cool air.

His smile faded as he approached the booth. "What the hell happened to your face?" he said, sitting across from me.

I decided to play coy. "Huh? What are you talking about?"

"Are you shitting me? It looks like someone hit you with a goddamn truck."

"Eat this," I said, pushing my plate in front of him.

When the waitress came by, he supplemented the meal with a heartstopper, the Quickman's specialty—a toasted parmesan bagel slathered in melted cheese and topped with a fried disc of salami that curled like burned paper around the edges.

"Seriously, man," he said, stuffing his face with egg. "What happened to you?"

I told him about the night before, and I could see the anger welling just below the surface of his face as the story progressed. By the time I'd finished, his normally ruddy complexion had transitioned to a purple rash-like blotchiness that seemed to originate somewhere below his neckline.

Peter pushed the half-eaten plate away. "That son of a bitch coward, jumping you when you're alone. He must have been following us and waiting for the right time."

I had been thinking the same thing. I even recalled seeing a pickup coast by the Harting Farms sign last night after we'd switched the letters. In hindsight, I thought it might have been Keener's truck.

"We gotta get that asshole. Like, for real. Payback's a bitch." Peter hooked one finger into his shirt collar and stretched it away from his neck. I nearly expected a cartoon mushroom cloud of steam to belch out. "What's his community service?"

"He and his friends gotta scrub the graffiti off the back of the Generous Superstore. Either that or paint over it."

Peter shook his head. "And that dumb fuck blames you?"

I shrugged, trying damned hard to look disinterested and not upset all of a sudden. "He thinks I ratted him out to my dad. He knows I saw them spraying the store."

"But, well, you didn't rat them out, did you?"

"Of course not."

"That overgrown fuck. We could set his truck on fire."

"Chill out," I said. "I'm in no mood to go to juvie over it."

"But you can't just not do anything about it."

"Well, if it's any consolation, I'm pretty sure I busted Carl Nance's kneecap before I got away."

Peter arched his eyebrows. "No shit?"

"I got him pretty good," I said, "and I think I heard it pop."

"Good for you. I hope he's in a wheelchair the next time I see him. Those assholes." Though still visibly angry, Peter's appetite had evidently returned, because he scooped up a mound of egg. "I'm assuming your dad doesn't know anything about this."

I snagged a strip of bacon off the plate. "Nope. Wasn't in the mood to get into it with him. That's why I left before he woke up."

"So then the plan is to hide from him all week until your face heals up?"

"I have no plan."

"Maybe we can catch a movie at the Juniper. They're showing all those old horror flicks for Halloween, remember?"

"Cool," I said.

"After that, we can figure out what to do about your face. Maybe Scott will have an idea. He's on his way over here."

When Scott arrived almost twenty minutes later, winded and chapped from biking halfway across town, he plunked down beside Peter, who was in the middle of eating a fresh order of breakfast.

Scott plucked a sausage link from his plate. "Jesus, Angie, what happened to your face?"

"Sorry," I said. "You missed the reenactment."

"Nathan Keener and his ballet troupe jumped him last night after we all split up," Peter informed him.

"Goddamn it. He tuned you up good."

I rolled my shoulders and pursed my lips. "Apparently it looks worse than it feels."

"What'd your dad say?" he asked, snatching another of Peter's sausage links.

This time, Peter shot him a disapproving look.

"He hasn't seen me yet."

"You think he'll arrest Keener and his friends for assault?"

"Christ," I said. "That's the last thing I need."

"Then what are you gonna tell him?"

"Beats me. You got any ideas?"

Scott narrowed his eyes and scrutinized my face while chewing slowly and methodically on the last bit of sausage. Then his eyes brightened and he snapped his fingers. "You could pretend it's fake. Like, it's your Halloween costume."

"What's he supposed to be?" Peter quipped. "A guy who got his ass kicked?"

"No, man," Scott said. "Your dad's got those old boxing gloves in the basement, right? You can say you're a boxer."

"Nice," I said, frowning. "And what am I supposed to do tomorrow? Pretend I'm still in character?"

"You can pretend you're one of the Piper's victims," Peter suggested. "The one who got away."

"That isn't funny," I told him.

"You guys realize he's real, right?" Scott said. "The cops finding that girl's body in Satan's Forest proves it. No one can say those other kids just ran away anymore. We're not dealing with runaways or even a kidnapper. We've got our very own serial killer." The look on his face suggested he was delighted at the prospect.

"Just because a girl was murdered doesn't mean those other three kids were killed," I said. "It doesn't even mean they're related."

"That's what everybody's saying," Peter added.

"Not everybody," Scott said. "The newspapers think they're all related. You should talk to your stepdad," he said, turning to Peter. Peter's stepfather worked for the *Washington Post*.

"Ed the Jew works in the goddamned classifieds," Peter countered. "What would he know? Unless the killer's taken out an ad because he's selling a bicycle or a used washing machine . . ."

"The cops haven't suggested that they're related," I said.

"No offense to your dad," Scott said, "but the cops, they don't know everything. I mean, if they did, they would have found those other kids, right?"

I sucked some of my Coke up through a straw and said, "Yeah, I guess."

"If those three other kids didn't run away," Peter said, "and they were actually murdered by some nut—"

"Serial killer," Scott interjected.

"Yeah, serial killer," said Peter. "If they were murdered, then where are their bodies? The police would have found them by now."

"Maybe they're hidden," Scott said. "Maybe they're down in the woods just like that Cole girl, only the cops haven't found them."

"Impossible," I said. "The police spent two days going through the whole woods. They had dogs with them and everything." I knew this because I had ridden my bike to the park and watched the uniformed police officers comb the area with cadaver dogs straining their leashes.

"Drug-sniffing dogs?" Peter said.

"Body-sniffing dogs," I said.

Peter raised his eyebrows and looked impressed.

"So maybe the other bodies are hidden someplace else." Scott was unwilling to be deterred. Once he wrapped his mind around something, he never let it go.

"Like where?" I said.

"Like anywhere. I don't know. Maybe he chopped the others up into fish food and dumped 'em in the Chesapeake."

"What about their bones?" Peter said. "You can't chop up bones and feed them to fish."

"You can smash bones. You can burn them, too. Or maybe the Piper just threw them in the bay, too. Do bones float or sink?" He looked at me.

"How the hell should I know?" I said. "How many bodies you think I've disposed of?"

"And where would he be doing all this chopping?" Peter asked. "In his house?"

"Sure," Scott said. "Why not?"

"If this killer of yours is chopping up bodies and dumping the pieces into the bay, how come he left that Cole girl in the woods?" I said.

"Maybe he didn't do it on purpose," Scott said. "Maybe she would have never been found if that drunk MacMillan chick hadn't driven her car off the road and into the woods."

"Okay," I conceded. "That's a good point. But it still doesn't mean those other three kids were murdered."

"Yeah?" Scott said. "So let me ask you. If there's no chance those other kids were killed, why were the cops searching the woods with cadaver dogs *after* they found the Cole girl? What else were they looking for?"

Peter and I exchanged glances.

Then, for the second time that morning, something slammed against the plate-glass window, causing the three of us to bounce up in our seats. Pressed against the glass, pink and hairless like two Easter hams, were the quivering twin lobes of Michael Sugarland's bare ass. Watching our expressions from over his shoulder, he exploded with laughter, his mouth so wide I could count the fillings in his molars. He dragged his buttocks along the glass, and the sound was like the rubber heel of a sneaker skidding on a gymnasium floor.

As luck would have it, this was at the same moment our waitress arrived and placed the check at the corner of our table.

"Lovely," she said and turned quickly away.

We caught a double feature at the Juniper, This Island Earth and The Incredible Shrinking Man.

During the intermission, Scott leaned close to me and said, "He must live right here in town."

"Who?"

"The killer," he said, his breath smelling of buttered popcorn. "The Piper. Don't you think so?"

I didn't answer.

There was a moving van in the driveway of the old Dunbar house next door by the time I pedaled home. It was about time, seeing how the new neighbors had been moving around inside the house for weeks now. I assumed they were old, since most of the old people I knew—including my grandparents—didn't venture outside the house very much.

I drew figure eights in the street on my bike as the movers hauled furniture and cardboard boxes into the house, hoping to catch sight of our new neighbors. At one point I thought I saw someone in an upstairs window peering down at me. I stopped in the middle of the street and looked up. There was certainly a face, white and round yet otherwise indistinct, in the window. To my surprise, it looked like a child, maybe even someone my own age. I waved, then immediately felt like an imbecile when the moon face retreated into darkness.

One of the movers grunted and stepped down the ramp at the back of the truck. He carried two cardboard boxes, one stacked on top of the other. Printed in block capitals in black marker on both boxes were the words *comic books*. One corner of my mouth tugged upward in a half smile.

I pedaled to my house, hopping the lip of the driveway and coasting up onto the lawn. The air smelled strongly of fireplaces, and a lazy plume of blackish smoke spiraled out of the Mathersons' chimney across the street. I stowed my bike against the side of our house, then went inside.

"New neighbors' moving van finally showed up," I told my grandmother as I flitted by her on my way into the kitchen. She was perched on a chair near the window in the living room, knitting. The curtains were swept back; apparently she had been spying on the comings and goings next door as well.

"I haven't caught sight of them yet," she called to me. "Have you?"

"No." I grabbed a Coke from the fridge and popped the tab, then joined my grandmother by the window. I strategically positioned myself behind her chair so she couldn't see the bruises on my face. "But a couple of the boxes were full of comic books."

"I've baked a fresh batch of oatmeal raisin cookies."

"Great," I said. "I'm starved."

"I meant for you to take over."

"To the new people? Do I have to?"

"Don't be impolite, Angelo."

"Okay. I'll do it after dinner. Did you make extra?"

"Yes," she said. "Save some for your dad and grandfather, though. And don't eat too many and spoil your appetite."

I went into the kitchen, snatched a handful of my grandmother's fantastic cookies, then pounded up the stairs to my bedroom. My dad and grandfather were in the backyard cleaning wet leaves from the barbecue pit. I watched them through my bedroom window but didn't want to alert them to my presence lest I'd be wrangled into their effort, not to mention I'd have to explain what happened to my face.

After I finished the cookies, I slipped a Bruce Springsteen cassette into the tape deck and picked up my acoustic guitar to strum along, keeping one eye on the window and the work being done in the yard.

When my grandmother called them both in for dinner, I shut off my music and darted into the upstairs bathroom to wash my face and hands. By the time my dad had come in through the back door, tired and breathing heavy, I had already dropped into my seat at the kitchen table, ready to face the inevitable.

"When'd you get home?" my father asked, peeling off his checkered flannel jacket and draping it over his chair. He went to the sink to wash his hands.

"Just a few minutes ago," I lied, grateful that my grandmother was out of earshot.

When he came back to the table, he paused once he got a good look at me. "What happened to your face?"

"It was stupid," I said. "We were playing baseball in the park, and someone hit a pop fly. I went to catch it, but the sun was in my eyes, and it hit me right in the face."

"Ouch." My father took my chin in his hand. He tilted my head to the side to examine my injuries. "One ball got you in the eye *and* the lip?"

In a small voice, I said, "I guess so."

"Must've been some hit." He smiled wearily at me. "I guess your friends had a good laugh at that one."

"Yeah."

"What park?"

"Huh?"

"What park were you playing at?" he said, sitting down across from me.

"Oh. December Park."

"Hmmm." He unfolded his napkin. "Do me a favor and stay out of that park, will you?"

"How come?"

"Just for a while. If you're gonna go to a park, go to one closer to home."

"Is it because of that girl? The dead girl?"

That weary smile reappeared but only for a second. "I'd just feel more comfortable if you stuck closer to home, Angie."

"Okay. I will."

As my grandparents filtered into the kitchen, I had to retell the phony story about taking a baseball to the face to each of them. My grandmother set the food on the table, and the four of us ate to the soundtrack of my grandfather's intermittent proselytizing about the tragic state of the country—there was a new clerk at the cigar shop he frequented who didn't speak English.

I thought about Scott's request of me—that I should ask my father about the disappearances of the kids from town. I had no idea how to broach such a topic with him—he never spoke of his work to me or my grandparents—and I didn't expect he'd even take my questions seriously if I did bring it up.

I supposed other guys my age would have fawned over the idea of their father being a police detective—it was no different than how my friends obsessed over the fact that there was a gun in my house—but I hardly ever gave it any thought. I had no clue if my father was good at his job or not (though I assumed he was), how he felt about the work he did, or how long he planned on doing it. I didn't even know if he had ever shot anyone. I never asked and he never brought it up. To some degree, he had shared those things with Charles, but that had been in a different lifetime.

After the table was cleared and my grandparents retired to the den to watch television, my father remained at the table, sipping a glass of red wine and gazing absently out the window. I refilled his wineglass and was about to replace the bottle in the cupboard when he said, "Was this your first fight?"

For a second, I didn't know what he was talking about. He had caught me with my guard down, as he so often did. There would be no use trying to convince him of the story about catching a pop fly with my face. "Uh, yeah, I guess. How'd you know?"

"You think I was never fifteen?"

"I just didn't want to get into it," I said.

"Who was it?"

"Some guys from school."

"Guys? More than one?"

"Well, only one of them hit me." I wasn't going to go into detail about how two of Keener's friends had held my arms while Keener pummeled me.

"Did this guy start it?"

"Yeah."

He smiled with just the corner of his mouth. "Did you finish it?"

I couldn't help but smile a little, too. "Sort of."

"You remember me teaching you and your brother how to fight?"

"Sure," I said. He had brought home sparring gloves from the police department's gymnasium and taught us the fundamentals of self-defense. Never start a fight, he'd told us, but never let someone put their hands on you, either. Know how to protect yourself.

My father looked at his wine, then peered out the window.

It had just started to get dark, and I could see groups of costumed children going door-to-door. They pounded down the twilit causeways, their pillow-cases bottom heavy with candy. Minivans prowled at a distance behind them, filled with parents who were more cautious this year.

"Grandma said I gotta go next door and take cookies to the new people who moved in," I said.

"Sounds good," said my father, still staring out the window.

A few minutes later I pulled on my Windbreaker and, balancing a plate of oatmeal raisin cookies in one hand, walked next door. The moving van had left sometime around dinner, and the whole house was once again deathly quiet. Even the trick-or-treaters knew enough to avoid it, although that was probably because it still looked like no one lived there.

For one split second, I wondered if I'd dreamed the whole thing—the moving van and the movers, the boxes of comic books, and, most implausibly, that pale moon face in one of the upstairs windows.

I walked up the porch and knocked on the door. Then I peeked in the narrow window running down the left side of the door but couldn't make out anything but dark, angular shapes. There were no lights on inside. I knocked a second time and continued to wait. Farther down the street, the Wilbers' Rottweiler barked at two young kids dressed as Aladdin and Jasmine.

I was just about to leave when the front door opened partway. A woman of indeterminable age stood on the other side. There was a look of distrust bordering on hostility on her face.

"Hello," I said quickly, almost robotically. "I'm Angelo Mazzone. I live next door. Here." I proffered the plate of cookies. "My grandmother made these for you."

The woman eased the door open a few more inches, the hinges squealing. She was haggard looking, with blonde streamers of hair framing her face. She wore no makeup and had very thin lips. Her eyes would have been pretty if only she adopted a softer countenance. I thought that maybe she looked older than she was.

She reached out for the plate of cookies.

I surrendered it to her, thinking, *There is no way she can pull that plate through the opening in the door. She will have to open it wider.* The thought was like cold water running down my spine; for some inexplicable reason, I didn't want her to open the door any wider.

"That's very kind," said the woman. She possessed the small, timid voice of a squirrel. The door squealed some more as she pulled it open farther. Behind the woman I noticed a heap of cardboard boxes and furniture covered in ghostly white sheets. "Please come in."

I wanted to say no, but my feet were already carrying me over the threshold before I knew what I was doing. When she shut the door behind me, it was like being sealed up in a tomb.

"I'm Doreen Gardiner."

"Hi."

"That's some makeup."

I made a sound that approximated, "Huh?" before realizing she was referring to my bruised eye and split lip. "Thanks," I said, allowing her to believe it was part of a Halloween costume. Maybe Scott had been right, and I should have draped my father's old boxing gloves around my neck.

"Do you want to wait here a moment while I get Adrian?"

"Sure, I guess."

"Have a seat inside and I'll fetch him."

The pronoun *him* threw me. The only Adrians I had ever known had been girls.

Doreen Gardiner waved me toward an adjoining room that, when the Dunbars had lived here, had served as a sort of parlor room, with plush chairs and a fancy love seat covered in clear plastic. It hardly looked like the same room anymore. There were no chairs, so I sat atop a box labeled *books* and watched as Doreen Gardiner mounted the stairs to the second floor. She walked with the hampered gait of someone suffering from osteoporosis, though she couldn't have been more than forty-five. Maybe even younger.

I looked around the room. The walls were barren and scuffed, the ceiling pocked with water damage. The carpeting was an ancient shag the color of oxidized copper. The Dunbars had been an elderly couple who'd been meticulous about the upkeep of their house, so I was surprised to find it in such poor condition.

Overhead, I heard footsteps followed by a muffled conversation. Then silence.

I must have sat on that box waiting for ten full minutes before I heard footsteps pattering down the staircase. I stood up.

The boy who appeared at the bottom of the stairs was small, thin, timid as a mouse. His hair was the color of wheat, and his eyes, swimming behind the lenses of thick black frames, were so pale they looked nearly colorless. He wore a Spider-Man sweatshirt that looked too small even for his insignificant frame, the sleeves stopping several inches above his frail wrists. I knew without question that it had been his face I had seen in the window.

"Hey, I'm Angelo. I live next door. You can call me Angie."

"I've got an aunt named Angie," he said, sliding his hands into his pockets.

I realized that we were two boys who both had girls' names. When he didn't introduce himself, I said, "Your name's Adrian, right?"

"Yes."

"Where'd you move from?"

"Chicago."

"Cool." I thought about sprinting out the front door. "How come you came to Maryland?"

"My mom's job moved her here."

While I found it jarring to think of that walking scarecrow of a woman holding down a job let alone being someone's mother, I merely continued to smile and nod like an imbecile.

"Is that real?" He pointed at my face as he leaned closer for a better look at the bruises.

"Unfortunately, yeah," I said, instinctively leaning away from him.

"What happened? Did you fall off your bike?"

"No. I got jumped by a couple of guys."

Adrian's mouth tightened into a knot.

"It's not a bad neighborhood," I said. "I mean, there are some jerks wherever you go, but for the most part everyone is cool."

"Oh. Okay. Do you have a lot of friends here?"

"Sure," I said. "There's a bunch of kids on this block, too."

He nodded impassively. "Do you like comic books?"

"Sure," I said, though I didn't own a single comic book. When I was younger, I used to buy them for a dollar and a quarter at the Newsoleum on Second Avenue, but I hadn't continued the practice once I started reading horror novels.

"I've got a bunch. I was just unpacking some of them upstairs. Do you want to come up and take a look?"

"Well, I sort of have to get back home. I gotta help my grandma hand out candy to the kids."

"Are you going trick-or-treating?"

My friends and I hadn't gone trick-or-treating since we were eleven. But this kid looked about my age, and I didn't want to make fun of him, so I just said, "Nah, I've got some homework and stuff to do, too."

"Where do you go to school?"

"Stanton. You probably saw it when you came into town. It's a big old building that looks like a medieval fortress."

"Oh yeah. That's my new school, too."

Great, I thought. I would probably wind up sitting next to this kid in half my classes. He would follow me around, inserting himself into my group of friends, and sit next to me at the lunch table.

"Well, maybe you can come by some time, and I can show you my comic book collection. When you have time."

"Okay." I feigned interest in the setting sun outside the nearest window. "But I should get back home now."

Without uttering another word, Adrian turned and led me to the front door. He twisted the doorknob with two hands, the way a small child would do it, and when he pulled the door open it seemed to weigh a thousand pounds. It was like watching someone open a bank vault.

"Well," I said, hurrying out the door, "I'll see you around."

"Hey," he said. "Does it hurt? Your face, I mean."

"No, not really. It's just sort of embarrassing."

"Wait here," he said, whirling away from the door and pounding up the stairs before I could say anything.

I turned and watched hordes of witches, ghosts, ghouls, and goblins rove up and down the street. Given all that had been happening in town since the Demorest boy disappeared in August, their joyful screams took on a sinister quality.

Adrian returned with something in his hand. "Sorry," he said, out of breath. "It took me a while to find it." He extended it to me and I took it. It was a pair of fake plastic teeth, all yellow and rotted and crawling with plastic bugs. "They're zombie teeth."

"Yeah?"

"You can wear 'em when you answer the door to hand out candy. This way, you won't have to be embarrassed about your face. People will think it's part of a costume."

"Oh." I didn't know what else to say. "That's a good idea. Thanks."

"Sure," he said.

"Later." I hopped off the porch and walked across his front lawn. When I glanced over my shoulder, I saw him standing in the doorway, watching me. He was still watching me when I walked through my front door.

CHAPTER FIVE
IN THE SHADOWS, IN THE SHADE

Following my altercation with Mr. Naczalnik, I was reassigned to Mr. Mattingly's English class. The polar opposite of the stodgy Naczalnik, Mr. Mattingly was young and looked more like a lacrosse player than a high school teacher. He spoke to his students as if they were peers. This was his first year teaching, and his slight Southern drawl made him seem as foreign and intriguing as someone from the other side of the world. I liked him instantly.

That Monday, I sat in Mr. Mattingly's class for a good forty minutes before I realized Adrian Gardiner was seated toward the back of the room. His presence surprised me; he looked completely out of his element here, like a ghost who'd just walked in from a graveyard. When he met my eyes he quickly bowed his head and stared at the top of his desk. I turned back around and faced the front of the classroom, inexplicably discomfited by his presence.

When the bell rang, I expected Adrian to follow me out, but he didn't. He gathered up his books, strapped a ridiculously large backpack to his shoulders, and bustled out of the classroom ahead of me. In the hallway, he vanished among the sea of students.

The following day, I said hello to him as I crossed the aisle on the way to my desk. He gazed up at me from his seat, his expression one of perplexity behind his thick glasses. When he recognized me, he offered me a partial smile that seemed to have no feeling behind it.

For the next fifty-five minutes, I wondered if Adrian would come up to me after class. But once again, the moment the bell trilled, he was up and out the door. Strangely, I found myself more troubled by his ignoring me than if he'd latched onto me and followed me around like a puppy.

One afternoon before class started, a kid named George Drexler strutted over to Adrian's desk. Adrian was staring absently at his textbook. Drexler, who was a stocky little prick with bad teeth, pointed to what looked like a doodle in the margin of a page, and said, "Hey, did you draw that?"

Adrian looked up at him. "Yeah." Then he smiled meagerly like he'd just befriended someone who appreciated his artistic talent.

"Cool," said Drexler before returning to his seat. Thirty seconds later, as Mr. Mattingly entered the classroom with his briefcase and a Dunkin' Donuts coffee cup, Drexler raised his hand. When Mr. Mattingly called on him, Drexler said, "The new kid drew all over his textbook."

I kept an eye out for Adrian in the cafeteria, but I could never spot him. Toward the end of the week, I wandered outside into the quad. It was a chilly November day, and there were only a few students braving the weather, mostly the hopheads who didn't get along with the rest of the student body. Adrian was not here, either.

Similarly, my friends and I never caught up with him as we walked home from school. Adrian lived right next door to me, but I never saw him walking along Worth Street in those first few weeks. On a couple of occasions I was tempted to knock on his door, but the thought of entering that stale, tomb-like house again caused my skin to break out into braille.

"Have you met him yet?" Peter asked me one afternoon as we walked home from school.

"Yeah. My grandma made me bring cookies over to the house the day they moved in. He's in my English class, too."

"What's he like?"

"Kind of strange. He's already missed a couple of classes."

"Your dad's not gonna make you hang out with him, is he?"

"Are you kidding? No way I'm hanging out with him. The kid's a spaz."

In fact, my father never said a word about the new neighbors. Not only was he overworked, but he was at his all-time lowest around the holidays. Charles's absence weighed heaviest on him this time of year, and I suppose he thought often of my mother around this time, too.

We maintained the family tradition of driving out to the Butterfields' where we bought apples for pies and Indian corn to decorate the front door. Yet my father moved through the Butterfields' cornstalks and bales of golden hay like a ghost, a humorless grin frozen onto his face. When he paid for the items at the register, he didn't engage Henry Butterfield in their ritualistic cheerful banter.

Thanksgiving morning, just as I had forgotten all about Adrian Gardiner, he appeared on our front doorstep holding a dish tented with foil. "It's lasagna, I think. I'm not sure. My mom made it."

My grandmother took the dish from him—it was our dish, the one that had been stacked with my grandmother's cookies—then invited him inside. The kid stood in the foyer, shifting from one foot to the other, his ski parka too tight around his shoulders while his glasses looked too big for his face.

"How are you getting along at school?" I asked him.

"It's okay."

"Do you like it?"

"Sure."

"Is it really different than Chicago?"

"I guess so."

"What about the town? I bet it's totally different than living in a big city."

"Yeah."

"Do you miss your friends?"

"I don't know."

Our conversation was strained to the point of breaking, so I wished him a happy Thanksgiving and ushered him out onto the porch. He said nothing in response and seemed relieved to be out the door. From the bay windows in the living room, I watched him cross the lawn toward his house. He dragged his feet and hunched his shoulders and looked like someone who felt uncomfortable merely existing.

The following Sunday, as my family and I drove back from church, I saw Adrian's narrow little frame packaged in that same undersized parka, marching up Haven Street. He had his bulky backpack strapped to his shoulders, and he walked with his head down, as if the effort of the exercise took so much out of him.

As our car glided past, I stared at him. It looked like he was searching for something in the patch of brownish grass that abutted the shoulder of the road. He did not see me.

Of course, I had more important things to worry about than Adrian Gardiner. In the weeks following my run-in with Keener and his gang on Mischief Night, I had seen Nathan Keener's truck cruising my neighborhood at odd hours of the day and sometimes in early evening. There was little doubt he was looking for me.

Every day for the remainder of that month Keener could be found with a handful of his friends at the Generous Superstore, whitewashing over the vulgarities they had spray-painted on the walls. I saw them there as my friends and I walked home from school, careful to stay out of their sight. Once, I saw Carl Nance among them. He sat on the hood of his Aries K, wearing a leg brace and balancing a pair of crutches across his lap. This gave me some dark satisfaction.

I had to be careful and anticipated an ambush at every turn. Like a fugitive, I kept to the shadows, kept to the shade.

One Saturday afternoon as I studied a display of pocketknives at Toddy Surplus, I spotted Keener, Denny Sallis, and Kenneth Ottawa strutting past the front windows. I prayed they wouldn't come inside. They paused just outside the store and lit cigarettes. A light snow was falling, and the sky beyond the parking lot was gray and brooding.

I sidestepped over to a rack of hunting gear, keeping my eye on the windows. When they ditched their cigarette butts onto the curb and entered the store, I felt a great waft of heat blossom up out of my coat. I faded toward the back just as Mr. Toddy, the pock-faced proprietor behind the counter, looked up and cleared his throat.

"Help you boys with anything?" Mr. Toddy asked Keener and his buddies.

"Just lookin' around," said Ottawa as he lazily spun a wire carousel displaying postcards, novelty magnets, and books of crossword puzzles. He wore a grease-stained military jacket and faded jeans. His jackboots left wet footprints on the linoleum.

I slipped down an aisle and stashed myself between two racks of old hunting coats. At the front of the store, Keener and Sallis snickered about something beside a display case of electronic equipment. Like a restless bear, Ottawa continued to rove around the store, absently picking up items off shelves, then shoving them back in place.

When Ottawa paused on the other side of the aisle where I was hiding, I glanced up at the antitheft mirror above the front door and saw that both Keener and Sallis were bent over one of the display cases with their backs to the front door. If Ottawa came around the aisle, I'd run in the opposite direction and head for the door. Hopefully I'd make it out before Ottawa could alert the other two.

But Ottawa meandered over to his friends, his boots still leaving wet tracks on the floor. The three of them muttered, and one of them—Sallis, I thought—tittered laughter like a hyena.

"Was there something in particular you fellas were looking for?" Mr. Toddy spoke up again.

From where I stood I couldn't see him, but I could certainly sense an air of apprehension in his voice.

"Nope," said Keener. He shoved his hands into his pockets. "Let's beat it."

They headed out. Before the door shut them out, I heard one of them mocking Mr. Toddy in a reedy parrot's voice: "'Was there something in particular you fellas were looking for?'" This was followed by guttural laughter.

I watched them cross the parking lot and walk up the sidewalk toward the highway. It was snowing harder now, and I soon lost sight of them among the crowd of holiday shoppers.

"Those boys friends of yours?" Mr. Toddy asked me after I'd come out from behind the rack of hunting coats.

"No, sir."

"I don't like them coming in here. You tell them I said so."

"They're not my friends."

"They come in here again, I'm calling the cops."

I nodded, then rushed out of the store.

On Christmas Eve, we celebrated *Festa dei sette pesci*, or the Feast of the

Seven Fishes. The house was pungent with the scent of scungilli and fried codfish while my grandmother butchered eels in the kitchen sink. My dad and grandfather sat in the living room drinking Chianti as Dean Martin and Perry Como took turns crooning Christmas standards on my father's old turntable.

I put the finishing touches on the Christmas tree and watched the snow spiral past the bay windows. Next door, Adrian's house was completely dark. I wondered if he and his mother had traveled back to Chicago for the holidays.

Yet the following morning, as my family and I climbed into my dad's car for Christmas mass, I saw Adrian sitting on the front stoop of his house. He was wearing flimsy-looking pajamas and fuzzy blue slippers.

My grandmother commented about how the kid was going to catch pneumonia sitting outside dressed like that, and wasn't his mother paying any attention? I thought of Doreen Gardiner's medicated stare and zombielike gait and decided that maybe paying attention was beyond her ability.

That night, we had the Mathersons over for Christmas dinner. They were a childless couple of middle age, plain and good-hearted. Mr. Matherson told the story about how a deer had gotten tangled in his Christmas lights one year and how he and my father and Charles had chased the deer up and down the street to try and get it untangled. I had been positioned on our front lawn with a broom; my dad had instructed me to swing the broomstick at the buck if it got too close. Mr. Matherson told the story every Christmas, as if none of us had ever heard it, let alone been there when it happened.

"Eventually," said Mr. Matherson, smiling ruefully if not a bit drunkenly, "the thing took off into the woods, trailing about one hundred feet of colored bulbs behind it. It's probably still out there to this day, its antlers strung up in lights."

Just as coffee was served, my grandmother ushered me into the kitchen and shoved a ceramic plate into my hands. It was filled with struffoli, which were little balls of dough glazed in honey and covered with colorful round sprinkles.

"Just go on over and wish those people a merry Christmas," she said and practically tossed me out the front door.

I crossed the snowy patch of yard. Paper-bag luminaries lit up the far end of Worth Street like an airport runway. As was typical, the worry about a heavy snowstorm this year had been for nothing, and we had received only three inches of snow, which was quickly melting. It was terribly cold, however, and the brief walk from my house to the Gardiners' was enough to numb my cheekbones and cause my nose to start running.

I climbed the porch steps of the Gardiner house, wondering once again if anyone was home. The lower level was dark, but there was a single light in one of the upstairs windows. I knocked on the door, then peered through the adjacent window, searching for any kind of festive lighting inside. I saw nothing.

Doreen Gardiner opened the door. Her face was pale and haggard, her hair tugged back on her head and tied in a tight bun. She wore a loose-fitting cotton shirt and flared pants with a wallpapery paisley pattern. The smell of stale, unwashed flesh combined with liquor wafted out onto the porch with me.

"Merry Christmas," I said, thrusting out the plate of struffoli.

"How nice," she said flatly and bent down to survey the sticky balls of dough. "Very interesting."

"It's called struffoli," I said. "I don't like it much, but the rest of my family does. My grandma makes it for Christmas every year."

As she leaned forward to take the plate, the frayed collar of her shirt gaped, and I saw what looked like a hideously pink scar twisting around the base of her neck. It was dark on the porch, and I thought it was maybe a trick of the light. Before I could get a better look, she straightened up, and the scar disappeared beneath the collar. "Do you want to come in? Adrian's upstairs."

"Uh, I need to get back home and help my grandma clean up," I said.

Doreen Gardiner smiled with much effort. She looked like a corpse brought to life by black magic, doomed to walk around still reeking of the grave. "Tell your grandmother thanks for the . . . What's it called again?"

"Struffoli."

"Yes. Tell her thanks. And merry Christmas, too."

CHAPTER SIX
AN INCIDENT ON BESSEL AVENUE

As was tradition on New Year's Eve, my father, grandfather, and I drove to the old rock quarry at the end of our street to watch some of the neighbors light off fireworks. The quarry was a large pit of excavated limestone surrounded by two layers of chain-link fencing topped in concertina wire. It took up several acres, beginning at the end of Worth Street, where Worth denigrated from paved asphalt to a narrow access road comprised of crushed white gravel, and stretching all the way out to the black curtain of stately pines in the west. It was hard to tell how deep the pit was, although you wouldn't be too far off estimating the drop at around two hundred feet.

It was eleven thirty when we arrived, still early for the fireworks show, but even at this hour I could see that there weren't as many people hanging outside the quarry fences as there had been in the past. It was easy to chalk up the poor attendance to the cold weather, yet I couldn't help but wonder if people had stayed home because of the Piper.

There had been nothing newsworthy that had come out since Courtney Cole's body had been recovered from the woods. No leads were reported in the news, and there had certainly been no arrests. If the police had any suspects in mind, they were keeping their suppositions close to the vest.

I wanted to ask my father about the investigation, since he was one of the lead detectives on the case, but his dour spirit and tired eyes kept me from opening my mouth. Conversely, when he was in a good mood and his laughter came more easily, I was loath to ruin it by asking him morbid questions. So I let it go and remained in the dark just like the rest of the citizens of Harting Farms. And although some people were hopeful that the person responsible for Courtney Cole's death—not to mention the disappearances of William Demorest, Jeffrey Connor, and Bethany Frost—had moved on, this belief did not seem to quell any concerns or lessen any fears.

My dad parked the car and we all got out. Beneath the three-quarters moon, the limestone on the other side of the fences appeared to radiate with an otherworldly light. A few people bundled in coats sat on lawn chairs, drinking beer or coffee from steaming thermoses. They sat in a rough semicircle around a slight concavity in the gravel where someone had already set up some impressive-looking fireworks. A battery-powered radio in someone's lap was tuned to a classic-rock station.

When we approached the small crowd, everyone said hello and a few of the older women waved at me. Looking around, I realized I was the only kid. It was a fact that this little fireworks display had always been more for the adults than for the kids, but in years past, a handful of teenagers and even some younger kids had been in attendance. Their absence was like a glaring hole in the fabric of the night, and I felt instantly self-conscious standing here among all my grown-up neighbors.

Mr. Matherson shook my dad's hand, a bottle of schnapps poking out from the side pocket of his Marlboro Man coat. He smiled at me, though he looked a little surprised to see me.

A man wearing a plaid hunting cap with earflaps, sort of like the one Elmer Fudd wears in the cartoons, came over and handed my dad and grandfather each a cigar. This man had a short and stumpy cigar, its tip glowing reddish orange like the blazing eye of a Cyclops, crooked into the corner of his mouth. "Merry Christmas, Sal," he said to my dad, squeezing his forearm.

"Hey there, Angie." It was Mrs. Wilber, seated in one of the lawn chairs.

She smiled at me. The Wilbers' Rottweiler, leashed to the arm of the lawn chair, lifted its head and gazed at me with something disconcertingly like contempt. "We've got some doozies this year," she said, nodding toward the assortment of fireworks in the gravel pit.

"Yeah," I said. "They look great."

"How's school going?"

"Okay, I guess."

"Wonderful, dear." She unscrewed the cap on her thermos, then poured some dark and steamy liquid into the cap and handed it to me. "Homemade hot chocolate to warm your bones."

I sipped the drink and knew two things instantly—Mrs. Wilber was drunk, and there was alcohol in the hot chocolate. I grimaced, coughed, and thrust the cup back at her, managing a strangled "thank you" as I did so.

Mrs. Wilber laughed and her Rottweiler glared at me again.

My grandfather sat on one of the large chunks of limestone that protruded from the earth, smoking the cigar the man in the Elmer Fudd hat had given him. He wore a tweed driver's cap and a heavy chamois coat trimmed in nicotine-yellowed wool. The tip of his cigar blazed beneath the brim of his cap as I approached and climbed up next to him.

"There were more people here last year," I said. "Kids, too."

"Well, it's a particularly cold New Year's Eve, don't you think?"

"Yeah."

"And people, they have long memories. They're mostly still . . . worried . . . about things." He looked at me. "You ain't worried, are you?"

"No."

"Good boy." He took the cigar from his mouth and held it out to me. "Wanna give it a try?"

"Sure!"

"You don't inhale it like you do cigarettes."

"I don't smoke cigarettes."

"Right." He winked at me.

I placed the wetted end of the cigar in my mouth, sucked on it until the ember burned a bright red and my mouth filled with smoke, then released it through puckered lips. It tasted like wet newspapers.

"Dad," my father said, joining us. He tucked his own cigar into the inside pocket of his barn coat.

"What? The boy's fifteen years old. When I was fifteen, Uncle Sam handed me a rifle and gave me an all-expense vacation to the South Pacific."

"Give the cigar back to your grandfather."

"Aw, man," I groaned, handing it over. "Can you blow smoke rings like they do in the movies?"

"Are you kidding?" My grandfather gave me one of his patented movie-star smiles; according to my grandmother, it was that very smile that had earned him quite a reputation among the ladies when he was younger. "Angelo, I practically invented blowing smoke rings."

My father laughed more loudly than I thought necessary, and I wondered if some subtle joke had just gone over my head.

After several unsuccessful attempts at blowing smoke rings, my grandfather cocked his driver's cap back on his head and scrutinized the half-smoked stogie as if it were defective.

Again, my dad laughed, and this time I laughed along with him.

At one minute before midnight, the woman with the radio on her lap cranked up the volume. Mr. Matherson, Mr. Wilber, and the man in the Elmer Fudd hat huddled together like revolutionaries preparing to conspire. They each brought out lighters and flicked them on, casting their faces in a mottled quilt of orange light and pitch-black shadows. I supposed they were deciding who had the best lighter to use for tonight's display. Both Mr. Matherson and Mr. Wilber tucked their plastic Bics back in their coats while the man in the Elmer Fudd hat, grinning, tapped his long-tipped barbecue lighter against the palm of one hand.

"Here it comes! Get ready!" shouted the woman with the radio.

A Beatles song had just ended, and a disc jockey was preparing to count down the New Year.

The man in the Elmer Fudd hat jogged over to the gravel pit where the fireworks were arranged.

Someone called out, "Don't set yourself on fire, Fred," and this was followed by a chorus of laughter.

"Ain't that the truth?" my grandfather mumbled, leaning close to my ear. "Old Fred there looks like he's got pure hundred-proof whiskey coursing through his veins. He might go up like a Roman candle."

"Ten . . . nine . . . eight . . . ," the crowd chanted along with the radio announcer.

My father and I chimed in with them, "seven . . . six . . . five . . ."

My grandfather removed his driver's cap and twirled it around.

"Four . . . three . . ."

Fred was on one knee in the gravel, the flaming tip of the barbecue lighter igniting the wick on a particularly nasty-looking cardboard rocket ship.

"Two . . . one . . . Happy New Year!"

We all cheered and applauded.

My grandfather tugged the driver's cap down over my ears, stood up off the chunk of limestone, and shouted, "Bravo! Bravo!"

A sparkly asterisk of fire ran the length of the rocket ship's wick as Fred retreated toward the crowd of onlookers. A moment later, on a cloud of black smoke, the rocket ship launched high into the night sky. I lost sight of it before it even cleared the tops of the trees.

As if reading my mind, my grandfather leaned his shoulder against mine and pointed toward a cluster of bright stars. "There!"

The rocket ship exploded in a dazzle of bright pink, orange, gold, and silver lights that rained down in glittering streamers. On the other side of the chain-link fences, the light show was replicated in miniature on the surface of the muddy black water at the bottom of the quarry.

The next fifteen minutes continued in such a fashion. Once the final set of fireworks had lit up the sky in brilliant colors that left smoky drifts in their wake, my throat was hoarse from cheering, and I was sweating from my excitement despite the cold. The air smelled of sulfur and my grandfather's cigar smoke.

My dad gripped me around the nape of the neck and tugged me closer to him. He kissed the top of my head and said, "Happy New Year, pal."

"Happy New Year. Can I go check out the leftovers?"

"Just be careful. They're still hot."

I slipped off the limestone and hurried over to the gravel pit, where smoldering black remnants littered the ground. Curls of black cardboard smoked in the gravel. There were coal-colored scorch marks at the base of the white-powdered pit. I touched the arrowhead cupola of the rocket ship firework, a partially melted cone of red plastic, and it was still warm.

When I stood and turned back toward Worth Street, I noticed a pair of headlights speeding down the narrow road through the encroaching trees. Drifts of hazy smoke softened the glow of the headlights. The car came to a jerky halt. I heard rather than saw doors swing open and slam closed. A woman hurried toward the semicircle of lawn chairs, inappropriately dressed in nothing but jeans and a sweatshirt whose front glittered with rhinestones. The woman shouted something and looked terrified. It took me a moment to realize she was yelling my father's name.

My dad intercepted her halfway across the gravel lot. My grandfather and Mr. Matherson came up beside him. My dad held the woman by the forearms and spoke slowly while looking her directly in the eyes. She appeared stricken, panicked. Her lips were nearly blue.

I rushed over to join them. I had missed the beginning of the conversation and struggled to catch up.

"No, no," cried the woman, "they're still there. They called the cops but I knew you were here."

"Okay. Get back home." My father turned to Mr. Matherson. "Can you—?"

"Yes, I'll take them home," Mr. Matherson jumped in, apparently reading my father's mind. "Go on, Sal."

"Go," my grandfather echoed.

My dad rushed past the frantic woman toward Worth Street and, presumably, his car.

"Dad," I shouted and took off after him. Both my grandfather and Mr. Matherson called my name, but I ignored them. I reached my dad's car as he was climbing in the driver's seat. I opened the passenger door.

"Stay with your grandpa," he barked.

"I'm coming with you," I said and slid into the car.

He stared at me for less than a heartbeat. Then, cranking the ignition, he said, "Okay. Let's go."

I slammed the door and fastened my seat belt.

My father jerked the car into Drive and gunned the accelerator while spinning the wheel. We carved a sharp circle across the narrow roadway, then headed up Worth Street at a surprisingly quick pace.

"What's going on?"

"The Ransoms," said my father. "Their son, Aaron, is missing."

I knew Aaron Ransom. He lived a few blocks over on Bessel Avenue and went to Stanton School. He was a smallish kid with a blond bowl cut who sometimes skateboarded in the Superstore plaza parking lot with other kids from school. It took me a minute to realize what my father's statement meant. "What happened?"

"Put your seat belt on."

"It's on."

He increased the speed, the speedometer's needle climbing toward forty-five through the residential street. Over the treetops at the horizon, more fireworks lit up the night sky. At Haven, my father slowed but didn't completely stop at the intersection. He hooked a sharp left and sped more or less down the center of the street. The high beams clicked on. I looked at my dad and saw that he was not just watching the road but the shoulders and the dark spaces between the houses.

As we approached Bessel Avenue, he slowed and coasted up the hill, checking the darkened yards of the houses we passed.

"Dad?" I said.

"What is it?"

But I couldn't think of anything. My throat dried up.

My dad glanced at me, then turned back to the road without saying a word.

There was a single police car in the Ransoms' driveway, its rack lights ablaze. A few neighbors in heavy coats milled around the front lawn, looking as confused as cattle in a hailstorm.

My father parked at the curb and told me to get out. I did, not wasting a second, and followed him up the lawn.

The front door opened before we reached it, and a man in a gaudy Christmas sweater waved us inside.

My dad marshaled through the doorway, and I trailed close behind him, my head down. I didn't meet the man's eyes.

We went through a cluttered family room with walls of ugly wood paneling and into a cramped little kitchen. A youngish police officer in full uniform stood before a woman sitting ramrod straight in one of the chairs at the table. I recognized her only distantly as Aaron Ransom's mother, since I'd seen her on only a few occasions. Now, she was hardly recognizable as that woman. Dark streaks ran from her eyes and muddied her cheeks. Her hands wrestled with each other in her lap.

She looked up sharply at my dad. When she recognized him, she stood.

The uniformed cop turned toward us, glancing at my dad, then me.

"It's okay, Rebecca," my father said, intercepting her and gripping her forearms just as he'd done to the woman in the rhinestone-studded sweatshirt by the quarry only moments ago. He turned to the cop. "We've got guys on the way?"

"Yes, sir."

"Get out front and check the nearby yards. Ask some of those people on the front lawn to help you out."

"Yes, sir."

"And have someone go over to the Torinos' place for statements."

The officer nodded, shot another glance at me—*Who the hell are you and what are you doing here?*—then hurried out.

"What happened, Rebecca?"

She began crying. It was miserable. Her face appeared to collapse straight down the middle, her eyes smeary and indistinct in their sockets.

For the first time I noticed a small black dog under the table. At the sound of Rebecca Ransom's sobs, the dog became frantic, running around the legs of the table and weaving around the chairs. It barked twice—more squeaks than barks—then fell silent.

My dad backed Rebecca Ransom toward one of the chairs and guided her into it. "Calm down, hon," he said, his voice impossibly calm. "Tell me exactly what happened."

I deciphered most of what happened through Rebecca's erratic retelling: at around ten o'clock, Aaron had gone over to the Torinos' house for a New Year's Eve party. She had instructed him to be home immediately after midnight. When he didn't show up, Rebecca telephoned Mrs. Torino and asked to speak with Aaron. Mrs. Torino informed her that he had never shown up. That was when Rebecca had called the police.

"Was he on his bike?" my father asked.

"No. He was taking over a rum cake and he walked. Oh, Jesus . . ."

"Did you tell all this to the officer who was here?"

"Yes."

"I'm sending someone to sit with you." He turned toward me. "Come on, Angelo."

I followed him through the house and out the door. More people had gathered in the street and on the neighbors' lawns, some of them carrying flashlights. The uniformed cop was speaking to a group of them, pointing in various directions around the neighborhood.

As my dad and I crossed the lawn to join them, two more police cars slid up Bessel Avenue, lights and sirens whirling. My dad paused by the Ransoms' mailbox and flipped back the flap of his barn coat. He took his handgun from the waistband of his jeans, jerked the slide, and stuck it back in his pants. When his eyes met mine, there was a confused mix of compassion, sorrow, and angst in them. Yet on the surface he remained calm.

All of a sudden, and to my great horror, I found that I was close to tears.

"It's okay," said my father in a calming voice. "You stick close to me. Right on my heels."

Numb, I nodded.

My father hurried into the street. He approached one of the police cars that had just pulled up and spoke to the officer behind the wheel. The officer handed him what looked like a trucker's CB radio handset. My dad brought it up to his mouth, keyed the button. When he spoke, his voice was transmitted over a loudspeaker hidden among the rack of lights on the roof of the car.

"We're looking for Aaron Ransom," he addressed the crowd. "Everyone, fan out. Check the streets and make your way through yards. If you see any neighbors, have them turn on all outdoor lights—floodlights, porch lights, anything. Four groups, searching north, south, east, west. You'll each have an officer leading the group. Stay with your group. No one should go off by themselves."

He looked out over the crowd, perhaps gauging the frightened and aggressive faces, then added, "Don't take any weapons. If you've got a handgun, leave it at home." He tossed the handset back in through the open driver's side window.

"What do we do?" I asked him when he faced me.

"Head up Bessel toward the Torinos' house," said my dad, already moving up the block. I hurried after him. Several neighbors joined us, the beams of their flashlights crisscrossing the night. Everyone jumped as more fireworks exploded over the horizon.

A woman shouted up ahead. A crowd gathered around her, and some of the men waved at us. One of the police cruisers drifted toward them, and several men—my father included—broke out into a run. I ran after them, my face burning.

My dad stopped when he reached the crowd. They stood in a semicircle around something in the street. As soon as I realized this, I felt my legs stiffen up. My heart was jackhammering. Shoulders thumped by me, jostling me as I slowed to a near standstill in the middle of Bessel Avenue. Up and down the block, porch lights came on.

"Oh, my God," said one woman. She wandered away from the crowd, her hands to her mouth, her eyes wide and fearful. "Oh, God, Rebecca . . ."

I approached the crowd, coming up alongside my dad. I spotted something small and dark, shoved up against the curb.

My dad placed a hand on my chest, arresting my progress. "Stay," he said, then pushed himself through the crowd. He bent down and examined the thing on the ground.

I managed to squeeze between two men and saw what he was looking at.

It was the rum cake. A ceramic plate lay in pieces in the gutter. It looked like someone had tried to kick the smashed cake and the pieces of plate into the sewer.

My dad stood, went to the nearest uniformed officer, and spoke quietly and very closely to his face. Once he backed away, the uniformed officer addressed the crowd, telling them to step back. More house lights came on farther down the block.

My dad headed down Bessel toward the Ransoms' house. I bolted after him, reaching him just as he went around to the driver's side of his car. "Go on. Get in," he said without looking at me.

I jumped in the passenger seat and slammed the door. My dad backed down the block, spun the car around, and gunned it toward Haven.

I wanted to ask where we were going, but I didn't. I thought it best that I sat there in the passenger seat and kept quiet. When we hit Haven, I expected him to turn in the direction of Worth Street. Instead, he swung the car around in the opposite direction. The fireworks were in the rearview mirror now. My dad reached down beneath the console and switched on his police radio. Static blossomed in the car. Unintelligible voices spoke in eerily calm tones to each other.

When my dad took a right onto an unnamed service road that ran through the woods, I knew what he was doing: circling Bessel Avenue on the far side of the woods. The service road was unpaved, and the sedan jounced like a roller coaster as we advanced deeper into the trees. The high beams caused the shadows to shift, and the trees looked alive.

When the service road forked, my father took the road that led deeper into the woods. He slowed the car to a near crawl and diligently surveyed the darkened landscape all around us. There was a floodlight affixed to the mirror on the driver's side of the car, which my father switched on. He directed the beam into the trees and manipulated its direction by thumbing a lever on the inside of the window. We drove like this for a while until our mutual respiration fogged up the glass.

The radio beneath the dashboard came alive with a man's official-sounding voice. "Intersection of Bessel and Waverly. Possible suspect. Need backup."

"Hang on," said my dad to me. He gunned the car through the trees and took a secondary dirt road. The decline was steep and bumpy, the roadway not designed for vehicular traffic. Tree branches clawed at the sedan's roof. At the bottom of the hill, the secondary road widened as it merged with a section of asphalt. This was Waverly Street, one of the single-lane beach roads on the far side of the woods behind Bessel Avenue. As the car's tires touched the pavement, my father placed a bubble light on the dashboard and hit a switch, turning it on. Blue light reflected off the windshield and blazed down the dark street.

When we took a sharp turn, I saw a police cruiser farther up ahead, the dome lights painting the nearby woods in red and blue. Two men, one of them in a police uniform, stood outside the vehicle. The cop's gun was still in its holster, but he was resting his hand on the butt, ready to draw at a moment's notice.

The other man looked to be about fifty. He had a neatly trimmed beard and wore a puffy brown parka and a Baltimore Orioles baseball hat tugged down on his head, flattening his ears. He held both hands up, though not in the reach-for-the-sky way criminals raise their hands on TV when cops tell them to freeze. There was a casualness to the whole thing that seemed strangely rehearsed.

My father had his door open before the car was fully stopped. "Stay inside," he told me and got out. He withdrew his gun as he approached the man in the Orioles hat.

I rolled down the passenger window so I could hear what was going on.

"Chester?" my father said, taking two careful steps toward the man. He kept the gun aimed at him. "The hell you doing out here at this hour?"

"Walkin.'" The man's voice was indignant. "Just what I was tellin' your protégé here."

"You been drinking?"

"Is that a crime all of a sudden?"

My father spoke to Chester in a low voice. I caught only a few words, among them Aaron Ransom's name.

Chester's expression changed from indignation to outright disbelief, then to something akin to horror. When he lowered his hands, the uniformed officer instructed him to keep them up.

"Turn around, Chester," said my dad.

When the man turned around, my father holstered his gun. I held my breath. My dad patted down the sides of Chester's parka, the pockets of his dungarees. They were still engaged in conversation, but I couldn't hear a word of it until Chester turned back around and said, "I've already told him that."

"Come on," my dad said. There was a pleading quality to his voice that sounded very informal given the situation. "Help us out here, okay?"

Chester sighed, waggled his hands like they were coming loose at the wrists, then placed them behind his back.

The uniformed cop closed in and handcuffed the man.

"I ain't talking to no one but you, Sal," Chester said as the cop led him into the backseat of the police car.

"I'll be there right behind you," said my dad. He got in the sedan, breathed warmth into his cupped hands, then smiled wearily at me. A nerve jumped below his left eye.

"Who is that guy?" I asked.

"Chester Vaughn. He works down at the piers."

"Is he being arrested?"

"No. I've asked him to cooperate and he agreed."

"How come that cop put handcuffs on him?"

"To be safe. You don't trust anyone." My father pulled away from the curb and drifted slowly past the police car.

The officer was in the front seat, talking on a radio. In the back, Chester Vaughn gazed at us. His eyes were bleary red holes in the doughy whiteness of his face. The cop had removed his baseball hat, and his wiry hair stood up in uncombed whorls.

"It's freezing out there," my dad said, despite the beads of sweat glistening on his forehead. "Roll that window up."

I rolled it up, then turned around in my seat. Through the rear window I watched the blue and red lights of the police cruiser alternating through the trees. Then the lights went dark.

"Shit." The word dripped from my father's mouth with undeniable defeat. He looked at me, and I thought I saw him trying to offer me another tired smile. But this time he couldn't manage it. Instead, he dug a Kleenex from his coat pocket and handed it to me. "Wipe your nose."

I blew my nose, then wiped my eyes, abruptly aware but not all that surprised that there were tears at their corners. The car's heater was blasting hot air, but my entire body was shivering.

Ten minutes later, we were driving down Haven Street. The radio continued to squawk until my father switched it off. The clock on the dashboard read 1:32 a.m.

"Was it the Piper?" I said. "What happened to Aaron, I mean."

My father didn't answer.

"What's gonna happen now?"

"I'm going to drop you off, then head down to the station to talk with Chester."

"I want to stay with you."

"Your grandparents are probably wondering what's going on. I need you to stay home with them."

"No," I said. "I want to come with you."

"I'm working now, Angie. This isn't a game."

I turned away and stared out the passenger window. The houses along this section of Haven Street were dark, with even the outdoor Christmas lights unplugged at this hour. Only the blue flicker of television lights could be seen in some of the upstairs windows. There were no more fireworks in the sky.

We turned onto Worth Street and glided up to our house. The porch lights and the kitchen light were on. As we idled at the curb, I saw the curtain whisk away from the window and a face peer out.

My dad looked at me. "Are you okay?"

"Yeah, I guess."

"I've got to go."

I nodded, opening the passenger door and stepping out into the street. My hands in my pockets and my head down, I walked around the front of the car and up the driveway. Before I was even halfway to the porch, my grandfather opened the front door. Once I was safely inside, my dad drove away.

They didn't find Aaron Ransom. Chester Vaughn was questioned but ultimately released, his alibi having checked out. Apparently, a midnight walk around the beachfront was typical for Mr. Vaughn, particularly after knocking back a few drinks.

However, word got out that he had been questioned by the police, and rumors circulated. It was common knowledge that some of Chester Vaughn's neighbors, emboldened after a night of drinking down at Shooter's Galley, arrived on the Vaughns' front porch, shouting for Chester to come out. Chester called the cops, who threatened to arrest them for trespassing and assault if they didn't go home, which they all did, albeit reluctantly. Two days later, Chester and his wife thought it might be a good time to visit relatives in San Antonio.

The day after Aaron Ransom's disappearance, I told my friends about it. Even though I did my best to relate to them all that had happened and how it had made me feel, I was powerless to really get it through to them. There were things I couldn't tell them, like how I hadn't realized I'd been crying until my father handed me a Kleenex and how my father had stood there holding his gun on someone. It wasn't just him pulling the gun and patting the man down; it was the beads of sweat that had clung to his forehead when he'd climbed into the car and that awful smile he had summoned for me, no doubt in an effort to give me comfort. But it had been a horrible smile, devoid of any trace of humanity let alone comfort.

Aaron Ransom's picture appeared in the newspapers, and his mother gave a tearful speech on television. I read in the *Caller* that the police had located the boy's estranged father, Henry Carlson, who lived in Milwaukee. On several past occasions Carlson had allegedly threatened Ransom's mother about snatching the kid and taking him to Canada. But after Carlson was apprehended by federal agents, he was cleared of any suspicion.

Some residents started up a neighborhood watch. My father joined, and sometimes he drove around the streets at night looking for anything—or anyone—unusual. I often asked to go with him, but he told me it wasn't something I needed to worry myself with. It didn't matter what he said; after seeing the Cole girl's broken skull followed by that sickening night on Bessel Avenue, things worried me.

Another search was conducted in the woods off Counterpoint Lane and in the surrounding park. Peter and I rode our bikes to December Park and watched the cops, along with countless neighborhood volunteers, comb the area for Aaron Ransom's corpse. Rebecca Ransom was there as well, propped up like a mannequin in the backseat of a police cruiser. We wanted to be there in the event they happened to find Aaron's body. But, of course, they didn't.

CHAPTER SEVEN
THE COMBINATION LOCK

Returning to school after the holidays was like resuming a death march after a brief respite to catch your breath. The halls had grown cold in our absence, the ancient furnace no match for the weather. Time itself seemed to get mired down in molasses, and even the clocks appeared to tick more slowly. Each footfall was duller; each gloomy corridor was somehow less hospitable. Stanton School was a mine shaft hundreds of feet below the surface of the earth. And it was haunted by Aaron Ransom's ghost.

As it always was, the first week back in class was torturous. Mr. Mattingly's class was the last one of the day, and when the final bell rang that Friday, it was like the report of a starter's pistol. The cacophony of desk chairs skidding across the scuffed tile floor was followed by a rush of students heading for the door.

"Angelo." It was Mr. Mattingly. "Do you have a couple of minutes?"

I swung my backpack over one shoulder. "Sure."

The remaining students filed into the hallway, Adrian Gardiner bringing up the rear. He walked quickly and with his head down, his backpack looking like something an astronaut would wear. He merged with the rest of the foot traffic in the hallway and disappeared.

Mr. Mattingly got up from his desk, smoothing out the wrinkles in his slacks. He went to the door and shut it. "Have a seat," he told me, nodding toward the chair directly in front of his desk.

I sat and he perched opposite me on the edge of his desk, the way cops on TV sometimes did when they were pretending to be sympathetic to a perp.

"Have you been enjoying the class?"

"Yes," I said.

"Have you started thinking about college?"

"No. It's still a few years off."

"Understandable. But do you have any notion of what you'd like to study in college? Where you'd like to go?"

"Not really. I mean, I haven't given it that much thought."

"Right." He prodded the cleft in his chin with one thumb. "I know you've been here only a short time."

For one sinking moment I thought he was going to ask why I'd been transferred from Naczalnik's class to his. I had just assumed he'd already known the reason. It seemed that Mr. Mattingly liked me, and I didn't want to tarnish that with what had transpired between Naczalnik and me.

"I just want to throw something out there and see what you think."

"Okay . . ."

"I'd like to recommend you for Advanced Placement English next year."

His statement caught me off guard. I didn't speak. Only nerds and members of the school marching band took Advanced Placement classes.

Mr. Mattingly laughed and rubbed the side of his face. "I see I shocked you a little. Sorry about that." He leaned over his desk and picked up a small stack of papers that he thumbed through but did not look at. He stared at me. "I've been very impressed with your work. You possess exceptional writing skills, and you never have trouble with any of the harder texts. I checked your transcripts and saw that you've been acing your English courses since your first semester of freshman year."

I shrugged. "I like to read a lot."

Again, Mr. Mattingly surrendered a warm laugh. "Yeah, I bet. And you do some writing, too, don't you?" His gaze shifted toward a copy of the school's creative arts magazine on his desk. A story of mine had been published in that very issue.

"I guess so," I said.

"So what do you think?"

I shifted in my seat. "You mean about the AP class? I don't know. I hear those classes are pretty tough."

"Not if you're willing to do the work."

"It's not . . . uh, I mean . . ."

"I get it. You want to be in class with your friends. Only nerds take AP classes."

"Something like that," I said sheepishly.

"Listen," he said. "You don't have to make up your mind right here on the spot. Go home and think about it, talk it over with your parents. Take some time to figure out what it is you want to do."

"It's just me and my dad," I said.

"Then talk it over with your dad."

"Okay. I will."

"Good." He clapped. Then he held a hand out for me to shake.

As I gripped his warm palm, it occurred to me that I had never shaken a teacher's hand before.

"Now get out of here and enjoy the weekend," he said, smiling.

Out in the hall the crowd had mostly died down. A few stragglers hollered down the corridor, and I had to duck to avoid getting dive-bombed by a paper airplane. I dumped some of my heavier textbooks into my locker, not up for hauling them on my back the whole way home.

Glancing at my new wristwatch, which had been a Christmas present from my dad, I saw that I was too late to meet up with Peter, Michael, and Scott in the parking lot. There was an unspoken pact between the four of us that if someone didn't show within the first five minutes, it most likely meant detention and the others were free to skedaddle.

I looked to my left. A few lockers down, Adrian Gardiner glared at his enormous overloaded backpack, which rested on the floor at his feet. After a moment, he turned and looked at me. Those large colorless eyes were like the headlamps on a VW minibus behind the thick lenses of his glasses. There was a blotch of dried ketchup on the front of his sweater that resembled a gunshot wound.

Because I felt like a deviant just standing there staring at him, I offered Adrian what felt like a conciliatory smile.

Adrian did not return my smile. He only stared at me, causing a wave of discomfort to rise through my body like steam.

"Did you do it?" he said, his voice quivering.

"Did I do what?"

He pointed down at his backpack. "The lock. Did you do it?"

I slammed my locker shut, tugged the strap of my backpack over one shoulder, and went over to him.

"Someone put it on there when I wasn't looking," he said. "I don't know the combination, and I can't get it open. All my stuff is in there."

Someone had locked his backpack by slipping a combination lock through the holes in both zippers.

"Oh." Half of me suddenly felt sorry for him while the other half was embarrassed by his weakness, his pathetic nature. "I didn't do that. Why would I do that to you?"

"Damn. Fuck." That second word squeaked out of him, and I wondered if it was the first time he'd ever said it. He glanced sideways at me, as if to see whether or not I was bothered by the curse word.

Dropping to one knee, I examined the lock and tried to tug it apart. No dice. Instinct told me to flee and leave this little twerp to suffer his own follies, but good sense intervened before I could take to my heels.

"I've got a friend who can get that open," I said finally, standing up.

"You do? Who?"

"Michael Sugarland," I said. "I'm gonna go meet up with him and the other guys now down at Drunkard's Pond. You wanna walk with me?"

"What's Drunkard's Pond?"

"A pond."

Distrust was more than evident in his eyes. I wondered if he had been avoiding me on purpose for some reason.

"Hey, man, it's up to you," I said when he didn't respond.

Wordlessly, Adrian hefted his backpack off the floor and put it on with both straps. He followed me down the hall, keeping at least one step behind me.

This kid's in for a tough year, I thought. Was it possible things had been easier for him in Chicago? It might seem that a big city would eat someone like Adrian Gardiner for breakfast, but I wondered if the anonymity might not prove beneficial for him. He could disappear. He would be one among countless other losers to choose from. But out here in Harting Farms, Maryland, the kid stood out like a turd in a punch bowl.

We exited the building, the frigid air rushing up to greet us. We cut across the parking lot, which was a traffic jam of bleating car horns and blasting stereos, and headed toward Solomon's Bend Road. Solomon's Bend overlooked Drunkard's Pond and the little spit of land in which it sat. Most of the neighborhood kids steered clear of this area, due mainly to the hobos who squatted beneath the tin bridge and the overpass, so my friends and I usually had the place to ourselves.

It was no different this afternoon; as Adrian and I reached the corner of Solomon's Bend Road, I peered over the guardrail and spotted Peter, Scott, and Michael skimming stones off the frozen surface of the pond.

"Those guys are your friends?" Adrian said. It was the first thing he'd said without being prompted since we'd left the school.

"They're cool," I promised him. I'd spent the duration of our walk talking aimlessly about movies and music, neither of which Adrian seemed to have any interest in, and I was suddenly grateful to dilute Adrian's awkwardness among my friends. "Come on."

I climbed over the guardrail and was halfway down the embankment before Adrian followed. Several times I thought the weight of his backpack would send him toppling down the hillside, but despite his ungainly approach, he managed to stay on his feet and reach the bottom without incident.

"Hey, slacker." Michael winged a rock in my general vicinity. "We had a bet you got detention again. Guess I lost."

"Not detention, exactly." But I let it drop there. I wouldn't mention the talk I had with Mr. Mattingly about the AP English class. There was no point in making myself an outcast among my own friends. In fact, I decided then and there that I would not take the class next year.

Peter and Scott were digging up stones from the bank of the frozen pond. They both looked at me, then simultaneously turned to Adrian.

I swung my backpack into the dirt and hunkered down on top of it. "This is Adrian Gardiner. He and his mom moved into the old Dunbar house next door to me. He's from Chicago."

"Hi," Scott said.

Adrian looked like he wanted to blink out of existence. "Hello."

"You go to Stanton?" Peter asked.

"Yeah."

"We're in the same English class," I said.

Michael whistled. "Jeez, kid, you picked a helluva time to move to town. You hoping to make the Piper's top ten list?"

"Cut it out," I told him. "He's got a bit of a problem with his backpack. You want to give us a hand here, Mikey?"

Michael drop-kicked a large stone halfway across the frozen lake, then clapped the dirt from his hands. "Sure thing. What's up?"

"Go ahead," I said to Adrian. "Show him."

I had expected him to point out the combination lock, but instead, he turned around so we could all view the ridiculous bulging backpack as it hung from his shoulders. He didn't say a word.

"Someone locked his backpack with a combination lock," I informed Michael.

"Ahh," Michael intoned. "You've been pack-latched, friend."

"I told him you might be able to help."

"I'll see what I can do."

Adrian jumped when Michael yanked the backpack's straps from his shoulders. If Michael noticed that he had startled the kid, he didn't acknowledge it. He tossed the backpack onto the ground and knelt beside it, fingering the combination lock.

It occurred to me that it was a child's backpack, made of cheap bright green vinyl with a decal of the Incredible Hulk on it.

This kid doesn't stand a chance, I thought again.

"How can you open it?" Adrian asked, peering over Michael's shoulder.

"Ees vetty deefficult," Michael said in his best German accent. "Das lock ees vetty stubborn."

Adrian stared at Michael like he was crazy. I couldn't help but grin.

"So what kind of music do you listen to?" Peter asked. He and Scott had finished excavating stones from the hard earth and were trying to stack the flatter ones atop one another without much success.

"I don't know," Adrian said. "I don't really listen to music."

Peter frowned. "Not *any* music?"

"No, not really. Well, my mom has some Bing Crosby records that used to belong to my grandma."

"Holy shit," Peter said in a low voice.

"How about movies?" Scott interjected. "You like horror movies?"

"I guess so. Some horror movies."

"Did you see *Jason Goes to Hell*? It's the last *Friday the 13th* movie." Scott was a Jason Voorhees fanatic. He had posters, T-shirts, and even a hockey mask he adorned with streaks of red nail polish so that it looked like blood. He owned every installment on VHS, and I couldn't count the number of times he made us watch them with him. He had all the lines memorized and knew which kill went with which movie.

"I'm not allowed to see those movies," Adrian said.

Scott literally gaped at him. Even Michael, who had been occupied with the combination lock on Adrian's backpack, turned to stare at him.

"You're kidding," Scott said. "What was the last horror movie you saw?"

"No, no—what's your favorite horror movie?" Peter jumped in.

I tried to catch Scott's and Peter's eyes and to mouth the words *leave him alone*, but they weren't looking at me.

"I guess maybe *Explorers*," Adrian said.

"Aw, fuck," Peter said. "That's not a horror movie."

"Those aliens at the end were pretty scary," said Adrian.

"They were like big rubbery puppets," Peter said. "They quoted TV shows."

"What do you mean you're not allowed to see 'em?" Scott pressed. Scott's parents worked long hours with little time for their kids. Shy of murder, Scott was pretty much allowed to do whatever the hell he wanted, which included watching any horror movie his little heart desired, no matter how gratuitous.

"My mother doesn't think they're neurologically stimulating," said Adrian.

Peter laughed. "What the fuck does that mean?"

"She says they're like junk food for your brain."

"Yeah," Scott said. "No shit. That's what makes them so great."

"Mmmmm," Michael moaned, climbing to his feet and thrusting his arms out like a zombie. "Fatty junk-filled braaaaaains . . ."

"Zombies would starve hanging out with this crew," I added.

Peter started laughing uncontrollably.

"Braaaaaains," croaked Michael as he stumbled toward Peter, casually dodging the stones Peter chucked at him. "Redheaded braaaaaains . . ."

Still laughing, Peter launched himself off the ground and tackled Michael around the waist, driving them both down to the hard dirt. The force of the hit drove a fart from Michael, who also burst into maniacal laughter.

Chuckling, I looked over to Adrian and was surprised to see him grinning. It was a goofy grin that made him look almost simple, but it was a grin nonetheless.

"Get off me, queer bait," Michael said, bucking his hips until Peter crawled off him.

"Jesus Christ," Peter said, looking just as eager to get away. "That fart reeks. What did you eat for lunch? An old lady's diaper?"

"Leave your mother out of this," Michael returned, though I could tell he was fighting off his own bout of laughter.

I watched Adrian watching my friends. He was so out of place among the four of us that he could have been a visitor from another world. All of a sudden I felt sorry for him.

Once everyone settled down, Michael returned to the combination lock. More focused now, he was able to open it in under two minutes. It came unhinged with an audible pop.

"Wow," Adrian said. "How'd you do that?"

"Magic." Michael tossed the lock at him.

Adrian attempted to catch it, but it rebounded off his chest and tumbled to the ground.

"Mikey's practically useless in all other aspects of life," I said, "but for some reason, the son of a bitch has a knack for popping open combination locks. Anyway, he's Michael Sugarland."

Michael executed a flamboyant bow and said in a cockney accent, "Atcher soy-vice, gov'nor."

I pointed to the others. "And that's Scott Steeple and Peter Galloway."

"Hey," Peter and Scott said in unison.

Then Peter punched Scott on the arm. "Jinx."

"Sweet mother, what in the name of holy hell *is* all this?" Michael pulled a jumble of random items out of Adrian's backpack—flattened soda cans, a single muck-streaked sneaker, several large stones that glinted with flecks of mica, a couple of audiocassettes, a paperback novel with its cover missing, and something that looked oddly like a plastic flute. "Our boy is a hoarder, it seems."

"It's just stuff," said Adrian.

"Yeah, but why are you hauling it around?"

"Because I found it. I collect it."

Holding the filthy sneaker by its tattered laces, Michael sniffed at it, then wrinkled his nose. "Oh, gross."

Adrian shifted from his right foot to his left. "I go on scavenger hunts. Like, I search for things that people lost or threw out or whatever. Sometimes you can find some really neat stuff."

"Find the other sneaker and you've got a pair. Good for you." Michael dropped the shoe, then produced a spiral-bound notepad from within the backpack. He opened it and thumbed through the pages until something caught his eye. He paused and scrutinized the page as a look of surprise overtook him. "Jesus," he said, his voice slightly more reverent now. It was rare to hear him speak in such a respectful fashion. "Did you draw these?"

"Yeah," Adrian said.

"Are you kidding me? Man, these are great." Michael tossed the book over to me, and it landed in my lap. "Take a look at those drawings. That's some serious shit."

They were pencil drawings of various muscle-bound superheroes swinging punches at each other while others wielded swords or prepared to fire an arrow from a bow. "Yeah, these are really great."

"Let me see," Scott said, and both he and Peter scrambled over to peer at Adrian's sketch pad. "Wow. Those are cool. Did you trace them or something?"

"No."

"Did you copy them from a book?" Peter asked.

"No."

"Did you make these characters up?" said Peter. "Like, from your head?"

"Some of them," said Adrian. "Some others are characters from comic books. But I changed them around and gave them different uniforms or different weapons or whatever."

"You think you could draw Bugs Bunny?" Scott said.

Adrian shrugged. "Sure. That's easy."

"Dude," Michael said, dropping to his knees and placing his hands together in a parody of prayer. "Do you think you could draw naked chicks as good as you draw those superheroes?"

"I guess," Adrian said. "I never tried."

Michael looked impressed. "If I could draw like that, I'd draw nothing but naked chicks."

"I'm shocked," Peter commented.

Everyone laughed.

Michael pointed to the notebook. "Let's see you draw one up right now. Give her huge titties. And make the nipples really detailed."

"Nipples," Adrian said, staring at Michael.

"Yeah, man, you know." He cupped a pair of invisible breasts.

"I'm not sure I know what they look like," Adrian confessed.

Michael froze, his hands still groping invisible breasts, and Scott's mouth hung open.

"Draw Michael's face," I suggested. "He's the biggest boob we know."

The five of us spent the rest of the afternoon pitching rocks onto the center of the frozen pond, telling jokes, and bitching about school. For the most part Adrian remained quiet, although I got the impression he was enjoying himself, too.

Later, as the sky darkened and the streetlights came on, we gathered our backpacks.

Scott clapped Adrian on the back hard enough to send the boy's glasses askew on his face. "I'm going to set up a marathon of *Friday the 13th* movies for us to watch. Trust me, man. You'll thank me for it."

On Solomon's Bend Road, we went our separate ways. Adrian and I bundled across the road toward the intersection of Point and Counterpoint.

"Your friends are funny," he said.

"They're cool, yeah," I said.

"What did Michael mean when he said I was hoping to make the Piper's top ten list? Who's the Piper?"

"Oh, that's just the name the newspapers gave to the guy who's supposedly responsible for grabbing all those kids and killing that girl."

Adrian stopped walking.

"What?" I said.

"Are you messing with me?"

"I don't . . ." And that was when it occurred to me that he probably knew nothing about what had been going on. So I told him about William Demorest, Jeffrey Connor, and Bethany Frost. I told him about Aaron Ransom, too, and what I had seen firsthand on New Year's Eve. "I'm surprised you haven't heard anything in school about him."

Adrian shrugged and said, "No one really talks to me at school."

"Yeah, but you haven't even heard his name?"

"I don't know. I wasn't paying attention."

"What about Courtney Cole? You must have heard something about her, right?"

He shook his head.

Given all that had transpired since last fall, it seemed impossible that any-one could live here and not know about any of it. And it wasn't like Adrian had just moved in last week; even though he never came out of his house, he and his mother had been here since early October, just before Courtney Cole was found dead in the woods.

"I haven't heard any of this," he said.

So I told him about the discovery of Courtney Cole's body in Satan's For-est. Since we were standing on the street above the woods at that point in the tale, I gestured toward the embankment. "They found her body down there. Me, Peter, and Scott saw them carry her out."

Adrian stared into the woods. "When?"

"Early October."

"Are you serious?" His voice trembled. "No way."

"Yes way. Why would I lie about it?"

"I mean, you guys saw her?"

"Yeah."

"What did she look like?"

"I don't know." Of course, the image of her smashed skull was imprinted on my own brain with perfect clarity, but I did not possess the words—or the desire—to explain it to him. "I mean, the whole thing just seemed sort of . . . surreal . . . you know? Like it wasn't actually happening . . ."

"And no one knows who did it?"

"No," I said. "The Piper's just a name the newspapers gave him, but no one knows who he is." We started walking again, heading straight for the highway. "You haven't even heard about this stuff on the news?"

"My mom doesn't want me watching the news," he said.

"Well, the news complains that the cops aren't doing enough, and the cops complain that the news is out to get them," I said. "My dad's a detective at the police department, so I hear him complain about that stuff sometimes, too."

"What do the cops think is going on?"

"They don't really know."

"Well, what do you think?"

I thought about New Year's Eve and what had happened to Aaron Ran-som. I pictured those cops carrying Courtney Cole's body out of the woods on a sheet-covered stretcher. Lastly, I thought of what Scott had said to us Halloween morning at the Quickman.

"I think there's probably a serial killer going after kids," I said.

We talked about the Piper for the entire walk back to Worth Street. He asked a lot of questions, and I was able to answer only a few of them, mostly from what I'd heard from other people or what had been in the newspapers. Adrian seemed mostly interested in Courtney Cole. Just as we reached the foot of his driveway, he said, "You said you saw them take that girl from the woods. Like, for real? You're not fooling with me?"

"I swear I'm not." I touched my nose. "I promise."

"Did you, like . . . know her?"

"No. She went to a different school."

"Are there pictures of her somewhere?"

I thought this was an odd question. "There was a picture in the newspaper after she was found. How come?"

"Just curious."

Adrian asked some more questions about Courtney Cole. I assumed his interest in what my friends and I had witnessed was purely sensationalistic—that any boy our age would have been curious as to the gory details of such an event.

It wasn't until two weeks later that I would come to understand Adrian's true obsession with the dead girl, and how that obsession changed everything.

BOOK TWO

THE DEAD WOODS
(FEBRUARY-MAY 1994)

February brought new snow, but it could not blanket old fears. "Towns like ours have good, long memories," my grandfather said, "and the people aren't so quick to forget."

Pink paper hearts went up in shopwindows. Stanton School held its annual Valentine's Day dance. The Bagel Boutique served their traditional pink bagels, and Mr. Pastore handed out Hershey's Kisses to anyone who came into his deli. The Kiwanis held their obligatory bake sale. Ice skaters took to Drunkard's Pond. The sordid bars in the industrial park served hot toddies, the smell of heated whiskey permeating the concrete alleyways and tenements straight out to the interstate. The homeless took refuge beneath the Solomon's Bend overpass. It seemed the world hadn't changed and that things kept on motoring along just as they always had.

But that wasn't the truth of it. Like hairline cracks in bone, tiny differences could be perceived if one looked closely enough. The skaters at Drunkard's Pond left each evening before the sky became fully dark, and there were no high school lovers camped out on the snow-covered benches, sharing kisses well into the night. The Valentine's Day dance was cut short so everyone could make it home before nightfall. The Butterfields let their Holsteins out and opened their fields for sledding, but very few kids came around.

People were on edge. Two men got in an argument over a parking space outside the Generous Superstore. A nervous woman struck a pedestrian with her car, breaking the pedestrian's leg in three places. Local taverns suffered an increase in barroom brawls. Break-ins occurred with more regularity at the industrial park, where there were nothing but liquor stores, pool halls, and pawnshops pressed against the banks of a soiled brown river.

At the Juniper Theater, Darby Hedges, the ancient and grizzled proprietor, continued showing old public domain horror films well past Halloween; it was as though he suffered from some lingering obsession with men in rubber monster costumes and bad dialogue. Meanwhile, several dogs ran away from home.

Eleven-year-old Callie Druthers claimed a stranger driving an old Plymouth tried to coax her into his car. A few hours later, police apprehended thirty-eight-year-old Kevin Topor who had gotten lost in Harting Farms, so he had stopped at an intersection and asked the nearest pedestrian, who happened to be Callie Druthers, if she could give him directions to Route 50. He offered to drive her home because the girl had been attending to a fresh cut on her knee.

Topor was from out of town and had no knowledge of what had been going on in Harting Farms over the past several months. Had he known, he would have never asked the girl for directions or offered to give her a ride home. It was a stupid thing to do, and he was gravely sorry.

When Kevin Topor was released, there was an outcry from the citizenry, this time on a much larger scale than when word got out about Chester Vaughn's interrogation and subsequent release. The people of Harting Farms wanted someone to pay for what had happened to Courtney Cole, and they wanted answers as to the whereabouts of the four other missing teens.

Chief of Police Harold Barber told the press that they had done a thorough investigation into Topor's background and found nothing suspicious. His alibis all checked out. His Plymouth was searched for fibers and hair, but there was nothing. They had no reason to believe he had been involved in Courtney Cole's murder or in the disappearances of the four other teens.

Rebecca Ransom appeared again on the news, pleading once more for the safe return of her son, Aaron. Hers was the ghoulish face of someone who is neither alive nor dead but some type of creature that exists between worlds, perpetually tormented.

. . . and the people aren't so quick to forget.

Two days after Topor was released by police, Courtney's mother suffered a nervous breakdown and was admitted to Sheppard Pratt for a full psychological evaluation.

CHAPTER EIGHT
THE SECRET

It was early evening, and I was out by the woodpile stacking firewood when I heard someone approaching. My first thought was, *Nathan Keener.*

I knew Keener and his gang were still prowling the streets for me, and I'd done an admirable job avoiding them since Halloween. Most recently I had seen Keener's truck idling outside school when classes let out (I took a shortcut through the woods, avoiding the main roadway), and one time I even caught sight of his pickup at the end of our block, its darkened headlamps facing our house. I had cut through the yards on the parallel block and came in through the backyard, avoiding Worth Street altogether.

I turned around and was relieved to see Adrian Gardiner walking around the side of the house. His pale skin seemed to shimmer in the fading daylight. He wore a puffy ski parka with lightning bolts on the sleeves and had his hands stuffed into the pockets.

"Man, you scared the crap out of me," I told him, catching my breath and stacking another log onto the woodpile.

"Your grandmother said you were around back."

"Yeah, well, you should know better than to go creeping up on people," I said. I hadn't meant to sound so exasperated, but I was exhausted from a day doing chores around the house.

Adrian shuffled a few steps closer, and I noticed how the arms of his glasses bent his ears down and how his legs looked like those of a flamingo poking out from the oversized bulk of his ski parka.

Since that day at Drunkard's Pond, Adrian had become a sort of de facto member of our little group. He came with us to the pond after school, pitched stones with us in the ravine behind the Generous Superstore, and had even spent two whole afternoons at Scott's house watching all the *Friday the 13th* movies back-to-back. We introduced him to Nirvana, Metallica, Pearl Jam, and Soundgarden, and he let us borrow his superhero comic books, which turned out to be pretty cool.

For the most part, Adrian remained quiet, but he seemed comfortable with my friends and me, and we didn't mind his company. We even began to like him, as much as anyone could like someone like Adrian Gardiner. In an effort to solidify our friendship, he had invited me over to read comic books, though I had politely declined, fabricating an excuse on the spot. (I had been in his house only once, and the thought of returning to that airless catacomb populated by his zombie-eyed mother still didn't sit well with me.)

Adrian was haunted. For one thing, he seemed constantly preoccupied with thoughts of Courtney Cole and the other missing teens. However, he brought it up only when he and I were alone together. He pushed me for details, though my details consisted exclusively of the broad strokes I'd gotten from Scott who had gotten his information from the various newspaper articles he'd read. Yet somehow Adrian's preoccupation with Courtney Cole and the missing teens was more troubling than Scott's. Scott approached it in a pragmatic, investigative way. Adrian, on the other hand, seemed obsessed. It wasn't until he asked if I had a photograph of Courtney Cole did I start to think he might be a little off in the head.

"You busy with chores?"

"Just stacking up some firewood," I said, stating the obvious. I tossed one final log onto the woodpile, then wiped the palms of my hands on my jeans.

"You going out tonight?" he asked.

It was a school night. My other friends would have known better than to ask such a question. But Adrian was new and didn't know the score. I wouldn't hold it against him.

"Wasn't planning on it. My dad's pretty strict about that. Anyway, I've got some homework."

"You finish that paper for Mr. Mattingly's class?"

"Not yet." I hadn't even started it, and I still hadn't mentioned Mr. Mattingly's suggestion that I bump up to AP English next year to my father. Thankfully, Mr. Mattingly hadn't brought it up to me again. If he had forgotten about it, well, that was just fine by me.

Adrian kicked a pinecone and kept his gaze on the ground. "I asked my mom about all the disappearances and about the dead girl, too. To see if she knew anything. She had heard about what's been going on in town."

I thought, *This is it. This is why he's here. Obsession.*

"She's not cool with me going out after dark until they catch whoever is, well . . . I guess, doing what . . ."

"Yeah." He was a chore to listen to when he groped for words. I learned to come to his rescue lest we both suffer under a barrage of fumbling sentences and half words that never came. He seemed sadly grateful whenever I did this.

"But there's someplace I want to go tonight before it gets dark. And I want you to come with me." Then he added, "If you can."

"Where?"

Adrian shivered in his parka. "I don't want to tell you just yet. I don't know how to tell it."

"What do you mean? What don't you want to tell?"

"First I need to know if you'll come with me. Then I'll tell you."

"You can't even tell me where you want to go?"

"Not yet. I want you to swear you'll come first."

I almost laughed at him. Michael had laughed at Adrian's horrified reaction to the *Friday the 13th* movies, and Adrian had looked like he'd been near tears. At first I thought it was because of the movie—someone's head had just gotten chopped off—but he'd sat and watched the rest of it without flinching. When the marathon was over, he had simply gotten off the couch and gone home without saying a word to Michael before he left.

I said, "What time?"

"As soon as you can." He glanced up at the sky, as if to alert me to the oncoming night.

"I'm covered in sap. Let me grab a quick shower, and then I'll meet you back out here. I'll only be fifteen minutes, okay?"

"Okay."

"You want me to call the guys and have them meet us here, too?"

"No," he said. "No guys. Just you and me."

"How come?"

"It's just how . . . I mean, it's just the way I need it to be for right now . . ."

I could hear Adrian breathing—his raspy little nasal respirations that sounded like a circus whistle was caught inside his sinuses—and I could even sense a slight tremor to his voice. I found myself confronted by a mixture of frustration and uneasiness. This happened often when I was around him; it went beyond simply being embarrassed for him or irritated by him.

But then I realized that it had taken great courage for him to come here and ask this of me, and I found myself apprehensive about what might be on Adrian's mind. Although I had never been a superstitious or prophetic person, I knew with a frightening certainty that the stars had aligned and afforded Adrian Gardiner the opportunity to meet and befriend me, because there was something fate needed him to tell me, to show me.

"Yes, okay," I said, even though I was still thinking things through. "Fifteen minutes."

Adrian bobbed his head like a spring-loaded toy. "Thanks, Angie. Thank you."

I didn't like the relief I heard in his voice.

Freshman year at Stanton School, a boy named Dennis Foley sat in the back of my biology class. Largely ignored by the rest of the students, Dennis was a chunky kid with a peppering of brown freckles on his cheeks. He carried a plastic lunch box with cartoon characters capering on its lid, and had he sat with anyone during lunch, he would have no doubt been made fun of. Every day after school the other students watched Dennis climb into the backseat of his mother's rattling old Escort because the family dog, who apparently took precedence, was belted into the passenger seat.

One afternoon, midway through one of Mr. Copeland's discourses on photosynthesis, a small commotion began toward the rear of the classroom. A few heads turned. Mr. Copeland frowned and spoke a bit louder. More heads turned.

Then one of the girls shrieked, "He's bleeding!"

Dennis had opened up his left wrist with one of the dissection scalpels Mr. Copeland had stored at the back of the classroom. There were dark splotches on the floor, and there was blood soaking into Dennis's polo shirt and rumpled khakis.

Dennis dropped the scalpel, which clattered to the floor where it reflected the sunlight coming in through the partially shaded windows. The look on his face was one of stupefaction. As I stared at him, I could see the color drain from his cheeks.

Dennis had been rushed to the hospital where he had recovered from his wounds. He never returned to Stanton School. His family lived in a dilapidated hovel along the Cape, not too far from the Keener farm, and on occasion people spotted him milling about the property.

One time, I saw Dennis walking by himself up Woolworth Avenue, his meaty hands wedged into the pockets of his too-tight corduroys, his attention focused on his feet. He had the same look of stupefaction from that day in the classroom. I wondered if it would be there until the day he died. However, I never found out, because his family eventually moved away.

Sometimes Adrian reminded me of Dennis Foley and of the look of stupefaction seated permanently on Dennis's wide, dull face.

Despite Adrian's request, I considered giving Peter a call and seeing if he'd tag along with us on whatever adventure Adrian had planned. I wasn't afraid, but Adrian's intensity and awkwardness were generally best diluted among others. To suffer him alone was to truly suffer.

However, in the end I decided to abide by Adrian's wishes and go it alone. I was certain he would refuse to show me whatever it was if Peter—or anyone else, for that matter—was present. And as wary as I was about the whole thing, I couldn't pretend that my curiosity wasn't also piqued.

I showered and dressed in warm corduroy pants, boots, a flannel shirt over a thermal one, and a hooded sweatshirt. My dad was in the basement, screwing around with the furnace, which seemed to cause trouble every February. He knelt in front of the open grate, peering at a wavering blue flame.

There were various tools spread out on a grease-spattered drop cloth on the floor beside him.

From halfway down the stairs, I watched him work for a few moments. When he stood to look around the back of the furnace, I heard the tendons popping in his knees—great audible cracks that sounded like twigs snapping. Listening to that sound, it occurred to me that my father would grow old and eventually die.

My mother had died, leaving nothing behind of her memory except a photo album with all her pictures in it in the den, wedged between an atlas and a thick leather-bound volume of Kipling stories, as well as the framed picture in my dad's bedroom. I scarcely knew my mother, so her absence meant little to me.

Charles had died in combat in 1991, and that had caused an indescribable darkness to come to our house—a darkness that could never leave. Charles's death had stripped something vital from my basic framework, my insides, simultaneously replacing it with a burning rod of anger. I often felt that parts of me had become translucent, turned to glass, since he'd gone.

But thinking of the inevitable death of my father instilled confusion within me. Despite our differences, I loved my father very much. I knew I would never be the son that Charles had been—my father would never be proud of me the way he had been proud of Charles and all that Charles had accomplished—but I also knew he loved me, too. Sometimes I wondered if our differences—and the mystery of our differences—forged the strongest bond.

"Hey, Dad. I'm gonna run out with that kid Adrian from next door for a little while."

He poked his head out from behind the furnace and mopped sweat away from his eyes with the heel of one hand. "Where are you guys going?"

"Probably just for a quick bike ride."

"Did you finish all your homework?"

"Mostly. I'm still working on a paper for English."

"I want you back before dark, okay?"

"Sure."

He nodded, scooped up a wrench from the drop cloth, and disappeared behind the furnace again.

Outside, the evening had turned cool and gray. The moon, a faint whitish pearl, was already visible over the Mathersons' house. I could tell by the current temperature that tonight would drop to damn near freezing, which was probably why my father had seemed so pressed to get the furnace up and running today. I crossed the yard and sat atop the woodpile where I had a cigarette while waiting for Adrian.

Nearly twenty minutes went by with no sign of him. I had nearly given up and gone back inside to finish my homework when I heard him rustling through the trees.

"Angelo?" he called.

"I'm back here."

"Is that you?"

"Who else would it be?" I said, sliding off the woodpile.

He stumbled into the yard, breathing heavily and adjusting his glasses. He had his backpack on, and the weight of it made him look unsteady. "I thought maybe you'd change your mind."

"I said I would, didn't I? So where are we going?"

"To the woods where they found that girl's body. Just like you said they did."

I stood there staring at him. "Why?"

"Because we have to. You said you'd come," he reminded me. "Are you gonna change your mind?"

Not that I had anything to prove to this mealy limp-wristed kid, but I couldn't go back on my word. Short of jumping off the Bay Bridge with him, I'd said I was in. And so I was.

"Yeah, okay." My tone should have alerted him to my displeasure in being duped. He'd tricked me into following him on some odd little escapade that served his morbid obsession. I hadn't expected to traipse out across the highway to what the neighborhood kids had started referring to as the Dead Woods. "Let me get my bike."

"We gotta walk," Adrian said.

I pulled my bike out of the ivy patch on the side of the house anyway. "It's too cold to walk and it'll take too long. Besides, I gotta be back before dark."

"We have to walk," he insisted.

Is this part of the game, too? "Why the hell do we gotta walk?"

"Because I don't have a bicycle."

I gaped at him, still clutching the hand grips of my dirt bike. "Are you kidding me?"

"No," he replied.

It occurred to me that I'd never seen him riding a bike. For the past couple of weeks, we had just happened to walk everywhere—to and from school, down to the Quickman, even to Scott's house on the days we all went over to watch horror movies. It had never crossed my mind that Adrian didn't own a bike. What kid didn't own a bike?

"Well," I said, "you can ride on my handlebars."

He eyed my bike warily. "How does that work?"

"You just get on and ride while I pedal and steer."

"Get on," Adrian repeated, his voice low and laced with uncertainty. Again he adjusted his glasses, then ran his tongue over his upper lip.

"Yeah, man. It's no sweat. Really."

"I don't know . . ."

"Listen," I said. "I promised to meet you out here and follow you to wherever without knowing a single thing. I think you can at least trust me to hop on the goddamn handlebars, chickenshit."

I thought the *chickenshit* was overkill and he might react to it the way he had reacted to Michael laughing at him. However, I was surprised to see an awkward grin crack one corner of Adrian's mouth—a grin I couldn't help but return.

"Yeah, okay, but if you drop me, I'm going to kick your butt."

"You couldn't kick my butt if you had a tractor trailer for a foot," I said, and we both started giggling.

I wheeled my bike across the yard. It was a green and white Kent with worn handgrips and Garbage Pail Kids stickers stuck to the frame. It paled in comparison to Michael's stellar Mongoose, but it was mine, and I couldn't imagine not having it. Out on the street, I straddled the bike and held the handlebars steady.

"What do I do?" Adrian said.

"Just hop on."

"Like . . ."

"With your butt. Climb on backward."

"I don't know if . . ."

Jesus Christ, I thought.

"You won't go fast, will you?"

"No," I said.

"Promise?"

"Holy shit, Adrian!"

It took him three attempts to hoist himself up. Once he had situated himself, I proceeded to pedal up Worth Street. His grip on the handlebars tightened. Since Adrian weighed less than my other friends he should have been easier to transport, but he possessed no sense of balance, so it was like transporting an unwieldy sack of potatoes on my handlebars. The backpack strapped to his shoulders didn't make it any easier.

Afraid of getting his feet caught in the spokes of the front wheel, he kept his legs straight out ahead of the front tire. I knew he wouldn't be able to keep it up for long, and I waited for his legs to give out. Yet he managed to keep those scarecrow legs out ahead of us all the way down Worth Street and halfway down Haven Street. By the time we reached Governor Highway, he was perched perfectly on my handlebars, his legs tucked up beneath him, like a chimp on a swing.

The streets were eerily quiet, which was not unusual for a Sunday evening. Even the highway was fairly calm. The shops in this part of town were shutting down for the night, their lights winking out one at a time.

I pedaled harder, running parallel to the highway, the cool early-evening air drawing tears from the corners of my eyes. On the handlebars, Adrian unleashed a strangled cry. *He's going to have a heart attack*, I thought, yet the notion did not cause me to slow down. In fact, I pushed us harder, and, accompanied by a second sheep-like bleat of fear from Adrian, I hooked a sharp right, hopped the shallow curb, and drove us straight through a copse of trees.

I'll have to explain to his mother, that creepy old witch, how I killed her son, I thought, pedaling faster. Around me, the world was a colorless blur. *She'll put a curse on me and turn me into a toadstool or a talking frog.*

Like a maniac, I threw my head back and laughed. No doubt little Adrian Gardiner was soiling his drawers right about now. Less than a second before we hit one of the highway intersections, the traffic lights changed. We bulleted through the intersection, and someone blasted their car horn at us.

Adrian groaned, and his feet shot out ahead of him again.

"Hold on!"

We crested a hill, and then it was nothing but a gradual downslope. I took the hill faster than necessary, the streetlamps smearing to runny blots of light in my peripheral vision. Of course, with Adrian hunkered down on my handlebars, I couldn't see directly ahead of me. But I had ridden this stretch of roadway since my early adolescence, and I knew every bump, groove, and pothole like I knew the contours of my own mattress or which floorboards outside my father's bedroom to avoid at night when sneaking out of the house.

I burned through the intersection of Point and Counterpoint and squeezed the hand brakes just as my rear tire fishtailed halfway around. We came to a stop mere feet from the guardrail that separated the roadway from the wooded embankment. The silence that filled my ears an instant later was like a sonic boom.

Almost wetly, Adrian dripped off my handlebars to the pavement. I eased my bike down on the ground and went over to where Adrian crouched in a ball. His shoulders hitched, and I thought, *Great. I made him cry.* All of a sudden I felt like a world-class asshole.

"Hey, man," I said, putting one hand on his shoulder. "Hey . . ."

Adrian sprung up, startling me. His face was red and wind chapped, and there were tears leaking from behind his glasses. The kid was laughing. "That was awesome!"

"Yeah?" I said.

"I can't believe it," he cried. "That was great. That was . . . fucking great."

"Jeez," I muttered, though I was smiling now right along with him. "You kiss your mom with that mouth?"

"Fuck," he said again, his laughter subsiding, his respiration heavy. "Fuck it, Angie. Fuck it."

I suddenly felt very sad for him. Had he had even a single friend in Chicago?

Once he got his laughter under control, we wheeled my bike through the break in the guardrail and then down the sloping embankment until the trees grew thicker and the ground leveled out. Broken bits of glass and shards of metal sparkled from a particular patch of dark ground, remnants of Audrey MacMillan's car accident in October. The scattered detritus would probably be here until the next ice age.

I let my bike fall into a nest of brambles, then swiped the hair out of my eyes. Even in the midst of winter and with the branches bare, the woods were still thick and insulated from the rest of the world. The ground was hard, and the tallest trees seemed to reach up with their skeletal branches to poke holes in the gray fabric of the evening sky.

"Okay," I said. "So we're here. You gonna tell me what's going on?"

Adrian kicked around in the dead leaves, turning over large stones with his shoes and bending down to examine the random whatnot that captivated his attention for a few seconds here and there. For all I knew, he was deliberately trying to ignore me. I didn't understand any of it, and I wondered what the hell I was doing out here with this strange kid, humoring his obsession about a murdered girl.

"Before I tell you," he said after I'd expelled a pent-up breath and dropped onto a moss-covered deadfall, "can you tell me something? Something personal, like a secret?"

"What?"

Adrian peeled off his giant backpack and tossed it on the ground beside a craggy-looking oak tree. "If I'm gonna tell you a secret, I want you to tell me something, too," he said, sitting down beside me on the fallen tree. "This way, we're even."

I had no idea what he was going on about. Every fiber of my being beckoned me to stand up, dig my dirt bike out of the bushes, and climb back up the embankment, yet it seemed like some outside force kept me plastered to my seat on the dead tree. Even down here in the woods, the wind was strong and biting, and I felt my cheeks growing numb and the moisture around my eyes freezing to solid crystals.

For one insane moment I thought about the time I'd nearly drowned in the Chesapeake Bay after falling over the side of a johnboat when I was seven or eight—how the black water had wasted no time swallowing me up and dragging me down, down.

It had just been Charles and me on the boat that day. We had puttered in and out of coves and eventually found our way into the open bay where the waves were great and angry beasts. Charles had pointed out the face of the immense cliff that was the ass end of Harting Farms. The cliff's face was pocked by countless bores in the rock, reminding me of photographs I'd seen in *National Geographic* of holes in the rock face where cave-dwelling Indians lived.

I'd gone overboard. My entire body suddenly went heavy, and then the cold attacked me and burrowed its way straight through my flesh and into the channels of my ears and the marrow of my bones. Ice water filled my lungs. I was rendered blind. Charles had fished me out and dragged me back onto the boat where I coughed and sputtered and vomited brackish water onto my sneakers.

And while I sat there gasping for air with Charles thumping a heavy fist against my back, I couldn't shake the sheer terrifying helplessness I had felt when I'd gone under that black and brine-tasting water. I could swim, but I could have just as easily drowned. The panic had set in as quickly as a pistol shot, and it consumed everything else. Everything.

I shivered at the memory. Glancing over at Adrian, I said, "Do you know the reason I'm in your English class?"

"I heard you shoved some teacher and they moved you."

"Mr. Naczalnik."

"They call him Nozzle Neck."

"Yeah, I know what they call him," I said. Even after all these months, I still hadn't told this to anyone. Not even Peter. I didn't know how I felt about telling it to Adrian, but it seemed like the right time, the right thing to do.

"Anyway, that's not what happened. See, we had to write an essay in class about something that had had a profound effect on us. I couldn't write anything at first. I kept staring at the clock and looking around the room. Then I thought of something and I began to write. But when Naczalnik asked to turn the papers in, I refused. He came to the desk and grabbed the pages from me. I pulled them back. I told him I didn't want to turn in the paper and to just give me an F. But he kept pulling the papers from me. The papers ripped and he fell backward over a desk. I didn't push him."

Adrian was silent for a moment. "What did you write about that you didn't want him to see?" he said eventually.

"I wrote about my brother, Charles, and the day he saved me from drowning in the Chesapeake Bay."

"Oh." His voice was so small it was nearly nonexistent. I could have been talking to myself in the woods. "I didn't know you have a brother."

"I don't anymore. He died in Iraq in '91, during an invasion. In Desert Storm."

"The war invasion?"

"Yes. He was . . ." My mind was suddenly filled with the image of Courtney Cole's caved-in skull. "He was killed there. It was a roadside bomb, so it must have been . . . uh, it's . . ." I cleared my throat. "We buried an empty coffin," I finished, hoping that would explain it all.

Across from me, Adrian said nothing.

"I wrote about the day I fell into the bay and almost died. I wondered if maybe I was the one who was supposed to die in our family and not Charles. If I had died, maybe Charles wouldn't have left home, wouldn't have left my dad, and would have never gone to war." My voice cracked. I felt like a helpless child.

Attempting to regain some control, I paused before continuing. "Anyway, it's stupid but that's what I wrote about. I don't know why I wrote it but I did. And I didn't want Naczalnik or anyone else reading it. It was for me to write and no one else to know."

Adrian turned away from me and stared at the ground, which was covered in dead leaves, pine needles, and a latticework of moonlight issuing through the canopy of naked tree limbs overhead. "That's a good secret. Did you ever tell anyone else?"

"No."

"I'm sorry about Charles."

"It's okay."

"Was he a good older brother?"

"Yeah," I said.

"I've always wanted a brother," Adrian said.

I just nodded, chewing my lower lip. My face burned.

When something rustled among the underbrush several yards to our left, we both spun our heads in that direction in unison, collectively holding our breath. The rustling fell silent.

We waited, listening for the sound to repeat. Of course, it was probably some forest critter—a deer or a skunk or something—but it still set me on edge. Suddenly, it was Mischief Night all over again, and I was hiding in the trees from Nathan Keener and the rest of those delinquents, when from nowhere I thought I'd heard a rustling noise directly behind me. I'd been certain that someone was right there in the trees with me, and I still hadn't forgotten that disquieting sense of violation.

"Probably just a big bird," I said, hoping to convince myself more than anything.

Adrian stared at his feet. "I know your dad's a cop. Please don't tell him, okay?"

"Tell him about what?"

"About this." He pulled one hand out of the pocket of his ski parka and extended it to me, his palm open. Something small and metallic glinted in the center of his palm.

I leaned over and peered at it. "What is it?"

"It's a locket. Here. Open your hand."

I reached out and opened one hand, and Adrian let the item fall into it. It was a locket, all right—a silver heart with a small loop at the top where presumably it had once been affixed to a chain. It was nearly weightless in my hand. I brought it up to my face and examined it more closely. "Does it open?"

"Yeah."

I stuck my thumbnail between the two halves, and the heart-shaped locket unclasped. I was careful opening it, expecting to find a small photograph inside—my grandmother owned a similar locket, and she kept a tiny photo of me on one side, Charles on the other—but it was empty.

"I found it when I first moved to town." Adrian pointed up the wooded embankment and in the approximate direction of Counterpoint Lane. "A car had crashed in the woods, and I watched the tow truck pull it out. When I looked down, it was right there in the ditch."

"Okay," I said, not sure why this was such a big deal to him.

"It's hers," he said.

"Whose?"

"The dead girl's," Adrian said. "Courtney Cole's."

"How do you know that?"

"I just know. Who else could it belong to?"

"Anyone could have lost it."

Adrian stared at me. His respiration whistled through the stovepipe of his throat. "Yeah, but it's hers. I didn't think anything of it until you told me about what happened to her. Before I knew, I thought it was just another piece of . . . well, something someone had lost."

"That doesn't mean it's hers."

Adrian took the heart-shaped locket back from me. He turned it over and over in his small, white fingers. There were black crescents of dirt beneath his fingernails. "It's hers. I discovered it right across the street from where her body was found. And here, look at the clasp," he said, holding it out. "See? It's broken."

I saw that the little silver hoop had been broken in two. "So what?"

"So maybe it happened when someone pulled it off her." His eyes were locked on mine. "Maybe it broke during a struggle."

"I guess it's possible," I conceded.

"No." There was a sharp finality to his voice. "It's not just possible. It's hers. I can feel it. I can tell."

I returned my gaze to the shimmering locket pinched between Adrian's thumb and forefinger. "Well, if you really think it's hers, we should take it to the police. We can give it to my dad, if you want."

"No," he practically snapped, clutching the locket against his chest. "No, Angie."

"If you're right and that did belong to her, it's evidence. We have to let the cops know you found it. It might have fingerprints on it or—"

"I wiped it down and cleaned it when I found it. There aren't any fingerprints anymore, if there ever were."

"There still could be—"

"There aren't."

A cold wind rustled the trees. I was suddenly aware of my exposed skin prickling in the chill air. My teeth had started to chatter at some point, though I wasn't entirely sure that was due to the temperature. "You didn't have to bring me down here tonight to show me that locket. So why are we here?"

"I want you to show me where the body was found," he said. "There might be other things like this locket down here, too. We could find them. I'm a good scavenger hunter."

"But what do you think we'd find?"

Adrian shrugged and suddenly looked as innocent as a newborn. "I have no idea. It could be anything."

"And why would we bother finding it? Because you like to collect junk?"

"No. Because we might find clues that tell us who the killer is."

The image of us traipsing around the underbrush looking for clues like the goddamn Hardy Boys nearly caused me to laugh. Not to mention how absurd it was that we might be able to uncover something the police had missed. "The police have already been through the whole area. They even had dogs down here. What makes you think we'll find something they missed?"

"They missed the locket, didn't they?" he retorted.

"The only reason you found it before the cops did was because they weren't looking for anything. Courtney Cole's body hadn't been found yet. If that's even her locket in the first place."

Adrian slowly closed his fingers around the locket. "I'm telling you, it's hers," he repeated, and I knew then that I was wasting my breath trying to convince him otherwise.

"So this is why you wanted to know about Courtney Cole," I said.

"Yeah. I mean, I didn't make the connection with the locket until you told me about her and said she had been killed here."

"I didn't say she was killed here," I said, although I wasn't sure if there was a difference. "Just found here."

Adrian nodded.

"You found the locket in October, so why did you wait until now to say something about it to me?" Yet one look at him—at the downtrodden puppy expression he perpetually wore—gave me my answer. It was the reason he'd asked me to share a personal secret with him: so he knew he could trust me. It had taken him all these months to build up his courage and his trust. I sighed. "Do you know anything about these woods?"

"No. What should I know about them?"

"They're huge. They start here, but they run along the highway and go all the way out to the cliffs that overlook the bay. I'm not sure where they found her exactly, because I only saw them carry her out. But even if they found her right here, that doesn't mean she was killed here. And that still doesn't mean there's anything left for us to find."

"You said they brought her body up at the intersection," he said. "If she was found a mile away, they wouldn't have brought her up over there, right? She must have been found close to this spot."

"But that doesn't mean she was killed right here," I repeated.

"It doesn't matter," Adrian said. "There still might be things left behind."

I sighed again, rubbing my palms against the thighs of my corduroys. I felt the cold radiating through my body. Darkness was drawing closer around us, and stars were beginning to poke through the sky.

"Some people say these woods are haunted," I told him, looking around at the ancient trees, their leafless black branches crisscrossing high over our heads and intersecting over the pale face of the moon. "December Park, too. They call this the Dead Woods now because of the Cole girl, but it had other names before: Satan's Forest, Ghost Park, the Black Lands.

"When I was younger, Charles used to scare me with stories about devil worshippers coming down here and sacrificing chickens and goats and whatever else they could get their hands on. I didn't necessarily believe him, but it worked in keeping me away from the woods until I was a little older. Fuck, those stories used to give me nightmares.

"Then there's the girls' school on the other side of the park, out by the cliffs," I continued. "People died in a fire there after World War II, after it had been converted to a hospital or something, and it's been closed ever since. It could be that the ghost stories originated from there. I think many of them did. Or maybe the history of a place like that tends to fuel those kinds of stories, makes them real."

He seemed unimpressed with the folklore of my hometown.

"Come on," I said, rising. "Let me show you something."

I led him deeper into the woods, wending around fallen trees and overgrown holly bushes that were full and prickly even in the dead of winter. I remained conscious of the daylight slipping away, and I knew we should head home soon.

We came to a narrow little brook that snaked through the underbrush, its water level shallow and crusted with muddy ice. "Watch your step," I warned and easily hopped over the brook. Adrian followed.

Eventually we arrived at our destination. I hunted around for several moments, sniffing like a bloodhound for a scent, until I came upon a scraggy overgrown mess of leafless bushes. I crouched down and pushed the poking branches aside, then waved Adrian over. He dropped to his knees directly beside me.

"What is it?" he asked, his voice just one notch above a whisper. This close, I could smell the sourness of his breath.

"One of the headless statues," I said.

Indeed, the thing that lay supine on the ground, entwined with brown veins of ivy, was a life-sized concrete statue of a man in a suit and tie, a square concrete base at the end of its tapered legs. It wasn't wholly intact, and there were crumbled bits of concrete scattered around the body as if leprosy had caused pieces of it to slough off. Most noticeable was the fact that the head was missing, a rusted metal pipe jutting up from the figure's concrete neck. "There's a bunch of them, and they're scattered all over the place. You can find them if you know where to look."

"Where'd they come from?"

"I don't know. They've always been here."

"Are all their heads missing?"

"Yeah. Creepy, huh?"

"Who did that to them?"

"I have no idea."

Adrian reached out, his fingers hovering over the concrete dummy. Eventually, he touched it. "It's cold." He removed his hand. White powder from the stone came off on his palm, which he rubbed down the length of his pants. "Do you think these were . . . I mean, you know . . . used in some kind of devil worshipping séance or something? Like black magic or conjuring spirits? That stuff your brother told you about."

"I guess it's possible. But like I said, I don't believe those devil worship stories anymore. That was just Charles trying to scare me." I straightened out my legs and felt the cold stiffening my muscles. "Anyway, what I'm trying to say is kids play down here in the summer, but hardly anyone knows these statues exist. Mostly, it's just me and my friends who know about them. So finding some tiny clue that connects to whatever happened to Courtney Cole or any of those other kids that the police have missed is a crazy long shot."

"But you found the statues, just like I found the locket." He smiled. "Things can be found."

I chewed at my lower lip while staring at him.

"You don't have to help if you don't want to," he said, the smile vanishing. Suddenly, I felt like a jerk. "Cut it out, man. Yeah, I'll help you look around." And there it was again—that crooked smile. "You mean it?"

"Sure. But not tonight. We need to get back. It'll be dark soon."

Adrian stuffed the locket back into his parka. "Do you really think these woods are haunted?"

"Nah. It's just superstition."

He nodded but his expression was not one of agreement. He surveyed the dark woods around us, a creeping unease all too evident on his face.

"Come on," I said, leading him back in the direction we had come.

Together we rolled my bike up the embankment and through the busted section of guardrail. I wheeled my bike across the street, then paused on the shoulder of the road. "Show me where you found it."

Adrian pointed down into the ravine, where the runoff had frozen to mud-streaked ice and the weeds were the color of straw. The mouth of the drainage tunnel that ran beneath the highway was curtained in dead ivy and brown vines and nearly four feet in diameter. Blackish water trickled from the mouth of the tunnel and turned the dirt to marshland. "Right down there."

"Let's get home."

I steadied my bike while Adrian climbed onto the handlebars. This time there was no quarreling. Dropping down onto my seat, I began pedaling, and with the cold firmly ingrained in my bones, it was like trying to start some enormous and antiquated machine.

By the time we arrived at the foot of Adrian's driveway, my leg muscles were sore and I was winded. I eased the bike to a halt, and Adrian hopped off the handlebars.

"Hey." He played with the zipper on his parka. "You're not gonna tell your dad about the locket, are you?"

"No," I said.

"You promise?"

I touched the tip of my nose. "I promise. But if it's really hers, then I still think you should turn it into the police. Or at least think about it. It may help them catch this guy. And that would be good. But, no, I won't say anything."

"Okay. I'll think about it."

"Cool."

Adrian looked lost in contemplation. I waited for him to say something more. When he didn't, I said, "See you later, skater."

"Yeah."

"No. You say, 'After a while, pedophile.'"

"What's a pedophile?"

"It's like a pervert."

"Oh . . ."

"So . . . see you later, skater."

"After a while, pedophile."

I turned and wheeled my bike up the slope of lawn that connected our yards. After I stowed my bike in the ivy at the side of the house, I watched Adrian mount the porch steps of the old Dunbar house. When he reached the front door, he cracked it open only the slightest bit and vanished into the slender band of blackness within.

CHAPTER NINE
THE HEART-SHAPED LOCKET

Late for school the following day, I eventually caught up with the guys in the cafeteria. Peter, Scott, and Michael were seated at a table in the back playing Uno.

"Missed you in first period," Peter said, dealing me in the next hand. "Thought you might be skipping the whole day."

"I had to finish a paper for English."

"Where's Poindexter?" said Michael. He used the nickname without malice. Since that day at Drunkard's Pond and the forging of our unseemly friendships last month, Adrian had sat at our lunch table every day.

"I guess he's not here yet," I said, looking around.

Michael laid down a card, leaving one left in his hand. "Uno."

Peter dropped a Draw Four on Michael, who let out a pathetic little groan. Apparently, Peter knew what color card Michael had remaining in his hand, because when he called red, Michael balked and accused Peter of cheating.

"Like hell," Peter said.

"Like hell, like hell." Michael glanced behind him. Directly at his back was one of the plate-glass windows that made up the east wall of the cafeteria. "You can see my card reflecting in the glass."

"Bullshit. Draw four."

"I'm not drawing shit. I want to switch seats. Angie, switch seats with me."

"Forget it."

"Draw," Peter cajoled. "Draw, draw, draw, draw, draw, you dork."

Scowling, Michael selected four cards from the deck. "I'd like to crowbar your face in, Galloway."

"You won't be able to lift a crowbar after I break both your arms," Peter countered.

"Okay," Michael said, suddenly beaming. He threw an elbow onto the tabletop, his open hand held out in front of his face, fingers wiggling. "Arm wrestle."

"I'm not touching that hand," Peter said.

Scott and I laughed.

"You big coward wimp bitch," Michael taunted. It was easy to see that he was fighting off laughter, too.

The truth was, no one in our small group would dare arm wrestle Michael Sugarland. Not just because he was freakishly strong—which he was, particularly for someone so wiry—but because we had all been present when he had arm wrestled David Schumacher in the cafeteria last year.

David had incrementally ratcheted Michael's hand closer and closer to the tabletop until a gleam flared behind Michael's wild eyes. He had darted forward and popped David's thumb into his mouth and sucked for all he was worth. David was obviously mortified and shocked. His wrist went limp, and the match was quickly overturned. The undisputed winner, Michael was awarded David's brown-bag lunch for the remainder of the week, which he opted not to eat. Instead, he wadded the bag into a ball and aimed for the industrial trash can beside our table, practicing his free throws, while David watched him with stormy contempt.

Peter won the hand, and the cards were collected, shuffled, dealt out again.

"Look," I said finally, "I gotta tell you guys something, but you gotta promise that it stays between us."

Michael rolled his eyes and said, "If you're gonna tell us you're gay, we already know."

I shot him a look. "Come on. I'm serious. Swear it."

Peter and Scott both put their index fingers to their noses and in unison said, "I swear."

"You, too, Michael," I said.

"Aren't we just a little bit old for the nose-swearing thing?" he said.

"Just do it."

Michael blew the loose strands of hair off his forehead, casually pressed his index finger against the tip of his nose, and intoned in a nasally resignation, "I swear. Okay?"

"Listen. Adrian found something. It might be important. I'm not sure."

"What is it?" Peter said disinterestedly.

"A heart-shaped locket," I said, "and he thinks it belonged to Courtney Cole."

They all looked at me over the fans of their cards. It was almost comical.

"Wait. What?" Peter said. "Are you serious?"

"Absolutely."

"A locket?" Scott said, furrowing his brow. "Like a charm for a necklace."

"Yeah."

"Why does he think it's hers?"

"Because he discovered it in the ditch beside Counterpoint Lane a couple of days before the cops found her body."

Michael slammed his cards down on the table. "Bullshit."

"And you saw it?" Peter said. "You saw the locket?"

"Yeah."

"What did it look like?"

Sliding my sandwich out of my lunch bag, I said, "Just a locket in the shape of a heart. It had a little clasp on top, like where you'd hang it from a chain, but it was broken. Adrian thinks it must have broken during a struggle with the killer."

"Holy shit," Scott said.

"What the heck does Adrian know?" Michael said. "That could be any-body's locket."

"I guess so," I said, unwrapping my sandwich. Peppers and eggs on a toasted roll. My lunch bag was always the greasiest at our table, but my lunches were the envy of them all.

"This is amazing," Scott said, looking intently at me from across the table. He had his Orioles baseball cap cocked backward on his head, and for the first time I noticed a fine fuzz of hair across his upper lip—very faint but certainly present. "Her actual locket? I gotta see this thing."

"Didn't you hear what I just said?" Michael scolded. "It isn't her locket. It's gotta be a coincidence. The police would have found it and taken it as evidence if it was hers."

"They wouldn't have been searching for evidence at that point," I informed him. "Her body wasn't found yet, remember?"

"It still sounds like bullshit to me," Michael grumbled.

"Yeah, well, I still wanna see it," Scott said. He looked at Peter. "What do you think?"

"As much as it pains me to say it, Michael's probably right. It's just a coincidence."

"A coincidence that Adrian found it just as she goes missing and in the same general area?" Scott countered. "Come on, guys. You've got to admit there's a possibility this actually is that girl's locket."

"We're not saying it isn't possible," said Peter. "We're just saying it isn't very probable."

"You guys are no fun." Scott grabbed his backpack off the bench and stood up.

"Hey," Michael said. "Where're you going?"

"To the library."

"For what?"

"Research," he said, turning his cap around to the front. He tugged the straps of his backpack over his shoulders, gave us a broad smile, then marched out of the cafeteria.

"Spoilsport," said Michael.

In fifth period science, Scott came into the classroom a few minutes after the bell.

Mr. Johnson, who had been scribbling nonsense on the big chalkboard at the front of the room, glanced over his shoulder as Scott sidled between the desks until he plunked down in his seat. "You're late, Mr. Steeple. I trust you have a hall pass?"

"No, sir."

Mr. Johnson turned away from the blackboard and folded his arms across his chest. Not one for fashion, he wore shit-colored slacks and a similarly colored polo shirt buttoned all the way to the top. The highlight of his ensemble was the toupee that sat crookedly on his head. "Care to provide me with a suitable explanation as to why you're late, then?"

"Well," Scott said, sliding his textbook out of his backpack, "I had diarrhea."

Murmured laughter greeted his response.

Mr. Johnson's face tightened. "I suppose you think that's humorous."

Looking as earnest as I had ever seen him, Scott said, "God, no. You should have seen it."

Full-fledged laughter erupted. In the seats behind me, Michael and Peter cackled like hyenas.

"Okay, okay," Mr. Johnson said, taking a piece of chalk from the pocket of his slacks. "Settle down." He bowed slightly in Scott's direction. "Thank you for that humorous little interlude, Mr. Steeple. It's quite refreshing to have someone other than your friend Mr. Sugarland performing for a change."

"Cock knocker," Michael whispered, leaning forward so that he was close to my ear.

I choked down a laugh and stared at my open textbook.

"Anyway . . . ," Mr. Johnson went on, returning to the chalkboard.

Moments later, I saw Scott hand off a folded slip of paper to the girl beside him. He pointed at me and she nodded, passing the paper along. It eventually found its way to me when the fat red-freckled hand of Margot Clementine dropped it into my open textbook.

I glanced at the front of the classroom to make sure Mr. Johnson was suitably occupied, then unfolded the paper. It was a photocopy of the article detailing the discovery of Courtney Cole, the one that had been published in the *Caller* in October. I recognized it right away by the black-and-white photo of Courtney. In it, she smiled prettily, her hair done nicely in a dark cascade that framed her attractive face.

Someone—presumably Scott—had drawn an arrow in bright red marker beside the photo, pointing to a slender chain that hung from the girl's neck.

"Big deal," said Michael. "Half the girls her age wear necklaces. That doesn't mean anything."

The four of us were heading across the quad to our next classes, our coats zipped up and our breath leaving vapor trails in the crisp afternoon air.

"But what if the newspaper cut the bottom half of the picture off?" Scott said. "The half that shows she's wearing a heart-shaped locket."

Michael plucked a drinking straw out from behind his ear and popped it into his mouth. "Well, I guess we'll never know, will we?"

"Maybe, maybe not," said Scott. He held the photocopied newspaper article and stared at the dead girl. "This photo looks just like the school pictures we all take. I bet it came from last year's yearbook."

"And do you happen to have last year's yearbook for Girls' Holy Cross?" Michael said, chewing on his straw.

"No," said Scott, "but I know where I can get ahold of one."

For the remainder of the day, I anticipated Adrian's arrival at school. It wasn't until last period English with Mr. Mattingly, when Adrian's desk remained empty, did I finally admit to myself that he wasn't coming.

On my walk home, I paused at the foot of Adrian's driveway and stared at the house. I felt a cold disquiet settle all around me like a shroud. The prospect of knocking on their front door and having it opened by Adrian's haunted and pale-skinned mother did not sit well with me. Instead, I lingered for a few minutes, kicking pebbles into the gutter, in hopes that I'd catch a glimpse of Adrian in one of the upstairs windows.

But he never appeared, and I eventually went home feeling strangely empty.

Scott's neighbor Martha Dooley went to Girls' Holy Cross and had been one of Courtney Cole's classmates. She was a short brunette whose unfortunate complexion resembled, in both hue and texture, the granulated surface of a brick. She also had an unfaltering crush on Scott and therefore did not question his motive when he asked if he could borrow her yearbook for a couple of days. She handed it over without hesitation.

In her little rectangular yearbook panel that in hindsight seemed all too much like a coffin, Courtney Cole looked very pretty and blissfully unaware that her life was quickly nearing its conclusion. It was the same picture as the one in the newspaper, though much clearer and in color. She wore a black gown cut low at the shoulders, exposing the soft tapered lines of her collarbones. And indeed, she wore a slender chain around her neck, but the charm that hung from it was not a heart-shaped locket; it was a gold crucifix.

"Well, there you go," I said. The two of us were in his basement, listening to one of the *Use Your Illusion* albums on the stereo and chugging cans of Jolt while Martha Dooley's yearbook sat spread out on the floor between us.

"I can't believe it," Scott said, slowly shaking his head. "I was so sure it would be the same necklace with the goddamn heart locket."

"That's because you're a morbid little freak show, buddy," I told him, though admittedly, I was a little bummed about the discovery myself. I had actually begun to psyche myself up about the possibilities: what if it really was her locket? What did that mean for us?

It had been three days since I told my friends about Adrian's find and an equal amount of days since I'd seen him. He hadn't returned to school all week. I still hadn't summoned the courage to knock on his front door, but things were getting ridiculous. My friends kept asking where he was, and Scott even suggested that perhaps our strange little friend had become the Piper's latest victim. The rest of us chuckled uneasily, hoping our uncomfortable laughter would turn Scott's very real concern into a joke.

Despite my reluctance, I knew I had to march up to Adrian's front door and knock on it. And if his mother opened it and stood staring at me from the other side like some lifeless crypt keeper, I would have to resist the very natural, very instinctual, very understandable urge to run.

Finally, after school let out Friday afternoon, the four of us stood at the foot of Adrian's driveway, staring at the dark and brooding Gardiner house. I was shaking and only partially from the cold weather. We had unanimously agreed that we needed to share the yearbook photo with Adrian, so he wouldn't go on thinking the locket belonged to the Cole girl.

"I don't think we should all go up there together," Peter said, breaking the silence.

"How come?" I said. I had Martha Dooley's yearbook under one arm.

"He told you about the locket, but he didn't tell us. Maybe he didn't want us to know."

"Yeah," Michael said. "You should go alone, Angie. We'll wait in your backyard."

"You guys are just too scared to knock on that door," I suggested.

No one disagreed.

After they'd gone around the back of my house, I took a deep breath and walked up Adrian's driveway. The windows were dark and partially shaded. The shrubs surrounding the front porch were dead; they looked dangerous and predatory in their prickly leaflessness. On the roof, a large crow peeled one of the shingles away with a sharp black beak.

I knocked on the door and steeled myself.

The door opened and Adrian stood on the other side. His glasses were off, and he looked somehow less present without then. I thought of blind baby rodents and the fused eyelids of featherless birds.

"Hey, man!" I said, overcompensating so that my voice came out sounding nearly maniacal with joviality. "Where've you been?"

"Sick," he said, a rasp to his voice. "I'm feeling a little better now, though."

"The guys have been asking about you."

"Yeah?" He hoisted one pointy shoulder and just looked bored. He opened the door more widely. "Come on in."

"Is your mom home?" I said, walking through the front door and glancing around. The false joviality was gone, the truer ring of apprehension back in my voice.

"No. She's at work."

I followed him through the main hallway. Amazingly, even all these months later, very little had been unpacked. Towers of cardboard boxes still lined the hallway and the living room. Clothing remained draped over the stairwell banister.

In the kitchen, a few pots and pans littered the Formica countertop, and there was a small table with only two chairs by the bay window that looked out onto the backyard. From this window I could see my own house and the three slouching shapes of my friends perched atop the woodpile. Around me, the Gardiner house was infused with that nonspecific staleness in the air, the same that I had registered on that day I'd dropped off my grandmother's cookies.

"You hungry?" Adrian asked, rifling through one of the cupboards.

"Not really." I looked up and noticed there were no lightbulbs in the ceiling fixture.

Adrian produced a box of Pop-Tarts from the cupboard. "You didn't get in trouble the other day, did you? For getting home after dark?"

"No, man. It's cool."

He ripped into one of the foil packages and had a Pop-Tart in his mouth

an instant later. He ate like a starving prisoner. "Whatcha got there?" He nodded toward the yearbook under my arm.

"Oh." I hadn't rehearsed this part. I hadn't rehearsed any of this. It was all I
could do to sound casual. "It's a yearbook." I set it on the counter and pushed
it over to him. "It's got a picture in it I think you should see."

Adrian looked at the yearbook cover. "Since when did you go to an all-
girls' school?"

"It's got Courtney Cole's picture in it. The dead girl." When I could tell by
his expression that he wasn't taking the hint, I said, "She's wearing a necklace."

Adrian tossed the box of Pop-Tarts onto the counter, and with the one
he'd been eating still protruding from his mouth, he opened the yearbook.
Big glossy pages glared up at us as I stepped beside Adrian and looked down
at the book with him.

"What page is she on?" he asked.

I flipped the book to Courtney's page, which Scott had tabbed with a yellow Post-it.

Adrian stared at the photo for a long time, not speaking, not making a
sound. Then he looked at me. Without his glasses his eyes appeared too small
for his head. "That's her." It was not a question but more like hearing someone
marvel to themselves over the secrets of the universe.

"Yeah," I said.

He returned to the photo. Squinting, he leaned closer to the page. "But
she's wearing the wrong necklace."

"I just thought you should know."

"That I should know what?"

"Well, uh . . ." I gestured toward the page. "She's wearing a crucifix. Not a
heart-shaped locket."

Adrian blinked at me. "So?" Then he looked past me and out the bay window. "Tell them to come in here."

"Who?" For a moment I had genuinely forgotten about Peter, Scott, and
Michael in my backyard, though when I glanced up I could see that they were
easily visible through the window. "Oh. Yeah." I fumbled for words. "They
thought . . . I mean, we thought . . ."

"It's okay. Call them in."

I opened the patio door and yelled to the three stooges to come up to the
house. They feigned ignorance and surprise before bumbling across the lawn.

"Hey, guys," Michael said, coming through the back door. He tried to
sound like this whole meeting was purely serendipitous and that they had
been shooting the shit on the woodpile in my yard without my knowledge.
"What's going on? Whatcha doin' here, Angie?"

"Cut it out, moron," I told him.

"It's okay that you guys know," Adrian said.

"Know what?" Michael said, keeping up the façade until Peter punched him on the arm.

Adrian carried the yearbook to the kitchen table and sat down in one of the chairs. The rest of us gathered around him. No one said a word, not even Michael. Then, just when the silence was becoming overbearing, Adrian rose from his chair and disappeared down the hallway. I heard his rapid little footfalls on the stairs.

Peter and I exchanged a look. Michael grew instantly bored and went to the box of Pop-Tarts on the counter. Scott continued to stare at the yearbook on the table.

"Is he all bummed out?" Peter asked me.

"I don't really know. I think he still thinks the locket is hers." I came up beside Scott and studied the photo again. It was almost unfathomable to think of that attractive young girl as the same one we'd witnessed being dredged up from the woods next to December Park, pale and gray beneath a sheet of white, the right side of her face punctured. Dented. Like a tin can.

"Poor little buffoon," Michael commented. I turned and glared at him as he hopped on the counter, half a Pop-Tart poking out of his mouth. He shrugged, then yanked the Pop-Tart from his mouth and gave me his best politician's smile—wide and toothy.

After several minutes passed and Adrian still hadn't returned to the kitchen, we all began to feel restless.

"Where is he?" Peter asked, peeking down the hallway.

I stepped into the hall. "Adrian?" My voice reverberated off the barren walls. I started down the hall but froze at the sight of him sitting on the bottom step of the staircase. He held the heart-shaped locket. He wore his glasses—he had probably gone to his room to retrieve them, I realized—and when he looked up at me, I had a hard time dissecting the mixture of emotion in his eyes.

Peter, Michael, and Scott came up behind me.

"It could still be hers," Adrian said, though much of the conviction had been stripped from his voice. I felt responsible for it. "That picture in the yearbook doesn't mean anything."

"Sure," I said. "Anything's possible."

"Can I see it?" Scott asked, approaching the front of the stairs. His shadow fell across Adrian's face.

After a pause, Adrian handed him the locket.

Scott held it with equal reverence, turning the small silver heart over in his fingers as though it were something unearthed from an archaeological site. "The eyelet is broken, all right."

"I think it happened when she was attacked," Adrian said.

Scott nodded, as if this made total sense to him. "I can take this home and fix it for you. I just gotta bend the clasp back into place. And if I can't do that, I can replace it with a new one."

"Yeah?"

"Sure. It's easy."

Adrian nodded.

"Hey," said Peter, breaking the tension. "Why don't we go catch a movie at the Juniper?"

"Sounds like a good idea," I said, anxious to get out of Adrian's house.

"Count me in," said Michael.

"Let me get my coat." Adrian stood and bounded up the stairs but then paused halfway up. He turned around and came slowly back down. "Can I keep that yearbook for a while?" he asked me.

"It's not mine," I said and looked to Scott.

"I guess so. I may have to take ugly Martha Dooley to the Quickman for a burger, though."

"Scott and Martha sitting in a tree, F-U-C-K-I-N-G," Michael sang, snapping his fingers like someone out of *West Side Story*.

We all laughed.

Just over a week later, after a Sunday dinner of spaghetti and meatballs, my grandparents retired to the den to watch television while my father remained at the kitchen table, going over stacks of paperwork.

"How's the case going?" I asked, grabbing an apple from the fridge.

He leaned back in his chair and ran his hands through his thinning, graying hair. "We've got a lot of people looking at a lot of different angles. I'm just double-checking to make sure all the lines have been connected."

I saw that his coffee cup was empty so I took it over to the pot and refilled it for him.

"Thanks, pal."

"Are you guys getting any closer to finding out who killed that girl?"

He made a face that approximated sad resignation. "I wish I could say we were."

"Do you think whoever did that to the Cole girl got those other kids, too? Like Aaron Ransom on New Year's Eve?"

"That was a bad night, wasn't it?" There was compassion in my father's voice, though I couldn't help but wonder if he was deliberately avoiding my questions. "I'm sorry you had to be in the middle of it."

"It's okay. I was just wondering about all those kids that nobody's found. Is it the same person who killed that girl?"

"It's hard to tell," my dad said with a sigh. "We've been talking to the other parents and getting as much info as we can. It might seem like too much of a coincidence that these kids seemed to vanish within months of each other, but maybe it isn't a coincidence at all, if you look at it in another way. There's always the possibility of a runaway pact or something like that."

"What's that?"

"Friends conspire to run away from home at the same time. They hide out someplace for a little while before eventually coming back home. Or more likely, a guy runs off with his girlfriend. The Frost girl kept a journal and mentioned a high school boy she had been seeing without her parents' knowledge. She doesn't mention the boy's name, but it could be the Connor kid, who disappeared around the same time. They could have gone off somewhere together."

"Oh," I said. I supposed it made sense to the police, but any kid at Stanton School could have told them that thirteen-year-old Bethany Frost had frequently been spotted sucking face with Tyler Beacham, a Stanton School sophomore, in the woods behind the middle school. Sixteen-year-old Jeffrey Connor probably didn't even know Bethany existed.

And then there was William Demorest, who hadn't been friends with either of the other two. That didn't explain how Aaron Ransom fit in, either. Wasn't it too much of a coincidence that all these kids had decided to run away around the same time a girl from town was found murdered? I wondered if my father actually believed this theory or if he was feeding it to me to quell my fears.

"Well," I said, "if it is the same person, do you think it's possible that the other kids, the ones who disappeared, were killed and left in the woods, too?"

"No. We searched the woods thoroughly with cadaver dogs. December Park, too. There isn't . . ." My father let his voice trail off. He had gone into cop mode and had temporarily forgotten that he was talking to his fifteen-year-old son. "Listen," he said, the timbre of his voice more conciliatory now. "As long as you keep away from deserted areas, stick in groups, and get home before it's too late, you and your friends have nothing to be afraid of. I promise. Okay?"

I nodded.

He winked at me, smiling wearily. Exhaustion seemed to radiate off him in visible waves. "You doing okay otherwise?"

"I guess."

"How's school?"

I shrugged. "Okay."

"You finish your homework for tomorrow?"

"Yeah."

"Good." Again, that weary smile. He turned back to his ream of paper-work, bringing the fresh coffee to his lips and slurping.

"Dad?"

"Hmmmm?"

"What do *you* think happened to those other kids? Do you think the same person who got Courtney Cole got the rest of them?"

He faced me, and I could tell he was debating whether he should pacify me or tell me the truth. "Yes. I think it's the same person."

I nodded. Only vaguely was I aware that I had dug my fingernails into the flesh of the apple while awaiting his answer.

That night, after everyone had gone to bed, I flipped the blankets off my per-spiring body and crept out into the hallway. It took an eternity to get past the traitorous floorboards outside my father's closed bedroom door and down the stairs. I didn't turn on a light until I made it to the kitchen, and even then the only light I switched on was the single tube light over the sink; it cast an almost iridescent penumbra across the length of the countertop.

My father's empty coffee mug was still on the table. The papers were gone, though I noticed his battered cordovan briefcase with the brass clasps propped up in the doorway. I picked it up, noting how heavy it was, and set it carefully on the table. I covered each clasp while I popped them open, muf-fling the sound.

Chewing on my lower lip, I opened the briefcase. Papers bristled out. Manila folders, industrial staples, large metal clasps on stacks of printed pages stared up at me. I thumbed through one of the packets. I wasn't sure what I was looking at. Another stack of pages, this one nearly as thick as a phone book, contained addresses and phone numbers, social security num-bers, license plate numbers.

I sifted through the rest of the paperwork until I located a blue case file at the bottom of the briefcase. There were no labels on the cover, though there were a lot of pages filed inside it. It was the file my father had been reading earlier that evening. I opened it and instantly recoiled at the sight of the dead, ruinous face of Courtney Cole.

I redirected my gaze toward the soft tube light humming above the stain-less steel kitchen sink. A sour breath exhaled through my flared nostrils. When I looked back down at the photograph, it was still just as gruesome, yet somehow I was able to look at it now without horror.

The photograph had been taken while Courtney Cole was still in the woods; I could see that her head, cocked strangely on her neck, still lay among a bed of sodden black leaves. Her two gelatinous eyes reminded me of automobile headlights after they had become foggy with moisture.

Mottled black-purple bruises ran from temple to jawline on the right side of her face.

I turned to the next page, which showed another photograph of the dead girl, this time with the head wound as the subject of the shot. I examined it in all its stark and morbid detail.

Dented, I thought again, same as I had on the day I saw the cops pulling her up the embankment, although I now found the word to be foolishly inadequate. It was a horrible, vivid gash, the skin busted apart and fringed in congealed black blood. At the center, whitish triangles of skull protruded through a terrible divot. Bits of dirt and little pebbles were stuck in the blood. There was a yellow ruler beside her head, measuring the diameter of the wound.

Similar photos followed. There were others taken at the morgue, for she was now splayed out on a stainless steel table with a white sheet draped to just below her collarbone. She looked more lifelike somehow under the fluorescent lights, though the discoloration of her flesh was more prominent. The photos toward the end were of the surrounding woods, but I couldn't identify what purpose they might serve the police.

I flipped to the next tab in the case file to find a stack of coroner's reports and various handwritten notes. I skimmed the typed parts and skipped the illegible handwritten notes. *Blunt force trauma*, it read in one of the boxes.

The sound of someone moving around upstairs caused me to freeze. I held my breath, listening. It had sounded like the groaning of bedsprings or possibly one of the noisy floorboards at the top of the stairs. I waited, anticipating the all-too-familiar sound of my father's tendons popping as he descended the stairs. But that sound did not come.

For a moment I considered closing the file and creeping back up to my room. But in the end, I decided to comb through the rest of it, pausing only to read the boldface type in various reports.

The final packet of papers contained more handwritten notes as well as a single-spaced typed sheet of paper. I realized that I was reading the statements made by Courtney's parents, Byron and Sarah Beth. There was no revelation in either statement—their daughter had simply failed to return home one evening—until I reached the end of Sarah Beth's. It was a simple recounting of the clothing her daughter had been wearing on the day she disappeared— a purple sweater, jeans with sequins on the rear pockets, a white knit coat, white tennis shoes.

And a heart-shaped locket.

I stared at the words until my eyes burned from not blinking. When another creaking sound from above filtered down the stairwell, I closed the file and stuffed it, along with the rest of my father's paperwork, into the briefcase. I set the briefcase back in its place on the floor, then took the stairs up

to my bedroom. Given the strength of my beating heart, I knew sleep would
be a long time coming.

CHAPTER TEN
THE REBELS OF ECHO BASE

My revelation about the heart-shaped locket convinced them all. How
could it not? Adrian beamed, and Scott joined him in crowing as if it
were some victory. Peter and Michael shared matching looks of amazement.
And then, of course, they wanted to go to the woods and see what else might
have been left behind, what clue may have been overlooked by the police.
They wanted to search.

The following Saturday morning, we all arrived at Scott's house around nine
o'clock to collect supplies. The Steeples' basement was a cornucopia of items
scavenged from yard sales, stockpiled by Scott's crazy aunt Willa who had
stayed a full summer with the Steeples while she sank deeper and deeper into
the quagmire of dementia. When she began bringing home stray cats, Scott's
parents had sent her to a home, but the stuff in the basement had remained.

We sifted through the junk like archeologists. Michael donned an old
World War II helmet, tied a fringed afghan around his neck like a cape, and
climbed on a chair. He assumed a posture reminiscent of Washington crossing the Delaware in that famous painting. "I'm totally wearing this helmet
today. In fact, I may never take it off again."

We uncovered some pitted canteens that looked like they had been used
during the Civil War, a pair of rubber galoshes, a pair of binoculars. I picked
up the heavy binoculars and peered through them. Everything was blurry. I
asked Scott if he knew how to work them.

"There's a dial on the top," he said. "Turn it to adjust the view."

I cranked the dial slowly counterclockwise, and it immediately brought
the wood-grain pattern of the far wall into detailed relief. "Holy shit. These
are way cool."

"Bring 'em along," Scott said. "I'm sure we can use 'em."

There were flashlights, too, though when we put batteries in them, only
one of them worked. Peter found what looked like an ancient transistor radio
with a hand crank on one side. He turned the radio over in his hands looking
for the battery compartment.

"It doesn't take batteries," Scott informed him. "It works off something called a dynamo."

"Yeah. That sounds made up."

"Seriously. Turn the crank."

Peter did, his tongue poking through his lips like someone taking a difficult math exam. The sound seemed to swell up inside the transistor radio like something in slow motion gaining normal speed until an AM station came through in surprising clarity. A disc jockey's disembodied voice crackled out of the speaker.

Peter stared at the machine with a look of astonishment. "That's awesome," he said, still turning the radio over in his hands and looking for the battery compartment like someone trying to find the hidden panel in a magician's magic box.

"What about these?" Michael held up a pair of walkie-talkies. They were the size and shape of bricks and looked equally as heavy. "Do they work?"

"I have no idea," said Scott, "but you have to charge them up first to find out. There should be chargers somewhere around here. I saw them once before."

"What do they look like?"

"Like plastic cradles that plug into the wall."

"Cool." Michael tossed me one of the walkie-talkies. I had been correct in estimating its weight. "Help me look, Mazzone."

I helped Michael search, pausing only when I came across a package of unopened typewriter ribbon. Spools of ribbon were becoming harder and harder to find, particularly after Second Avenue Stationery had closed, and the one on my typewriter at home had begun to fade months ago. I held up the package and called over to Scott, "Hey, man, do you mind if I take these?"

He frowned. "What are they?"

"Ink ribbons for my typewriter."

"Shoot, you're still using that old thing? I've got an extra word processor up in my bedroom. You can have it if you want it."

It was like telling an antiques collector to get rid of all his junk in order to make room for brand-new things. When I wrote, I entered a fantasy world. That old typewriter was the machine that took me there and brought me safely back. I didn't know if I could get there from someone's spare word processor. Moreover, I thought that once you stopped writing words and started processing them, those wonderful fantasy worlds became harder and harder to visit.

"No, thanks," I said. "I'll stick to the typewriter."

Scott hoisted his shoulders. "Suit yourself. Sure, go ahead and take 'em."

The entire morning, Adrian sat on the basement steps, Martha Dooley's yearbook open on his lap, and scrutinized Courtney's school photo. As I stared at him, he looked up and met my gaze from across the room. Magnified behind the thick lenses of his glasses, his eyes looked like two searchlights beaming into the fog of a wintry midnight.

After a hasty meal of pizza rolls, microwaved salami sandwiches, and Kool-Aid, we were on our bikes heading across town to the Dead Woods. We rode beneath the sun of midday, our backpacks heavy with items from Scott's basement, the air warming up all around us with the oncoming spring. With Adrian perched once again on my handlebars and the binoculars swinging from my neck by a leather strap, their weight oddly comfortable, I pedaled twice as hard as my friends just to keep pace.

"Go, go, go!" Adrian shouted, clutching the handlebars.

The wind whipped my face and burned my skin. I hunched behind Adrian's Incredible Hulk backpack to avoid the slipstream. Tears leaked from the corners of my eyes and carved burning paths toward my temples. *Go, go, go*, I thought, echoing Adrian's sentiment. *Go, go, go.* I pedaled harder.

At Woolworth Avenue, Michael's rattling Mongoose came up alongside us. His jacket billowed in the wind, and he still wore the World War II helmet. Without saying a word, he turned and grinned at me, his eyes hidden behind mirrored sunglasses. It was the biggest, stupidest grin he could muster, and I burst out laughing. Arching his eyebrows above the frames of his sunglasses, he gave me a thumb's-up.

We coasted down the street toward the highway, the spires of St. Nonnatus jutting up beyond the skyline like a medieval parapet. The binoculars thumped weightily against my breastbone.

At Augustine Avenue, Peter and Scott began singing Creedence Clearwater Revival's "Run through the Jungle" off-key. Peter was wrapped in a neon green ski jacket and had headphones on. He pedaled hard, his ass off the seat of his bike, his strong legs working like the wheel arms of a locomotive. Despite the chill in the air, Scott wore only a flimsy Orioles Windbreaker over a tattered T-shirt. He had headphones around his neck, and his shoulders were burdened with the weight of his JanSport backpack.

We didn't need words between us. We rode, our little quintet, and in that moment we were the only living creatures traversing the streets of Harting Farms.

When we hit the road behind the Generous Superstore plaza, Scott motioned toward the ravine on the side of the road. We fell into a straight line and veered one by one off the road and down the embankment into the rocky ravine. On my handlebars, Adrian jolted like someone being pumped full of electricity. At one point, just as we struck a particularly aggressive rock, he shouted something that sounded perplexingly like, "My coolie!"

As we approached the highway intersection, I shouted, "Hang on!" and didn't slow down a bit. Neither did my friends. Scott, who was leading the charge, knew the highway's traffic lights better than the county workers who repaired them; he had timed our arrival so the lights changed in our favor just as we hit the intersection. We blasted through it at top speed to the accompaniment of bleating car horns and shouts from open windows.

On the opposite side of the highway, we dipped down a second small embankment, whipping through scraggly underbrush and cattails that rose like tiny minarets from the muck. Scott and Peter launched up the embankment toward Counterpoint Lane, and Adrian and I followed. Close at my back, Michael whooped like a loon. Our bike tires printed wet streaks on the asphalt as we cruised toward the intersection of Point and Counterpoint.

When we reached the busted section of guardrail, we all skidded to a stop. The intersection was eerily clear of cars. Adrian dropped off my handlebars and, his legs wobbly, walked to the middle of our circle of bikes. His backpack looked like it weighed two hundred pounds easy.

"I'm vibrating like a live wire," Michael said.

"What was it you said when we went down that first ravine?" I asked Adrian.

"Coolie," Adrian said.

"What's a coolie?"

"It's my butt," he said, reddening.

I laughed.

"So where exactly do we start looking?" Peter asked, peeling the headphones from his ears and dropping them around his neck. I heard the tinny resonant drone of John Lennon issuing through the orange foam earpieces.

"They took her out of the woods here." Scott wheeled his bike to the cusp of woods and peered over the guardrail.

"Okay," Michael said, "so let's get down there first."

We rolled our bikes through the twisted rent in the guardrail and carefully descended toward the bottom of the woods, where the tree trunks grew thickest and the kudzu, even in winter, was a Gordian tangle of brownish vines. This time, Adrian led the charge.

"The Dead Woods," Peter marveled, suddenly right beside me. He was breathing heavily. "Satan's Forest."

When we reached the bottom and the ground leveled out, we simply dropped our bikes into the foliage and continued following Adrian deeper into the woods.

My friends and I were no strangers to Satan's Forest, of course. We had spent much of our summers here, smoking on tree stumps and catching brine shrimp in the shallow rust-orange water of the creek. By midsummer, the trees were so thick and full it was impossible to see to the bottom from the streets above, and sometimes we secreted ourselves down there from early morning until dusk when the mosquitoes and black flies finally drove us home.

In all that time, none of us had ever ascribed to these woods the preternatural sense of power I felt in being here now. It was as though we'd crossed a great and secret threshold, and things—important things—were finally being set into motion. I wondered if the others felt it, too.

"We should set up camp." Adrian paused beside an oak tree. "Like a home base or something. You know, a place where we can set up our base of operations."

"The statues," Peter and I said at the same time.

Adrian grinned. "Right."

We walked deeper into the woods toward the clearing with the statues, the spot I had taken Adrian on that first evening.

"What about an ambush?" Michael said from the rear of the line.

"What do you mean?" Peter said.

"Like, what if he's still down here? What if this is his home?"

"The Piper?"

"Yeah. If you were a crazed serial murderer, where else would you hide?" Michael glanced up at the treetops, his army helmet sliding back on his head. "You ever hear of nut bags living in the forests in camouflaged tree houses and things like that?"

My father's voice from so many months ago resonated in my head: *You stay away from remote places—the woods, the locks down at the poorer end of town, the bike path, and all the parks after dark. Stay away from those empty cabins along the Cape and the Shallows and the old railway station at the end of Farrington Road. And that bridge by Deaver's Pond where the homeless go in the winter. I don't want you hanging around by that underpass, not with your friends and certainly not alone.*

In a town like Harting Farms, with all its honeycombs and shadowed, forgotten places, a serial murderer could hide literally anywhere.

Scott produced his butterfly knife. He flipped it open in one graceful swipe. "I'm prepared in case of an attack."

"Terrific," Michael commented. "I feel safer already. If the Piper comes after us, you can give him a nice shave."

When we reached the clearing, we stopped and looked around. I thought, *Yeah, this is right. This is the perfect spot.*

Adrian dropped his backpack onto the ground. Sunlight speared through the trees in narrow shafts, creating golden pools of light along the dead, wet leaves that carpeted the earth. Scott, too, set down his backpack. He was still twirling the butterfly knife, his dark eyes sharp and alert.

Michael stepped around the clearing while looking down, as if to examine the ground for booby traps or evidence of enemy armies. He removed the army helmet, and his hair fell down in that perfect right-sided part. His sunglasses hung from the collar of his University of Maryland sweatshirt, which was about two sizes too small and stippled with holes.

I sauntered over to one of the headless concrete statues hidden beneath the underbrush. I felt around for it with my foot. *Thud.* I practically collapsed onto it, suddenly taken aback at the strength of my exhaustion. I took the binoculars from around my neck and dropped them at my feet.

Peter joined me on the statue. His exhaustion was evident in the drawn-out expulsion of air that issued from his lungs. Sweat beaded his forehead.

Adrian remained standing, his back toward us, his backpack sinking into the muck at his feet. The outline of his frame was silvered in sunlight and veined with the shadows of interlocked tree limbs. There was nothing but an endless wealth of trees ahead of him, but he seemed focused on something the rest of us could not see.

Scott knelt down and dove into his backpack. I watched him withdraw the canteens, the walkie-talkies (we had found the chargers in Scott's basement, and the handhelds worked commendably), a spiral-bound notebook with a ballpoint pen clipped to the front cover, some items wrapped in tinfoil, an alarm clock, and the dynamo-powered radio. He caught me staring at him, smiled, then tossed something white in my direction that I originally mistook for a baseball. When I caught it I was surprised by the sponginess of it. It was a pair of gym socks rolled up into a ball.

"I brought some for everyone. I figured the ground would be wet. No reason to catch frostbite, right?" Scott tossed balled-up socks at the other guys.

"You should have been a Boy Scout," Peter told him.

"I'm too smart to be a Boy Scout."

"Hey. I was a Boy Scout," said Michael, catching the pair of gym socks that Scott launched at him.

"Yeah," Scott said coolly. "See what I mean?"

Michael flipped him the bird.

In the end, Scott was left holding the remaining pair of socks that was meant for Adrian because Adrian was still staring off into the trees. Scott eventually dropped the socks into his backpack, then shrugged when he caught my eye again.

"Poindexter," Michael called. "You okay, man?"

Adrian turned. With his sweatshirt hood over his head and the shadows of the overhead tree branches crisscrossing his face, I couldn't make out his expression—couldn't tell if he even had one.

"Sure," Adrian said after a moment. He went over to a carved-out niche in a nearby tree and hoisted himself into it, pulling his knees up to his chest. He wore imitation Converse sneakers, the kind with the cheap soles that looked overly white and were made of uncomfortable plastic instead of rubber. When he held his legs straight out before him, I could see that someone—his mother, I supposed—had printed in permanent marker an *R* on the sole of his right sneaker and an *L* on the sole of his left.

Scott distributed the canteens. There were five so we each got our own. "It's just filled with water. In case, you know, we get thirsty or whatever. But I also brought something to keep us awake, too." He returned to his backpack and produced two six-packs of Jolt Cola. "Extra caffeine to keep us going."

"I love this man," Michael said. He was seated on his army helmet like a soldier on break, drumming his hands against his thighs. "Toss me one of those, Scotty boy."

"Just what he needs," Peter commented. "More caffeine."

Scott pulled some cans of Jolt free from the pack and tossed them around. Adrian was the only one who didn't take one.

A moment later when Scott took out a pack of Camels and offered a cigarette to Adrian, the smaller boy recoiled into the niche in the tree and said, "Those things give you cancer."

Scott cocked his head and didn't seem like he cared all that much. He stuck one of the smokes between his lips, then chased it with his lighter for several seconds before catching and lighting the tip.

Silence overtook us. Even Michael was uncharacteristically quiet. We all sat in our rough circle about the clearing as a cool wintry wind shook the skeletal tree branches and rattled the remaining leaves like maracas. In the far distance, I heard children shouting somewhere across December Park. Beyond the park and the woods, Harting Farms ended abruptly at the edge of a cliff that overlooked the Chesapeake Bay.

Again, I recalled that day so many years ago when Charles and I had gone out on the boat and he had pointed up to the cliff and at the giant holes bored into the face of it. Some had looked large enough to drive a car through. With terrible clarity, I saw my brother's tanned chest and the flecks of bay salt that crystalized in his dark eyelashes. I shivered.

After a moment, Scott cranked the transistor, and soon we had an AM oldies station to keep us company. The reception was horrible, and Scott kept the volume low, but at least it was something.

"I wonder if it's anyone we know," Scott said. He used the blade of his butterfly knife to scrape the dirt out from beneath his fingernails.

"Who?" Peter said.

"The killer. The guy who got Courtney Cole. And the others."

"Possibly the others," Michael added. He was laying on his back now, his hands laced behind his head and his army helmet on his stomach, rising and falling with his respiration. "We don't know that for sure."

"You sound just like the goddamn news," Scott scolded. "Is it so impossible to believe?" He turned to me. "What does your dad think?"

"He thinks it's the same person," I said, "but the cops don't have any real proof."

"What else did your dad say?"

"That's about it. He didn't seem like he really wanted to talk about it."

"Man, you gotta ask him for some details," Scott said.

"I went snooping through his work papers. Isn't that enough?"

"You gotta ask him if he has any suspects," Scott continued. "Find out if he has any idea who it might be."

"Leave Angie alone," Peter said. "His dad ain't gonna tell him anything important. That shit's all confidential, anyway."

Scott feigned a jab at Peter with his butterfly knife.

"You're pretty tough sitting all the way—" Peter quickly shut his mouth as Scott flung the knife at him. It pinwheeled through the air before planting itself, blade down, in the dirt between Peter's sneakers. "Holy shit! You could have killed me!"

Scott laughed. "Yeah, right."

"You could have cut my fucking balls off."

Scott laughed harder. "What balls?"

Michael sat up and grinned. He had his mirrored sunglasses back on, and he looked like someone enjoying a day at the beach.

"Dickhead," Peter said, plucking the knife from the ground. He examined the blade, then attempted to flip it shut. He managed to do it on the third try, but it wasn't nearly as graceful as when Scott did it.

"What if it isn't a man?" Scott spoke up.

"What do you mean?" Peter said. "Like, it could be a woman?"

Michael shook his head. "That's horseshit. Chicks don't have the balls to pull off this kinda madness."

"Literally," commented Peter.

"I'm serious. Only men can be that sadistic. You ever hear of a female serial killer?"

"Aileen Wuornos," Scott said without missing a beat.

"Shut up," Michael said. "You made that up."

"Did not. She killed a bunch of guys and was arrested a few years ago."

Michael waved a hand at him. "Well, it sounds like bullshit to me. And, anyway, I'd bet anything that the Cole girl was . . . I don't know . . . raped or . . . like, molested or something . . ."

"She wasn't," I said.

"Yeah? How the hell would you know?"

"Because I read the coroner's report, dummy."

"Anyway, I didn't mean that the killer's a woman," Scott said. "But what if the killer is something that's . . . maybe not human . . ."

"What's that mean?" Peter said.

"Maybe there's something else here in town taking everyone."

"This isn't one of your horror movies," Peter told him.

Michael piped up: "I once read a story about a rogue lion in Africa that went around killing villagers. The thing would wait for someone to go wandering off from the rest of the tribe and then attack. It was almost human in how it hunted. You know, like it waited for the right time and everything. Creepy as hell."

"Or like an alligator or something," Peter suggested.

Across the clearing, Adrian nodded almost imperceptibly. "I've heard about alligators in some areas getting really big and eating children. It happens down south a lot. They put up big fences around the yards in Louisiana to keep the alligators out."

"Or the sewers," Scott said. "Like that movie we saw at the Juniper. The one where someone flushed a baby alligator down the toilet, and it lived in the sewers eating all kinds of stuff—"

"Like turds," Michael interjected, chuckling.

"—until it got so big that it broke through the street and started eating all those people."

"Whoa," said Adrian. "Cool."

"It was awesome," Scott assured him.

"Don't forget about the Chesapeake Bay," Michael said. "Man, there could be *anything* living down there."

"Like that story Angie wrote about Chessie," Peter said.

"What's Chessie?" Adrian asked.

"It's the Chesapeake Bay version of the Loch Ness Monster," I said. "It's a myth, like Bigfoot."

"That shit's real," Michael contested, jabbing a finger at me, then sliding his sunglasses down the bridge of his nose. "Chessie's no myth. Uncle of mine saw it a few years ago at the Cape locks, right here in town—two big humps rising out of the water. Swear to God."

"You're a big hump," Scott said.

"Hey, I'm dead serious," Michael said.

Beside me, Peter began carving his initials into the stone statue with Scott's knife. "Remember when they caught that huge shark by the Naval Academy? It was a great white, wasn't it? Like in *Jaws*."

"I think it was a sand shark," Scott said. "Some fishermen caught it on a line from the academy bridge."

"Well," Michael said, "unless the thing's got legs, it ain't crawling on land and snatching up kids, jackass."

"I didn't say it was, jerk face," Peter said.

"Douche nozzle!"

"Ass muncher!"

"Gorbachev's wife!" This had been Michael's favorite insult for as long as I could remember. When he first started using it, none of us even knew who Gorbachev was, let alone his wife.

Peter ignored him. "Ed the Jew used to tell us stories about a thing called the White Worm, something that his old man used to scare him with. He never described it in much detail, just that it was a worm about the size of a sofa, really fat and bulbous."

"Bulbous," Michael echoed, snickering.

"It lives in the bay and attacks watermen who fall asleep on their boats overnight. It climbs into the boats and eats them. Oh, and it has a big mouth on one end filled with a ring of teeth, all jagged and pointy like a shark's."

"Awesome," Scott intoned.

"Whenever you see an old johnboat or Sunfish floating across the bay or down the river with no one on it, that means the White Worm got 'em."

Michael's eyes widened. "I've seen those boats."

"That's a fuckin' cool story," Scott admitted.

"He used to tell it to me when I was just a kid and acting up," Peter said. His eyes grew distant and he smiled. "He liked to mess with my head."

"How did it climb onto the boats if it was just a worm?" Michael asked.

Peter shrugged. "Well, it was a *giant* worm."

"Worms don't have hands. Not even giant ones."

"This one did. It had skinny little arms like you, and it would drag its fat body up onto the boats."

"Aw, you just made that up," Michael said, waving him off. "I'm being serious. How can a giant worm climb onto a boat?"

"Dude." Peter shook his head. "It's just a story. The whole thing's made up."

Adrian got up from his perch and went over to his backpack. He unzipped it and withdrew the Girls' Holy Cross yearbook and a slimmer volume I recognized as his drawing tablet. Then he returned to his tree and crawled back into the niche. He moved with the litheness and delicateness of a girl. His entire body looked fragile, as if he might break apart into pieces at even the slightest nudge. He opened the yearbook and slowly turned the pages.

"Here," Peter said, handing me the knife.

I started to engrave my initials beneath his.

"The question I'd like answered is what happened to their bodies," Scott said. The radio at his feet changed songs, the soft lilt of "In the Still of the Night" crackling from the speaker. "There's only been one body found, but there are still four kids missing. Where are their bodies? Down here somewhere, too?"

We looked around at the looming, sun-silvered trees and the serenity of the woods that surrounded us. All of a sudden, it seemed like a false quiet, a façade designed to lull us into false security. This place could be a graveyard, a land for the dead and buried. Were any of them beneath our feet—just mere inches under the soil—at this very moment?

But then I remembered what my dad had told me, and I said, "The cops took cadaver dogs down here. They would have found bodies if there were any."

"Even if they're buried real deep?" asked Scott.

"I guess."

"Gah!" Michael shouted, grabbing his throat and struggling on the ground. The army helmet bounded off his stomach and rolled away. "They got me! They got me!"

"Cut it out, fuck face," Scott scolded him.

Finished with my carving, I closed the knife and tossed it to Scott. He got up, came over to the statue, and began inscribing his initials into the concrete below mine.

I slid off the statue and onto the ground, the coldness of the earth radiating through my jeans and numbing my buttocks—*coolie*, I thought, smiling to myself—and popped the tab on my can of Jolt. The soda was warm and too sugary. Perfect.

"Why do you guys make so much fun of each other if you're friends?" Adrian said.

"We're just screwing around," I said. "We don't mean it."

"Although Michael *is* a fuck face," Scott said from over his shoulder. "That's just a fact."

"We've all been friends for years," Peter said. "It's just joking, Adrian. No one means anything by it."

Adrian pursed his lips and nodded slowly, watching us.

We must look like alien creatures to him, I thought, *a kid who's never had any close friends in his life . . .*

"Get over here, Sugarland," Scott called, rising off the ground and holding out the knife. "Your turn."

Michael snatched the knife from him, feigned slicing open one of his wrists, then dropped to his knees in the muck, gurgling and frothing from the mouth. A glob of spittle hung from his lower lip, slowly lengthening to a fine white thread that eventually touched his sweatshirt.

"Gross," Scott remarked casually. He'd seen enough of Michael's stunts to remain unimpressed.

His tongue poking from his mouth, Michael crawled toward the statue.

Adrian continued to turn the pages of the yearbook. On occasion he would lift his eyes and gaze off into the darkness of the woods. Once, he caught me staring at him and turned hurriedly away.

I stood and, brushing debris off my backside, went over to him. "Whatcha doing?"

"Just looking," he said.

"Is something wrong?"

He shook his head but didn't look at me. He had his writing tablet balanced on his other knee. I deciphered what appeared to be hasty sketches of Courtney Cole. Even as a sketch, the likeness was unmistakable.

Then he looked at me—a lost babe in the woods of some horrific fairy tale. His big fishy eyes appeared sloppy and unfocused, perhaps muddled by too many thoughts. I noticed a thin piece of shoestring around his neck and saw that Courtney Cole's heart-shaped locket hung from it. This struck me. Scott had fixed the clasp for him, but it never occurred to me that Adrian would actually wear it.

From the corner of his mouth, Adrian said, "I'm okay, Angie. I'm just doing some thinking. We should probably designate areas and spread out, start searching."

I chewed my lower lip, then looked over at Michael, Peter, and Scott. Michael was still carving his initials into the statue while Peter watched over his shoulder. Scott was fiddling with the dynamo radio and balancing a can of Jolt on one knee. They all looked young but also strangely old, too. It occurred to me that there wouldn't be many more days like these, hanging out in the woods without a care in the world.

"Yeah, okay, but you gotta do something first," I told him.

"Do what?"

"You gotta carve your initials," I said.

In the end, they ran down the trunk of the statue like this:

PG

AM

SS

MS

AG

Once we finished, the five of us stared at our work in silent appreciation. Seeing our names on that statue seemed to solidify the notion that these

woods, these Dead Woods, were now ours and ours alone. We held steward-
ship over them.

"Scott's got Nazi initials," Michael said.

Scott slugged him on the arm.

Adrian nodded at the statue, a satisfied little smile on his thin lips. Then he
pushed his glasses up his nose and looked at Michael. "Did you bring the map?"

Michael took out of one his maps from the rear pocket of his jeans and
handed it to Adrian. Adrian unfolded it and splayed it out over the statue.
The rest of us gathered around and dropped down on our haunches in the
cold earth.

The legend said this map had been created by the Harting Farms Parks
and Recreations Department in conjunction with the Maryland Department
of Natural Resources. It was a map of the surrounding woodland as well as
the coastal waterways that filtered straight out into the bay.

"The Dead Woods are here," Michael explained, tracing a dark green
horseshoe on the map. Next, he addressed a pale green rectangle surrounded
on three of its four sides by the Dead Woods. "And this is December Park,
smack in the middle. That means we're probably . . . right about . . . here." He
pointed to a spot in the dark green horseshoe that was bordered by two intersecting roadways toward the northwest—Point and Counterpoint Lanes—
and by December Park to the south.

"This is great." Adrian retrieved a black felt-tipped marker that he'd clipped
to the cover of his sketch pad and returned to the map. As he uncapped the
marker, he glanced at Michael. "Do you mind?"

"Shoot, I've got a dozen of these," Michael said.

Drawing a series of vertical lines in one corner of the map, Adrian divided
the woods into sections. When he finished, he admired his work for a moment
before retrieving some more items from his backpack. He handed us flashlights, some plastic bags with the Generous Superstore logo on them, small
notepads, and rubber gloves.

Michael snapped one of the gloves on his hand. "These for the proctology
exam?"

"This is how they do it on TV," Adrian explained. "You wear gloves in case
you find evidence and don't want to ruin the fingerprints that might be on it."

Examining his own pair of rubber gloves, Peter nodded. "Makes sense.
Good thinking."

Adrian tapped the marker against the grid he'd drawn across the Dead
Woods. "See how I broke it up into squares? We each search a different
square, then check them off on the map when we finish. But then we rotate,
so that we can search someone else's section after they're done in case that
person missed anything."

"That's gonna take a long time," I said.

"Yeah, but it's important." He held up one of the small notepads. "We use these to mark down anything we find. Like, the location of it. And then we can mark it down on the map, too. One of us should stay here, too, at home base. It's like when you call 911 and you get that operator on the phone . . ."

"A dispatcher," Scott and I said at the same time.

"Yeah. So the person staying at home base can have one of the walkie-talkies."

"Who gets the other one?" I asked. "We've only got two."

"My sister has some toy ones at home," Peter said. "They work just like real walkie-talkies, though maybe they don't go as far."

"You can bring those tomorrow," Adrian said.

"So who stays back at home base?" I said.

"Do we have to call it 'home base'?" Michael groaned. "Can't we come up with something cooler? Like Zanzibar Outpost or Ice Station Zero or something like that?"

"What about Echo Base?" Peter suggested.

Michael's bright eyes widened. "Yes! That's perfect."

"What's Echo Base?" Adrian asked.

We all gaped at him.

"It's the Rebel Alliance's base on Hoth," Peter explained. When Adrian's confounded expression didn't change, he added, "From *The Empire Strikes Back*."

"Oh," Adrian said, and it was obvious he didn't know what Peter was talking about.

"It's the second *Star Wars* movie," I said. "Haven't you ever seen it?"

Adrian shook his head.

"Holy shit, this is a travesty," Michael wailed. "I don't believe it."

"Have you ever even heard of *Star Wars*?" Peter said.

"Sure," Adrian said. "It's spaceships and stuff, right?"

"Good Lord." Michael moaned, holding his stomach. "The boy's a caveman."

"It's cool," I told Adrian. "Don't worry about it. I've got all three on videotape. You can come over and watch them sometime."

"Okay, thanks."

Michael blurted, "Darth Vader is Luke's fa—"

"Shut up!" Peter, Scott, and I shouted. Then we all laughed.

Adrian stared at us as if we'd lost our minds.

"So Echo Base it is," Scott said. "Who stays at the base first?"

I grabbed a longish twig off the ground, broke it into five pieces of varying sizes, then tucked the pieces into one fist so that just the tips of the sticks poked out. "Shortest stick stays back."

They each picked a stick, leaving one in my palm. Peter had drawn the shortest. Adrian gave him one of the walkie-talkies.

"There's one last thing," Adrian said. "I came up with jobs for everyone, too. Something we can do on our own when we're not down here in the woods."

Michael looked skeptical. "Jobs?"

"Yeah," Adrian said. "Like, Michael, you'll be the listening tower."

"Ironic title for a guy who never listens," Peter joked.

Michael shot him a look, then turned to Adrian. "So what do I do?"

"Keep an ear out around town and at school for anything that sounds suspicious."

"Like if I overhear someone talking about a stranger they saw at the park or something?"

Adrian nodded. "Exactly. And you're good at talking to people, so maybe you can get them to tell you stuff, if you think it's important. But that's not all. You should come up with a list of possible suspects."

"Oh, man," Michael said, chomping at the bit, "how do I do that?"

"Deduction," said Adrian. "Based on what you hear, you keep a list of potential suspects. When you have enough names on it, we'll review it and see if we can add any names or maybe take some away. Then we can narrow it down to a few realistic suspects."

"What about me?" said Scott.

"You're the weapons guy." He addressed us all now. "We have to be safe, to be able to protect ourselves. We'll need weapons."

"Yes," Scott trumpeted. "That's what I've been screaming about for months."

Adrian nodded. "If we're gonna hunt down a serial killer, we're gonna need more than walkie-talkies and headphones."

"What kind of weapons are we talking about?" I said.

"That's up to Scott," said Adrian.

"Blowtorches and chain saws for everyone," Scott said, grinning from ear to ear.

"What's my job?" asked Peter.

"Make a list of all the possible places in town where the killer could hide," Adrian said. "Dangerous places, too, where we might stand a chance of running into him."

"That's a lot of places," Peter said. "You're talking about the whole city or just the local neighborhoods?"

"At least within the perimeter where the kids have gone missing," Adrian said. "We need to pinpoint the locations where they disappeared as best we can and search around those areas."

"How do we do that? The newspapers don't give specifics."

Adrian turned to me.

Oh, boy, I thought.

"That'll be Angie's job," he said.

"Is it?" I retorted.

"You need to keep talking to your dad and get details about the missing kids that haven't been in the newspapers," he said. "If we can find out the specific places where the other kids went missing, it could help narrow down our search."

"I'm not sure the cops even know where they disappeared. No one saw anything. There aren't any clues."

"As far as we know," Adrian said.

"Yeah," Scott chimed in.

"Don't you think the police have already searched those places?" I said. "And besides, my dad's not gonna tell me anything that wasn't already on the news."

"Lazy bastard," Michael said. "We all got jobs, Mazzone."

"I'm not being lazy. I'm just saying I don't know how you guys expect me to—"

"Big fat lazy jerk," Michael continued. The others were grinning along with him. "You don't hear me bitching about *my* job, do you?"

I sighed. "Fine. I'll see what else I can find out." I looked to Adrian. "What are you gonna do?"

"Bring the killer out of hiding."

"Whoa," said Scott. "How you gonna do that?"

"Well, I've got an idea, but I'm still working it out in my head." He rubbed his chin. "Lastly, we need to establish a rendezvous point."

Peter looked around. "I thought *this* was the rendezvous point."

"No, this is home base."

"Echo Base," Michael corrected him.

Adrian shrugged. "Whatever it's called, we need a separate rendezvous point. It has to be a place we all know to go if Echo Base is compromised. Like if someone is following us and we don't want to lead them back here."

"Or if we're attacked and we have to meet up someplace else," Scott added.

"Then it should be out in the open," Michael said. "Some place safe."

"But close to Echo Base, too," Peter said. "Our stuff's here. We'll need to protect it."

"The park," I suggested. For Adrian's sake, I pointed due east through the trees. "December Park is straight through there on the other side of the woods."

"That's perfect," Peter agreed.

"There's a big tree beside the baseball diamond," Michael said. "It's right in the middle of the park."

"That might be too out in the open," Scott said. "What about the underpass?"

"Underpass?" Adrian said.

"It's at the far end of December Park under Solomon's Bend Road," Scott said. "It's like a big tunnel with a cobblestone road running through it that goes right out to Solomon's Field."

"Okay, good," said Adrian. He put his backpack on. "So, are we ready to start searching these woods?"

Michael clapped. "Let's do it!"

We searched until dusk fell upon the woods like a dreadful shadow. The woods darkened and grew colder, and our respiration exited our throats in visible clouds. I stomped through my section of the Dead Woods in silence while examining every bit of ground. When the foliage became too thick, I bent down and sifted through it.

Occasionally I heard the distant laughter of Scott or Michael searching in their own remote parts of Satan's Forest or Peter back at Echo Base fumbling with the dynamo-powered radio and singing off-key with the songs.

And of course, we found nothing.

"It's getting dark," Adrian said, coming toward me through the trees. We both glanced at the darkening sky through the interlocked boughs of the high trees. "We should probably round up the others and call it a night."

I had been given the second walkie-talkie. I unhooked it from my belt and keyed it now. "Hot Stuff to Big Red. Come in, Big Red. Over."

Peter's voice came over the static-laden radio: "Who the hell is Hot Stuff?"

"You gotta say 'over' when you're done talking, Big Red," I told him. "Over."

"You're a dickhead. Over."

I laughed. "Heading back to Echo Base, Big Red. We're calling it a night. Over."

"About time. I'm starving. Over."

Fifteen minutes later, after all our stuff was packed and we had wheeled our bikes up the embankment and onto Counterpoint Lane, thunder rumbled. We each cast a wary glance at the darkening sky. Before us, light traffic shushed through the intersection of Point and Counterpoint. We waited for a break in traffic, then sped across the intersection, back down the ravine on the other side of the street, and headed out toward Governor Highway and home.

We parted ways at our respective streets until it was just Adrian and me coasting down Haven. I slowed my pace as we hooked the corner onto Worth, the lights of the houses along the block looking yellow and warm and welcoming. Except for Adrian's house.

We coasted up his driveway, and I skidded to a stop beside Adrian's front porch. He climbed off my bike, his hair sticking up at random angles, his glasses askew on his face. We had beaten the thunderstorm home, though not by much; large raindrops began to fall, leaving darkened asterisks on the driveway.

"Is anyone home?" I asked him.

He glanced over his shoulder at his darkened home. "I guess. Sometimes Mom keeps the lights off."

What a head case, I thought.

"You know, I was thinking," I said. "We shouldn't limit our search to the woods. We should look around where you found that locket, too. Just because her body was found down there doesn't mean that's where the Piper got her."

"Yeah. That's a really good idea. Did you get that from your dad?"

"What do you mean?"

"A talent for investigating things," he said.

"I don't know. It just seems to make sense, doesn't it?"

"It sure does."

"You want to come over and watch *Star Wars* with me?"

Adrian glanced at his house again. When he looked back at me, I saw storm clouds in his eyes. "Not tonight. I should get home." He readjusted the straps of his backpack, still staring at me. "It's not a monster or anything who killed that girl and took the other kids. Not like your friends were saying."

"Of course not," I said. "They were only joking."

"Because it's a man, and he's very careful and very smart, and that makes him dangerous."

"Okay . . ."

"We shouldn't pretend like he's some bogeyman. We shouldn't let our guard down like that."

"Like I said, they were just joking around. They know it's some guy. Of course it is."

"Good. Because men are more dangerous than monsters." Then, wholly unexpectedly, Adrian said, "You're a putrid fart nose, Angie."

I blinked at him. "Uh, what?"

His face instantly reddened. "Um . . . I mean, you and your friends and all that name-calling . . ."

But then I understood. And laughed. In his own awkward way, Adrian was telling me he trusted me and that I was his friend. "Oh, okay, I get it. But putrid fart nose? That's the best you've got in you?"

Adrian made a sour little face that sent me laughing again.

"You should take lessons from Michael. He can come up with some whoppers."

"Yeah," he said. "And what's a Gorbachev's wife, anyway?"

I laughed even harder. I couldn't stop.

Soon Adrian was laughing, too.

Later that night as I lay in bed staring at the darkened ceiling of my bedroom while Bruce Springsteen issued softly out of my Walkman headphones, I thought about Adrian's obsession. It had begun mysteriously with him asking more and more questions about the Cole girl. That was explained away after he told me about the heart-shaped locket.

But now there was a new obsession: finding the killer. His interest seemed different than the rest of ours. More intense. My friends and I were doing it for fun; Adrian had another agenda. I kept seeing Adrian's determined face from earlier that day and those storm clouds roiling in his eyes. *Because it's a man, and he's very careful and very smart, and that makes him dangerous.*

I wondered what darkness clouded Adrian Gardiner's soul.

CHAPTER ELEVEN
THE NIGHTMARE

For the first time since Charles's death, I suffered a nightmare of such vivid, visceral proportion that it would cling to my psyche for days to come. It was dark. I was lying in the dirt in Satan's Forest surrounded by my friends while a smoky mist crept over us. I saw the moon through the trees, and I breathed in the scents of the woods and distant cigarette smoke and the even more distant dead fish smell of the Chesapeake on the far side of the wooded peninsula.

Angry winds bullied the trees and whipped up whirlwinds of dead leaves and gritty debris off the ground. I felt the wind, probing and unforgiving, its icy fibrils veining across my sweaty flesh beneath the layers of my clothes, which ballooned out from my body as if they had been pumped full of hot air.

Then the ground began to vibrate. Subtly at first but it amplified with increasing and frightening speed. Trees trembled. I sat up off the ground, my bones shaking loose in my flesh. Looking around, I expected to find my friends gone, but they weren't. They were scattered around me and sitting up as well, staring at the trees as their branches shook apart high above us.

Someone said something. I opened my mouth to scream but succeeded only in emitting a high-pitched keening that caused the lenses of Adrian's glasses to fracture and explode. Behind the shattered lenses, Adrian's eyes were missing. Bloody pits gaped back at me, black gore drooling down his cheeks from his eye sockets. His flesh purpled to the color of carbon paper. Graphite-colored veins bulged in his neck.

Then Adrian vanished into the ground fog. It was as if a large hole had opened up in the ground directly beneath him, swallowing him whole. Even the fog on the ground whirlpooled around the unseen hole like water going down a drain.

Beside me, Peter shrieked. It sounded many octaves too deep, like a record played at the wrong speed. I turned and saw that his normally full cheeks were sunken and jaundiced, networked with burst blood vessels. His eye sockets widened until his eyeballs jostled loosely in the expanding divots. Dark red fluid dribbled out of one nostril. I opened my mouth to speak his name but managed only a foghorn sound that blended with the increasing vibration radiating through the ground. Then Peter was sucked into the ground, too.

Michael shouted across the clearing. The mist parted, and I saw his blazing white face twisted in agony, his crystal blue eyes straining in his skull, his mouth stretched so wide I could see the flesh beginning to tear. Before I could attempt to speak to him, he disappeared through a hole in the ground.

To my left, Scott's countenance was distorted into idiot madness. He produced his butterfly knife, then drove the blade into the soft white flesh of his forearm. Blood spurted out, incongruous in its greenness, and oozed in slimy ropes to the mist-shrouded ground. When he looked at me, he was no longer Scott but the awful Dennis Foley, the haunted boy who had opened up his arm with a scalpel in biology class freshman year. Foley's yellow eyes blazed as a hideous grin stretched across the lower half of his face. The greenish blood steamed and bubbled out of his wound like lava. But then it was Scott again. Just as he lifted the knife out of the wound and brought it up to his neck, he dropped through the earth just as the others had.

I stood and prepared to run, but just as I took that first step, something gripped my right ankle and yanked. The force sent me sprawling forward while my ears echoed with the horrific sound of my bones not only breaking but actually coming apart—a sound like rubber bands snapping overlaid with the crunching of gravel beneath heavy truck tires.

On my stomach and pawing at the ground, I managed to look behind me in time to see my entire foot and lower half of my leg pulled through the fog and into a gaping wound in the earth. The serrated maw at the end of my severed thigh trailed ribbons of flesh and the wormlike, rubbery tubes of my arteries. A whitish knob of bone protruded from the center of the mess.

And that was when the earth opened up beneath me.

CHAPTER TWELVE
THE GHOSTS OF LOST CHILDREN

We spent the remainder of that winter among the headless concrete statues of the Dead Woods. On the coldest days, some sparkling with snow or raining icy pellets onto the dull pavement of the city streets, one of us would bring a thermos of hot chocolate to share, and once I brought some of my grandmother's escarole soup. (My friends examined the seaweed-like ribbons of escarole with skepticism bordering on distrust, but then they tasted the soup, and their eyes lit up.)

A heavy snowfall buried the city near the end of February. We got a few days off from school, a rare event, and since there was no searching that could be done, we went sledding in December Park, had snowball fights with Sasha Tamblin and the Lambeth twins at Solomon's Field, and Michael peed Nathan Keener's name in the snow in front of Principal Unglesbee's house.

By mid-March, we met in the woods by early morning on the weekends. On the days we had school, we walked to the woods after classes and hung out at Echo Base until the sky darkened and we had to depart for our homes.

We continued to hunt for clues, alternating our locations throughout the woods, forging our way through all the far places where human feet rarely—if ever—traversed. Per my suggestion, we searched the length of the culvert on the opposite side of Counterpoint Lane, too, since that was where Adrian had found the locket. We didn't limit ourselves to that specific area, either, but instead we went all the way down to Point Lane (where the culvert became a muddy swamp) and all the way up to Solomon's Bend Road (where the culvert was eventually paved over and elevated as part of the walkway that flanked the overpass above Solomon's Field).

Several times I caught Adrian staring at the open mouth of the drainage tunnel that ran under Counterpoint Lane, a disquieting look of detachment on his face. Once, I nudged him on the shoulder and asked if he was okay. He turned and smiled at me, but there was no feeling behind that smile. I thought I could see the gears and wheels and cogs moving about inside his head.

All this searching, yet we still hadn't found any clues. The treasures we uncovered included an old *Star Trek* lunch box, scores of hubcaps, heaps of busted bottles and beer cans crushed like accordions, the maggot-riddled corpse of a house cat with a nametag that read *Dillinger*, a single gold hoop earring, an outboard motor for a johnboat, plenty of moss-slickened sneakers, the deflated wind socks of used condoms, and even a discarded toilet.

We found countless articles of clothing, too—mostly moldy and in tattered ribbons, which we supposed could have belonged to any of the missing teenagers, but most likely had been dumped in the woods by vandals or homeless people. Nonetheless, Adrian didn't want to uniformly dismiss these bits of clothing, so he stowed the clothes in garbage bags for later inspection, if it ever came to that. We stored the garbage bags at Echo Base, among the statues.

Peter managed to steal his sister's Little Mermaid walkie-talkies. There were two of them, plus a headset that worked just as well, so now we had five radios—one for each of us. The headset remained at Echo Base, and the radios were divvied up between the four doing the searching. We rotated the radios, so the same people didn't always get stuck with the embarrassing Little Mermaid ones.

Somewhere along the line, Scott, Peter, Michael, and I lost interest in searching for clues that were not there—clues to a murder that had happened over five months ago. Hours spent peeking beneath bushes, under rocks, or digging through the softening muck that flanked the creek dwindled. As spring marched on, we spent most of our time sprawled out in the statue-laden clearing listening to music, reading horror novels and comic books, climbing trees, telling stories. Sometimes we slipped out onto the brownish lawn of December Park and tossed a football around.

But Adrian's dedication to the cause did not falter. He continued exploring the surrounding woods. Throughout the day he returned to Echo Base, sweating through his clothes and looking grim, to chart his progress on Michael's map. If it was around lunchtime, we passed out cheeseburgers from the McDonald's on Second Avenue, and Adrian ate and laughed along with us, his obsession seemingly in remission for the time being. Yet as soon as he finished eating, he shouldered his backpack, tightened his shoelaces, and stomped through the foliage. Never in my life had I witnessed such determination. It would have been admirable if it hadn't been so unsettling.

Adrian didn't become irritated by our lack of commitment to the search because, for the most part, we all continued doing the jobs he'd assigned to us.

Scott showed up one Saturday morning with dulled and rusted switchblades he'd gotten at a discount from Toddy Surplus. They weren't as cool or fearsome as his butterfly knife, and mine often jammed when the release lever was depressed, but there was an undeniable ceremonial air that overtook us when, among the headless statues in the clearing, Scott distributed them to us.

Michael took to his job with the zeal of a religious fanatic. He stopped sitting with us in the school cafeteria so he could make the rounds at various other tables, intent on overhearing poignant tidbits of information that might reveal the identity of the Piper. Like a beat reporter, he kept the small notepad Adrian had given him in the breast pocket of his shirt. I often caught him jotting down notes in it while in class, and he was reprimanded by Mr. Johnson several times for not paying attention.

Michael came up with a list of possible suspects, although his rationale for arriving at these outlandish conclusions was more than just questionable. Half the teachers from Stanton School, including Mr. Johnson, Mr. Mattingly, old Nozzle Neck, and even Principal Unglesbee, made the list.

Down in the woods, we passed the list around so we could all view it.

I raised one eyebrow. "Old lady Schubert?" The elderly woman who lived on Shore Acre Road and whose lawn was populated with an entire army of ceramic garden gnomes was certainly a mean old witch, but in no way was she capable of anything more malevolent than shouting at kids from her front windows.

"Is that so impossible?" Michael said.

"She's like a hundred years old," I said. "And besides, weren't you the one who said the killer has to be a man?"

"Hey," he said, hands up, "that was the old sexist me. I'm new and improved. I'm a modern man now."

"This is just a list of people you don't like," Peter said, leaning over my shoulder to look at the list. "Or people who don't like you."

"Explains why it's so long," Scott said.

"Why Mr. Mattingly?" I asked. "What has he done to you?"

"Nothing. But he's new to town. I figured that had to count for something." When Michael saw that none of us understood his rationale, he said, "Think about it. Do you really believe the killer is someone who's lived among us for years and just, wham, one day decides to start kidnapping and murdering kids? Highly unlikely. It's more plausible that the killer is fairly new to town. Maybe he'd been killing where he came from and things got too hot for him, so he had to move on."

I had to admit, the theory made a lot of sense. However, I couldn't picture Mr. Mattingly with the cleft in his chin and the clean-shaven face as a murderer of children.

Adrian dropped a hand on Michael's shoulder. "I think you're onto something. Put little stars next to the names of the people who are new to town."

"That doesn't mean anything," Peter remarked. Looking at Adrian, he said, "You're new to town."

"Yeah," Michael said, gripping Adrian around the wrist and shaking his thin little arm. "But look at this thing. He couldn't choke the life out of a teddy bear."

We laughed.

Since I had been avoiding my own job, I helped Peter with his—namely, coming up with a list of all the possible places a child killer might hide out. On a Thursday afternoon after school, the two of us hopped on our bikes and coasted through the streets of the city. We visited the houses of the missing kids and checked out the general vicinity where each one had last been seen.

Peter stopped to write in his notepad whenever we saw an abandoned house with a For Sale sign in the front yard or a run-down hunting shack that stood haunted and empty along Peninsula Drive. There were some vacant storefronts on Second Avenue, their windows dark and soaped over. Some of them had been that way for years. We made note of all of them.

We marked down the boathouses along the Shallows, and on our way back home, the weathered remnants of the Werewolf House beyond the Butterfield homestead made the list, too.

On a different day, we rode out to the Palisades, with its whitewashed gazebos and manicured lawns, and down to the playground where, when we were just toddlers, Peter and I had played together in the sandboxes. The sandboxes were gone, as were the jungle gyms and tire swings, and the small lake that had once looked so beautiful had greenish scum on the surface through which sickly looking mallards carved their passage.

We located the Coles' house, which was only a few blocks from the modern-looking Girls' Holy Cross High School, and we straddled our bikes outside the quaint cottage-style home with the peach siding and the dark green shutters, wondering what the last horrible moments of Courtney's life had been like. The house looked dark, and the only thing in the driveway was a large oil stain. I felt some of the adventure seep out of me. This wasn't a game; this was real.

"What are you kids doing?" a screechy voice called from across the street, startling us both. I turned and saw an elderly woman in curlers and a floral housedress admonishing us from over a white-picket fence. She had a newspaper tucked under one arm, and she pointed an accusatory finger in our direction. "Get away from that house!"

Without a word, Peter and I pedaled away.

Down at the Cape, we peeked into the grimy windows of the watermen's shacks along the shore. Not much bigger than outhouses, these sloppy, poorly constructed hovels reeked of rotten fish, urine, and sweat. There were rubber waders in some, dirty calendars pinned to the walls of others, and even a pot-bellied stove in one of them. We wrote them down in the notepad, although we couldn't imagine someone willingly hiding out in one of those claustrophobic and foul-smelling little coffins.

Peter motioned to the water and the rank of winter-proofed boats suspended by winches near the docks. "What about those?"

"Do you think someone could live in one of them?"

"Don't know. Let's mark 'em down, anyway."

"Yeah," I said. "Let's."

Afterward, we were heading down Magothy Road before I realized we were biking right past the Keener farm. At least a dozen scarecrows had been tied to the fence surrounding the property, some with burlap-sack faces, others wearing dime-store Halloween masks. The house stood a distance away, closer toward the river. It was a ranch with a wraparound porch made of natural logs. Junked cars were lined up along one side of the house, their windshields opaque with grime and webbed with cracks. Big black dogs loped about in a pen in the backyard. I scanned the property for Nathan Keener's truck but couldn't spot it.

"Let's get out of here," I suggested, and Peter didn't protest.

We spent an hour cruising the streets of Shipley's Crossing, where Courtney's friend Megan Meeks lived. There was an old neighborhood clubhouse that had closed down, its black windows arced with soap, large two-by-fours hammered over the entrances. A number of the boards looked new, and I recalled seeing police walking around the place one afternoon as we came home from school.

"I think the cops may have checked this place out already," I said.

Nevertheless, Peter marked it down in his notebook.

On another day, we biked all the way out to the industrial park, where the houses stood closer and closer together, separated by barrooms, pawnshops, billiard parlors, and squalid brick tenements that overlooked squat warehouses with bars on the windows. On every street corner we came across the hollowed-out shells of abandoned automobiles. There were literally hundreds of places someone could hide in this part of the city—and where bodies could be hidden, too, and most likely never found.

We biked down North Town Road, crumbling storefronts ticking by like landmarks. At the edge of the neighborhood was a miserable little trailer park set among tall blond weeds and crumbly drifts of white gravel. There were ATVs and satellite dishes in nearly every yard.

"Write this place down," I suggested. We had paused in a deserted intersection made of disintegrated asphalt. In one of the yards across the street, a piebald pit bull barked at us, ropes of saliva whipping about its snout. I felt eyes spying on us through darkened windows.

"What place, specifically?"

"The whole lousy neighborhood," I said.

During Mass one Sunday morning, Father Evangeline brought Rebecca Ransom, the parents of Jeffrey Connor, and Courtney Cole's father and younger sister, Margaret, up to the pulpit where he blessed them. Margaret wept when Father Evangeline pressed his thumb to her forehead and prayed with her.

"There is a scourge that has come to this town," the priest announced. "It is the devil in human form, and he walks among us. He is the beast who wears the mask of a man while cloaking himself in darkness."

Rebecca Ransom fell to her knees. Two men in the first pew rushed over and helped her up. Her cries were heart-wrenching.

After Mass, I met up with the guys at Echo Base. As I came through the woods, the four of them were gathered around the statues playing Uno while the dynamo-powered radio crackled out "Man in the Box" by Alice in Chains.

Michael noticed me first. He had the Little Mermaid headset cocked jauntily on his head. "Ahoy!" he called, and the others whipped their heads around and looked at me over their shoulders.

"Deal me in," I said, going over to Scott's backpack and fishing out a can of Jolt.

My friends all set their cards down. "Tell him," Peter said.

Scott leaned over and grabbed a can of Jolt from his backpack. "We've got a new place to search."

"Yeah?" I said. "Where's that?"

Scott pointed across the woods toward the embankment and Counterpoint Lane. "The tunnel that goes under the highway. We've looked for clues down here and in the ditches and ravines, but Adrian found the locket right by the opening of that tunnel. It was Adrian's idea to check it out."

I looked at Adrian and his swimmy, magnified eyes. I recalled how he had stared at the mouth of that tunnel as if in a trance. How long had he been considering this before saying something?

"Isn't that like a sewer pipe or something?" I said.

"It's a drainage tunnel," Scott said. "It's there so the highway doesn't flood during a big storm."

"I don't know," I said. "I'm not too crazy about crawling through some underground pipe."

"It's wide enough so we won't have to crawl," Adrian said, a professorial tone to his voice. Yes, he had been planning on how to approach this for some time. "Maybe just hunch over a little but not crawl."

"You know what I mean," I said.

"Well, it's part of our new theory," Adrian said.

"What theory is that?"

"That the cops are wrong," he said.

The others nodded.

"They've been looking for clues in December Park, in the woods, and back toward the school. They assume she was abducted and murdered either in the park or in the woods. But that's because they don't know about the locket. They don't know I found it on the other side of the street by the ditch. Which means maybe she was abducted after she walked out of the woods."

"But the cops don't know that," Scott added, still nodding. "They can't know what we know. We're ahead of the game."

"And you guys think we'll find more clues in that tunnel?" I said.

"It's worth a shot," Scott replied.

"That girl was killed in October," I said. "That's almost six months ago. Even if there was something in there, it would have washed into the sewers by now."

They were all looking at me. They wanted to do this, and suddenly I was the one roadblock in their way. How had that happened? Hadn't I been on board with them from the beginning? In my mind's eye, I saw Margaret Cole weeping while Father Evangeline prayed with his thumb against her forehead and Aaron Ransom's mother being led out of the church, her body wracked with sobs.

"Yeah, okay," I said. "I'm in."

Scott handed out flashlights to each of us while Adrian passed around plastic shopping bags he'd gotten from the Generous Superstore.

"What are the bags for?" I asked.

"For collecting whatever we find," Adrian said.

"Let's leave the backpacks here," Scott said to Adrian. "I don't want to get stuck crawling through that tunnel."

"Good idea."

I checked my flashlight and made sure the light came on, which it did, then stuffed the shopping bag into the rear pocket of my jeans.

The five of us crossed through the woods and ascended the embankment toward Counterpoint Lane. We waited for a break in the traffic, and when we got it, we sprinted across. The opening of the tunnel was in the muddy ravine, where we had previously trampled the weeds and imprinted the soles of our sneakers in the mud while searching for clues.

A curtain of ivy hung in front of the mouth of the tunnel. Staring at it, I felt a needle of apprehension at the base of my spine. All too clearly I remembered my nightmare of being sucked down a hole in the Dead Woods and buried underground. I quickly chased the thought away.

"We'll have to go in single file," Peter said. "Who goes first?"

"Don't look at me," I said. "This wasn't my bright idea."

"I'll go." Adrian climbed down into the ditch. The flashlight Scott had given him was one of those hefty black Maglites, like policemen carry, and it looked ridiculous in Adrian's small hands. As he approached the mouth of the tunnel, the rest of us slid down the hill to the swampy earth.

It had been colder when we first searched this area, but in the warming weather of spring, the aroma of flowers mingling with the foul-smelling runoff from the pipe was enough to make me light-headed.

Adrian clicked on his flashlight, then swept away the curtain of ivy and vines from the tunnel's opening. A circular black eyelet, perhaps four feet in diameter, stared back at us.

Stories my grandfather had told me about World War II suddenly flitted through my brain, particularly those of the Japanese soldiers hiding in L-shaped tunnels under the villages to escape the American troops. My grandfather had said they'd shoot the first few Japanese at the opening of the tunnel, and that was all they needed to do to trap the others inside, where they would all eventually die of suffocation, dehydration, or starvation.

"Wait," I called to Adrian, but he had already gone into the hole. The curtain of ivy and vines swung back over the opening.

Scott went next. The tallest of us, he bent over and paused halfway into the opening. I thought he might back out and call it off. But he didn't.

I took a breath, stepped onto the concrete lip, and urged myself forward into the darkness. The air was stagnant and thick, the temperature at least ten degrees warmer since there was no breeze inside. Bent forward at the waist, I inched my way into the pipe, the soles of my sneakers grinding on the accumulated debris while the concrete ceiling brushed against the top of my head. Just ahead of me, the beams of Scott's and Adrian's flashlights ticked back and forth along the walls. I heard their respiration clearly, their sneakers scuffing over muddy grit.

"Hey," I half whispered, and even that was like a shout in this tomb-like echo chamber. "Do you see any opening up ahead, Adrian? At the other end?"

"No," he returned, his voice the disembodied drone of a ghost.

Wonderful, I thought.

Directly behind me, the beam from Michael's flashlight projected my shadow against the curved wall to my right. One of his hands fell against my back. "Jesus," he whispered. "There's probably bats down here. And rats. Possums, too. Shit. There could be anything." He wasn't saying this to spook me, I realized; he was saying it because he was suddenly fearful of all those things. "Don't walk too fast, Angie." And I felt him ball up a fistful of my shirt.

I took another step and felt my sneaker sink down into something. I paused and pointed the flashlight to the ground. Moist black sludge had engulfed my foot. Grimacing, I extracted it with a squelching sound. Bits of gunk pattered to the curved floor of the pipe.

"Just what exactly are we collecting from down here?" I said to no one in particular.

"Anything," Scott said. "Anything at all."

I reached down and fingered something shiny and metallic out of the muck. It was the pull tab from a soda or beer can. Holding it between two fingers, I was about to pitch it when Michael's face came up close to mine.

"He said anything. That's anything."

"Yeah, yeah," I said, unraveling the plastic shopping bag and dropping the pull tab inside it.

"Stinks in here, too," Michael went on. "It's like walking through a giant anus."

"Don't make me laugh," Peter said from the back of the line. "I might throw up."

A few feet ahead of me in the darkness, Scott paused. I sensed him moving around, the beam of his flashlight washing across the confined walls of the pipe.

Peter asked what was going on.

"The walls," Scott said. "Check 'em out."

I shined my light on the wall to my left. It looked like corrugated concrete, nothing special. I kept walking, running my hand along the wall, until the concrete ended and my hand fell on jagged brown stone. "What just happened?" I muttered.

"This isn't a pipe at all," Scott said. "It's like some natural tunnel under the street. The concrete was just the end cap."

I grazed the rock with my fingertips. All of a sudden I was a little kid again in the johnboat out on the bay with Charles. Charles was pointing up to the face of the cliff and at all the openings in the rock. Holes. Tunnels.

"Just keep moving," I urged Scott.

We pushed on. The toes of my sneakers unearthed rusted soda cans, bottle caps, and the rubber heel of a boot from the river of muck that ran down the center of the pipe. Not sure what role any of these items might play, I stowed them in my plastic shopping bag along with the pull tab.

"Shit," Scott said. He froze, his light trained on something on the ground. With one foot, he moved the gunk around.

"What is it?" I said.

"A hypodermic needle."

"Oh, Christ. Don't pick that up."

He crouched right above it, staring at it. When he looked up, he said, "Adrian? What do you think?"

"I'll pick it up," Adrian said.

"Dude," Michael said to him from over my shoulder, "that thing could have hepatitis or AIDS or some shit on it."

"I'll be careful." Adrian bent down in front of Scott and gingerly lifted the item out of the muck. I glimpsed the translucent tubular body and the gleam of the needle. Pinched between two fingers, Adrian studied it.

"What is he doing?" Peter said.

"Here." Scott twisted the head off his flashlight. The bulb went dead, and he slid two chunky batteries out of the flashlight's shaft and into the pocket of his jeans. "Put it in here," he told Adrian.

Adrian dropped the hypodermic needle into the flashlight, and Scott twisted the cap back on.

"Great," Michael said. "Now all we gotta do is get that sucker to the CDC and we're golden."

"I've got no light now," Scott said to Adrian. "Go slow. I'll stay close behind you."

Just then, a low resonant moan resounded through the tunnel. I felt the hair on the nape of my neck prickle. Michael tightened his grip on my shirt.

"What is that?" Peter said.

"The ghosts of lost children," Michael responded. No doubt he'd meant it to be humorous, to break the tension, but no one laughed.

"It's just the wind," I said, "blowing through the tunnel."

"No," said Adrian. "That's the Piper's song."

Scott paused and said, "You guys got your knives, right?"

"For what?" Michael said. "To cut our way out of here when the whole fucking tunnel collapses or to ward off a swarm of mutant-sized sewer rats when they come in for the kill?"

"Pleasant thoughts," Peter commented, his voice hollow.

"Seriously," I added. "You're not cheering me up, Mikey."

"Don't call me Mikey."

We kept moving. One thing was for certain: I wouldn't be able to remain hunched over like this for an extended period of time. I already felt the muscles tightening in my back, and my neck was beginning to hurt. "Any light up ahead yet?"

"No," came Adrian's response.

I cast my flashlight's beam on the ground as I walked. There was nothing but crumbled bits of rock covered in a mat of putrid black sludge. Whitish weeds sprouted like hair from the sludge. Rivulets of water trickled through it. The smell reminded me of the watermen's shacks along the Cape. Also, the boys' restrooms at school.

"What's that?" Michael said, his arm shooting out past my head as he pointed to something on the floor of the tunnel.

I turned the flashlight on it. "An old tennis ball." It was brown with age and slimy with blackish-green moss.

"I spotted it," he said. "It's mine."

"Be my guest," I said, stepping over the reeking tennis ball.

That ghostly moan rose up again, sounding all too human and causing my heart to beat faster.

"Boom-boom diddum daddum waddem shoo," Michael sang in a low voice, as if in concert with the moan. "And they swam and they swam right out to the sea—"

"Shut up," Peter told him. "You're creeping me out."

The windy moan eventually tapered off, but now a much deeper sound seemed to be coming from all around us. It reminded me of the hum the washing machine made when I would lie in my bed and listen to it through the floor.

"What is that?" Peter said.

"It's the traffic up above, I think," Scott said. "We're probably heading beneath the highway."

"Holy shit," Michael whispered.

As we progressed, the droning grew louder and more resonant. Soon the rush of passing automobiles was perfectly audible directly above our heads through the layers of bedrock. We were beneath Governor Highway. With each passing vehicle, the tunnel seemed to vibrate, and I imagined I could feel the heat from the cars' exhaust as they zoomed by. I was sweating profusely, the stillness of the air in the tunnel like that of a locked mausoleum.

"Where do you think this tunnel comes out?" I said to the darkness.

"What if it doesn't?" Peter said. "What if it goes on for miles until it dead-ends?"

"I can't walk like this for miles. My back's gonna break."

"Or what if the floor breaks apart and we fall into it?" he went on. "We'd be down there with broken necks waiting to die. It could take days. Weeks, even."

I ran one hand along the rocky wall. "Is it me or is this tunnel getting smaller and smaller?"

"No one would ever find us," Peter went on.

"Hey," Michael broke in. "I feel like the filling in an asshole sandwich. How 'bout talking about something else, huh?"

"If this goes straight across the highway," I said, "then we're heading toward the Superstore plaza."

"What if we came up through the floor of a bank vault?" said Scott. "That would be awesome."

"Or a sub shop," said Peter. "I'm starving."

After the drone of the highway traffic receded into the darkness behind us, Adrian said, "I think I see light up ahead. A little pinpoint of daylight."

"Thank God," Michael groaned. He hadn't let go of my shirt the entire time.

I pushed against Scott's back, feeling the sweat that had dampened his shirt. It was a lot of sweat. But then I realized there was water dripping from the crevices in the rock above our heads. Like walking straight into a spider-web, I frantically swiped the cold water off my face and out of my eyes. When I opened my eyes, I thought I could see the widening disc of daylight at the other end of the tunnel, too.

"Shit," Scott uttered. This was followed by the sound of something metal clanging on the floor of the tunnel. Ahead of him, Adrian's flashlight clattered to the ground.

"What happened?" I said.

Scott said, "Adrian?"

"There's . . . something . . . ," Adrian mumbled.

I shined my flashlight beam over Scott's shoulder as Adrian bent down and picked something up off the ground. I took a small step, and my right foot came down on something that threatened to roll out from under me. Glancing down, I saw that it was Adrian's flashlight. "Here," I said and toed it over to Scott, who grabbed it and handed it to Adrian.

"Look," Michael said. "Can we get out of here or what?"

"Yeah," Peter seconded.

We hurried toward the circle of daylight, spilling one by one out into the cool wind and silver-gray skies of an overcast afternoon. It had started to rain while we were underground, the raindrops feeling like blessed salvation on my sweat-sticky flesh. I massaged rainwater onto my hot face and breathed the fresh air. Thunder cracked.

We were in the ditch behind the Superstore parking lot. Muddy water swirled about my feet, soaking the cuffs of my jeans.

Adrian stood beside me, casually examining the item he had just found in the tunnel. It was an iron fleur-de-lis, and it looked heavy.

"Cool," I said.

Adrian opened his shopping bag and dropped it inside.

Just then, lightning burst on the other side of the plaza. The rain came down harder. We climbed out of the ditch and crossed the narrow band of asphalt that ran behind the Superstore's loading docks. Green and silver awnings hung over the loading bays, and we crowded beneath one just as the rain came down in a torrent.

Peter dug a pack of Pall Malls out of his pocket. Peering into the pack, he said, "Shoot. I've only got one left."

Another whip crack of thunder caused us all to jump.

"Well," Michael said, slinging an arm around Adrian's neck. There were streaks of black mud on Michael's face. "Was it everything you hoped it would be?"

Rain had speckled the lenses of Adrian's glasses. He grinned at Michael, then turned and looked toward the ditch. "What if the killer got her right here?"

Peter sucked on his cigarette, then passed it to Scott. "What do you mean?"

Adrian pointed to the ditch. "What if Courtney Cole made it out of December Park, across the highway, and was crossing the road back here when she ran into the killer? He could have killed her over there, then carried her through the tunnel to the woods to throw off the police. Did you guys see the way the water flowed through the tunnel? Maybe the locket broke right here and got washed out to the other end of the tunnel."

"That still doesn't help us any," I said.

"But if that's what happened, then the police were definitely looking in the wrong place for clues." Adrian took his glasses off, wiped the lenses with the hem of his shirt, and slid them back on. He motioned toward the far side of the ditch. "What's beyond those trees?"

"More trees," I said, plucking the cigarette from Scott's mouth and sticking it into my own.

"There's neighborhoods back there, too," Peter said, pointing to the west.

"Which neighborhoods? Like, did any of the missing kids live there?"

Peter and I had ridden our bikes through all the missing kids' neighborhoods, so we both nodded.

"Two blocks over is Shore Acre Road," I said. "The Demorest kid lived out that way. He was the first one to go missing back in August."

"But it's totally residential," Peter countered. "Angie and I went up and down every street. Unless the killer lives in one of the houses, he ain't hiding out anywhere."

"Maybe he does live in one of those houses," Scott interjected. "For all we know, he could just be a normal guy most of the time, right? Isn't that why Michael's been making a list of suspects?"

"My list!" Michael dug his notepad out of the rear pocket of his jeans. He flipped through the pages, scanning the notes. "Old lady Schubert. She's the only one who lives on Shore Acre Road."

"Yes, of course," Peter said. "She probably ran the Cole girl over in her wheelchair, then clubbed her to death with her cane."

Michael frowned. "Why would she have a cane if she's in a wheelchair?"

Peter rolled his eyes.

"If the killer lives on this side of the highway and also killed the Cole girl here, why was her body found in the Dead Woods?" Scott asked, taking the cigarette back from me. "It doesn't make sense."

We all considered this in mutual silence for nearly a full minute. The rain continued to come down in sheets.

"Unless," I suggested, "the cops are right, and he killed Courtney in the park after all, and he was planning to carry her body back here, where maybe he lives."

"Yeah?" Adrian said.

"Well, think about it. He kills her in December Park, carries her through the woods toward Counterpoint Lane but decides not to risk it and leaves her there. Maybe he takes the heart-shaped locket with him but drops it as he crosses the street."

"Not the street," Adrian said. "The tunnel. He would have used the tunnel so no one would have seen him."

"But why would he just drop her in the woods?" Peter said. "He didn't do that with anyone else. Why leave her body for police to find but hide the others?"

No one had an explanation for that.

Adrian pointed east, toward the heavy black shroud of trees. "What's over that way?"

"More woods," I said.

"Okay, but what's beyond the woods?"

"The Butterfield farm. Then the Shallows."

"What's the Shallows?"

"An inlet with a beach and a marina. Some houses."

Adrian sucked on his lower lip and looked west, where Shore Acre Road and the Demorest house were hidden behind the rain and the trees.

"What's the plan for all this junk, anyway?" Michael said, holding up his mud-streaked shopping bag. He opened it, and I peered inside, glimpsing the mossy tennis ball, a soggy cardboard juice box, and several rust-orange bottle caps.

"We hang on to it, keep it as evidence," said Adrian.

Michael shrugged.

We stood around in silence, listening to the rain. We had reached an impasse.

"So what do we do now?" Scott asked eventually.

"I'm out of cigarettes and I'm hungry," Peter said. "Let's run over to the Quickman."

We sprinted across the loading docks in the rain and hopped onto the awning-covered sidewalk of the plaza's strip mall. Lightning slammed down beyond the trees on the far side of the highway. A moment later, the sky roared.

"Hey," Scott said, pausing in front of the RadioShack. A TV in the window informed us of Kurt Cobain's suicide, and we all watched in silent disbelief. Scott undid the Nirvana patch he had on the sleeve of his jacket and pinned it over his heart.

"What happens now?" Peter asked no one in particular. It seemed that while we weren't looking, occupied as we were with the Piper, the world had stolen something important from us.

After a time, and in contemplative silence, we continued on our way toward the Quickman, though none of us felt much like eating anymore.

CHAPTER THIRTEEN
DISCOVERIES

The following day, I was bum-rushed by Mr. Mattingly out in the hallway after his class let out. "Do you have a minute, Angelo?"

"I guess," I said. I nodded at Adrian to go on without me.

Adrian looked at Mr. Mattingly with something akin to distrust in his eyes. Then he turned and merged into the sea of students.

Mr. Mattingly's smile was warm. "We've got about two and a half more months left before the end of the school year. I was wondering if you'd given any further thought to what we'd discussed about next year."

"AP English?" I shrugged and tried my damnedest to look disinterested when, in truth, I had been dreading this confrontation since Mr. Mattingly had first approached me about it. It had been so long, I had mistakenly thought he'd forgotten about it. "No, not really. It kind of slipped my mind."

"I have to turn my recommendations in next week. I'd like to put your name on the list but only if you want to do it."

"Aren't those AP classes for kids going to college next year? Seniors, I mean."

"Don't you plan to go to college eventually?"

"I guess," I said. "The community college."

Mr. Mattingly rubbed at the cleft in his chin. "What does your father think about it?"

"He said it's up to me. Whatever I wanted to do." Which sounded like absolute bullshit, especially to anyone who knew my father. Thankfully, Mr. Mattingly did not.

"Maybe he could come in after school one day? The three of us could sit down and discuss it."

Not a chance, I thought, knowing damn well my father would kill me if he found out I'd been shucking an opportunity to advance to an AP class.

"You know, he's pretty busy," I said, and it sounded so impossibly weak I expected him to laugh in my face.

"I'm sure he'd make the time for something this important."

I sucked at my lower lip. It was decision time. "Okay, sign me up for the class. Might as well give it a shot."

Mr. Mattingly nodded and seemed suddenly pleased with himself. When he slipped back into his classroom, it occurred to me that the son of a bitch had called my bluff. For a few extra seconds I watched him through the doorway as he shoved papers into his briefcase and swept the blackboard with a big fuzzy eraser.

I thought of Michael's list of potential murderers and how Mr. Mattingly had been on it. It had made some sense at the time, because he was fairly new to our school and to Harting Farms, but standing here now and watching the man go about his daily routine, the notion seemed utterly preposterous.

"How come you don't want to take AP English?" It was Rachel Lowrey, who had materialized like a ghost beside me.

"What do I need with AP classes?" I said, moving across the hall to my locker. The place was mostly cleared out by now, though a few students remained shouting at each other at the far end of C Hall.

"I think you'd be good at it. I read that short story you wrote for the school magazine last year. The one about the girl who falls off the ladder."

This surprised me. My friends hadn't even read it, though in fairness, I hadn't told them it had been published, and they never picked up copies of the school magazine. "Oh yeah?"

"I thought it was really great."

"Thanks."

"Do you like to write?"

I pulled my books from my backpack and stuffed them into my locker. "Sometimes."

"I think that's really cool."

"Really? Well, thanks."

"I write some poetry but it's pretty horrible. I'd never let anyone read it. I'd be too embarrassed to ever have it published. Not that anyone would actually publish it."

"I'm sure it's not that bad."

"Maybe. Maybe not. I don't know."

"I feel that way about my stories, too. But I thought it would be cool to see one in the school magazine, so I sent it in. I mean, they publish anything they get, but it was still neat." Thinking I sounded like a blathering idiot, I willed myself to stop talking.

"Well, I still thought your story was way cool."

"Let me read some of your poems," I said. "I'll tell you if they're horrible." Rachel laughed.

I remembered kissing her during the Kiss War. I wondered how much different it would be to kiss her now. Her face was narrow and soft, her eyes dark around the edges from the fullness of her lashes. I couldn't help but look at her lips, too—small, pink.

"You'd really do that for me?" she said.

"Read your stuff? Sure."

"No," she said. "Tell me if it's horrible."

"I'd give you my honest opinion about it, if that's what you mean. Besides, what does it matter what I think? I'm not a poet."

"That's not true. You were a poet in that story. Anyway, have a good weekend."

"Later, skater," I said and watched her go.

My friends were waiting for me in the quad. Scott and Peter were smoking cigarettes while Michael and Adrian sat cross-legged in the grass playing Uno.

"What happened?" Adrian said. "You get in trouble or something?"

"No, it's cool." To tell them that Mr. Mattingly wanted me to transfer to AP English next year was to invite unrelenting ribbing. Michael might even start calling me Poindexter instead of Adrian. So I kept my mouth shut about it. "He just wanted to go over one of my papers. No big deal."

"We still gonna head to the library?" Scott asked.

Over lunch we had decided to go to the public library and pull up all the newspaper articles on Courtney Cole to glean some insight that might better direct our next course of action. Scott had already tried to look them up in the school library, but they didn't have any newspapers older than a couple of months, and none had been archived on microfilm.

We headed down Broad Street, then turned onto Solomon's Bend Road.

School buses farted by, their brakes squealing as they approached the intersection. At the bottom of Solomon's Bend Road, we took a shortcut through the underpass and cut directly across December Park. As we entered the mouth of the underpass, its black cobblestones still glistening from yesterday's downpour, I wondered if Courtney Cole had come this way the day she was approached by the killer. The thought gave me chills.

Scott and Peter stopped walking as they exited the underpass. Michael quickly followed suit.

I glanced up to where they were looking and felt my stomach sink. Beyond a rickety wooden fence and a line of trash receptacles that separated December Park from the Dead Woods sat Nathan Keener's pickup.

"Son of a bitch," Michael muttered. "What the hell is he doing here?"

"Who?" said Adrian.

"Nathan Keener," Peter said. "He's just about the biggest asshole you'd ever want to meet."

"We still owe that bastard for what he did to you, don't we, Angie?" Michael said.

"Just forget it," I said. I felt a needling chill at my spine.

"What'd he do to you?" Adrian said.

"Forget it," I repeated, not wanting to go into it.

"They clobbered him," Michael said anyway.

"Oh." Then something dawned on Adrian. "Are those the guys who jumped you and beat up your face?"

Resigned, I uttered, "Yes."

"That goddamned guy," Peter said.

"I don't see anybody there," Scott said. "The truck looks empty."

"We owe him," Michael repeated.

"No one owes anything," I said.

"Says you," Michael said, then took off running toward Keener's truck.

The rest of us didn't move at first. In fact, Michael was already scaling the wooden fence on the far side of the park before we sprinted after him. We hit the fence simultaneously and scrambled over it like rats, our backpacks doing their best to weigh us down.

"He's gonna get himself killed," Peter shouted.

We approached Keener's truck together. The driver's window was down. I touched the hood and found that it was cold. The truck had been sitting here for a while. There was no sign of Keener anywhere.

Scott withdrew his butterfly knife from his coat. He twirled it around with impressive dexterity. "We can slash his tires."

"Tires are tires. Big fucking deal." Michael gripped the side mirror and planted one foot on the narrow running board.

I shook my head. "Mikey, what are you doing?"

Michael extended one finger, held it straight up in the air. "I love you, Angie. Do you know that? I would die for you, if that's what it came down to. Shit," he said, his voice rumbling with laughter, "I would die for any of you guys. You hear me? You dig me? Also, don't call me Mikey, you shithead."

With that, he unbuckled his belt and dropped his pants. Then he hoisted himself up and forced his pasty white ass through the open driver's side window. "Lucky for us it was taco day in the cafeteria," Michael said and proceeded to evacuate his bowels onto the driver's seat of Nathan Keener's truck.

Peter exploded with laughter. He doubled over, clenching his stomach and crying so hard tears wrung from his eyes. His face turned a mottled purple.

Scott stared in astonishment, his butterfly knife suddenly limp in his hand.

Adrian clutched both straps of his backpack at his shoulders, his eyes as large as saucers behind his glasses. He uttered a singular laugh that came out like the chirp of a tiny bird.

I felt a laugh threaten the back of my throat, too. And by the time I surrendered to it, Scott and Adrian had joined in, and soon we were all laughing like lunatics.

"Socks!" Michael cried when he'd come to the end, tears bursting from the corners of his eyes now, too. "I need socks to wipe!"

"God!" Peter howled, rolling his back along the grille of Keener's truck. "Oh please oh God oh stop it please oh please oh God!"

Scott and Adrian stripped their socks off and tossed them at Michael. He wiped his ass with them, then pitched them into the open window. By the time Michael hopped down from his perch and tugged up his pants, I was mopping tears from my eyes and my stomach ached from laughter.

"He ever finds out that was you," I said after I'd regained some of my composure, "he's going to end your life."

Michael grinned. "Let the games begin."

The Harting Farms Public Library was a dark brick building with smoked windows. It catered not only to the residents of this part of town, but it also served as the primary library for students who attended St. John's on the other side of Center Street.

On this day in early April, the manicured front lawn was populated by St. John's students in their pressed khakis and purple polo shirts with the school's crest embroidered in gold over the breast. Some of them sat on the wall that flanked the curving driveway, and they eyed us with marked suspicion when we arrived. We must have looked awfully conspicuous in our T-shirts, torn jeans, and muddy sneakers.

I loved everything about the library—from its shelves crowded with books and its uncomfortable chairs of molded plastic to the inspirational posters of astronauts clutching volumes of Shakespeare and Mark Twain. Charles and I had come here often to listen to librarians read Roald Dahl and Beverly Cleary in the Children's Corner. When I first learned to read, my grandmother helped me fill out a form for my very own library card—a faded yellow bit of cardboard that I still carried in my wallet—and I recalled the relish with which I stalked the aisles, hunting for the perfect book to check out. It was a great adventure, a grand mystery.

As my friends went to the stacks of local and national newspapers, I wandered over to the Children's Corner. It was much as I remembered it: beanbag chairs spread out across the maroon carpeting, posters of Judy Blume book covers on the walls, copies of *Where the Wild Things Are* and *The Mouse and the Motorcycle* and *The Trumpet of the Swan* on the shelves. I had checked out all those books as well as countless others.

Maybe someday my own books will be on these shelves, I used to think once I started writing my own stories. It was a thought I still entertained, though with dwindling certainty. I was already halfway done with high school. College would be next, and then I would have to get a job—a *real* job, as my dad was fond of saying. Where would the writing go? Would there be time? Some nights, when I closed my eyes, I was terrified to imagine myself in middle-age while my old Olympia typewriter collected dust on a basement shelf.

I blinked and for a moment could see Charles and me sitting Indian-style on the floor as a soft-voiced librarian read us a chapter out of *The Enormous Egg*. The ghosts of lost children, indeed . . .

I joined my friends. Michael and Peter were snickering over an issue of *Mad* magazine. Scott and Adrian were talking to a librarian who had just handed them spools of microfilm. The librarian, who was a skinny bearded man in an ugly striped shirt, pointed to the three microfilm projectors against the wall. Before departing, he cast a disapproving glance at Michael and Peter, whose snickering had risen slightly in volume.

Adrian, Scott, and I pulled three chairs in front of one of the projectors and sat down.

"He gave us a weird look when I asked for last October's paper, so I told him we were doing a research project for school," Scott said, loading the film into the projector. He clicked it on, and milky yellow light flooded the oversized screen. He spooled over until the *Caller'*s masthead appeared.

I leaned over the back of my chair and waved Peter and Michael over. "Stand behind us," I told them.

We couldn't remember the exact date Courtney Cole's body was discovered, but we knew it had been on the front page of the newspaper, so it didn't take long to find it. Her yearbook photo was larger on-screen, and I felt a chill looking at it. Behind me, Peter and Michael stood closer together so no one passing by would be able to see the screen.

In a low voice, Scott read the article. There were no details in it that we didn't already know. When Scott came to the end, we continued staring at the screen in deferential silence.

"Back up," Peter suggested, "and see if you can find when she was reported missing."

It was two days before her body was found. This headline was also on the front page—Local Girl Reported Missing. Again, Scott read the article in a quiet voice while we all leaned closer to the glowing screen. As with the previous article, there was nothing in it that we hadn't already heard on the news or, for that matter, in the halls of school and around town. The article continued on the next page, but when Scott scrolled over to it, I said, "Wait. Go back."

Scott scrolled back.

"There," I said, pointing at the screen. "The story toward the bottom."

The story's headline read, Car Crash Injures Local College Student, and it summarized Audrey MacMillan's inebriated slalom off the road and into the woods. The photo that accompanied the article showed a pair of taillights wedged in a net of tree branches.

"Courtney Cole was killed the night she went missing," I said. It had been staring us in the face since October, yet no one had connected the pieces. "It wasn't part of his plan for her body to be found. He was in the woods when that MacMillan girl drove her car off the road. He couldn't risk taking the body anywhere and being seen with it, so he left it there and ran away."

"Holy shit," Scott said.

"So maybe it's true," Adrian said, "and he was planning to bring her back across the road to the other side of the highway. He would have used the tunnel—"

"And dropped the locket in the ditch," Michael interjected.

"—on his way back to . . ." Adrian's voice trailed off.

"Back to where?" Peter said.

We didn't know.

CHAPTER FOURTEEN
AFTER THE STORM

As April progressed, our town was accosted by a torrential downpour that lasted nearly three full days. The sky remained the color of soot, and a furious and unrelenting wind blew shutters off houses and cast small tornadoes of dead leaves down neighborhood streets. My friends and I avoided the Dead Woods, which turned into a swamp as the creek overflowed and flooded December Park, and we got rides home from school for much of the week so we didn't have to walk.

Down by the Cape, the tide came in past the locks and rushed up onto the shore where it smashed against the watermen's shacks, reducing a number of them to piles of sun-bleached wooden boards and flapping sheets of tar paper, and some of them were washed clean out into the bay. Deaver's Pond swelled like a balloon and flooded the surrounding culverts and ravines, causing a massive clot of dead leaves, fallen tree limbs, and great clumps of trash to clog the underpass beneath Solomon's Bend Road. Frogs popped out of the swamp grass of Solomon's Field, for a brief time ruling the world.

The television news spoke of doom when a grim-faced reporter detailed how one of the massive stained glass windows of St. Nonnatus was struck by lightning and exploded into a dazzling array of colored blades of glass. Lightning also blew out a transformer on the second night of the storm, cutting the power along Worth and Haven for nearly twelve hours.

There was concern from the mayor's office about the rising waters of the Chesapeake. Sewers backed up, bubbling out into the streets. Boats were demolished in the channels and along the Shallows; weeks after the storm passed, pieces of these boats were found scattered as far inland as the Palisades. One kid from Stanton School claimed to have discovered a wooden steering wheel from a pirate ship up in a tree in his front yard.

On the fourth day, the world finally began to dry up. My friends, agitated at being cooped up inside for half a week, skipped out after lunch period to enjoy the weather.

I wanted to join them, but I had to give an oral presentation in Mr. Mattingly's English class. My report was on Ralph Ellison's *Invisible Man*, which, in my ignorance, I had chosen based strictly on the title that I had apparently interpreted too literally. The book was not about an actual invisible man, like Claude Rains in that old black-and-white movie, but it was a commentary on racism and society. Nonetheless, I had surprised myself by enjoying the book, and I thought my presentation went pretty well. Mr. Mattingly seemed pleased.

When the bell rang, I was the first one out of the classroom, though, in my haste, I'd forgotten to zip my backpack, and my textbooks spilled out across C Hall like a fan of playing cards. I dropped to my knees and gathered up my books.

Rachel appeared beside me. "Hey."

"Oh. Hey." I suddenly felt like an imbecile.

As the rest of the classes let out, C Hall exploded with students eager to evacuate into a brightening day. Some asshole kicked my math book down the hall, and I chased after it like a dog. When I returned, Rachel was there holding my backpack. She had piled all my books into it.

"Shoot. Thanks, Rachel."

"Sure." She handed over my backpack.

I stuffed my math book into it, zipped it up, then slung the strap over one shoulder.

"I brought you some of those poems I wrote," she said. "You know, if you still want to read them."

"Yeah, I'd really like that."

"You're sure? Because you don't have to. I'll let you off the hook."

"I want to." And I meant it. I didn't know anyone else who enjoyed writing. My friends complained if they had to write anything more substantial than a two-page book report.

"Okay. Here." She gave me a few folded sheets of lined notebook paper. "Just promise not to laugh."

"I won't. I promise."

Some lummox knocked into me with his shoulder, and I nearly crashed into the lockers. C Hall was ripe with assholes this afternoon.

Rachel laughed.

"Glad I could amuse you," I said, stuffing her folded pieces of paper into the rear pocket of my blue jeans.

"So, I gotta run," she said, backing down the hall. Her smile shook something inside me. "Have a good weekend, Angelo."

"You, too," I said and inadvertently took another shoulder to the chest.

Cutting across December Park, I surveyed the debris the storm had left in its wake—felled trees, lawns strewn with garbage, soil so saturated that it squelched with every footstep. It was like traversing a field of quicksand.

I kicked a Taco Bell cup until I reached the fence that separated the park grounds from the woods. The storm had ravaged the fence, plucking pickets out at random intervals and launching them like spears into the nearby trees.

A glance at the mud revealed such random items as a license plate, a lone red rubber boot, busted terra-cotta pottery, a few cushions from someone's outdoor furniture, and a deflated basketball that appeared to be frowning at me. I hopped the fence, my backpack thumping against my back and straining on my shoulders, and dashed into the trees.

Peter, Scott, and Adrian were in the clearing. The dynamo-powered radio was tuned to a classic rock station, and the air was haunted by recently smoked cigarettes. I could smell the stink from the sewers' backwash, too; it hung in the air like a wet and fetid cloud.

Scott shouted my name from a perch in a tree. Below him, seated on one of the headless statues, Peter curled over a sketch pad. Inspired by Adrian's artistic talent, Peter had taken to drawing his own doodles lately—mostly trucks with heavy artillery guns mounted on them.

Adrian sat in his usual spot—the opening in the bole of the tree—and scribbled furiously in his notebook. I saw that he still wore Courtney Cole's heart-shaped locket around his neck on a length of shoelace. He barely looked up as I approached.

"Where's Michael?"

"Detention," Peter said. "He won't be gracing us with his presence anytime soon."

"What'd he do?"

"Got caught wiping boogers in Kiki Sullivan's history book."

I crossed the muddy clearing and sat down next to Peter on the headless statue. All around us was the sound of water dripping from the trees. The foliage looked overly green and heavy after the storm, the leaves bright and shiny, the boughs sagging from the force of the past days' unrelenting rain. There was trash everywhere, washed down from the streets above and snared among the bushes and weeds. I spied a pair of boxer shorts flapping like a battlefield flag in one of the high branches of an oak tree.

Some of the trash couldn't be attributed to the storm, however: five plastic shopping bags, filled with the random junk we had collected that day we trekked through the tunnel under the highway, sat in a mound between two of the headless statues. We had gone through the items, but we couldn't discern any significance from them. In hindsight, traveling through the tunnel hadn't been about finding clues; it had been about realizing someone could actually go from one side of the highway to the other while completely hidden underground.

"Check it out," Peter said, tapping his pencil on his sketch pad and grinning.

"You've moved on to fighter planes with big guns," I said, looking at his drawing.

"The big guns have little guns mounted on them. Pretty cool, huh?"

We lounged around for about an hour, pretty much just wasting time, when Scott shouted from his perch in the tree, "Hey! Someone's coming!" He pointed at the trees. "Identify yourself!"

"Identify this, jack face," Michael said, coming through the trees with his middle finger extended. He got caught up in a tangle of bushes, cursed, stumbled, then righted himself with one hand against the trunk of an oak tree. He stepped in a puddle of mud, splashing filth up the leg of his khakis. "Christ. It's like a toilet down here."

Scott scrambled down the tree, then clapped the loose bark from his hands. He had his Orioles baseball hat turned backward, and he wore what we referred to as his Oh Shit Shark Shirt, a T-shirt depicting a giant cartoon shark about to devour a tiny scuba diver whose little cartoon thought bubble proclaimed, "Oh, shit!"

"We weren't expecting you today. You get time off for good behavior?" Peter asked, closing his sketch pad.

"Fuck it," Michael said. "I snuck out."

"You snuck out of detention?"

"I was bored." He bent down and fiddled with the knobs on the radio. In freshly pressed slacks, a buttoned oxford shirt, braided belt, docksiders without socks, and his hair neatly parted as usual, he didn't look like the type of person who would wipe boogers in Kiki Sullivan's history textbook. Which was part of his charm.

"It's detention, asshole," Peter said. "It's supposed to be boring."

Michael located a station playing a Huey Lewis song, then grinned. "Besides, when I heard old Poindexter was sneaking out of class, I thought that was cause for celebration."

"Your face is a cause for celebration," Adrian said, pushing his glasses up the bridge of his nose. There was a thumbprint of mud on the side of his face.

"Ha! Holy shit!" Michael cried. "Was that an insult? That's great. I'm proud of you, man. Lousiest fucking insult I've ever heard, but goddamn, it's the thought that counts, right?"

We all laughed. Even Adrian.

"Anyway, come here," Michael said, waving him over. "I got somethin' to tell you guys."

Adrian closed his sketchbook, tucked it under one arm, and joined us on one of the headless statues.

Scott dug a can of Jolt from his backpack, popped the tab, downed a mouthful, and then passed it over to Peter.

"So I'm in detention with Tommy Orent," Michael said. "We got to talking about the Piper and everything that's been going on around town—"

"You didn't tell him about the locket, did you?" Adrian said.

"Heck, no. Am I an idiot?"

"Well . . . ," both Peter and I said at the same time. Michael kicked the can of Jolt out of Peter's hand, which set Peter laughing.

"You guys wanna hear what I gotta say or what?"

"Go ahead," Scott said, though he was smirking.

"So we get talking about the missing kids, and Tommy, he says, hey, you wanna hear something fucked up? And you know I always wanna hear something fucked up, so I say sure. He says he was friends with a kid from Glenrock named Jason Hughes. Mostly he said he just used Hughes for cigarettes, since Hughes had a fake ID and would buy cartons of smokes down at Lucky's and sell 'em to his friends."

Lucky's was a sundries shop not far from the city limits, where Harting Farms ended and the depressive blue-collar community of Glenrock began. There were a few bars in that area, too, renown for attracting the lowest common denominators from Glenrock's working class.

"Well, anyway, Orent says this kid Hughes took his money but never showed up with the smokes. This was back in June of last year, right? Orent figured Hughes would turn up eventually, and he wasn't too pissed at first. But then he heard that Hughes had run away from home and he owed a bunch of other guys money, so Orent said he got real pissed. He thought Hughes had dicked him over."

Scott said, "No shit. I'd be pissed, too."

Michael nodded. "But when those kids went missing in the fall, Orent says he started to wonder if Hughes really ran away. Like, maybe something bad happened to him."

"How come this Hughes kid's name hasn't been in the papers with all the others?" I said.

"Don't you pay attention? This was months before the Demorest kid disappeared, so no one was talking about the Piper yet, and everyone, including Hughes's parents, figured he ran away, which he'd done a bunch of times before."

"That would mean the Piper was in Glenrock before coming here," Peter said.

"Or maybe the Piper got him when he was here in town," I offered.

Michael shrugged. "I don't know what the fuck it means, but it's something, isn't it?"

"How can we find out more about him?" Adrian asked.

Michael shrugged again.

"We can look him up in the newspapers," Scott added. To Michael, he said, "You said this happened last June?"

"Yeah."

"That should narrow it down."

"But would there be a newspaper article on some kid who was thought to have just run away?" I said. "Especially if his disappearance happened months before any of the others here in town."

"I don't know," Scott admitted, "but it couldn't hurt to check and see."

"You could ask your dad," Adrian suggested, looking at me. "See if the local cops know about Hughes and if they consider him one of the Piper's victims."

"I could try," I said.

Just then, a strong wind swooped into the woods, stripping leaves from the trees and blowing grit and pebbles into our eyes. Thunder rumbled directly overhead.

"Christ," Michael said, gazing heavenward. In a matter of seconds the sky had gone from sunny and blue to rumbling and overcast.

Then the rain hit, a sound like gunfire rushing down through the trees. We all pulled our jackets over our heads and shrieked like girls.

Heavy thunder woke me in the middle of the night. I remained lying there and staring at the ceiling, listening to my locomotive heartbeat, fearful I might succumb to a heart attack if I didn't force myself to calm down.

The filaments of my nightmare, though quickly fading, still pulsed inside my head. The dream had been a combination of memory and make-believe. It was of the time Charles and I had run relay races during a neighborhood field day in December Park. I had been seven or eight, but in the dream I was my current age. Also in real life I had pissed my pants in my nervousness while standing on the starting line with the other runners. I had run, come in last place, then hid behind some trees where I had cried, mortified. Charles had comforted me, telling me that sometimes he gets so scared about things that he cries, too, and it made me feel better.

Standing at the starting line in my dream and anticipating the starter's pistol, a warm wetness spread through my crotch and down my legs. I looked up at the crowd of ogling onlookers, a dreadful sense of shame radiating from my face so that it actually burned, and tried to make out Charles's face in the crowd. But Charles was not there.

The starter's pistol went off, the report echoing in my head like the blast of a cannon, and the runners took off. I stumbled forward, my dream muscles as uncooperative as rusted machine parts. The other runners were far ahead of me, but I soon closed the distance despite my rusted legs. Flanking me on either side of the track, the spectators watched me in silent condemnation. I felt their burning stares firmly on my sodden crotch.

As I closed in on the runners, I realized they were corpses, and one of them was Courtney Cole, her head caved in on one side, her right eye milky and dead and turned outward toward the sky. The other runners were the missing children—Bethany Frost, her nude body blue and so skinny I could see every twist of vertebra, every xylophonic rib, the asteroid knobs of her knees and elbows; William Demorest, his colorless, featureless face leaking blackish gore that spewed across his boyish chest from what looked like a slender, proboscis-like appendage dangling from beneath his chin; Jeffrey Connor, his eye sockets wriggling with doughy white maggots and his decomposing flesh being ravaged by enormous horseflies.

There was the boy I knew to be Aaron Ransom, too, though he possessed no identifiable features. I ran up alongside him just as he turned and grinned at me. His face was nothing but a gleaming skull, bits of gray flesh still clinging to it in places. A number of teeth had been busted out. His nose was missing, leaving behind a dark, spongy cavern in his face. Only his eyes were alive—bright blue, leering, soul-searching, and terribly hideous in that fleshless skull.

Sweating beneath the blankets, I sat up in bed and propped open the nearest window to let some fresh air into my room. I imagined I saw a man standing in the yard, looking up at my bedroom window. His was the flimsy, insubstantial frame of a scarecrow, with tendrils of inky black hair whipping about in the wind. The longer I stared at the shape, the less it looked human. And after what must have been a full minute, I realized there was no one down there and my overworked imagination had created this stark character out of tree limbs and shadows.

Once my heartbeat returned to normal, I eased back down on my mattress and listened to the spring wind blow through the leaves of the trees in the yard.

CHAPTER FIFTEEN
NEIGHBORHOOD WATCH

After dinner a few nights later, my father called to me from the foyer where he stood by the front door tugging on a Windbreaker.

I saw the butt of his pistol poking out of the waistband of his jeans as I came up behind him. "Yeah?"

"You finish all your homework?"

"Yes. Are you going on another patrol?" It was his night to take part in the neighborhood watch.

"Just for an hour or so," he said. "I thought you might want to take a ride with me."

"Really? I sure would."

My dad rubbed the nape of his neck. His were the weary, red-rimmed eyes of a bloodhound. Based on the noises I'd heard coming from his bedroom at night, I knew he hadn't been sleeping. "Go grab a jacket. It's chilly out."

I raced upstairs, stripped a nylon Windbreaker from its hanger, drove my feet into a pair of Nikes, and a minute later followed my dad to his car in the driveway. The sedan started with a grumble. We backed out onto Worth Street, my dad turned left, and we coasted down the block toward the old rock quarry.

"How come we're going down here?" I asked.

"Just checking up on all the quiet places," said my dad.

Houses fell away, and the roadway narrowed as tree boughs stretched out toward the car. Through the windshield, wisps of clouds threaded in front of the full moon. When we reached the fences around the quarry, my dad turned on a side-mounted floodlight and panned its beam back and forth across the grounds. On the far side of the quarry, giant limestone monoliths looked like something on a lunar landscape.

"Hang tight a sec," my dad said, leaning over my lap and opening the glove compartment. A flashlight rolled into his hand. He winked at me, then climbed out of the car. Clicking the flashlight on, he went over to the gates in the fence. The flashlight's beam reflected off the large No Trespassing sign screwed into the fence. A large, rusted chain was knotted around the posts and secured with a padlock. My dad checked the lock by tugging on it. Seemingly satisfied, he returned to the car.

"Do you ever see anything when you're out patrolling?" I asked.

"Not really. Usually teenagers getting into trouble. Nothing exciting." He tucked the flashlight between the door and the driver's seat, then turned the car around. We headed back up Worth Street. "Got a birthday coming up, huh?" His voice was low, resonant.

"Yeah," I said. "I almost forgot."

"Anything special you want to do?"

"Maybe we could go to The Wagon Wheel." It was my favorite steak house in town.

"Don't see why not." He cracked the window to get some air circulating in the car, then depressed the cigarette lighter under the dashboard. "Your English teacher left a message for me this afternoon. I'm gonna give him a call on Monday, but before I do, is there anything you want to tell me?"

"Oh."

He took a cigarette from the breast pocket of his shirt and stuck it between his lips. When the lighter popped, he touched it to the tip of the cigarette. Bluish smoke whirled out the partially open window. "Something bad?"

"Well, no. Mr. Mattingly wants me to take Advanced Placement English next year."

"Is that right?"

"I don't think I'll be able to cut it, but he seems to think so."

"Why don't you think you can cut it?"

"It's mostly seniors in those classes."

"Don't you think you're smart enough? You're always reading. You're a smart kid."

"I guess."

"Is it up to you? Your choice to take the class?"

"Yeah."

"What will you do?"

"I told him to put my name in for it."

He exhaled smoke out the window. "That's good. I'm glad."

We drove up Bessel Avenue past Aaron Ransom's house. At the far end of the neighborhood, my father turned onto one of the wooded roads. He clicked the floodlight on, causing shadows to shift deep in the woods.

"Can I ask you something?" I said.

"Sure, pal."

"My friends and I heard about this kid Jason Hughes from Glenrock, who went missing last summer. People thought he just ran away back then, but now some kids from school are thinking something might have happened to him."

"So what's the question?"

"Just that, well . . . is he part of all this, too?"

"All this?"

"You know—the Piper."

My dad frowned. "Well, Glenrock isn't our jurisdiction. But, no, we know nothing about this kid from Glenrock."

"Do you think the killer's from town?" I asked. "Like, has he lived here very long? Or are you guys looking for someone new, someone who just moved in around the time the murders started?" Michael's theory still haunted me. I hated that my mind summoned Mr. Mattingly's considerate face as I asked the question.

"You interested in law enforcement all of a sudden?"

Because Charles had been a good student, a football player, a soldier, and because my father had had a closer relationship with him than he had ever had with me, I said, "Yes."

"Isn't that something," my dad said, and I couldn't tell if he was pleased or making fun of me.

"But what do you think? The cops, I mean. What do the cops think?"

"It's good thinking on your part. But are these the questions you really want to ask me? Because if you ever want to talk to me about stuff . . . The department has a therapist who's been speaking to some of the kids at the local schools. If you want, you could speak with her, too."

"A therapist?"

After Courtney Cole had turned up dead, Stanton School had brought in a psychologist to speak to any students who needed to talk. The psychologist, a meaty-armed woman with an alcoholic's ruddy complexion, spent a few weeks in the front office. A few kids had actually sought her out.

"She's just there to listen and to answer any questions or concerns you might have. I'm talking about serious things, Angie, not rumors you and your friends hear in school." He glanced at me. "Do you have any questions?"

"Did you ever shoot anybody?"

He laughed. "I didn't mean those kinds of questions. I meant about what's been going on in town. You were friends with the Ransom boy, weren't you?"

"Sort of," I said. I knew him from school, and he had seemed cool enough, but we hadn't exactly been friends.

"In case you were worried about things," my dad went on. "I wouldn't want you to keep things . . . you know . . . bottled up inside. If you were afraid."

I looked out the passenger window and watched the shadows peel away from the trees as we drove by.

"Are you afraid?" he asked.

I looked at him. After a time, I said, "No."

"Because it's okay if you are," my dad said.

"I'm not afraid."

"Okay. But you'll talk to me if you get afraid? Or if you just want to talk?"

"Sure," I said, considering. "But did you?"

"Did I what?"

"Ever shoot anybody?"

He squeezed my knee. "Would it disappoint you if I said no?"

"Maybe."

"Well, then I've shot . . . let's see . . . maybe a hundred perps. No, no—that's not right. It's more like two hundred. Yeah, that's it. Two hundred perps. Maybe more. You lose count after the first fifty."

I smiled and he tousled my hair. As we drove out of the woods and hit one of the darkened beach roads, my dad fired the cigarette butt out the window. The houses here were small duplexes with overgrown yards and boat trailers in the driveways.

"Do you guys have, like, a suspect list or anything?" I asked eventually.

My dad arched one of his eyebrows. "A suspect list, huh?"

"How do you figure out who to put on that list?" I asked.

"It's not necessarily a list of suspects. Remember the man we saw walking down here on New Year's Eve?"

"Chester somebody," I said.

"Yes. Chester Vaughn. He was out here so we needed to find out why. We needed to make sure his answers made sense and that he had an alibi. You know what that is, right?"

"Sure. It's an excuse for where he's been."

"Right. But it's an excuse that can be verified."

"His excuse was verified?"

"Yes. That's why we let him go."

"Have there been other people you've questioned like Chester Vaughn?"

His lips went firm, and I thought he wouldn't answer my question. "Yes," he said finally, "we've spoken to quite a few people."

"How come the newspapers haven't mentioned that?"

"Because we try to keep that info away from the press."

I watched the houses give way to sloping black lawns dripping with moonlight. "Do you think that Cole girl was killed in December Park?"

My dad patted down his shirt, probably looking for another cigarette that he didn't have. "We don't really know, buddy. It's one of the things we're considering."

"Not the police," I said. "You. What do you think?"

He exhaled greatly through flared nostrils. "It seems to make the most sense."

"Is that why you don't want me hanging around down there?"

"One of the reasons. You haven't been playing down there, have you?"

The lie jittered out of me. "N-no."

My father cut the wheel, and we took one of the nameless gravel roads toward the beach. On the incline, the bay opened up before us—dark velvet rippling with stars. A white mist roiled across the beach.

My dad eased down on the brake, then shifted the sedan into Park. "I'll just be a minute," he said, climbing out. He already had his flashlight on. I watched him advance over the dunes and toward the beach. With his shoe, he turned over empty beer bottles in the sand. When he shined his light down the length of the beach, the mist swirled in the beam like smoke.

He had left the driver's door open. A cool breeze entered the car, causing me to shiver. I peered out the open door, across the gravel roadway toward the incline of trees that ran along the cusp of the beach. Their branches waved in the wind.

I imagined someone standing just beyond that line of trees, staring right at me. Because the door was open, the interior dome light was on, casting me in conspicuous yellow light. All of a sudden, I felt vulnerable and naked. I leaned across the driver's seat, gripped the door handle, and slammed the door.

My dad's flashlight jerked in the direction of the car. The circle of light widened as he approached. "You okay?" he said, getting back in.

"Yeah. I was just getting cold."

He geared the sedan into Drive, carved a semicircle in the gravel, and headed toward the main road.

After a few more stops, my dad slowed to about ten miles per hour as we went by the Butterfield farm. The pens were empty, the cows and sheep having all been brought into the large red barn for the night. Two large grain silos extended over the distant veil of trees, their matching cupolas like dulled arrowheads. As we passed the entrance to the Butterfields' winding driveway, two carriage lights came on at the house, most likely on motion sensors.

Then there were the wide fields and the lighted houses far in the distance. There were the bats carving erratic helixes across the face of the moon and the heavy-limbed trees that drooped down into the roadway. There were the power lines bowing along the shoulder and the shimmering white eyes of a raccoon as it stood on its hind legs and stared into the sedan's headlamps.

And then there was the Werewolf House. Beneath a full moon and wreathed in ground fog, it looked even more like its namesake than it ever had in the past. It sat a distance away from the road on a weedy patch of land that shone silver in the moonlight. My dad slowed the car, hobbled over the shoulder, and drove onto the lawn. There were No Trespassing signs staked in the ground and more of them posted on the boarded-up windows of the house.

"Should we be coming out here?" I said.

"The place is abandoned. No one owns it. The police department put those signs up to keep kids out." He pointed to a mud-streaked placard nailed to the peeling front door that read Beware of Dog. "That one was my idea."

"Oh. Cool."

My dad stopped the car in front of a four-foot wrought iron fence that surrounded the house. There was a hinged gate in the front of the fence, but it was ajar and hung at an angle that suggested it was no longer properly attached to the post. Expulsions of weeds sagged over the fence and burst through the rickety front porch. The boarded-up windows looked like the mouths of mine shafts that had been deemed too dangerous for entry. The siding peeled in great curled shavings of wood, and the roof was a patchwork quilt of rot, missing shingles, and leprous holes. Half a stone chimney stood against one side of the house, its other half scattered amongst the weeds in ruinous crumbles of mortar and stone.

"Wait here." My dad grabbed his flashlight and opened the door. "I'll be right back."

He shut the door on me, probably thinking I had really been cold earlier, and went through the busted gate. As he approached the house, something dark and fairly large loped fluidly through the underbrush. It looked a little bigger than a fox, and I wondered if there were wolves out here.

My dad walked around the side of the house. He shone his flashlight on the porch balustrades, casting vertical shadows against the rotted siding. When he disappeared from my view, I held my breath. I followed the beam of his flashlight until that, too, disappeared behind the house.

In the glare of the sedan's high beams, the house looked fake, like a movie prop. Straw-colored grass rippled in the wind. With the driver's side window open a crack, I heard an owl hollering forlornly from a nearby tree.

And then I saw them—the fence posts, the wrought iron staves twined with stiffened brown vines. The spear-shaped heads of each post . . .

My father came around the other side of the house. His flashlight swept back and forth along the overgrown grass. Shielding his eyes against the glare of the headlights, he stepped over tangles of kudzu and crabgrass, opened the car door, and climbed inside. He clicked the flashlight off and tucked it between the door and his seat.

"You okay?" he said, looking at me. His eyebrows knitted together with concern. "Something wrong, bud?"

The release of my pent-up breath fogged the windshield. "I'm okay." It was all I could do to pull my gaze from the fence and offer him a smile.

My dad nodded and patted my knee. Then he proceeded to back down the lawn toward the street. Shadows swarmed across the front of the Werewolf House as the headlights pulled away from it. It was like watching a curtain of darkness close on a stage.

As we headed home, he looked at me one more time. "You sure you're okay?"

I felt amphibious with sweat. "Yeah," I lied. "I'm fine." But my heart was running a marathon, my breath coming in hard-to-stifle shudders.

"You and your friends should never play by that house," he said. "It's dangerous. The thing should be torn down."

"Yeah," I said, glancing into the rearview mirror where the Werewolf House retreated into the darkness. "No problem."

CHAPTER SIXTEEN
THE WEREFOLF HOUSE

The following morning, Adrian was sitting on the curb between our two houses, waiting for me so we could walk to school together. It was twilight and the air was cool. The lampposts were still on, and the world was as silent as a distant star.

"Hey." Adrian stood as I came down my driveway. "I was wondering if you were gonna show. We're gonna be late for class."

"We're not going to school today," I told him.

"How come?"

"There's something I gotta show you."

We crossed the street and cut through the Mathersons' yard. I had my headphones around my neck, and I maxed out the volume on my Walkman so we could both hear Mellencamp singing "Small Town."

"Where are we going?" Adrian asked as we went through the trees and out onto the bike path.

"The Werewolf House," I said.

"Whoa. What's that?"

"It's a run-down old house on the other side of the woods. We call it the Werewolf House because it looks like the house from a werewolf movie we saw. But there's something there I gotta show you."

"You guys know all the secret ways to get to places." He looked up through the canopy of trees. Daylight in the form of pink and orange striations had begun to rib the sky. "Have you lived here your whole life?"

"Mostly. We moved here when I was around three. After my mom died."

"Oh. I didn't know your mom died."

"Yeah. She got cancer. I sometimes think that maybe I remember her—like, I can see these blurry images of her in my head—but then I wonder if that's just my brain making stuff up, you know?"

Adrian nodded, his gaze trained on the ground now.

"My grandparents moved down from New York to help my dad take care of Charles and me. It's been like that ever since."

"So you lost your mom and your brother," Adrian said.

"Yeah." It was a different feeling having lost Charles, but I didn't possess the words or the desire to explain that to him. I hardly understood it myself.

"My dad killed himself."

I looked at him.

"He didn't do it in a messy way, like you sometimes hear about," Adrian went on. "Some people take their heads off with shotguns or swan-dive out of an office building or something. Or open up their wrists."

Inwardly, I cringed. *Open up their wrists.* I thought of Dennis Foley again and how he'd cut himself with a scalpel in freshman biology. I thought too of how much Adrian reminded me of him.

"He turned the car on in the garage and just, like, sat in it. He died of carbon monoxide poisoning. It's the least painful way to do it, I guess. That's why we moved here. My mom wanted to get away from Chicago and our old house and all."

I thought of Doreen Gardiner's haunted eyes and expressionless face, of the zombielike way she moved, and wondered if this explained it. What drives a man with a wife and a son to take his life? I wanted to know but I couldn't ask. Anyway, I wasn't sure Adrian would know the answer.

We walked the rest of the way through the woods without talking, content listening to the Mellencamp tape on my Walkman. By the time we stepped into the large field that flanked the road, it was as if we'd left the ghosts of our dead parents behind us among the trees.

"There it is," I said, pointing at the decrepit remains of the Werewolf House. "Creepy, huh?"

"Wow. You're right—it looks like something out of those hockey mask movies." It was what Adrian called the *Friday the 13th* franchise.

"I've ridden my bike past this place like a billion times," I said as we walked toward it, "but it wasn't till last night when I came out here with my dad that I noticed it."

"Noticed what?"

"Come on," I said and broke into a jog.

"Hey! Wait up!"

The overgrown grass whisked against my shins as I ran. By the time I reached the wrought iron fence surrounding the property, Adrian was only halfway across the field, struggling to maintain a steady pace with that over-burdened backpack weighing him down. When he finally joined me, he was out of breath.

"We shouldn't be here," he said, no doubt reading the No Trespassing signs.

"Don't worry about those. Look." I closed my hand around one of the iron staves in the fence; it was loose and I rattled it like a saber. Then I motioned to the top of the stave, where it was capped in an iron fleur-de-lis.

"That's . . . ," Adrian began. He dropped his backpack on the ground at his feet and rooted around inside it. He produced the matching fleur-de-lis that he had found in the tunnel beneath the highway. He held it up against one of the others, and we both saw that it was a perfect match.

"How could one of these make it all the way into the tunnel?" he said.

"Someone would have had to bring it down there," I said. There were plenty of staves missing from the fence, and some of the ones that remained had their fleur-de-lis missing. "I think we should look around inside."

Adrian studied the house. I did, too. It somehow seemed less ominous now, almost inviting . . . but it was a false front, a subterfuge. As if it were saying, *See? I'm just a harmless old house. You two boys are on the right track. Why don't you both come inside? I promise not to bite. I promise not to have my roof cave in and crush your little skulls. I promise not to have my floor fall away under your feet and swallow you whole . . .*

I swung my backpack around and took a flashlight from the front pocket.

"Do you think there's really a dog?" Adrian said. I didn't know what he was talking about until I realized he was looking at the Beware of Dog sign nailed to the front door.

"No. My dad put that up. The police want to keep kids away from the place."

"Smart thinking," he said and didn't seem any less apprehensive. "How do we get in?"

"Let's try the front door."

I went through the opening in the fence, where the gate hung lopsided from its rusted and broken hinges. Adrian followed close behind me. The ground was a cushion of matted weeds, and the porch steps were so overgrown that they hardly existed anymore. The porch slanted toward its center where a gaping hole bristling with tall yellow weeds was visible.

I was contemplating the best way to mount the porch when Adrian came up beside me and said, "Why don't we go to the back and see if that would be easier?"

We circled around to the rear of the house much in the same way my father had the night before. The yard was festooned with spiny-looking bushes, the boughs weighted down by countless birds' nests. Much of the siding had rotted away, exposing weather-blackened boards and bent carpentry nails. Nests made of dead leaves and twigs burst from between the boards like stuffing from an old car seat. They weren't birds' nests, I knew, but probably some mammal, like that fox-like thing I'd glimpsed arcing through the underbrush last night.

There was a rabbit hutch—a rectangular box of unpainted two-by-fours standing on a quartet of splintered wooden legs. Wire mesh covered the front of the hutch, though its corners had been pulled away from the frame, most likely so some animal could come and go as it pleased. The floor of the hutch was a mat of sodden brown hay topped with bird feathers and graying turds roughly the size and shape of shotgun shells. In the grass sat a large rusted contraption that reminded me of the pump handle on an artesian well, like the kinds they had on the Butterfield farm.

"What are these?" Adrian asked. He was staring at a pyramid of wire cages.

"Crab pots." I pointed out the hole on one side of the cage. "Crabs go in there, where you put the bait, but then they can't get out."

"I didn't realize crabs were so stupid."

I recalled all the times Charles and I had gone crabbing with my grandfather. Once we returned home, we dumped the crabs in the kitchen sink where my grandmother cleaned them. She cracked off their shells while they were still alive, and they tried to pinch her with their claws even with their fibrous white gills exposed and their eyes missing. Crabs might be stupid but they were fighters.

There was a back door at the top of three rickety wooden stairs. A pair of two-by-fours had been nailed in an X across it. Half an iron railing ran down one side of the stairs, bowed out at an angle. I tested the first step with one sneaker and was surprised to find that the wood was strong enough to hold my weight.

This close, I could see that the nails fixing the boards to the doorframe had come loose. I wedged a hand between one of the boards and the doorframe and pulled. The nails groaned as they came out of the wood. I let go of the board, and it swung like a pendulum from the upper left corner of the doorframe. I repeated this with the other board.

"Whose house was this?" Adrian stood on his tiptoes, trying to peer between the boards over one of the windows.

"Beats me. It's been empty ever since I've known about it."

"It's pitch-black inside."

I jiggled the doorknob but it didn't budge. Yet the frame looked about as sturdy as wet cardboard, so I shoved my shoulder against it . . . and nearly sent myself sprawling face-first into the house.

"Angie!" Adrian bellowed and chugged up the stairs behind me.

"I'm okay," I uttered, pushing myself to my knees. The palms of my hands came away speckled with sand, tiny stones, and black pellets that looked disconcertingly like mouse turds. I clapped the debris from my hands, wincing.

I'd dropped the flashlight during the fall, yet there was enough light coming through the tears in the roof to glimpse heaps of junk—washing machine parts, a pile of busted chairs that nearly touched the ceiling, automobile tires stacked against one wall. A clotted, mildewing stench seemed to register not only in my nose but way back in my throat. I could almost taste the staleness of the place.

I stood up and brushed the dirt from my jeans as Adrian came through the doorway behind me.

"Whoa," he said. "Look at this place."

I retrieved the flashlight from under sheaves of old plaster. There was a spiderweb suspended in one corner of the front room that looked as big as a soccer goal. When I turned the flashlight beam on it, I noticed spiders the size of peach pits vibrating in the silken strands.

"Let's stick close together," I said.

The floor was spongy in places. We moved carefully through the main room. Up ahead, doorways stood crookedly in the walls. One room was a kitchen. I was troubled to find the dry-rotted frame of an old wooden high chair shoved against a row of cabinets that had no countertop. Wires spooled out of gaping holes in the walls, and a single chain hung suspended from a pair of iron hooks in the center of the ceiling. Copper pipes jutted from one section of the wall at angles, attached to nothing. Beneath the pipes, the floor was stained a deep russet color. Deduction told me it was from rusty water, but it looked a whole lot like dried blood.

Adrian opened one of the cupboard doors and screamed. I whirled around in time to see him back up and knock over the high chair, which broke apart the moment it struck the floor.

Something hissed from within the cupboard. I glimpsed rows of bared teeth and the soulless black eyes of a shark. It was a possum, its back arched, the patchy black-and-white hair of its hide bristling like porcupine quills. It sat on one of the cupboard shelves, its tapered fleshy tail dangling toward the floor. It was devouring something small and furry, stringy entrails spilling to the shelf below.

Adrian backed out of the kitchen. The moment he was out of sight, the possum swung its enormous conical snout in my direction. Pinkish meat was stuck in its teeth. Slowly, I backed out of the room, too, the flashlight stuttering in my hands.

The other rooms were nondescript. The boarded-up windows cast zebra stripes of daylight on the opposite walls, and the floorboards were alternately soggy or brittle as bone. Graffiti had been spray-painted across various surfaces, including the ceiling, most of it illegible. Empty beer bottles were found in another room. An empty carton of Marlboros had been appropriated as part of some animal's nest wedged into one corner of another room. The whole house stank of shit.

"When was the last time you think someone was in this place?" Adrian asked. He peeked down a gap in the floor into infinite space.

"I have no idea."

"I mean . . . do you think the Piper. . . ?"

He didn't need to finish the thought, and I didn't need to answer him.

In the front hall the remnants of a faded floral-patterned wallpaper peeled away from the walls. The front door and windows were boarded up from the inside, too. One section of the hall floor was buckled and broken, and strange leafless vines spooled out of the opening and trailed snakelike across the floor. I crept to the edge of the opening and shined the flashlight down into it. The vines, thick as telephone cables at their bases, spiraled down farther than I would have thought.

"There's a basement," I said.

Adrian went over to a closed hallway door. The doorknob was gone, but he found a stick on the floor, which he used to pry the door open a few inches. The grinding sound suggested its hinges had been rusted to stone. A dark well appeared on the other side of the door. Warped stairs descended into a black pit.

"Forget it," I told him. A smell came up those stairs—a reeking odor like shit fermenting in an outhouse. "I don't care what we might find. I'm not going down there."

To my relief, he toed the door shut and said, "Me, either. Yuck."

I peered into an adjoining room. What must have once been sofa cushions were strewn about the floor, their fabric glistening with black mildew. Intestinal cables of wet stuffing spilled out of torn stitching in the fabric. As I stared, I noticed a small gray mouse, carrying a hunk of something red in its jowls, scurry along the baseboard and disappear into a knothole at the far end of the room.

"Did you hear that?" Adrian said from the opposite end of the front hall. He stepped over trash to one of the windows, bent down, and tried to look out the slatted boards.

"What was it?"

"Sounded like voices."

"Outside?"

"I-I don't know," he stammered.

I glanced up at the ceiling. Brown stains were eating away at the plaster. More wires spooled out of ragged holes.

"Hey," I said, coming back down the hall. "Let's get out of here, okay?"

Adrian nodded. His glasses had fogged up, so he removed them, wiped them with his shirt, and put them back on.

We retreated through the house, careful to leave a wide berth between us and the kitchen where the possum was presumably still enjoying its breakfast.

Adrian went through the back door, sighing once he touched the grass. He stepped around the side of the house as I came out, breathing the fresh air. Despite the chill in the morning air, my armpits were swampy with perspiration. I clicked off the flashlight and was about to shove it into my backpack when Adrian said, "Hey, Angie. There's people here."

I joined him at the side of the house to find Nathan Keener's pickup and
Eric Falconette's Fiero parked in the front field. They were laughing loudly,
and Falconette was lounging on the hood of the Fiero. I counted seven of
them, including Nathan Keener, before Falconette sat up, shielded the sun
from his eyes, then pointed at us.

"Hey!" one of the others screeched.

Adrian, the ignoramus, smiled and waved at them.

I grabbed one of his backpack straps and yanked him backward. "Come
on. We gotta get out of here."

Falconette jumped off the hood of his car. The others ambled in our direction. Like jackals, they wouldn't run until we did.

Instead of running, I dragged Adrian toward the rear of the house.

"Let go," he said, trying to shake me loose.

"Remember those guys who banged up my face?"

"Yeah . . ."

"That's them."

Proving my theory wrong, Keener and his friends started running in our
direction.

"Come on!" I shouted, shoving him around the side of the house. Adrian
staggered and would have probably lost his footing had I not let go of his
backpack strap and snared him around the forearm.

Instinct told me to bolt for the woods and try to lose them among the
trees on the way back to Worth Street, just as I had done in October. But
now I had Adrian to worry about. He was not as fast or as agile as me, and he
would get lost too easily. Not to mention we were both weighed down with
backpacks. So instead of running for the woods, I spun around and dragged
Adrian into the Werewolf House.

"They had . . . I think . . . one of them had a gun," Adrian blurted.

"I didn't see a gun."

"It was like a rifle or a shotgun," he said. "A long gun."

"You're imagining things."

I headed toward the kitchen, then paused. My hope was that Keener and
the others would assume we had run off into the woods and would pursue
us accordingly. However, if they came in here, Adrian and I would be sitting
ducks unless we found the best place to hide.

I released Adrian's arm, moved swiftly down the hall to the front of the
house, and peeked through the cracks in the boards over the windows. I could
hear their shouts through the flimsy walls. In another few seconds I would see
them streaming past.

I turned and saw that the basement door was still slightly ajar. Taking
a deep breath, I yanked it open. A twisted white stairwell disappeared into

lightlessness. I could see nothing beyond those stairs—not even the bottom of the staircase—but I could certainly smell whatever was down there: a foul concoction of rotting vegetation, fecal matter, and decaying corpses.

Adrian appeared beside me. His eyes looked like flashbulbs, and panic colored his cheeks red.

Outside, a sharp thunder crack of sound exploded and echoed across the valley. This was followed by maniacal laughter.

I met Adrian's eyes. *Gun*, he mouthed and I nodded.

I ran down the basement steps two at a time.

Midway down, I realized I was still holding the flashlight. I fumbled for the switch and clicked it on just as my right sneaker dropped into several inches of cold, shit-brown water. I trudged forward, hardly registering the mounds of debris that floated by nor the paddling of large sleek-furred rats as they fled the flashlight's beam.

Adrian splashed down behind me. Air wheezed out of his lungs like an accordion.

Frantically, I swiped the cone of light around the room and saw that it was hardly a basement at all but a festering root cellar. Jungle plants plumed out of the sewer water. The helix of sturdy vines that carved up from the ground and through the rent in the flooring above looked so much like a beanstalk from a fairy tale that I momentarily wondered if I was dreaming the whole thing.

"Here." Adrian was maneuvering around floating garbage to hide beneath the stairs.

I wasted no time joining him. The two of us huddled beneath the stairwell, the angled risers pressing against the tops of our heads, our necks, down our backs. I thumbed the flashlight off, dousing us in blackness. We held our breath and listened.

Someone banged through the door at the rear of the house. Someone did a Ricky Ricardo impression—"Hey, Lucy, I'm home!"—which was followed by cackling laughter. Their heavy footfalls thundered the floorboards overhead.

"You in here, Mazzone, you queer?" It was Keener. The sound of his voice caused my teeth to clench and my face to burn. "I got somethin' for you."

"Queers like surprises," someone else chimed in. It might have been Denny Sallis.

Heavy feet stomped slowly across the floor, directly above our heads. Then they paused. I thought I heard whispering, though I couldn't imagine why. My heart was thundering.

The footfalls moved again. They came closer to the stairs. Then I heard the grinding rasp of the hinges on the basement door.

Adrian tensed up.

In my mind's eye, I saw Keener descending the stairs with a rifle, catching the two of us cowering under here, and leveling the rifle first at Adrian, then at me. He would be grinning the entire time.

"You down there, Mazzone?" It was Keener, all right. The serenity in his voice troubled me more than any aggression he had ever shown. "I got something you can sit on. Just come on up here."

Then silence. Was the son of a bitch actually waiting for me to respond?

Seconds ticked by. I waited for him to say my name again or come down the stairs . . .

But nothing happened for what seemed like an eternity. Then someone shouted and threw something to the floor. Rapid stomping commenced. All too easily I pictured those lunatics smashing mice beneath their boot heels.

Next to me, Adrian released a shuddery breath. "I wet my pants," he whimpered. Not that it mattered: I was pretty sure we were both crouching in raw sewage.

There was more muffled chatter, but I could make out none of it. It wasn't until their footfalls moved across the house did I catch the next phrase, clear as day: "Jesus fuck, look at that monster!"

Boots hurried along the floorboards. Something fell over and broke.

"Get back from there," Keener said. "Those things give you rabies."

"The possum," I whispered next to Adrian's ear. The thing had indeed looked like a monster, but now I pitied it, left to defend itself against Keener and the rest of his shit-eating friends.

"Fucker gives me rabies, I give it the clap," someone yelled, and this was followed by more laughter.

"Gimme your gun," Keener said.

I recognized Kenneth Ottawa saying, "You gotta pull back on the—"

"I know how to work a fucking gun, you shit pipe," Keener barked.

"Don't take off its face," Eric Falconette said clearly. "I wanna keep the jawbones."

"Move." It was Keener's voice again.

The silence that followed was filled with tension. I closed my eyes and sucked my lower lip between my teeth.

A resounding explosion caused dirt to rain down from the floorboards into the muddy water all around us.

Keener's friends whooped and hollered. More dirt rained down from the boards overhead.

When I opened my eyes, I was staring once again at absolute darkness.

"Look at that fucker's tail whip around," someone shouted—a high-pitched, girly squawk. "Goddamn!"

"You got fucking guts on my shoes," someone else protested. It sounded like Denny Sallis.

"Shut your mouth," Keener said. "You're lucky I don't open your head for you."

"I'll do it," Falconette said. "Gimme the gun. I'll blast that fucker's head around backward."

"Fuck you," Sallis spat, although there was no strength to his voice. In that instant I could tell Sallis was afraid of Eric Falconette.

"Fuck me?" Falconette tittered laughter—another strangely girlish sound, though his seemed laced with some dark poison. "I'll ram my boot up your pussy, you dipshit."

"Cut it out," Keener growled. He said something else, but his voice was too low for me to make it out.

More fumbling reverberated through the floorboards. Something else was knocked over. Their heavy footfalls retreated to the rear of the house. The door slammed as they exited. For several moments, they could be heard cackling and jeering out in the yard. Then, something like twenty minutes later, there came another gunshot. After that, things went quiet.

Adrian and I remained under the stairs, not moving, hardly breathing. Even when the vehicles started up in the field, I gripped one of Adrian's knees and whispered, "Don't move. It might be a trap. They may not really be leaving."

So we remained where we were even after the engines faded down the street, leaving nothing but empty silence in their wake.

"Did they shoot that possum?" he whispered.

"Yeah. I think so."

"Those guys are crazy."

I resisted the urge to click on the flashlight. For one thing, if it was a trap, I didn't want Keener or whoever else to see the light come on. For another thing, I didn't really want to see what we'd been crouching in for the better part of half an hour.

Something moved upstairs. It was a subtle sound, like the shushing of stocking feet across the floor. I felt Adrian tense up beside me again. I tensed up, too. I was just about to convince myself that it was nothing more than a rat when footsteps moved down the hall. As they drew nearer, I held my breath.

They stopped directly overhead. At the basement door.

He won't come down here, I thought, desperate to convince myself with logic. *He was too chickenshit to come down here before, so he won't come down here now. He's trying to scare us out of hiding, but if we just wait him out, he'll get bored and go home.*

A heavy foot came down on the first step. The whole staircase creaked.

Sweat leaked down my forehead and stung my eyes.

A foot on the second step. The staircase—*reeeek.*

I wouldn't sit here and watch him leer at me from behind the barrel of a rifle. If it came to it, I would jump at him, attack him, bite and claw and tear and pull. I would be a wild animal if I had to be.

It was Charles's voice I heard in my head: *I would never let anyone hurt you, Angelo.* He had always protected me.

But now Charles was dead.

I clenched my fists. My whole body trembled.

The person on the stairs came down two more steps, then paused. The silence was as loud as the rifle blast had been. Louder, even.

In one second—*He won't come down here.*

In the next—*I'll fight him if he does. Even if he kills me in the end, I'll hurt him and make him remember me for the rest of his miserable—*

The footsteps went back up the stairs.

At first, I thought I'd misheard. But then I heard soft footfalls in the rear of the house. I heard the back door squeal. And although I didn't hear it bang against its frame, I was overcome by the sensation of being sealed up, so I knew the door had closed.

I shut my eyes and was powerless to move.

Somehow, astoundingly, Adrian and I had fallen asleep. I awoke with a jolt, gripped by a nameless terror that only intensified when I realized I couldn't see and that I was crouching in freezing water. Then it all rushed back to me.

I was still gripping the flashlight with both hands, so I turned it on. A jittery milk-colored beam issued out across the cellar. The walls were exposed cinder block. The water we were crouching in looked so much like cocoa that I felt my stomach tighten up in revolt. What appeared to be disassembled machine parts leaned against the walls and hung from large iron hooks.

I jabbed Adrian with an elbow. "Wake up."

His head jerked and slammed against the bottom of the stair. He rubbed his head, then looked around. "This water smells like poop."

"Congratulations. You win the prize."

"Are they gone?"

"I think so."

"What time is it?"

I checked my wristwatch with the flashlight. "Crap. It stopped working." I shook my wrist. "There's water in it."

"I can't stay down here any longer. My muscles are sore, and the smell is making me nauseous." Adrian climbed out from under the stairwell, his backpack spilling water like a sieve.

I handed him the flashlight so I could climb out, too, and was instantly greeted with a tightening pain beginning from the base of my neck all the way down to my tailbone. It felt like someone had driven an iron rod through my spinal column.

"Angie. Look."

Adrian had the flashlight trained on a series of large wooden crates that had been stacked against one cinder-block wall. They looked similar to the rabbit hutch out back. But it wasn't the crates he wanted me to see. It was what sat on top of them, molded out of concrete, its features buffed to rudimentary suggestions. Where its neck should have been was just over two feet of rust-red pipe threaded like a screw.

"Holy shit," I said. "Do you know what this is?"

Adrian's voice was surprisingly calm. "One of the missing heads for the statues down in the woods."

The head was heavy but we got it out of there. I carried it up the stairs and through the house. Before we left, I paused to peer into the kitchen. The back wall of one cupboard had been blown out, and there was blood spattered all over the place, even on the ceiling. But the possum's carcass was not in attendance, which could only suggest that Keener and his buddies had taken it with them. What had Falconette said before Keener pulled the trigger? *Don't take off its face. I wanna keep the jawbones.*

Outside, the afternoon looked gray and drawn-out. We walked through the woods, conscious of every snapping twig and falling acorn. When a flock of blackbirds burst from the ground and took to the treetops, both Adrian and I unleashed simultaneous cries. Then we laughed nervously.

We took turns carrying the head out of the woods. Finally, when we could see the back of the Mathersons' house, I unzipped my backpack and we stuffed the head inside it. We didn't want anyone stopping us and asking us questions about where we'd been and what we'd found there.

When Adrian saw that his mother's car wasn't in the driveway, he said, "My mom's still at work. You can come over and we can put our clothes in the wash. Then we can get down to the woods with the statue head and wait for the guys to get out of school."

The Gardiners' house was just as dark and unwelcoming as it had always been, but after spending however long cowering like mice in the basement of the Werewolf House, stepping inside was like being embraced by a loved one.

CHAPTER SEVENTEEN
WHAT ADRIAN SAW

The concrete head we had found in the basement of the Werewolf House didn't match any of the headless statues in the Dead Woods. For one thing, the head had a metal pipe jutting from it. All the bodies did, too. The corresponding body wouldn't have a pipe but rather a hole for the pipe to fit in. It felt like we were overlooking something very simple, but no matter how we considered it, the head just did not belong.

"So what does that mean?" Scott asked.

"It means it belongs to some other statue," I said. "There must be one we're missing."

"What do we do with the head in the meantime?" Peter said. The head was on the ground, and he was rolling it back and forth with his foot.

"We keep it here at Echo Base," Adrian said. "This is our place. It's protected."

"What the heck were you guys doing at the Werewolf House, anyway?" Peter asked.

We told them about the fleurs-de-lis on the fence posts.

We also told them about Keener. It was decided that we all lay low for a bit.

The near confrontation with Keener left us shaky and nervous, and for the next several days, I glanced over my shoulder every time I stepped out of the house. This wasn't paranoia—twice in the following week I'd seen Keener's pickup idling at the end of Worth Street. After seventh period, we left school from the back doors. This way, we were able to avoid the main roads.

It was necessary to keep away from the Dead Woods for a while, too, since we spotted Keener's truck down there again toward the beginning of May. Adrian was unhappy about this—we were all unhappy about it—but to return to Echo Base so soon was to court further trouble. So instead, we killed the hours in someone's basement, listening to music, watching TV, and playing board games until dusk beckoned us home.

And spring ushered us closer to summer . . .

I read Rachel's poems and thought they were quite good. I told her so in class, and she seemed genuinely pleased. She asked if I had written any new stories. I told her that I had been thinking about it.

(The truth was, I had been setting aside an hour each night before bed to hammer out fresh pages. I typed quickly but too hard, pecking at the keys with enough force to pop paper circles out of the O's, which littered my desk like confetti. After just a few weeks, a sizable stack of typed manuscript pages had materialized on my desk, smelling of ink from the new typewriter ribbon. What began as a short story soon grew into something larger and more dangerous, and I wondered if I had unwittingly crossed into the precarious and intimidating territory of a novel.)

My family and I piled into my dad's unmarked police sedan and headed to The Wagon Wheel, the gaudy steak house where life-sized ceramic cattle grazed in the parking lot, for my birthday dinner. I had a fat, juicy sirloin with sweet potato fries and a milk shake for dessert.

When we got back to the house, my grandmother placed one of her wonderful apple pies speared with sixteen candles on the kitchen table. We all had several pieces, dollops of vanilla ice cream on the side. My grandparents gave me some sweaters and slacks—"church clothes," my grandmother called them, since she was constantly complaining that I dressed like a beggar—as well as a birthday card with fifty dollars flapping out of it like a party favor.

My dad gave me a CD player and stereo, along with a bunch of CDs and paperbacks. The novels were cool—Stephen King, Peter Straub, Mark Twain, Ernest Hemingway—but the CDs were from groups I'd never heard of, groups my dad probably listened to when he was a kid. Nonetheless, I cracked them open and plugged the player into the wall. Soon we were eating birthday pie and listening to such mysterious groups as The Guess Who and The Lovin' Spoonful.

"Next gift," my grandfather announced, kicking his chair back from the table, then disappearing down the hallway.

"What gift?" my grandmother called after him. Shaking her head, she looked at me and said, half in jest, "I really think that old fool is losing his mind."

When my grandfather returned, he held his samurai sword horizontally in both hands. As I watched with widening awe, he set the sword on the table among the plates of uneaten pie crusts and mugs of steaming coffee.

"No way," I said.

"Salvatore," said my grandmother, "is that really such a good idea?"

"The boy's old enough. When I was his age, I was being shot at by the Japanee in the jungles." As far as my grandfather was concerned, there was no *s* in *Japanese*. "No one said I was too young, did they? When the Japanee started shooting from the trees, they didn't think I was too young, did they?"

I looked at my dad to gauge his approval. His expression was one of resignation. He knew better than to argue with the whims of my grandfather, though it was obvious he disapproved of the gift.

"Can I hold it?"

"It's yours, isn't it?" said my grandfather. "But be careful with it."

It was heavy. I needed both hands to hold it. The prospect of wielding it and chopping things up with it like they did in the movies struck me as virtually impossible. Nevertheless, I was anxious to give it a try. "Can I go chop at the woodpile with it?"

"Are you outta your head?" my grandfather barked. "That thing's a goddamn priceless souvenir!"

"Watch your language," my grandmother scolded him.

"A family heirloom," my grandfather continued.

"Not *our* family," corrected my grandmother.

"Go put it in your room," my dad said evenly. He ran his thumb along the rim of his coffee mug. "Keep it under your bed for now. When I get a chance, we can hang it on your wall."

"Over my bed?" I asked, hopeful.

"Lord," commented my grandfather, stomping into the living room with an extra slice of pie. "The kid's gonna decapitate himself."

On some random night, Adrian called me up. Living right next door, he'd never telephoned me before, so it took me a few moments to place his voice.

"Why are you calling?" I said. "You wanna hang out, just come over."

"Can't," he said. "Doing a puzzle with Mom."

"So what's up?"

"Don't freak out," he said, "but I think there's someone outside your house."

I thought I'd misheard him. "What?"

"I thought I saw someone walk around the side of your house just two minutes ago. I went outside to take a look but I couldn't see anything. And then my mom called me back in."

"Jesus. Was it Keener?" I went to our own kitchen windows and peered out onto the street. It was dark, and I could see no sign of Nathan Keener's truck. However, had he the foresight to park at the end of the street, where the asphalt concluded at the fenced-in rock quarry, I wouldn't have been able to see him.

"I don't think so," Adrian said.

"Okay. I'll go check it out. Call me back if you see him again."

"Yeah, I will. Just be careful."

"Sure will."

I hung up, then went to the rear of the house. I saw nothing through the windows. The porch door squealed when I opened it. I swiped the wall for the light switch. The porch lights came on, illuminating the wicker chairs and a few feet of lawn near the porch. But beyond that, the world was a black and sightless void.

"Somebody out here?" I called, and instantly felt foolish.

I crept down the porch steps and out onto the lawn. It was a warm night, the air scented with honeysuckle and spruce. I went around to the side of the house where the big pin oaks brushed against the aluminum siding. Suddenly I was no longer thinking about Keener but the kids who'd disappeared. I remembered the dream I'd had and how I had woken and looked out my window where I had imagined—or thought I had imagined—a man standing in the yard, staring at my bedroom window.

I went around to the front of the house. The light from the windows threw illumination on the lawn. The street was just as dark and empty as it had appeared from the kitchen window. Lights were on at the Gardiners' house, and I thought I glimpsed Adrian's round head silhouetted in one of the downstairs windows.

I stood perfectly still and even held my breath while I surveyed the property. There were certainly enough places to hide, especially at night. Anyone could be out here. When a slight breeze rustled the trees, I tried to decipher human speech in the issuance but knew that I was only making shit up. Scaring myself.

"Angelo!" My father's voice echoed over the rooftop from the backyard. I heard the back porch door swing shut on its spring-loaded hinges. "Are you out here?"

"Yeah," I called. "I'm . . . I'm taking out the trash."

He said something unintelligible. Then the porch door squealed and slammed shut again. I heard his heavy footfalls through the house's aluminum siding.

There's no one out here. Adrian's eyes were playing tricks on him, and now my mind is playing tricks on me. The place is desolate.

I was trying to convince myself. It wasn't working.

Shivering despite the warm night air, I dragged the trash cans down to the curb, then hurried inside, glancing over my shoulder as I went.

BOOK THREE

THE PIPER'S SONG
(JUNE 1994)

From the Harting Farms *Caller*, June 2, 1994:

ANOTHER MISSING CHILD, STILL NO LEADS

Howard Matthew Holt, 13, was reported missing by his mother, Susan Holt, when the boy failed to return home from school yesterday afternoon. This is the most recent in a string of disappearances that have plagued Harting Farms since last autumn. Holt's disappearance is the first since another local boy, Aaron Ransom, 15, went missing on New Year's Eve and the body of Courtney Cole, also 15, was discovered in the woods by December Park last October. Previously, three other teenagers had disappeared from the city. No other bodies have been found.

Holt, an eighth grader at Cape Middle School, was walking home with fellow classmates yesterday when he left the group to continue home on his own, according to other students.

"There is no evidence of foul play," Chief of Police Harold Barber said last night. "Right now, we are handling this as an unrelated incident."

Roger Dollins, an attorney and spokesperson for the Courtney Cole Memorial Charity, disagreed with Barber's assessment. "It is naïve to think these disappearances are unrelated, particularly after what happened to Courtney," Dollins said. "This is simply a case of local law enforcement turning a blind eye because they are ill-equipped to handle a situation of this magnitude. They have no leads."

"Instead of placing blame, we should remain vigilant as a community," Chief Barber responded. "We are not ruling out the possibility of abduction at this point, but to assume these other children came to the same fate as Courtney Cole is irresponsible and presumptuous. No evidence exists to suggest this."

Nonetheless, county executives have expressed their displeasure with

Barber's handling of the situation, and parent groups are calling for Barber's resignation.

"I think it's time the city bows out and allows federal investigators to take over," Dollins said. "How many more children have to vanish before someone does something?"

From the Harting Farms *Caller*, June 3, 1994:

HOLT BOY'S BACKPACK FOUND

Police discovered the backpack of Howard Matthew Holt, 13, yesterday evening in the woods off Magothy Road in the section of Harting Farms known locally as the Cape. Holt was reported missing June 1 by his mother, Susan Holt, when the boy failed to return home from school.

Police said the backpack was discovered after conducting a thorough search of the area surrounding Cape Middle School and the route Holt would have taken to walk home. Holt's mother had informed police that it was a route her son had taken every day to and from school, usually with a group of his friends.

"We spoke to a number of Howard's friends who had been with him on June 1 when school let out," explained Detective John Ebbett of the Harting Farms Police Department. "The consensus is that Holt went off on his own when he and his friends reached Muraco Street. Howard's friends said he turned and walked up Magothy Road alone. That was the last time they saw him."

The backpack was discovered in a shallow section of woods beside Magothy Road in view of some tenements and a small park, police said. The backpack was searched, then sent to a laboratory for analysis. According to police, it is too early to determine if the backpack contains any evidence that would assist police in uncovering what has happened to the boy.

A search continues for more evidence in the surrounding area.

Chief of Police Harold Barber had no comment.

From the *Baltimore Sun*, June 5, 1994 (Sunday edition):

CHILD ABDUCTIONS, MURDER PLAGUE BAYSIDE COMMUNITY

Howard Matthew Holt, 13, of Harting Farms, Maryland, has been missing since June 1. Holt's disappearance marks the sixth adolescent to vanish from the streets of the small bayside community since last August. Fears about a child predator were finally confirmed last October when the body of Harting Farms resident Courtney Cole, 15, was found bludgeoned to death in a wooded area off one of the city's main thoroughfares. To date, no other bodies have been found.

Harting Farms Chief of Police Harold C. Barber has stated that his department is looking into the possibility that these disappearances are related, although there exists no evidence to suggest they are.

"The only thing that links all these cases," Chief Barber said at a recent press conference in Baltimore, where he was rallying support from Baltimore County police, "is that the children have gone missing. We are exploring all avenues and aren't ruling anything out."

Concerning the specific details of Holt's disappearance, Chief Barber declined to go into the matter, though he insisted that his department is doing everything within their power to find out what happened to the boy. "We have recovered Howard's backpack and have sent it to the lab to be analyzed," said Chief Barber. "We have been conducting interviews and are following up on a number of leads."

As to what leads the department has received thus far, Chief Barber wouldn't comment.

The Harting Farms Police Department came under strict criticism last October when the body of fifteen-year-old Courtney Cole was discovered in a wooded area near Governor Highway, the city's main thoroughfare. To date, the department has no suspects in Cole's death, and it seems from an outside perspective that all leads have reached a dead end.

"My heart breaks," said a tearful Byron Cole, father of the deceased. "Someone should have been arrested by now."

Meanwhile, parent organizations and city council groups are in an uproar at what is perceived to be a cavalier attitude taken by Barber and his department.

"These are children," said Holly Dangliano, spokeswoman for the Protect Our Children Foundation. "It is deplorable how dismissive the local police have been throughout the past year."

Chief Barber was asked if the FBI should be brought in to assist in the investigation.

"This isn't a single investigation," Chief Barber said. "These are six separate investigations."

When a reporter at the press conference repeated the question about possible FBI involvement, Chief Barber ended the interview without further comment.

From the Harting Farms *Caller*, June 7, 1994:

BARBER RESIGNS

Chief of Police Harold C. Barber announced his resignation yesterday during a press conference outside the county courthouse. County executives and parent organizations have been calling for Barber's resignation since the body of fifteen-year-old Palisades resident Courtney Cole was discovered in the woods by December Park last October.

"I feel I have done right by the community," Barber said, his wife, Janet, by his side. "I feel I have done everything within my power. I am a servant of the people, and the people have voiced their opinion loud and clear."

Barber has served as chief of police for the Harting Farms Police Department since 1988, after replacing Arnold McDowell following McDowell's retirement.

Barber had come under close scrutiny last fall after the disappearances of thirteen-year-old William Demorest and sixteen-year-old Jeffrey Connor, both of Harting Farms. Police had no leads in either case, and Barber was criticized in the media and by several community organizations for his cavalier attitude and reluctance to address the situation with the urgency many thought necessary.

"This [resignation] is long overdue," Freeman Demorest, the father of William Demorest, said following Barber's press conference. "Communication with the [police] department has been deplorable to say the least. It was clear from the beginning no one at the department took my son's disappearance seriously. I was told many times that my son would eventually 'turn up' and that my wife and I were overreacting. I find that disgusting."

County selectmen will discuss the process for naming an interim chief later this week.

"We've got quite a few candidates stepping up to the plate," said Selectman Robert Gordon. "We will be appointing someone who understands the platform of the community and the concerns expressed by this unfortunate situation."

"It's too little too late," Demorest said. "I have been in touch with private investigators who have all told me the chances of finding my son alive are slim. The trail has gone cold. I blame the police. I blame Barber."

Many others have echoed Demorest's sentiment.

"There has been discussion about filing a lawsuit against the [police] department," Gordon said. "We are not blind to this. Our hope is that with this transition we can avoid any legal ramifications and focus all our attention on finding these children and bringing the person responsible to justice."

Headline from the Harting Farms *Caller*, June 10, 1994:

No Prints, Evidence on Holt's Backpack

From the Harting Farms *Caller*, June 11, 1994:

Solano Named Interim Chief

Deputy Chief of Police Michael Solano, twelve-year veteran of the Harting Farms Police Department, has been named interim chief of police last night by a vote of 4-0 from the county selectmen.

"Solano possesses all the qualifications to best serve this community," said Selectman Robert Gordon.

"I hear the people of this city loud and clear," Solano said during a press conference last night, following his selection. "Your concerns will not fall on deaf ears."

Solano's first order of business is to institute a 9 p.m. curfew throughout the city.

"This will go into effect immediately for anyone under the age of eighteen," Solano said. "Exceptions will apply for anyone with summer jobs or other unavoidable circumstances."

Solano was asked if this curfew should be interpreted as the police department finally acknowledging the possibility that children have been abducted and not simply run away.

"The time for ignoring the obvious is over," Solano said.

CHAPTER EIGHTEEN
FEAR CLOSES IN

S chool was out.

Yet summer was hesitant. As if tempered by the events of the past year, it was reluctant to push the gray and mild spring away, letting it linger like bad memories. Highways shimmered with a mixture of rainwater and oil while flowers refused to bloom, disillusioned by the terminal skies.

The disappearance of thirteen-year-old Howie Holt caused the city to fold in on itself. Distrust was palpable; it was in everyone's eyes now. Courteousness was replaced by suspicion. Father Evangeline quit bringing people up on the pulpit; his Masses were cursory and without feeling, as if he was in a hurry to be done with the whole ordeal. At the deli, Mr. Pastore no longer engaged me in idle chatter when I picked up my grandmother's groceries. People made anonymous phone calls about their neighbors' so-called suspicious activity. Our neighborhood watch tripled in size.

My father spoke little of the changes in the police department, though his face betrayed the stress and exhaustion from which he suffered on a seemingly daily basis. On his days off, which were few and far between, he spent much of his time trimming the shrubs and the pin oaks that had become saggy because of all the recent rain, mowing the lawn, chopping firewood we wouldn't need until late September, or smoking Romeo y Julieta cigars in one of the old wicker chairs on the back porch. At supper, he tried to affect a pleasant demeanor, engaging in conversation as best he could, but his eyes had begun to deaden with strain and, I thought, bitter reflection.

His distancing troubled my grandmother, who complained about it not to my father but to my grandfather. She felt the job was wearing at my father. She often said, "It's eating him up." I wondered how much was the job and how much was Charles. Charles's birthday was fast approaching, and with each passing day my father grew darker.

The police-enforced curfew put a damper on the opening of summer vacation. Most nights I was home before the nine o'clock curfew, having come home for dinner only to remain there for the rest of the night.

The search for Howie Holt curtailed our visits to the Dead Woods, too, since there were always cops around. Uniformed officers patrolled the park grounds, dump yards, and schoolyards on foot. Sometimes they walked German shepherds on leashes. There were county police cars stationed at various intersections, helping to augment local law enforcement. Men in dark suits were spotted around town, usually one or two at a time, although they could be found having lunch or dinner together in some establishment, their matching suit jackets draped over the backs of their chairs, their voices conspicuous in their quietness.

There were rumors that plainclothes policemen wandered the streets, pretending to be average Joes, buying coffee at The Bagel Boutique or chatting with the greasy, nervous salesmen at the OK Used Kars lot. My friends and I frequently saw them in December Park, strolling by themselves while pretending to admire the walnut trees or sometimes pausing to watch a pickup baseball game. They stood out like gorillas someone had dressed up in people clothes.

Our little city had made the national news, and there was even an exposé about the disappearances on one of those weekly news programs. An attractive woman with coiffed hair and glossy pink lips interviewed some of the parents of the missing children, as well as the spokespeople for the Courtney Cole Memorial Charity and the Protect Our Children Foundation. Former Chief of Police Harold Barber was demonized while the interim chief, Michael Solano, declined to be interviewed.

As we had done with the other missing children, Peter and I took to our bikes one sunny afternoon and rode out to the Holt household on Ridgley Avenue. Scott came with us. Adrian hadn't been waiting on the curb for me this morning, so I wasn't sure where he was, and Michael was enjoying a stint in summer school.

Yet unlike with the other kids, we happened on the scene when it was still fresh and new, and we weren't prepared for it. The Holt house had balloons, stuffed animals, and bouquets of flowers on the front lawn, up the driveway, and around the perimeter of the front stoop. It looked like a parade float. The small two-story house was dark, the window shades drawn.

There was an HFPD cruiser parked farther down the block, a dark shape propped up behind the wheel. In thoughtful silence, the three of us assessed that we had about two minutes before the cop got out of the car and informed us that this wasn't a carnival attraction and we should get lost. So we got lost.

We purchased two six-packs of Jolt from the Generous Superstore, and Peter, Scott, and I went down to Solomon's Field. We sat in the shade of the underpass, drinking sodas like dockworkers chugging beer on lunch break. We had dropped our guard after learning that Nathan Keener had started working days at the Ralston-Redmond Brothers junkyard and wasn't out patrolling the neighborhoods for us anymore.

"Ed the Jew says the FBI has been hanging around town," Peter said. "He thinks they're helping the local cops work the case on the Piper behind the scenes."

Scott handed me a fresh can of Jolt. I popped the tab and chugged half the can, wiped my mouth on my arm, and handed the can to Peter.

"There were some guys in dark suits checking out the quarry at the end of my block the other day. They drove by in an unmarked police car." I knew what one looked like since my dad drove one, and I had easily spotted the red and blue lights hidden behind the Crown Vic's grille. "If there's FBI in town, I don't think they're working with the local police. My dad seemed surprised to see them."

"The Piper got that Holt kid in broad daylight," Scott said. "What's the point of a nine o'clock curfew if kids are being swiped in the middle of the day?"

The Cape was an alternating panorama of farmland, beaches, and woods sequestered from the rest of the city not only by distance but by economic status. It was one of the poor neighborhoods, separating our section of Harting Farms from the industrial park. Nonetheless, it was still a risky move approaching a kid in the middle of the day. Particularly just as school let out.

"The news is saying that the Piper could be someone from town that these kids know," Scott said. "They would go with him and not feel threatened. That's how he's able to take them so easily and without leaving any clues behind. Not even signs of a struggle."

"Like a teacher," Peter suggested.

"Or a cop," I said.

Later that afternoon, we hung around Fairway Court where Michael lived, waiting for him to come home from summer school. We had the remaining cans of Jolt Cola stowed in Scott's backpack and our headphones on.

Michael, lanky in khaki shorts and a *Ghostbusters* T-shirt, met us at the end of the block an hour later. Water-soluble tattoos, which he'd been collecting from boxes of Cracker Jacks for weeks, covered his forearms. He had his backpack slung over one shoulder.

Scott looked at the digital clock on his Walkman. "Did you actually get detention in summer school? Is that even possible?"

"Miss Huber loves me, didn't want to let me go," Michael said. "The poor lady said she'd miss me too much if I didn't hang around an extra hour to clean up the classroom and wash the blackboard. Who am I to break her heart? Anyway, where's Poindexter?"

We all shrugged.

"I called his house this morning," Michael said, dropping his backpack to the curb, "but his mother said he wasn't home. It wasn't even seven yet. Where would he go that early?"

I tried to imagine Doreen Gardiner's dead voice over a telephone line. I imagined it sounded like the automated phone calls we sometimes got at the house confirming my grandparents' medical appointments.

"You think she would report him missing if something happened to him?" Scott said as we hoisted our bikes off the pavement and Michael ran up to his garage, where he threw his backpack inside and came out riding his Mongoose. "Like, if he vanished? Angie, you said she was a weirdo, but do you think she wouldn't—?"

"I don't know what she'd do," I said truthfully, hopping on my bike. "And what are you saying? That something might have happened to Adrian?"

"I don't know. It's just weird that we haven't seen him all week."

"Should we go to his house and see if he's okay?" Peter suggested.

I shrugged.

Our ride to Worth Street was shadowed by the seed that Scott had inadvertently planted in all our heads: would we have any idea if Adrian had been abducted by the Piper? It was possible, wasn't it? I suddenly felt like a coward for not knocking on the Gardiners' door sooner.

When we arrived at Adrian's house, we pulled slow figure eights in the street on our bikes. No one wanted to knock on the door. It had been many months since I'd told my friends how creepy Adrian's mother had been, but my description must have been vivid enough to ward them off permanently.

Eventually Scott stopped his bike and shot daggers at me. "We're here now. Someone needs to do something."

"Don't look at me," I told him.

"Shoot," Michael said. "Mothers hate me."

"So does everyone else," Peter said, but we were all too wound up to laugh.

Scott asked Peter for four cigarettes, and Peter reluctantly handed them over. Scott broke one in half—"Hey!" Peter said, frowning—then tucked all four into one fist so only the filters poked up. He held his fist out, and we brought our bikes in around him.

"Who wants to draw first?" Scott said.

Michael plucked one from Scott's hand. It was whole.

"Gimme that." Peter snatched the cigarette from Michael and tucked it behind one ear. Then he looked uncomfortably at the remaining cigarettes in Scott's hand.

"Just pick one," Scott urged him.

"Fine." He did. It was also whole. Relief spread across Peter's face.

Scott repositioned his fist in front of me. Like someone just handed me a gun in a round of Russian roulette, I stared at his hand and felt my mouth go dry.

Peter lit his cigarette and blew smoke in my face. "Do it, Mazzone."

Turning my head away, I blindly snatched one of the cigarettes from Scott's hand. I heard my friends make an "ooh" sound. I looked at the cigarette in my hand to find that it, too, was whole.

Scott revealed the broken cigarette in the center of his palm. "Crap. Best two out of three?"

"No way," Peter and Michael harmonized.

Scott set his bike down and threw the cigarette at Peter on his way up the Gardiners' driveway. It was like watching someone forced to walk the plank of a pirate ship.

"Ditch the smoke," I said to Peter.

He tossed the lit cigarette on the ground.

Scott knocked on the door and waited. Nothing happened. He knocked again. Finally, when it seemed we might all wait around until the world ended, Scott turned and looked at us. He held up his hands in a sign of surrender, then turned his ball cap backward on his head.

Michael used his finger as a gun and pretended to shoot at Scott, and Scott proceeded to do a commendable rendition of a cowboy tap-dancing over bullets. That was when the front door opened.

"Shit," I muttered. "His mom."

Scott faced the woman. He readjusted his ball cap and shifted from one foot to the other while he spoke to Ms. Gardiner.

She listened, cocking her head like a snow owl, her face carved in half shadows. She was gaunt, cadaverous, her movements like a Disney animatronic slowly winding down. Then she said something to Scott. He nodded dumbly.

Out of nowhere I wished for Scott's benefit that he would suddenly blink out of existence—*Please, God, let him vanish and not have to talk to that scary witch for one more second.*

The door closed, and Scott moved slowly back down the slope of the lawn. His dejection was evident in every fiber of his body. "He's not home," he said, picking his bike up off the pavement.

We all looked at each other.

"Then where is he?" Peter said eventually.

"She didn't say."

"You didn't ask?"

"Fuck, no."

Peter retrieved his cigarette off the ground. It was still lit. "You should have asked."

"You would have asked? Give me a break. You didn't even want to go up there." Then Scott looked at me. "She had this huge fucking scar on her neck." He ran one finger across his jugular.

"Yeah," I said. "I've seen it."

Michael turned his bike around and faced the intersection of Worth and Haven. Scraps of paper and street sand blew across the pavement. "Let's get out of here."

We spent the remainder of that week—that first week of summer vacation— not hearing a word from Adrian Gardiner. It was like he'd vanished. We pretended it didn't bother us. In the daytime, my friends and I prowled the city, not letting the pall of the Piper impinge upon us, ruin us, frighten us. We biked to the Cape and threw rocks at the barges that turtled through the murky waters. We ran relay races between the stone hovels at the bottom of Milkmaid Street, pounding divots into the dirt with our sneakers.

We rode out to the Blue Pirate Restaurant, which was an old weather-worn tavern near the Shallows, and listened to the garrulous laughter of the shipyard workers and watermen who patronized it. Sometimes they left dirty magazines in the cabs of their trucks. One afternoon, the proprietor of the Blue Pirate, a tattooed and crinkle-faced swashbuckler in his own right, turned on his hose and chased us away, his booming laughter following us down the boulevard like cannon fire.

Each night, after splitting from my friends, I found myself pulling circles on my bike in the street outside the Gardiners' house. Lights flicked on and off in different parts of the house. One night I stayed out a few minutes past curfew only to ignite the ire of my grandmother, who peeked out the front door and shouted my name.

I returned her cry with one of my own—"I'm right here!"—before pedaling up the driveway, pitching my bike in the ivy alongside the house, and going inside.

I was itchy. Agitated. I watched shitty black-and-white horror films on TV late at night. Every noise in the house reminded me of that phone call from Adrian about the stranger outside. I couldn't stop thinking of the man I thought I saw standing in my yard that night after waking up from a nightmare.

Another afternoon, it was just Peter and me heading to the Juniper Theater on our bikes to catch a double feature. Darby Hedges was showing *Prophecy* and *It's Alive*. It seemed we were in store for hours of mutated killers, and we couldn't have been happier about it.

"How long do you think this curfew is gonna last?" Peter asked. We were biking past Tiki Tembo, a Chinese restaurant with garish stone lions positioned outside the entranceway.

"I guess until they catch the guy," I said.

"What if they never catch the guy? I mean, they can't have us in at nine for the rest of our lives, right?"

"Just until we're eighteen."

"I don't know if I can wait that long." He smoked a cigarette down to the filter, then cast it in the gutter. "I fucking hate this town. It's like an extension of my house. A bunch of strangers telling me what to do. I don't belong here."

"Do you ever think about what you're going to do after high school?"

"What do you mean?"

"About college, I guess," I said. I thought about the AP English class I'd reluctantly be starting in the fall.

"Fuck if I know," he said. "I just want to get out of here."

"Yeah. Me, too. So you better not leave without me."

"No way, man. We'll leave together. We can go someplace cool, like New York City or Las Vegas. Get an apartment. It'll be awesome. You could write your stories, and I could become the world's greatest blackjack player."

I laughed. "That would be cool."

"So let's promise. Neither of us leaves without the other."

I touched my nose and said, "I promise."

Peter did the same. Then he spat on the sidewalk while we pedaled uphill. "If I don't get out of here someday, I feel like I'll go crazy."

"Maybe that's what happened to the Piper," I suggested. "Maybe Michael's theory is totally wrong, and the killer isn't someone new to town but someone who's been here all his life and was never able to get out."

"Yeah, man, I can believe that. It's this town, this whole city. I can see it making someone into a monster. Someone like the Piper couldn't happen in a city like Baltimore or anywhere else. Only here."

"Harting Farms is like Sugarland's train village," I said.

Two summers ago, Michael had set up a model train village in his basement using his father's old Lionel locomotives. He'd organized several dozen plastic army men throughout the landscape, their plastic rifles pointing at the wedges of hand-carved buildings while troops of green men prepared to hijack the trains.

"Like an entire world set up on a table in the middle of nowhere," I went on. "In the middle of someone's basement."

"Yeah, that's good. Model train set. Shoot," Peter continued, grinning, "you remember when Michael brought the garden hose through the basement window to flood the village? He called it a tsunami and wound up soaking all his father's law books."

"He hit the fuse box and blew the power out in the house, too."

"No, the fuse box thing was when he tried to make an indoor swimming pool in the basement," Peter corrected.

I laughed. "I thought his old man was gonna kill him."

"It was the same summer we found that old water heater in the woods, and Michael tried to cut it in half to make a bobsled, remember?"

"That's right."

"Goddamn, that was fun." Peter shook his head and rose off the seat of his bike, his back arching like a cat's. I could tell something was on his mind.

"What is it?" I said.

He knew better than to lie to me. "It's just something I've been thinking about. I don't want you to take it the wrong way because I know you like him and everything . . ."

"Michael?" I said, confused.

"No, dummy. I'm talking about Adrian. I mean, I like him, too, but do you think . . . I mean . . . do you think there's something wrong with him?"

"What do you mean?"

"Well, he's so intent on this whole thing with the Piper. You know, figuring all this stuff out on our own."

"It's just something to do," I said.

"No, it's more than that. I've been thinking about that locket he found and the top of that fence post and how it belonged to the Werewolf House."

"What about it?"

"What if those things are really important? Like, important enough to solve that girl's murder and find those other missing kids?"

"Isn't that the point? Isn't that why we're doing it?"

"Maybe at first. But it was just for fun. If we found stuff that could help the police catch this guy, we should probably tell someone."

"We can't tell the police," I said. "I'm not even supposed to be hanging around in the woods or going out to the Werewolf House, let alone inside it. My dad would kill me."

Peter looked at me. I suddenly remembered him from Charles's funeral, how he'd shown up with his mother and stepfather at the church in a suit that didn't quite fit him and a clip-on necktie with boats on it. It had been the only time I'd ever seen his wild red hair combed. He had said nothing at all to me that day, but he sat down next to me on the church steps afterward. We had watched the traffic creep along Augustine Avenue, and he'd given me a Tootsie Pop, which he'd produced from the inner lining of his too-big suit jacket.

"Do you really think something's happened to him?" Peter asked. "Something bad?"

"His mom would have contacted the police if he's been gone this long."

Though saying this, I wasn't sure whether I believed it or not. When I glanced over at Peter, I could tell something else was needling at his brain. "What is it now?"

"Tell me," he said. "Why do you need this so badly?"

"Need what?"

"To find the Piper."

"I don't," I said, realizing as I spoke the words that I didn't believe them myself. Yet I repeated them nonetheless. "I don't."

That night during dinner, I casually mentioned to my dad that I hadn't seen Adrian all week.

"Maybe he got a summer job," said my dad, scraping the tines of his fork against his plate as he shepherded his peas. "In fact, I'd like to hear your thoughts on that matter."

"On where Adrian went?"

"No. On getting a summer job. Have you put in any applications?"

"No, I haven't." I'd been so preoccupied with my friends and with what we pretended was our investigation that I hadn't even thought about it.

"Got any ideas where you could go?"

"I don't know."

"What about that bagel place you worked at before?"

"They're not hiring," I said, not knowing if this was the truth or not. I didn't want to drag my butt out of bed at four in the morning during my summer vacation.

"Well, you've got to go somewhere."

My grandmother got up, refilled everyone's coffee, then sat back down.

At the head of the table, my grandfather watched me. It looked like he wanted to say something, but in a rare display of restraint, he kept his mouth shut.

"But what about Adrian?" I said, bringing the conversation back around. "Would the police know if something happened to him?"

My dad sipped his fresh coffee, then set it down on the table. "Is that what this is about? You think something happened to your friend?"

"Which friend is this?" asked my grandmother.

"The boy next door," said my dad. "I'm sure he's fine, Angie."

Later, as I cleared the table and helped my grandmother do the dishes, I couldn't help but wonder how brilliant it would be for the Piper to strike again so soon after his last abduction. While it seemed the whole world was looking for Howie Holt, the Piper could have swooped in, gobbled up Adrian, and no one would even know he was missing. Unless, of course, his mother went to the police.

When I was done with the dishes, I brought my grandfather's pipe and tobacco pouch out to where he reclined in one of the wicker chairs on the back porch. The yard was dark, silent. Cicadas and crickets exchanged dialogue.

My grandfather smiled as he took the pipe and tobacco from me. I turned to go back inside but he said, "No, no—have a seat."

I sat beside him. My father had gone upstairs for an early shower, and my grandmother was just settling into the den to watch *Murder, She Wrote* on the tube, so the house was quiet through the open porch windows.

My grandfather tamped his pipe against one arm of the chair, and flecks of white ash drifted to the floor. With gnarled and lumpy fingers, he opened the tobacco pouch, pinched out some tobacco, and used his thumb to shove it way down into the pipe's bowl. Next, he took a box of wooden matches from the breast pocket of his flannel shirt—since he was on blood thinners, he always wore heavy clothing, even in the summer—and shook it so that the matches inside sounded like maracas.

"I've got a thought," he said as he opened the box of matches, "but I didn't want to say anything in front of your dad."

For a moment, I thought he was going to tell me that he saw something horrible happen to Adrian. It was ludicrous, but that was the first thing my mind jumped to.

He took out a wooden match, then tucked the box into his breast pocket. Using one rough purple thumbnail, he ignited the match while setting the stem of the pipe in his mouth. Tilting the pipe down, he touched the flaming match head to the packed tobacco and made wet mawp-mawp-mawp sounds with his mouth as he puffed.

"My friend Callibaugh owns that thrift store on Second Avenue," he said once he'd gotten the pipe sufficiently lit. Phantomlike smoke curled from the pipe, which he took from his mouth and examined. "You know the place I'm talking about?"

"Yeah."

"Well, I happen to know for a fact that old Callibaugh is looking for someone to work around the place for the summer—stock shelves, take out the trash, maybe man the cash register when he's busy. That sort of thing."

"Oh," I said.

"Best of all, I don't think he needs someone full-time. Knowing old Callibaugh, he probably couldn't put up with anyone for more than a few hours, so it could be a good thing for both parties."

"Okay," I said.

"Seeing how I'm so goddamn old and wise, I know how precious summer vacation can be for a boy your age. That's why I didn't bring this up in front of your father. But seeing how I also don't know where you stand on this whole summer job thing, I figured I'd let you know on the sly, in case that's something you decide to look into. You hear me?"

"Yeah, Grandpa. Thanks." It was thanks for not bringing it up in front of Dad, not for telling me about it. And I think he knew as much.

"I won't stick my nose in it further. Just consider yourself advised of the situation. You have some interest in it, you can go on in, introduce yourself, and handle all the details yourself. You're practically an adult now, ain't you?"

I smiled. "Well, I'm sixteen."

"Jesus. You know what I was doing when I was sixteen?"

"Shooting Japs and Nazis."

"Hell." He made a sour face and waved a hand at me. "I ain't never seen a Nazi in my life. Was too warm for them where I was. Nazis got cold hearts and mercury for blood, so they stuck to the colder hemispheres. No, son, when I was your age and I was overseas in the war, I did some time as a lifeguard in Australia. There was a whole team of us Americans keeping in shape as lifeguards."

"Yeah, I've seen the pictures."

"You know what a winch is?"

"It's like a big . . . I guess, crank that you turn."

"Yeah, all right. It was this giant spool made of wood with a rope around it, and the locals had constructed it from all these trees that had come down after a big storm. See, that's how poor they were, that they had to build their own winches from deadfalls. But—"

"What was the winch for?"

"Well, when there was a shark attack, you'd tie a rope round your waist and swim out to rescue the victim—or, in most cases, what was left of the victim—and the guys on the beach would wheel you in with the winch."

"You swam *toward* shark attacks?" I asked.

Again, my grandfather waved a hand at me. "Wasn't nothing. But let me tell you about how the locals built this winch . . ."

That night, I dreamed I was trudging through the wet forests of some South Pacific island, my small frame burdened with heavy gear, my hands outfitted in the cold steel of a maple-stock rifle. There were other men with me, but when I looked at them I saw they had no faces beneath the greasy pith helmets they wore . . . or at least I couldn't make out their faces with any detail.

—Don't move, said a voice right beside me. A hand shot out and pressed against my solar plexus. I stopped walking and held my breath. Then the hand pointed with one grease-blackened finger at a fan of thick ferns sprouting from the earth.

—What is it? I asked.

—It's where they hide.

—Who?

The man didn't answer me. Instead, he looked out across the jungle and whistled high and sharp to the other men. They surrounded us like ghosts summoned in a séance.

I turned to see the man beside me. It was my grandfather. In this dream, he looked both old and young. And while I knew him to be my grandfather, I felt no grandfatherly emotions for him.

—Watch and learn, Poindexter, said my grandfather as he crept closer to the nest of ferns, his footfalls soundless and his movements as lithe as a cat's. When his shadow fell over the ferns, he sucked in a great swoop of air, then swung his rifle down in an arc through the brush just as the men surrounding us pointed their weapons at the spot on the ground where the ferns had been just a second before.

What lay exposed in the ground was what looked like the rectangular opening of a ventilation shaft sans faceplate. It was dark within, but I could clearly see two startling, wet eyes blazing out at me and the bronze nubs of eight fingertips protruding from the opening.

Rifles roared and the glade filled with black smoke.

I stumbled backward until something took my legs out from under me, sending me crashing to the ground. My rifle and pith helmet spun away, and the sweat that poured from my scalp was so profuse I thought I'd suffered a head wound. I rolled onto my stomach and crawled through the muck until I saw the maple stock of my rifle through the thinning smoke. I reached for it, galloped my fingers across the wood and up along the steel of its flank. Just as I grasped it, someone plunked my helmet on my head and jerked me by my collar to my feet.

It was my grandfather, eye-to-eye with me now. I could smell the war on him, the way butchers smell of the abattoir, and it singed the hairs in my nose and caused my eyes to fill with water.

—Are you some kind of coward? my grandfather barked. Take a look there. See what we done. That's how you get 'em, Poindexter.

I looked. As the smog cleared, I saw the ruined hamburger meat of the man's face wedged in that hole, the shattered splotches of blood where his fingers had been. Those wet, blazing eyes were gone, leaving behind fleshly pockets filled with squid ink. Blood, thick as syrup and the color of motor oil, drooled out of the opening and saturated the earth.

—There could be two dozen of 'em in that hole, my grandfather informed me, but you only need to do the one up front. The rest of them slope-headed bastards are stuck back there for good and will die there.

A thunderous noise somewhere behind me caused the trees to shudder. I could smell death on the air, and it was even stronger than the gunpowder.

—Something's coming, I said. Something big.

—Come on, boy, said my grandfather, and he grabbed my hand.

A second later, we were flying through the jungle at a clip so fast my feet weren't touching the ground. Literally flying. We'd left the bloody mess in the hole behind us, along with that platoon of faceless soldiers. Whatever giant monster was pursuing us through the jungle was still on our heels, though; I felt each of its footfalls reverberating in the earth and in my bones. For some reason, I knew that if it caught us it would turn us to—

(statues)

—stone.

The man that was my grandfather only younger snatched a fistful of my shirt and thrust me toward a path that wound through the wet, dripping trees.

My feet crashed through puddles and swampy pools of mud. Each foot felt like it weighed a thousand pounds. In my fury, I glanced down and saw I was clad in military boots that looked many sizes too big.

We came onto a clearing studded with fragile-looking straw huts. A village. Embers smoldered in pits formed of white stone, and scraps of muddy clothing lay strewn around in the dirt. Upon closer scrutiny, I saw that those clothes weren't caked in mud at all but blood and flecks of whitish tissue, and the white stones around the smoldering pits had eye sockets and teeth. Even in the dream, I felt my gorge rise.

Behind us, the giant creature crashed through the trees in pursuit of us.

—In there, said my grandfather, pointing to the nearest hut.

I realized he wasn't my grandfather but my dad. That explained why he looked like a younger version of my grandfather . . .

My dad thumped me hard on the back. Go, he shouted.

I ran across the clearing and ditched into the triangular cutout at the front of the nearest hut. Darkness engulfed me. I crouched in the stuffy, enclosed little space and stared out the opening before me. The camouflaged figure that had been my father/grandfather was nowhere to be seen.

Beside me in the darkness: breathing.

A vague silhouette of a human form, outlined in a shimmering nacreous light, hunched down beside me in the straw hut. I heard the figure's respiration wheezing up through the narrow smokestack of his throat (for I knew this figure was male), smelled the fetid, almost fecal, pungency of the man's unwashed flesh, the sour griminess of his breath. A hand much like the talon of a giant bird gripped me high up on the arm; fingernails like the hooked beak of a squid punctured my flesh, drawing blood.

He was the Piper, the Harting Farms child killer. Panic bubbled up my throat, and I wanted to scream—to pull free of that talon-like claw and run the hell out of that hut. Yet outside, the enormous unseen creature had finally broached the clearing, its massive nostrils flaring as it attempted to sniff me out among the massacre of the villagers.

—You will open a door, said the Piper. His voice sounded like gravel sliding around inside a cardboard box. You will open a door.

I felt my skin tighten. In the dim light that spilled through the hut's doorway, I watched the flesh of my exposed arms pucker and brown like paper in a fire. Sores appeared on the backs of my hands, oozing a yellowish, snot-like fluid. My fingernails thickened and turned opaque. When I examined my palms, they looked like the hands of an old wizard, a mummified Egyptian king.

—You will crawl through, said the Piper, his grip on my upper arm tightening. I felt my own blood soaking down my arm and my ribs, plastering my tunic to my torso. You will find a tunnel, he said, and you will crawl through.

An enormous shadow fell across the hut's pyramid-shaped doorway. I heard the creature's respiration, a sound like air being let out of tractor tires, and I could smell it just like I could smell the Piper, though it was a rotten fruity smell.

As I peeked out the doorway, I saw a massive tri-toed foot plant itself into the blood-drenched soil, each toe roughly the size of a skateboard, each claw a hooked blade crested with spade-shaped growths that reminded me of the bony plates running along the back of a stegosaurus. In fact, had the foot been covered in scales I would have imagined it to be a dinosaur's. As it was, the flesh of the tri-toed appendage looked like human skin, and I could discern the fat blue veins and arteries just beneath the skin's surface.

And I thought, *There are no smells in dreams.*

The talon crushed the bone in my arm.

There is no pain in—

I shot upright in bed, my flesh burning up and nearly boiling the sweat on my body to steam. The filaments of the nightmare still clung to me. Clumsily, I pawed at my left arm, holding my breath until I was confident no one was gripping me there and drawing blood.

A shadow passed across the window.

I flipped the sheet off and practically spilled to the floor in my rush to the window. Pressing my nose against the glass, I looked down into the yard. Moonlight crisscrossed the black lawn, dripping between the interlocked limbs of the tall maples.

There was a man standing in the yard. He was halfway hidden in absolute darkness, and I could make out only the tapered yet undeniable slide of an arm, the protrusion of one shoulder, and, planted in the summer grass, the shape of a foot. I held my breath, unable to pull my nose from the glass, unable to shout for my father. I knew that the moment I saw the figure move I would find my voice and shriek like a girl.

But the figure never moved. I stared at it for such a long time the dark shapes began to lose their solidity, their realness. Things blurred into other things. The patches of moonlight turned everything into ghosts. There was no one down there. The remnants of my nightmare had caused me to see things. It fooled with my head. And despite my relief, sleep had a hard time reclaiming me.

CHAPTER NINETEEN
THE SEARCH PARTY

Callibaugh, the proprietor and sole employee of Secondhand Thrift, was a foulmouthed old cur with three fingers missing from his right hand. Grizzled, barrel-chested Callibaugh was approximately my grandfather's age and was a veteran of the Second World War. I wasn't sure if Callibaugh was his first or last name, so I simply addressed him as "sir," which seemed to please him the way not kicking a cat might please the cat.

"Ah," he said after I'd introduced myself. He was perched on a swiveling stool behind the front counter, one fat index finger bookmarking his place in a creased and dog-eared paperback novel with battling warships on the cover. "You're Salvatore's grandson, eh?"

"Yes."

"And you're looking for a summer job?"

"Yes."

Callibaugh waved one hand across the space between us. "Look around, son. What's the first thing that comes to your mind?"

In fact, two things came to my mind. One, that the store was in absolute shambles, with junk piled ceiling high in spots while random items hung off shelves and lay scattered about in incongruous heaps on the linoleum floor. And two, that he and I were the only two living creatures in the place, with the possible exception of the rodents that had left behind a Morse code trail of black turds along one baseboard.

But I said neither of these things. Instead, I surveyed the cluttered, schizophrenic amassment of junk with feigned contemplation before turning back to the proprietor. "It must be hard to remember where any specific thing is."

"Yes," Callibaugh said. He possessed the voice of a 1930s radio announcer, though one who had spent a lifetime sucking on unfiltered Camels. "I have no charts. I have no inventory. Do you know how this place started?"

I shook my head.

"I wanted to have a garage sale but don't actually own a garage. It started with one old man's lifetime of accumulation that, I suppose, at one point served a purpose and had a meaning but no longer does. The accumulation, I mean. Not the old man's life."

He set his book down on the countertop. "Walk around the store. Smell the place. Get a feel for it. See what junk pops out at you. If you work here, all this stuff will be yours until someone comes along and buys it out from under you. It's important that you think of it in that way."

"Is there an application or something I should fill out, too?"

Callibaugh's laugh was as sharp and as brief as the report from a pistol. "Application," he croaked, phlegm rattling deep down in his throat. "That's rich."

Somewhat bewildered, I turned away from the counter and proceeded to walk up and down the aisles. As I'd first gleaned, there was no rhyme or reason for how the items were placed on shelves—old textbooks slid into videogame cartridges which leaned against bags of potting soil which sat upon scruffy pairs of cleated sneakers. The only orderliness seemed to be in the way all the larger items had been shoved toward the back of the store. Sofas and love seats were packed against scuffed pieces of furniture. An old upright piano, its keys gray and furry with dust, slouched in one corner. I pressed one of the keys, only to be rewarded with a metallic and unmelodious clunking sound.

After I'd wasted what seemed like an obligatory amount of time wandering around, I returned to the counter where Callibaugh still sat on his swiveling stool, the open paperback mere inches from his face. When he didn't set the book down, I made a show of clearing my throat, then offered him a guiltless smile when he peered at me over his book.

"Well?" he rasped loudly. "What say you?"

"It's, uh . . . neat," was the best I could come up with. Some wordsmith was I.

"It's a war zone. It's a sunken ship at the bottom of the sea. It's a goddamned space station on the dark side of the moon." The book rose to cover his eyes again. "You can start on Monday."

That afternoon, with Michael's parents having gone into Ellicott City for a day of antique shopping, the four of us gathered on the Sugarlands' screened-in back porch to discuss what we should do about Adrian's mysterious disappearance.

Though not nearly as creepy as Adrian's house, the Sugarlands' home was a cold and eerie museum, spotless and regal like a European church. Michael's father was a lawyer, his mother a college professor, and to look upon their house one might surmise that the Sugarlands had never had any intention of having children. The few times I'd witnessed the Sugarland family together, their formality with one another bordered on palpable discomfort, like strangers trapped in a stalled elevator forced to make conversation. Even Michael, who was normally a live rocket ready to blast off into space when hanging out with his friends or among our peers at school, appeared uncharacteristically reserved in the company of his parents. I often theorized that his acting out at school was the equivalent of a valve letting off steam to prevent a systemic meltdown.

After returning home from what passed as a job interview with Callibaugh, I had gone up the walk to the Gardiners' front door and knocked loudly. The car wasn't in the driveway, and I knew Adrian's mom worked on weekdays, so I had no concern that she would answer. She didn't. Neither did Adrian. He had been missing now for nearly a full week.

"If he had been taken by the Piper and was seriously missing, his mom would have called the police by now," Peter rationalized. "I don't care how crazy she is."

The four of us were sucking down neon-colored ice pops in little plastic sleeves. Michael's backpack sat on the patio table spewing textbooks across the pebbled glass, and the sight of such incongruity—schoolbooks in summer!—was nearly blasphemous.

"Angie said she's a zombie," Michael responded. "She might not even know how to use the phone."

"Don't be an ass," I countered.

"It's just so weird," Scott spoke up. "I mean, if he was going to go someplace, don't you think he would've told us?"

"Maybe he didn't know," Michael suggested. "Maybe his mom sent him away somewhere."

"Why would she do that?"

"To keep him out of the hands of the Piper, for one thing."

"But where would she send him?"

"Maybe he's spending the summer with his dad," Peter said.

"His dad's dead," I said. I hadn't mentioned the suicide to my friends because I felt it had been told to me in confidence, but I didn't think I was betraying Adrian's trust by surrendering this one morsel of information.

"Yeah?" Peter said. "I just assumed his folks were divorced."

I waited for them to ask how he had died, but they didn't. I was silently grateful.

"Hey," Scott said. "You don't think he's dumb enough to go off searching for clues on his own, do you? That could be dangerous. Even if the Piper didn't get him, he could have gotten lost somewhere. Hurt, even."

I considered all the places in the Werewolf House that, were someone not careful, could bring about serious injury or even death.

"Still," Peter said, "his mom would have called the police when he didn't come home."

"But we don't know that." Michael's tongue, electric green from the ice pop, lashed out to moisten his lips.

"Maybe we should look for him," I said. "We can check the places he might have been searching on his own. If something did happen to him, we might be able to find him."

"Good idea," Peter said. "Who's got the walkie-talkies?"

"They're at Echo Base," Scott said.

Because it had become too laborious to lug all our stuff back and forth every day, we left the equipment, including the walkie-talkies and the dynamo-powered radio, in the woods. Peter had salvaged an old nylon beer cooler from his garage, and we had packed the stuff inside it, then wrapped the whole thing in a trash bag so that anyone who might accidentally stumble upon it wouldn't think twice about it. The only time Scott brought the walkie-talkies home was when they needed to be charged.

"Great," Michael said, standing up so fast that his chair fell backward and clacked against the floor. "Let's ride."

Less than three minutes later, the four of us were pedaling like demons. Peter was nearly sideswiped by a blue van on Ridgley Avenue. Two policemen with a German shepherd on a short chain gaped at us from beneath the sagging awning of the drugstore as we whizzed through City Center and burned up Second Avenue.

When I heard the deliberate growl of a car's engine behind me, I realized I'd been hearing it for the past several seconds without actually registering it. I whipped my head around and saw Eric Falconette's mud-streaked Fiero grinding its gears as it came up quickly behind us.

"Hey!" I shouted, alerting my friends to the danger.

They all turned and saw the Fiero just as its front bumper lurched out in an attempt to thump the rear tire of my bike.

I swerved across the street, nearly losing it and spilling myself to the pavement in the process, but still managed to avoid the collision. I hopped the curb onto the sidewalk, my bike chain rattling.

The car's passenger window went down, and someone shouted at us. Then an empty Budweiser bottle cartwheeled through the air and shattered on the sidewalk mere feet in front of me.

Unable to avoid it, my bike tires crunched over the broken glass. I winced. All I could do was hold my breath and hope I wouldn't blow a flat.

More bottles launched into the air; they smashed all around us like the blitz, leaving sunbursts of colored glass glittering on the pavement. One struck Peter's thigh, and he howled like a wounded hound.

In the car, I heard a pair of thugs cackling like hyenas.

Then the Fiero pulled up right alongside me. The driver's side window was down, and when I glanced over, I saw Falconette's greasy white face gibbering at me like a wind-up Halloween toy. His long hair was slicked back from his face, and I caught the shimmer of a cross-shaped earring in his left ear.

Nathan Keener had it in for me because he thought I had ratted him out to my dad. Eric Falconette, on the other hand, had no reason to come after any of us, except one: he was an evil son of a bitch who was more than just a little bit crazy.

"You queers should really watch where you're going," Falconette shouted. "Shouldn't drive in the middle of the street."

The Fiero jumped the curb, nearly forcing me into the bushes. Gears shrieked and exhaust burned in the air. Falconette leaned on the horn, which had been modified to sound like the air horn of an eighteen-wheeler. It nearly sent me shooting out of my skin.

Shrieking with laughter, Falconette dumped the Fiero back down onto the roadway.

At that point, Michael pulled a risky move: he cut across the street directly in front of Falconette's car. The sudden unexpected maneuver caused the driver to slam on the brakes. As Michael hopped up the opposite curb and joined me on the sidewalk, the Fiero fishtailed, leaving streaks of black rubber on the pavement. The burning scent of the car's tires flooded my nostrils.

The rear of the car swung far enough to one side that I could easily see it slamming into one of the shop fronts. Yet somehow Falconette regained control, and the Fiero slowed and thumped like a crippled racehorse alongside the curb. Then I heard the distinct report of a blown tire.

Michael cried out in triumph.

"Here," Peter yelled and cut sharply down an alleyway.

One by one, we all followed him.

By the time we reached December Park, we were all giddy and high-strung. We hid our bikes in the woods, then trudged through it to the clearing and Echo Base. It was June, and the floor of the clearing was lush with new grass. Ivy had sprouted out of the ground and snaked around the headless statues, keeping them well hidden and protected.

Scott went to the trash bag concealing the nylon beer cooler packed with our gear and untied it while Peter and I stood around and shared a cigarette.

Michael grabbed the concrete head with the pipe jutting from its neck and held it up to his face. "Where do you belong, big fella?" he said in a creepy singsong voice, as if he were talking to an infant or a small animal. Then he proceeded to croon a few bars of "I Ain't Got Nobody."

"Let's stick together in pairs," Scott said. He took the two big walkie-talkies from the beer cooler and handed one to Peter.

Peter glanced at Michael, who was now pretending to French kiss the decapitated concrete head, then turned to Scott. "I'll go with Angie; you go with Mikey."

"Wonderful." Scott rolled his eyes and clipped the walkie-talkie to his waistband. He rifled around inside the beer cooler until he found one of Michael's maps of Harting Farms. He unfolded the map and spread it out on the trunk of one of the statues.

Scott traced a line down the center of town. "You guys take this side. Michael and I will take the other. We don't have to go far. Adrian doesn't have a bike, so if he went anywhere, it's probably within walking distance. When we're done for the day, let's meet back here." He clicked on his walkie-talkie. "Keep these on the whole time. If we don't go too far we shouldn't be out of range."

We retraced our steps back to our bikes. Out in December Park, some kids had gathered on the baseball diamond with gloves and a ball. Farther across the park, where Solomon's Bend Road was veiled behind a curtain of walnut trees, a few younger kids flew kites under the guidance of their parents.

A terrible feeling squirmed around inside my guts. "Listen," I said as we prepared to split up. "You guys be careful, okay? And stick together. Don't separate."

"Yes, mom," Michael quipped.

"He's right," Peter said, bouncing an acorn off Michael's forehead. "Quit being a prick."

"Can't," Michael said. "It's my nature."

Scott straddled his bike and headed across December Park. Michael gave Peter and me the finger, then turned and went after him. They carved a serpentine path through the overgrown grass while gathering speed and blasted right through the baseball diamond, kicking up clouds of dust and eliciting a barrage of swears from the older kids. A moment later, they both vanished beneath the underpass.

"Where to first?" Peter said, adjusting the volume on the walkie-talkie.

I didn't have to think about it. "The Werewolf House."

* * *

Since that day Adrian and I had cowered in the basement shin-deep in fetid brown water, my perception of the Werewolf House had changed. It was no longer just a creepy old house at the far end of a vacant lot. It was something more sinister now.

As we rode through the field and stopped before the wrought iron fence that surrounded the property, I felt my eyes glued to the house. It was as if to take them from it—even for a second—was akin to turning my back on a growling lion ready to pounce. It was nothing more than a collection of sun-bleached boards held together by scores of rusted carpentry nails, but I felt—no, I *knew*—that its whole was greater than the sum of its parts.

"That door looks pretty sealed up," Peter said.

"We went in through the back door."

We set our bikes down in the grass. I walked through the opening in the fence, grass seed and small bugs adhering to my clothes, and headed around the back. Peter followed close behind me.

"I can't believe you guys went in there," he marveled, gazing up at the crumbling roof and the hornets' nests that hung like Chinese lanterns from the eaves. Then he froze. "What if Keener and his friends are in there?"

"I don't see their cars anywhere. Besides, I didn't get the impression that this is a place they typically hang out. I think they went in looking for us."

"Are you sure you weren't bullshitting about the rifle?"

"I'll show you where he blew a hole in the wall," I said, approaching the back door. The boards still hung loosely, just as Adrian and I had left them. The door was shut.

"Do we really have to go in there?" Peter said.

"It's why we're here," I said, climbing the steps. I gripped the knob and shoved one shoulder against the door. It popped open without much effort. "Come on."

It was like a dream, entering that house again. Indeed, I'd suffered nightmares about it, though I only now remembered them.

Peter came up behind me, looking around at the ruined interior in awe. "It stinks."

"I think there's a busted sewer pipe in the basement," I said.

Stepping over random debris and avoiding the blackened floorboards, I went into the kitchen. Peter was practically piggybacking on me, he was so close.

"Right there," I said, pointing to the blast hole in the cupboard. The possum's blood had dried to brownish muck on the wall and the floor. Amazingly, I thought I could still smell gunpowder in the air.

"Holy shit." Peter shook his head slowly. "Keener's a psycho. I know we've joked about it before, but is it possible he's the Piper?"

"I don't think stealth is Keener's style. The Piper is someone more"—I wanted to say *cerebral*, but it didn't quite fit—"cautious. You don't stay hidden from the cops for the better part of a year by stomping around town in steel-toed boots and spray-painting grocery stores. It's too obvious."

"Where are you going?" he called to me.

I hadn't realized that I had been slowly making my way down the hall toward the basement door. I turned around and saw Peter standing at the opposite end of the hallway. Grainy harpoons of daylight filtered into the room behind him, creating the unsettling illusion that he was semitransparent.

"I need to check the basement," I said.

"Do you really think Adrian would have gone into the basement by himself?"

"I don't know."

I approached the basement door, took a breath, opened it. The stink of the rancid water rushed up and slapped me across the face. They say the olfactory sense is the one connected most closely with memory, and I believe it; by just catching a whiff of that fecal stench, I was back down there in the dark, crouching beside Adrian while heavy footfalls tramped the boards above our heads. My sneakers were submerged in it, my jeans soaked, my heart strumming frantically. I had to take a step back from the doorway to convince myself that I wasn't actually still down there.

"You all right?" Peter said, joining me. "You look like you're gonna be sick."

"I just had a weird thought," I said.

"What's that?"

"Remember how I said Keener had tried to trick us into coming out? How he'd had his friends drive the cars away while he stayed here, waiting for us? And then he'd come halfway down the stairs?"

"Yeah."

"Well," I said, my throat suddenly dry, "what if it hadn't been Keener?"

"What do you mean?"

"I don't know," I said, only because I couldn't bring myself to say it.

The house creaked.

"Hey!" Peter shouted down the mine shaft of the open basement door. "Adrian! You down there?"

His voice echoed in the fetid chamber—*there . . . ere . . . ere . . .*

"I don't like this place," Peter said, his voice nearly a whisper. "Let's get out of here."

We hurried back through the house, and Peter was out the door first. I followed, shutting the door behind me. After some consideration, I readjusted the two-by-fours and pressed the nails back into the nail holes in the frame.

"Why'd you do that?" Peter asked.

"So we'll know if someone goes inside," I said.

"If we ever come back out here, you mean."

"Well, yeah."

"Come on."

We went around the side of the house, absently swatting at wasps that orbited our heads . . . then froze as we stepped out into the overgrown front yard.

A man stood on the other side of the fence, a red baseball cap tugged down low over his face. He wore carpenter's pants and a gray T-shirt with a faded emblem on the chest. He was looking directly at us. "What are you two doing?"

I couldn't speak. If his silence could be construed as evidence, I don't think Peter could, either.

"Angelo?" the man said, his voice cracking slightly. "Angelo Mazzone? Is that you?"

The man pushed back the bill of his hat. Instantly I recognized his face, although I couldn't place his name.

"Y-yes," I managed.

"You guys shouldn't be hanging around out here. It's dangerous."

"Oh," I muttered. In my head, I was gauging the distance to our bikes. The man was closer to them than we were; we wouldn't be able to get on them without him stopping one or both of us.

"Seriously," the man said. He turned and looked at the house. If we were to run for it, now would be our chance. "This place should be torn down. It's asking for trouble."

Just as I was about to break into a sprint, I realized who the man was: Mr. Mattingly, my English teacher. Something like relief washed over me. I must have uttered a pathetic little mewl, too, because Mr. Mattingly turned back to me.

"Hey, Mr. Mattingly," I said.

He laughed. "Didn't recognize me, huh?"

"Not at first, no."

"You kids think that after the school year's through, all the teachers are packed away in crates filled with Styrofoam peanuts," he said not unkindly.

It wasn't that at all. Rather, it had been the inability to fully recognize someone when they were out of their usual place—in Mr. Mattingly's case, the classroom.

"Forget it," he said. "No hard feelings. But seriously—you guys shouldn't hang around this place. Know what I'm saying?"

I nodded like an imbecile. "We were just leaving."

"How come you're out here?" Peter said.

"I'm looking for my dog." The abrupt change in his tone was unmistakable.

"You want us to help you find him?" Peter said.

"That isn't necessary," said Mr. Mattingly.

"It's no big deal. What's his name?"

When I realized I was holding my breath, I released it in a shuddery exhalation.

"Brindle," Mr. Mattingly finally said. "And he's a she." He glanced at the road, then back at us. "We were out for a walk when she saw a rabbit run by. She can't resist a good chase."

"If—," Peter began.

But he was cut off as a black-and-white cocker spaniel bounded toward Mr. Mattingly through the grass. Mr. Mattingly hunkered down and rubbed the dog's face.

The dog barked twice, then cut through the grass and came over to Peter, where it proceeded to sniff at Peter's sneakers.

"Hey, pooch," Peter said, bending down to stroke the dog's back.

"Do you live around here?" I asked Mr. Mattingly.

Mr. Mattingly pointed in the direction of the gridded little neighborhood beyond the Butterfield farmhouse. "Back there. It's just my wife and me," he said. I must have been staring at him too intensely, since he laughed, possibly to break the tension, and added, "Yeah, I know. Students don't think of teachers as having wives or husbands, either, right?"

"Right," I said flatly.

"Well," Mr. Mattingly said, crouching back down in the grass. He patted his thighs. "Come on, Brindle. Let's head home."

The cocker spaniel darted between Peter's feet and scampered over to Mr. Mattingly.

Mr. Mattingly removed a leash from the rear pocket of his pants and hooked it to the dog's collar. When he stood up, he smiled. "I guess I'll see you guys around. Have a good summer."

"See you," I said and watched him walk across the empty lot.

"That guy's your teacher?"

I nodded.

"What do you think he was doing out here?"

"I don't know, man."

"You don't think. . . ?" Peter let the unfinished thought hang in the air.

When Michael had listed Mr. Mattingly's name among the suspects, it had struck me as a ridiculous and far-fetched assumption. Now I wondered why I had thought so . . .

Static burst through the walkie-talkie. It was garbled nonsense.

Peter plucked it off his belt and keyed the Talk button. "We didn't make out a word of that. Repeat. Over."

We waited but the static burst did not repeat.

"Maybe they didn't hear us," I suggested. "We might be too far away."

"Let's head back," Peter said, clipping the radio on his belt. He went over to his bike and pulled it out of the weeds.

I grabbed my bike, too. As I climbed on, I glanced toward the road where Mr. Mattingly and his dog walked in the direction of the Shallows.

We were riding down McKinsey when the walkie-talkie came alive again.

Peter brought the radio to his mouth. "Is that you, Scotty? You're breaking up, man. Repeat. Over."

". . . to the woods," Scott's voice crackled over the radio.

"Go to the woods?" Peter said into the radio. "We'll be there in a bit. Over."

"Don't," Scott's voice returned, and the word was crisp and clear. "Don't . . . woods . . ."

"*Don't* go to the woods?" Peter asked me.

"That's what it sounded like," I said.

Peter brought the handheld up to his face again. "Hello? Guys? We can hardly understand you."

Scott's static-laden voice answered: ". . . dezvous . . ."

"Rendezvous," Peter translated. "He wants us to meet at the rendezvous point instead of the woods."

"Where's the rendezvous point?" I asked. After all this time, I had forgotten. "Is it the tree by the baseball field?"

"No," he said, clipping the walkie-talkie to his belt loop. He arched his back, lifting his butt off the seat, and pedaled faster. "The underpass."

When we reached December Park, we flew through the intersection and hooked a left onto Solomon's Bend Road. Evening crept across the horizon, making the distant trees look like woodcut carvings, and the baseball players and kite-flying kids had gone.

Riding side by side, Peter and I took the bike path that curved down into Solomon's Field. Drunkard's Pond was wreathed in three-foot-tall cattails, and the water appeared dark and mysterious in the encroaching dusk.

"There they are," Peter said, pointing to a figure standing before the mouth of the underpass waving his arms. It was Scott.

Our bike tires eating up the earth, we cut across the field and coasted to a bumpy stop next to the underpass. Michael stood just inside it, halfway cloaked in shadow. Their bikes leaned against the black stone walls of the tunnel.

"What gives?" I said, still straddling my bike.

"There's someone in the woods," Scott said.

"At Echo Base," Michael added.

"Who is it?" Peter asked.

"Some guy," Scott said. He described him—a man in his thirties with short, sandy hair, wearing dark-colored cargo pants and a black shirt. Neither Scott nor Michael had recognized him.

"We were walking through the woods over to Echo Base when we saw him just kind of . . . well, looking around at all our stuff," Michael said. "He was opening one of the trash bags when he looked up and saw us watching him through the trees."

"He didn't say anything," Scott said. "That's when Michael and I took off and came here."

"Is he still there?" Peter asked.

"How should we know?" Michael said.

"Well, should we go back and look?"

"Seriously?" Michael said. "It'll be dark soon and I gotta get home. Besides, you really wanna be in those woods with some weirdo who's rooting around in our stuff?"

"What if it's the Piper?" Peter said.

"All the more reason," Michael said. "I'm not keen on having my skull bashed in tonight."

"Mikey's right," I said. "I need to get home, too. We can check things out tomorrow."

"All right," Peter said, though he seemed uncertain.

"Who's there?" someone called and we all jumped. A man walked toward us through the underpass, his legs spaced wide apart, his hands loose at his sides. "Let's see you."

Michael jumped out from beneath the tunnel and joined us on the grass.

"Let's see all of you." The man raised one hand and made a come hither gesture. When he stepped out from beneath the underpass, we could see he was a uniformed police officer. "What are you kids doing down here?"

"We're just hanging out," Michael said. Then, as conversational as you please, he added, "What's up, dude?"

Looking right past Michael, the cop pointed at the walkie-talkie on Peter's belt. "What do you got, son?"

Peter glanced down at the handheld. "Uh, a walkie-talkie, sir."

"You boys vandalizing anything?"

"No, sir."

"Got any spray paint? Anything like that?"

"No, sir," Peter repeated.

The cop jerked a thumb over his shoulder but kept his eyes on us. "That backpack belong to one of you?"

"It's mine," Scott said.

"School's out," the cop said, as if he'd caught us in a lie. He had a tired, creased face with cold eyes beneath heavy lids.

"It's for scavenger hunting," Michael piped up. "We're looking for treasure."

"Yeah?" the cop said. "Find anything?"

Michael frowned at the irony of it. "No, sir. Not a thing."

"You kids shouldn't be down here, especially after dark. You know you're supposed to stay away from enclosed places like this, don't you?" He outlined the opening of the underpass with one finger, in case we were ignorant about what "enclosed places" meant.

"Yes, sir," I vocalized from the back of my crew. "We're sorry, sir."

"You boys should know better."

"Yes, sir."

"You're Sal Mazzone's boy, ain't you?"

I swallowed a lump of spit that felt like a walnut. "Yes, sir."

"I know *you* know better than to play down here."

"Yes, sir. I'm sorry, sir."

"Don't be sorry. Just skedaddle. I won't tell your pops."

"Thanks."

The cop glanced at Scott's and Michael's bikes leaning against the wall of the underpass. "Then get on home."

Scott and Michael got their bikes out and joined Peter and me in the grass.

"Do me a favor and don't cut across the park." The cop pointed up the embankment toward Solomon's Bend Road. "It's getting too dark. Stick to the roadways."

The four of us rolled our bikes across Solomon's Field. Still standing at the mouth of the underpass, the cop watched us go.

When we hit Solomon's Bend Road, Michael said, "That guy came out of nowhere. Gives me the creeps."

It was true that it had been creepy, but we had gotten used to the presence of law enforcement all over town this past year. Sadly, it had become commonplace.

As we walked our bikes, Peter and I told them how we had run into Mr. Mattingly outside the Werewolf House.

"He scared the shit out of us even worse than that cop," Peter said. "I still don't understand what he was doing all the way out there."

"He was going after his dog," I said, though I didn't think I was completely convinced of this, either.

"Mr. Mattingly at the Werewolf House and some strange guy going through our stuff in the woods," Scott mused. "It can't just be a coincidence."

We all looked at him.

"One of them must be the Piper," he explained.

"Where's the logic in that?" Peter asked. "I'm not saying you're wrong. I just don't know how you made that connection."

"We've been going to all the places the Piper goes," Scott said. "The Dead Woods, where the Cole girl's body was found. The Werewolf House where that fence post thing came from. Not to mention the statue head. Maybe it was only a matter of time before we crossed paths with him. Which was sort of the point of this whole thing, right? To figure out who the killer is?"

Michael cleared his throat and said, "I think you guys are just trying to scare the shit out of each other."

"I'm not scared," Scott said.

"Yeah? Well, then you're scaring the shit out of me. Cut it out. I don't like talking about the Piper once it starts getting dark."

When we reached the intersection of Point and Counterpoint, we waited for a break in traffic before pushing our bikes across. Behind the Superstore plaza, we climbed on our bikes.

Scott said, "What if the Piper had nothing to do with Adrian's disappearance? What if his whacko mother actually did something to him? That would explain why his mom hasn't reported him missing. Right?"

We all looked at him for a long time. Doreen Gardiner was certainly strange, but was she capable of that? I couldn't fathom it.

Could you fathom someone's father poisoning himself in the family car? a voice spoke up in my head. *And what about that hideous scar on her neck? What awful things have happened to Doreen Gardiner? Were they things that could have warped her mind so terribly, so completely, that she would do something unthinkable to her own son?*

"Okay, enough of this," I said. "I'm going over there tomorrow and asking Adrian's mom where he is."

They nodded, the relief evident on their faces. It was as though they had been waiting for me to make this suggestion all week.

CHAPTER TWENTY
WHERE ADRIAN WENT

As it turned out, there would be no need for me to confront Doreen Gardiner.

That night, while clearing the table after dinner, I saw through the kitchen window the Gardiners' car pull into their driveway. Doreen Gardiner got out and skulked to the porch. Then the passenger door opened and Adrian climbed out.

At the sight of him, I was momentarily overcome by disbelief. I went to the window and watched his small fragile-looking silhouette follow his mother into the house. It wasn't until the Gardiners' front door closed and lights came on in the windows that I felt myself relax. I expelled a shaky breath against the windowpane.

My dad and grandparents were sitting on the back deck with some of my grandfather's friends, drinking wine and telling war stories.

I poked my head out and said I was running next door for a minute. "Adrian came back," I finished.

"Right next door," said my dad. "No place else."

I agreed, then ran through the house and out the front. As I crossed the lawn, I saw lights come on at the back of the Gardiner house. Someone was in the kitchen. Adrian's silhouette appeared in the window. I felt that he was looking right at me. Then the curtain swished back into place, and my friend's silhouette moved away.

The Gardiners' backyard was overgrown and buggy. Clay flowerpots were scattered about a concrete slab in front of the back doors, and a hollowed bamboo wind chime hanging from the eaves clinked in the wind. A garden hose lay unspooled in the grass like a cobra.

I went up to the porch doors and knocked lightly. The blinds had been swept to one side, and I could see the whole kitchen—the dishes stacked on the counter, the pots in ranks and towers on chairs, unopened cardboard boxes under the table. Something went *zzzt-zzzt* in the bushes nearby. I was about to knock again when Adrian came to the door in a bathrobe and fuzzy slippers that looked like bear feet, claws and all. He popped the lock on the door and whooshed it open.

"Hey," he said, the word coming out slow and disinterested. It was as if we'd just hung out yesterday.

"Where the hell have you been?" I blurted.

He stepped aside and waved me into the house. "Come on in."

I entered, surprised that after all these months the air still smelled stale and there were unpacked boxes shoved against the walls in the adjoining hallway.

"Where've you been?" I said again. "Me and the guys have been trying to get in touch with you all week. We thought something bad might've happened. We went looking for you."

Adrian leaned forward on the balls of his feet and peered through the doorway and down the hall. "Come on upstairs," he said in a low voice, and I followed him down the hall and into the foyer.

"Adrian?" It was Doreen Gardiner's voice, funneling down the stairwell. It cracked on each syllable and sounded like the noise a large bird might make when agitated. "What are you doing?"

"I have a friend over, Mom," he called. We were at the bottom of the stairs now. I paused but he proceeded up them.

Doreen Gardiner appeared at the top of the stairs in a bathrobe. Her hair looked like a bird's nest that had been struck by lightning, and her eyes were outlined in purplish circles. Her mouth was nearly lipless, a firm and blood-less gash bisecting the lower half of her face. "What friend is this?"

Adrian paused midway up the stairs. I was behind him but still standing in the foyer. "It's Angelo from next door."

"Who?"

"Angelo Mazzone," he repeated. "From next door."

She seemed to waver, and for one horrifying moment, I was certain she would take a header and topple down the stairs. "Shoes," she said.

"We're not—"

"Shoes, Adrian."

I realized she was staring at me. I was, after all, the only one wearing shoes.

Adrian turned and brushed by me on his way to the foyer. "Come on," he said, kicking off his bear slippers in what could only be an exercise of solidar-ity. "Take your shoes off."

"Sure." I climbed out of my sneakers and left them by the front door next to his slippers. My hackles rising, I followed him up the stairs.

His mother was still there watching us, leaning against the wall with her arms crossed over her chest like she had something to be pissed off about. Her robe was open enough at the top so that the puckered pink scar that circumnavigated her neck was all too visible. When we shrugged past her I caught a whiff of stale cigarette smoke and unwashed flesh. She eyed me distrustfully. I braced myself for one of her claws to reach out and clutch at me. Blessedly, nothing happened.

Adrian led me to his bedroom and shut the door behind us. It was the first time I'd been in his room. There was a mattress on the floor, moving boxes bursting with clothes shoved against one wall, his Incredible Hulk backpack tucked in one corner, and several stacks of comic books arranged in a hopscotch grid around the grimy carpet. There were more comic books tacked to the walls in protective Mylar sleeves, the characters on the covers completely alien to me. Some of the comics looked very old, and they were probably worth some money. Holes had been punched in the drywall, and the light switch hung from wires like an eyeball dangling from a socket. The smell— Christ, it was like a locker room.

"Is your mom okay?" I asked, marveling over the warped rationale of having to take my shoes off in order to stand on a stained carpet crusted with dried bits of food.

Adrian dropped to his knees and sifted through a mound of smelly clothing. "Yeah, why?"

"No reason." I faced him. "Where have you been all week?"

He pulled a three-ring binder out from beneath the clothes, then sat on the mattress. "I want to show you something."

I dropped down beside him on the mattress.

"Promise you won't laugh."

I touched my nose. "I promise."

He raised his eyebrows. "Why do you touch your nose like that when you promise?"

"It's just something stupid me and the guys used to do when we were kids. But don't worry, I promise. I won't laugh."

Adrian opened the binder. The first page was a detailed drawing of five superheroes, slightly foreshortened as they flew straight out of the center of the page. They wore elaborate costumes with twirling capes and masks that tied around their eyes, like the kinds the Ninja Turtles wore. The detail was remarkable, and their expressions were not only realistic but identifiable.

"Wow. Is this us?"

"Yeah," he said. "All five of us. It's the cover page. I haven't thought of a title yet."

"A title for what?"

"The comic." He flipped to the next page. It was divided into a series of square panels in which the superheroes posed in a variety of heroic positions. "I'm drawing a comic book about us."

"Holy shit." I slid the binder from Adrian's lap and pulled it in front of me. "These are incredible. How'd you. . . ? I mean, how the heck. . . ?" I didn't have the words. Adrian Gardiner had rendered me speechless. "This is really great, man."

"Thanks. I can draw, but I don't really know how to write a story for it. I was wondering . . . maybe you would want to work on it with me?"

"Really? Yeah, that would be great." I looked at him. "Why would you think I'd make fun of you for this?"

"I don't know." Adrian raised one small shoulder, then took the binder back from me, shut it, and slid it beneath the heap of clothes on his mattress.

"Is that where you were all week? At art school or something?"

"No."

"Well, then where'd you go?"

"I had to talk to some people." He got up, went to a stack of comic books, and selected one from the top. He dropped back down on the mattress and flipped through the pages.

"What people?"

"Just some people."

"Was it cops?" I said. "Did you tell them about what we found, what we've been doing?"

"Heck, no," Adrian said, glaring at me. "I'm not stupid, you know."

"So who was it?"

"Just some doctors."

"For a whole week?"

"They're specialists."

"For what? Is everything okay?"

"Yeah, I'm fine. My mom just gets weird about stuff. They're not real doctors, anyway. They're, like, psychiatrists and stuff."

"Like that lady they brought into school to talk to kids about what's been going on in town?"

"Sort of like that. But it has nothing to do with the Piper. This was about my dad."

"Oh."

"My mom gets all freaked out and wants to make sure I'm not upset about it or anything."

"About his . . . his suicide, you mean," I said.

"Yeah."

"Are you?" The words were out of my mouth before I knew what I was doing.

"Not really. Not anymore." He put the comic book down. "Do you want to see some pictures of him?"

"I guess so. If you want to show me."

Adrian rolled off the mattress and dug through one of the cardboard boxes shoved against the wall, pulling out random items and dropping them to the floor until he found a small scrapbook with a dark blue vinyl cover. He brought it over to the mattress and sat down beside me again.

"Here," he said, opening the scrapbook. There were photos pasted to the pages, and I could tell by the clothing and the hairstyles that even the most recent were at least a decade old. Adrian pointed to one photo of a smiling man with a dark moustache and kind eyes who held a toddler on his lap. "That's my dad. And that's me."

What struck me was that Adrian's father looked like a regular guy. In my head, I had made him out to be a lunatic, a social outcast who had taken a zombie for his wife, then ended his life by sucking on poisonous fumes in the family car. Yet the man in the photos could have been a baseball coach, a high school guidance counselor, a scoutmaster.

There were photos of Adrian's mother, too. She was a different woman in these photos—prettier, more alert. Absent were the dead eyes, the frazzled hair, the parchment-colored flesh.

We were only a few pages in when a shadow appeared beneath Adrian's bedroom door. Adrian noticed it, too. A floorboard creaked.

Adrian closed the scrapbook, got up, and stuffed it back into the box. When he turned around to face me, he said, "Wanna read some comics for a while?"

CHAPTER TWENTY-ONE
COURTING A KILLER

The next day was Saturday, and Michael had no summer school, so the five of us convened at the Quickman around noon. When Michael arrived and saw Adrian, he raced up to the smaller boy and enveloped him in a bear hug that lifted him clear off the floor. Adrian laughed.

"We thought you were dead, Poindexter," Michael said, once we were all seated at a window booth. We had ordered nothing but Cokes, which we now sipped at our leisure. "We were really starting to think the Piper got you."

"Where the heck have you been?" Scott asked.

I wondered how Adrian would tell it since, to the best of my knowledge, he had never spoken of his father to the guys.

"My mom sent me to a hospital, so some doctors could talk to me, ask me questions," he said.

"Doctors?" Peter said.

"My mom overreacts. After my dad died, she had me talk to doctors all the time. Now it's just every once in a while, whenever she thinks I need to talk to someone."

"You can talk to us about stuff, too," Scott said.

"Thanks," Adrian said. "But I'm not really upset about anything anymore."

It was the *anymore* I thought my friends would key in on. But if they did, they didn't ask him about it. Part of me was grateful while another part of me felt uncomfortable being the only one who knew what happened to Adrian's father.

"We gotta tell you about yesterday," Michael said and proceeded to describe the man he and Scott had come across in the woods, going through our stuff.

When he finished, Peter took over and explained how we had gone to the Werewolf House looking for him and had run into Mr. Mattingly.

Adrian looked at me. "Our English teacher? What was *he* doing out there?"

"Walking his dog," I said.

"Did he recognize you?"

"Of course."

"He's been on the suspect list from the beginning," Michael reminded us.

My apprehension and suspicion about running into Mr. Mattingly yesterday afternoon had worn off. "Mr. Mattingly's not the Piper," I said.

"How do you know?" Michael said. "We can't rule anyone out. And it's pretty fuckin' strange that he was hanging around that old house."

"So were Keener and his friends, remember?"

"Keener could be the Piper," Michael offered.

Peter tossed a balled-up napkin at him. "You think everyone's the Piper."

Michael shrugged. "Maybe everyone is. Maybe we're the only five people in the whole city who aren't responsible for the deaths of all those kids." Then his eyes narrowed. "Except you, Mazzone. If I had to guess, I'd say you're in on it, too."

I jerked a thumb at Scott. "He's the morbid obsessive, remember?"

Michael rubbed his chin, his gaze shifting to Scott. "Hmmm . . ."

"We need to go to Echo Base and see why that guy was snooping around," Scott said.

"I'm gonna be pissed if he stole our stuff," Michael said.

"It's mostly garbage we found in the woods," Peter said. "Why would someone want to steal it?"

Our waitress swaggered over to our booth, planted both hands flat on the table, and glared at us. "Okay, here's the deal. You little fuckers always sit here and order sodas or share a plate of fries, then stiff me on the tip. Order some real food and pay for the goddamn service, or go haunt another dive. You get me?"

Her brazenness shocked us all into temporary silence.

"I've got . . . uh . . ." Michael fished around in his pocket. He tossed a few coins, a plastic army man, and a button that said Eat Bertha's Mussels on the table.

"Here," Peter said, rolling a half-eaten package of Life Savers onto the table.

"Oh, wait." Scott beamed. From one pocket he produced a mix tape that was covered in stickers, and from his other pocket he took out a few Pogs.

The waitress's expression did not falter.

I pulled ten dollars out of my pocket and slid it over to her.

She eyeballed it like it was a trap, then shot her cool glance in my direction.

"It's all I got," I told her.

"Brilliant," she said flatly, scooping up the ten-spot as well as the Life Savers before sauntering away.

Michael examined the army man and the button. "I don't think these are my pants," he said after a minute.

When we arrived at Echo Base, we were surprised to find that our stuff was pretty much how we left it. We checked the trash bags and the nylon beer cooler to see if anything was missing, but it didn't appear as if anything was.

Scott walked around the clearing, searching for footprints. But the ground was overgrown with bushes, weeds, and ivy, making it impossible to locate a single footprint in the dirt. Defeated, he gave up after only ten minutes.

"Maybe it was just some guy out for a walk through the woods who happened to stumble on this stuff," Peter said. He sat down on the concrete statue head and rocked back and forth on it.

"No, man," Scott said. "A guy just out for a walk wouldn't start opening up muddy trash bags, would he? It was like he was looking for something."

"But nothing's missing," I said. "What would he be looking for?"

"This," Adrian said. He pulled taut the length of shoelace he wore around his neck. Courtney Cole's heart-shaped locket twinkled in the sunlight.

"But how would he know we had it?" Peter asked.

"Because he's been following us," Adrian said. "How else would he know we've been hanging around down here?"

"You're just trying to give me the heebie-jeebies," Michael said.

I looked around, wondering if there might in fact be someone secreted away beyond the depths of trees. A person could hide anywhere. My grandfather's voice spoke up in my head, talking about shooting snipers down from trees during the war. Unnerved, I glanced up at the treetops.

"It makes sense," Scott said, nodding. "If we've been doing this right, then we've been visiting all the places the Piper would have gone, too."

"And there was that day Angie and I were at the Werewolf House," Adrian said. "Remember those footsteps that came halfway down the stairs?"

"Yeah," I said, certain I knew where he was going with this. Because I had already said it to Peter yesterday . . .

"What if it wasn't that bully after all?" Adrian said.

"Keener," I said.

"Yeah. What if it wasn't him? What if that was the Piper instead?"

"Man," Michael said, turning toward me with an oddly forlorn expression. "Your English teacher is a homicidal child killer. Bummer. Personally, I was holding out hope it was Principal Unglesbee."

"It's not Mr. Mattingly," I said. "He's got a wife."

"Serial killers can't have wives?" Michael said. "They can't be married? Is that some rule or something?"

"John Wayne Gacy had two wives," Scott said.

Michael frowned. "At the same time?"

"No, dummy," Scott said. "And Ted Bundy had a serious girlfriend."

"Quit making shit up," Michael scolded him.

"It's not Mr. Mattingly," I said again, ignoring them.

"He *was* at the Werewolf House yesterday," Peter added, though skeptically.

"Yeah, but he wasn't the guy who was down here going through our stuff. So which one is it? They can't both be the Piper."

"What if they are?" Adrian said. He tucked the locket inside his shirt. "Who's to say the Piper can't be two people?"

"Two crazy child killers who happen to be terrorizing the same city at the same exact time?" Peter said, wrinkling his nose. "That sounds highly unlikely."

"It would be too much of a coincidence," I added.

"Unless it's not a coincidence at all," Scott said, already buying into Adrian's theory.

Michael said, "What do you mean?"

"Like, what if they're working together?" Scott said. "We've got a guy down here checking out our stuff and Mr. Mattingly hanging around the Werewolf House. They could *both* be the Piper."

Peter made a sour face that suggested he didn't believe it was possible. I silently agreed with him.

"So what do we do about all this?" Michael sat on the ground and crossed one ankle over the other.

"I don't know," Adrian said.

"We could go knock on the English teacher's door, tell him we know who he is and what he's been doing," Michael said.

"Yeah," Peter groaned, "that's brilliant."

"Wait a minute," Scott said, his eyes brightening. "That's not such a bad idea."

At Scott's house, we put the plan into action. Among the junk that Scott's aunt had salted away in the Steeples' basement were countless magazines, everything from *National Geographic* and *Newsweek* to more obscure periodicals with tattooed men and marijuana leaves on the covers. We flipped through them, cutting out letters from the pages, which we then glued to a sheet of typing paper.

Once we finished, we had something that looked like a ransom note from a movie.

WE *know* who YOU are & what *you* HAVE done

Wearing a pair of rubber dishwashing gloves, Scott folded the letter and tucked it inside a plain white envelope. He wet a sponge at the kitchen sink, then daubed the glue strip with it to seal the envelope. With more than just a hint of pride, he grinned at us, claiming to have seen it in an old black-and-white movie. Probably Hitchcock.

"What the hell are you dweebs doing?" Kristy, Scott's older sister, stood in the doorway. She was twenty and home from college for the summer. She wore black leggings and a satin blousy thing that clung to the contours of her breasts. She was attractive in a dark and devious way—what some people might misconstrue as slutty—and, like her brother, was unpredictably intelligent.

Her voice startled the five of us. We were seated around the table like conspirators. Scott yanked the envelope off the table and hid it in his lap.

"Seriously," she said, snapping gum. "What are you bozos up to?"

"None of your business," Scott shot back. "Get lost."

"You can't bullshit me. You're up to something." She looked around the table. "You," she said to Adrian. "I don't know you. What's your name?"

"Adrian."

"You part of this sordid cabal now?"

Adrian said, "What?"

"Never mind."

Scott scowled at his sister. "Don't you have some pituitary case you should be humping in the back of a car somewhere?"

"You're fucking puerile."

"Hey, Kristy," Michael said. "Show us your tits."

"You'd have a heart attack, you spaz." She went to the fridge, grabbed a can of Diet Coke, then stalked out of the kitchen.

"She's your sister?" Adrian said. He remained staring at the doorway, as if in anticipation—or hope—that Kristy would return for an encore performance.

"Unfortunately," Scott grumbled.

"Aw," Peter cooed. "Our little buddy's got a crush."

Adrian blushed. "I do not."

"You're right," Michael jumped in. "He does. Look—he's turning red as a tomato."

"They grow up so fast," I said, adding my two cents.

"I don't," Adrian insisted. "I don't have a crush. No way."

"Cut it out, guys. You're making me sick," Scott said, placing the envelope back on the table.

Our plan was rudimentary at best. Nonetheless, Adrian, Scott, and Michael were all completely on board. Peter thought we were wasting our time. I had a deeper resignation—namely, that if we got caught perpetrating this foolishness, I could never look Mr. Mattingly in the face again. And I had been kicked out of one English class already.

None of us knew exactly where Mr. Mattingly lived, so Scott retrieved the most recent Harting Farms phone book from the pantry. However, there was no Mattingly listed.

Scott went into his father's study and returned with a pamphlet supplement to the phone book, which some of the neighborhoods released midyear to keep the comings and goings updated. Scott flipped through the pages. "Here it is. David and Tina Mattingly, 1597 Beauchamp Drive, Parliament Village. It says they moved into town on August 5."

"When did William Demorest disappear?" Peter asked.

"It was the end of August. I don't remember the exact date."

Peter moved his lips as if he were chewing something.

"Okay, we got the address. Let's do it already," Michael whined.

We all got on our bikes—Adrian on my handlebars—and rode out to the section of town designated as Parliament Village. It was a nice June day, the heat index slowly creeping toward ninety. Kids zipped up and down the streets on bikes. On Beauchamp Drive, four young girls sat on someone's front lawn around a circular wooden table having a tea party. Amidst all this summertime normalcy, it was almost possible to believe that the Piper was nothing more than a figment of a paranoid town's imagination.

We slowed down as the numbers on the houses grew closer and closer to 1597.

"There it is." Peter executed a casual arc in front of the driveway, then headed back down the street.

The rest of us followed suit and came to a stop a few blocks away.

"So how do we do this?" I asked. This neighborhood had very few nooks and crannies to hide in. I felt like we were overly conspicuous just being on the street corner.

"We do it like ding-dong ditch," Michael said, "only we leave the letter behind."

"Who goes?" Peter asked.

"Scott, you're the fastest," I said. "You can knock and run away quicker than any of us."

He nodded.

"What about the rest of us?" Adrian asked. He had dropped off my handlebars and was now sitting on the curb. "We need to hide, but we should be someplace where we can watch what happens."

We all looked around.

Peter pointed at a high fence between two houses across the street. "We can hide behind the fence."

"Yeah, okay," Adrian said. He turned to Scott. "Do you think you can knock and make it all the way back here before Mr. Mattingly opens the door?"

Scott looked at the fence, then the Mattingly house, gauging the distance. Scott had never been part of an organized sports team in his life, though pretty much every coach at school was after him to go out for their respective teams. "I think I could do it," he said finally.

"Just be careful," I told him.

We wheeled our bikes across the street and down the narrow strip of lawn that ran between the fence and a two-story Victorian with puke-green aluminum siding.

Scott came with us, holding the sealed envelope. He kept glancing over his shoulder, perhaps trying to convince himself that he could make the run without getting caught.

"You gotta wedge the envelope in the doorframe," Peter told him. "This way, when he opens the door, it'll fall at his feet."

Scott bent one knee and held his sneakered foot against his butt for a few seconds. He repeated this stretch with the other leg. When he finished, he took a deep breath, and both Michael and Adrian clapped him on the back.

"I'll be back in thirty seconds," Scott said, then he was off.

He jogged up the block toward the Mattingly house, a two-story A-frame with sky-blue siding and charcoal shutters flanking the dormer windows on the second floor. In the driveway was a maroon Subaru with a Stanton School bumper sticker that read Go Cows! in navy-blue lettering on a gold background.

Scott leaped up the porch steps in one long-legged stride. He tucked the envelope between the door and the frame, then banged the brass doorknocker against the door three times. The sound echoed down the street. Scott turned, jumped off the porch, and sprinted in our direction.

We watched through slats in the fence. Somewhere a dog barked.

Come on, come on, come on, I willed Scott.

"Come on, come on," Michael whispered. It was as if he were narrating my thoughts.

Scott hopped the curb, dashed across the lawn, and joined us behind the fence a mere second before the Mattinglys' front door opened.

A slim woman with blondish hair piled high on her head came out. When the envelope fluttered to her feet, she stared at it without moving. Then she picked it up and examined both sides of the blank envelope. She looked up and down Beauchamp Drive. For a second, I thought she stared straight at me, capable of locking onto my eyes despite the distance and the fence between us. Then she retreated into the house and shut the door. The brass doorknocker jumped.

"That must be his wife," Adrian said.

I turned to Scott, who was bent over with his hands on his knees. He was breathing heavily, but when he saw me looking, he gave me a calm and confident smile.

"What do we do now?" Peter asked.

"We wait and see how Mr. Mattingly reacts," Adrian said, pushing his glasses up his nose.

"What if his wife just throws the letter out without showing it to him?" Michael asked.

Adrian looked at him. "Would you?"

The five of us sat behind that fence for over an hour, watching Mr. Mattingly's front door. We expected anything to happen at any minute—Mr. Mattingly to burst out of the house clutching the letter, climb into his Subaru, and peel out into the street while leaving streaks of rubber on the driveway. But that didn't happen. No one came out of the Mattingly house.

When a face appeared in an open window of the puke-green house beside us and someone said, "Hey, you kids," we all got up, gathered our bikes, and took off. As I biked, balancing Adrian on my handlebars, I glanced over my shoulder at the Mattingly house one last time. There was nothing to see there.

Because Michael had to go back to summer school on Monday, we let him pick what we would do for the rest of the afternoon. He elected to catch *The Killer Shrews* at the Juniper. Even though the titular shrews were actually mangy-looking dogs donning ridiculous oversized teeth and strands of fake hair woven into their fur, we all laughed and had a great time. For the time being, we forgot about Mr. Mattingly and the Piper, content to lose ourselves in the nicotine-soaked upholstery of the theater seats, the patches of molasses on the floors, and the indiscriminate scatter of popcorn that stuck to the soles of our Adidas. When the protagonists attempted to escape the killer shrews by lugging around old oil barrels on their heads, we shouted and tossed Jujubes at the screen.

It was dusk when the movie ended. We biked back home, going our separate ways once we crossed the Superstore plaza. I was exhausted from riding Adrian all over the city, and the two of us walked my bike the rest of the way. We talked excitedly about the movie. Then we talked about what kind of story line I could come up with for the superhero comic book he was drawing.

"It should be something like the Fantastic Four," he said. Then added, "Only, you know, with five of us."

"The Fantastic Four," I said. "That's like with Iron Man and the Incredible Hulk and all those guys, right?"

Adrian gaped at me. "Are you kidding? No way! You're thinking of the Avengers."

"Oh."

"But we can be like the Avengers, too. I can lend you some comics so you can see how the stories go."

We hadn't talked about the Piper for the entire walk home, and it was refreshing. After all, it was summer vacation. It was a time for running wild in the parks and racing bikes in the streets. It was a time for jumping off the docks at the Shallows and swimming out to the barges. It was a time for losing yourself in the air-conditioned darkness of the Juniper Theater, watching public domain horror movies and shouting at the actors on the screen.

"Do you think I could spend the night at your place?" Adrian asked when we approached his driveway.

"I guess so," I said.

"Thanks. My mom's been in one of her moods lately. She's been staying home from work, sitting around the house in her robe, drinking."

"Do you need to get some stuff from your house?"

Adrian looked at his house, contemplation etched on his otherwise expressionless face. "I'd rather not."

"I think we've got a spare toothbrush you could borrow."

He wrinkled his nose. "Ew. *Borrow*?"

"I mean, you can keep it," I said and slugged him playfully on the forearm.

Inside, the TV was on in the den and the smell of my grandfather's pipe wafted through the open porch windows. My grandmother greeted us in the hallway, a cup of steaming coffee in her hand. "Well, you two look like you've been through the wringer. What have you been up to all day?"

"Not much," I said, catching Adrian's sidelong glance in my direction. For whatever reason, I felt very close to bursting out in a gale of laughter. "Can Adrian stay over?"

"I don't see why not. Should I heat up some food? There are plenty of leftovers. Your father ate nothing."

"Sounds great," I said.

Adrian nodded vehemently, a keen hunger in his eyes.

My grandmother reheated a dinner of veal cutlets and peppers for us, then went upstairs to get clean sheets for my bed.

As we ate, my grandfather came in, paused in midstride as he saw Adrian shoveling a second helping of peppers onto his plate, then said, "Are we adopting neighborhood children now?"

"Hi, Mr. Mazzone," Adrian said.

"Hi, Grandpa," I said.

"I hope you two are aware that you're eating my lunch for tomorrow."

"Where's Dad?" I asked.

"He had to drive to Baltimore for work."

"Why Baltimore?"

"Do I look like the chief of police?" my grandfather said, then ambled out of the room.

After dinner, we played Uno at the kitchen table for an hour or so. We talked about ideas for Adrian's comic book while we played, but what I really wanted to know was what was going on with Adrian's mom.

"I'm sort of writing a story about us already," I said, laying down a Draw Four card. "Maybe we can work it around your comic book drawings."

"What do you mean?"

I set my cards down. "Come on. I'll show you."

We went past the living room where my grandparents exchanged snores from dueling recliners, then up the stairs to my bedroom. This was the first time he had been in my room.

Adrian looked around in awe. "Do you know how to play that?" he asked, pointing at my acoustic guitar.

"Sure." I picked it up, sat on the edge of the bed, took a second to tune it, and then strummed the first few bars of "Glory Days."

"Wow." He actually leaned forward, staring at my fingers splayed across the frets. "I didn't know you could play the guitar."

"It's not hard. I can teach you."

"Really?"

"Sure. Watch." I strummed a G-C-D progression, calling out the chords as I hit them.

"That sounds familiar," he said.

"It's just like every single song ever written. Do you see how I move my fingers?"

"Yeah, but I couldn't do something like that."

"Of course you could. It's not hard. I taught Michael."

Adrian sat on the bed beside me. I slid the guitar into his lap, and it suddenly looked like an oversized novelty instrument. I reached over and finagled Adrian's fingers onto the strings so they approximated the fingering for G major.

"That's a G chord," I said, handing him the pick.

"What's this?" he said, pinching the pick awkwardly between two fingers and holding it up to his face.

"It's to help you strum. Go ahead. Try it."

He dragged the pick down through the strings. Some of them made stunted plunks while others rang out sourly.

"That doesn't sound like what you did," he said equally as sour.

"It just takes practice." I got off the bed and went to my desk. As I gathered up the typed manuscript pages of my story that was slowly expanding into novel territory, Adrian continued down-strumming the guitar. "Yeah, you're getting it."

"What's that?" he said as I set the manuscript down on the bed beside him.

"It's the story I'm writing."

"You wrote this? Like . . . you made it up?"

"Yeah."

He set the guitar aside. "It's like a hundred pages. I thought you just wrote short stories and stuff for the school magazine." He flipped through the first few pages. "What's it about?"

"Well, it's sort of about what we've been doing all year. You know, going after the Piper. Only in the story, I call him the Chesapeake Bay Butcher. He hacks people up with a machete, like Jason Voorhees."

"Neat."

"I thought maybe we can use this story idea for your comic book."

"Comic books don't have this many words."

"Well, maybe we can do a bunch of comic books. Like a whole series of them."

"Or maybe I can draw pictures for your story," Adrian said. "I could read it and draw scenes from what you wrote."

"You could do that?" But I had already seen what he could do, and I knew it would be easy for him.

"Yeah, it would be fun."

"Does your mom get like this a lot?" I'd asked the question before I realized what I was doing.

"She used to do it a lot after my dad killed himself. Now it's only every once in a while. Sometimes I lock myself in my bedroom, but last time she broke the lock on the door." His tone sounded so easy and casual and collected that he could have been discussing box scores or the plot to the latest comic book he'd just read.

"Does she . . . like . . . hit you?" I said, trying hard to sound equally as collected. I wasn't sure I pulled it off.

"Not really. Like, not on purpose. Sometimes she throws stuff and I get in the way, but that's about it. Mostly, she just wants to hug me until she cries and falls asleep. It usually doesn't bother me, but I didn't feel like dealing with it tonight." He hoisted his small shoulders and stared at the manuscript in his lap. "I guess I feel bad for her."

I flopped down on my bed.

Adrian stood and put the manuscript on my desk. Then he picked up the guitar and looked at the way the strings were wound into the tuners, as if to divine some secret into how the instrument might be conquered.

"You can stay more than one night, if you want," I told him. "Like, if you need to."

"Thanks. But just tonight should be fine. She'll be okay by tomorrow." He propped the guitar against the wall.

"Come on," I said, rolling off the bed. "I'll get you some clean clothes and show you where the shower is."

We stayed awake for hours that night, side by side in my small bed, telling ghost stories and hypothesizing about the Piper. The more we talked about the Piper, the less he seemed like Mr. Mattingly. The less he seemed to be real at all. And in that cold, black witching hour, it was almost possible to convince ourselves that we had made him up and that he was no different than the bogeymen we saw on the big screen at the Juniper Theater.

I fell asleep with images of the Piper's unknown face flashing through my subconscious while in real life the Piper was taking his next victim.

CHAPTER TWENTY-TWO
THE BRUBAKER GIRL

The circumstances surrounding the disappearance of Tori Brubaker echoed those of William Demorest and Jeffrey Connor in that she wasn't known to have gone missing until nearly a full day later.

This was because fifteen-year-old Tori had lied to her parents about spending the night at her friend Madeline Probst's house. In reality, she had planned on spending the evening with her seventeen-year-old boyfriend, Zach Garrison, because his folks were out of town. But Zach and Tori got into an argument, and Tori walked home along the banks of the Magothy River at some point in the night. What happened after that has been left to speculation.

Police were dispatched. Zach's parents were contacted and hurried home, cutting their vacation short, so they could be present when the police questioned Zach. In the meantime, the surrounding woods and the banks of the river were searched. One of Tori Brubaker's slip-on shoes was discovered in the mud along the river. Fears mounted.

Detectives questioned Zach Garrison over and over again (and I believe my father questioned him, too). Ultimately, he was released into the custody of his petrified parents. There was videotape of Zach coming out of the police station with his head down, his parents hurrying him down the sidewalk toward the family car.

Interim Chief of Police Michael Solano gave a press conference at the Cape while divers dredged the marrow-colored waters of the Magothy and the Shallows. Though it was a horrifying sight, no one actually believed that Tori Brubaker had drowned.

"Tori Brubaker was last seen walking through the woods toward the river, presumably toward home." Solano was dark and tight jawed and looked somewhat cunning in his dark suit, unlike his predecessor, Barber, who was a nervous-looking individual possessing the ruddy, gin-blossomed complexion of a career alcoholic. "While nothing has been ruled out at this point, we are certainly aware of the concerns of this community, and we will close no doors on any possible leads until they have been exhausted to my personal satisfaction."

For a moment, my father was visible in the background of the televised broadcast, a slender, dark-suited man speaking with one of the uniformed police officers on the beach.

Tori Brubaker's body was not recovered. Her name was added to the list of missing children, and her parents were seen on TV begging futilely for the safe return of their beloved daughter. It was terribly reminiscent of Rebecca Ransom's televised pleas.

Speculation abounded throughout the media. What had caused the brief respite in abductions only to have them start up again, with the Holt boy and the Brubaker girl vanishing within two weeks of each other?

Like some great forest beastie, I imagined the Piper hibernating throughout the long, cold winter, tucked away in an underground burrow far below the panicked streets of my hometown, gnawing on the bones of Aaron Ransom, Bethany Frost, and the rest. Other suppositions were more practical: Scott suggested that perhaps the Piper didn't want to leave footprints behind in the snow. Regardless of the reason, the Piper hadn't moved on. He had been hiding among us all along.

Two days later, a torrential downpour kept us holed up like prisoners in our homes. The storm had also made things difficult for those involved in the search for Brubaker, and there was concern that if the girl had drowned, it was possible the storm had washed her body out to the bay by now. Regardless, her body was not recovered from the river, and the search ultimately made its way out into the open gray waters of the Chesapeake Bay.

Adrian had gotten roped into doing some chores for his mom, Michael was still in summer school, and Scott was held hostage on a family outing, so it was just Peter and me that afternoon in the woods, chucking rocks into the flooded creek and smoking cigarettes. The dynamo-powered radio was wedged into the V of a maple tree, and the sounds of Springsteen singing "No Surrender" made us both feel like we were wrapped in some invisible blanket of comfort.

"You think a person could actually die from fear?" he asked, staring into the woods and watching the rainwater drip off the sagging green leaves. "Like, have a heart attack or whack themselves out because they're so scared of something?"

"I don't know. I guess maybe it's possible."

"You used to get letters from Charles when he was overseas, right?"

"Yeah." It was weird hearing him bring up Charles. I couldn't remember my brother coming up in a conversation among my friends since the funeral.

"He ever mention being scared?"

"No. He mostly talked about the people in his squad or platoon or whatever you call it and the people from the villages they went to."

"Oh." Peter sounded disappointed.

"Also, he talked about home a lot. He kept telling me not to grow up too fast like he did, even though that's all Dad ever seemed to want me to do. He kept saying he wished he could stay young forever, but he never realized that was his wish until he was too old and it was too late."

I could tell by his silence that he wanted to ask me more questions about Charles but didn't know how. I allowed him the silence because I didn't like to talk too much about Charles, either.

After a long while, Peter said, "My sister's scared."

"About what happened to Tori Brubaker?"

"About all of it. She went to Cape Middle School with Howie Holt, and she's friends with Tori's sister. She was crying last night. I didn't know what to do."

"There's nothing you can do," I told him.

"Yeah, that's just it. I'm completely helpless. My sister's scared shitless and I can't do a damned thing."

It occurred to me that what had been happening not only affected the victims and their families, but it affected every man, woman, and child who walked the streets of Harting Farms, smiling in the daylight, cowering at night. It affected the police, who had been turned into a joke by the press. It affected my friends and me because we had made it something important and convinced ourselves that we were the only ones who could end it. Somehow we had persuaded ourselves that we needed this. That it was ours.

"Can you do something stupid for me?" Peter said.

"You know it."

"Promise me we're on the right track and that we'll end this thing. Promise me, Angie."

"I promise," I said. Then repeated it: "I promise."

Picking up a line from the Springsteen song on the radio, Peter sang, "No retreat, baby, no surrender."

When I got home, I found that morning's edition of the *Caller* on the kitchen table. It was unfolded, and the smiling faces of the missing kids took up the entire front page. The bold headline asked simply What Is Going On?

Listed, in order of their disappearance—

Demorest, William
Connor, Jeffrey
Frost, Bethany
Cole, Courtney
Ransom, Aaron
Holt, Howard
Brubaker, Tori

* * *

The article recapped each teenager's disappearance in a gruesome highlight reel. The summaries were continued on the next page, along with an eighth photo of a teenage boy with feathered brown hair and a devious smile, which was actually more of a smirk. I didn't realize who the boy was until I scanned the headline that accompanied the photo:

COULD MISSING GLENROCK BOY BE PIPER'S FIRST?

What Michael had found out from Tommy Orent was apparently true: Jason Hughes had gone missing last June, and since no one was looking for a serial abductor back then—and because Hughes had a penchant for running away—it was assumed he had taken off on his own accord. When the boy didn't return after a week, Glenrock police searched the surrounding areas and interviewed Hughes's friends. If the Glenrock PD ever made it to Harting Farms to conduct these interviews, the article did not say. Neither had Tommy Orent.

When I heard my father's sedan pull into the driveway, I refolded the newspaper and placed it back on the table, as if I'd never touched it. As if I'd been doing something wrong.

While dragging the trash cans to the curb after dinner, I heard my dad talking on the phone.

I went over to the open kitchen window and crouched beneath it, eavesdropping. It was a work call; I could tell by the tone of my father's voice. Much of what he said was difficult to hear, but I managed to glean what may have been the most important bit of information to date in the investigation into the missing teenagers: the cops had found what they believed to be the Piper's footprints in the mud down by the river.

CHAPTER TWENTY-THREE
THE ABANDONED RAILWAY DEPOT
(PART ONE)

On a cool afternoon near the end of June, Peter and I biked down Farrington Road, an unused and forgotten strip of asphalt that eventually dead-ended at the defunct railway depot.

Folded up in the back pocket of my shorts was the recent article about Jason Hughes from the *Caller*. Peter and I planned to see what we could learn about his disappearance. If Hughes had been the Piper's first victim, then there was a pretty good chance he had run into the Piper on the day he had come into town to buy cigarettes for Tommy Orent and his friends. It was possible that the folks at Lucky's might have seen something. Since the police had never spoken with Orent or his buddies, they might not know that Hughes had been out this way the day he disappeared. If that was true, our intel put us one step ahead of the police.

It was a long ride to Lucky's, and we had wanted to leave earlier, but I'd spent the morning at Secondhand Thrift, organizing Callibaugh's shelves as part of my new summer job. In the short time I'd been there, I had already managed to knock over a display case, punch in the wrong digits on the security alarm, and clog the ancient-looking toilet.

Before we reached the outskirts of town, we spotted the tar paper shack that was Lucky's Sundries, so we cut through the woods and came out on the winding B&A bike path. Lucky's sat in a gravel parking lot between the bike path and the road, its back lot corralled within a scrim of spindly trees. With its slouching placard over the entranceway that read Lucky's Sundries in painted red script and its warped wraparound porch complete with hitching posts, it looked like something out of an old John Wayne western. Beneath the placard, some wit had spray-painted the phrase *B-more girls give Natty Boh jobs*.

Peter and I propped our bikes against one of the posts and went inside. A handful of men in blue jeans and sleeveless T-shirts hung around by the register, one leaning on the countertop while the others sat in canvas-backed folding chairs. They glanced at us: a jigsaw of wiry beards stained piss yellow from chewing tobacco and swarthy black eyes crowded beneath the creased bills of camouflage baseball hats. On the wall above the men's heads, and matching their vacuous expressions, taxidermy animals stared down at us.

The air was clotted with cigarette smoke and the headier stench of unwashed bodies.

Peter and I slipped down the first aisle, feigning interest in a row of toilet paper. With the possible exception of Secondhand Thrift, never in my life had I seen such a confused assortment of items jammed together in one store—household items, camping gear, auto parts, canned goods, cheap toys, a rack of clothing that looked like it had been rejected from the Salvation Army. There was even a whole shelf dedicated to pet products, where small bored-looking fish floated in plastic cups.

"Check it out," Peter whispered, snagging a copy of *Penthouse* from a nearby magazine rack. Normally pornographic magazines were packaged in cellophane, but this one was loose, and Peter wasted no time flipping it open to the centerfold. His eyes bugged out comically, and then he turned the magazine around so I could see the tri-panel photo of a nude woman with breasts like cantaloupes and a stripe of dark pubic hair.

When someone cleared his throat farther down the aisle, Peter nearly dropped the magazine.

"He'p you boys?" a man drawled. He was potbellied, with a wide, whiskered face and hands like clubs. There were fish silk-screened to the front of his T-shirt.

"Uh, we were looking for someone," I uttered while Peter stuffed the magazine back on the rack.

"Yeah? Like who?"

I produced the newspaper article from my back pocket and handed it to the man. "He's a friend of ours but he disappeared."

A lump formed against the inside of the man's cheek, either from his tongue or a ball of chewing tobacco. "Been happenin' a lot lately."

"We thought maybe you might have seen him," I said.

A nerve jumped in the man's right eyelid. "How would I have seen him?"

"He used to come here and buy cigarettes," I said.

The man gazed down at the paper. Then he thrust it back at me. "Not this boy. Too young."

"Well, maybe you've just seen him around the store," I said. "This would have been around last June when he—"

"I ain't never seen this boy."

"Well, I mean, he sometimes—"

"Ain't sold no smokes to a kid that young." It sounded like there were stones rolling around in his throat. "Ain't let no underage boys come in this store." His eyes narrowed. "Boys like you."

"They shoplift," one of the man's cronies shouted, evidently eavesdropping on our conversation.

"We're not shoplifters," I said.

"Maybe you boys should get on now," said the man.

"Could you maybe ask your friends if they recognize him?" I said.

The man called to his friends from over his shoulder. "Any of you fellas ever see a young kid come in here buying cigarettes?"

A chorus of negatives rumbled from the front of the store.

"There you go," said the man.

"If you could show them the picture." I extended the piece of newspaper toward him.

"I told you boys to split," he said.

We didn't need further invitation. Without another word, Peter and I shoved out the front door and down the steps.

"Buncha dicks," Peter murmured.

There was a man leaning against one of the hitching posts, dressed in dingy carpenter's pants and an unbuttoned chambray shirt with the sleeves cuffed past his elbows. He eyeballed us as we went to our bikes. "Hey, amigos," he said, his voice like sandpaper.

Peter and I glanced at him as we rolled our bikes across the gravel parking lot.

"You trying to buy cigarettes?" the man said amiably enough. The sun was directly in his eyes, causing his features to scrunch up into a grimace.

Thinking of all the plainclothes policemen hanging around town lately, I feared this might be a setup, even though this guy looked about as far on the other side of the law as one man can get. "No, thanks," I said.

"How 'bout beer? You amigos want some beer?"

Peter stopped pushing his bike. "Yeah? You got beer?"

The man's squinty face broadened into a smile. "Oh yeah. I got some I can sell you. Real cheap. Pennies on the dollar."

"Where is it?" Peter asked. There was no beer anywhere in sight.

The man jerked a thumb over his shoulder. "Behind the store. Lucky don't like me undercuttin' his prices, so's I gotta keep out of eyeshot. Like, do it on the sly, right?" When neither of us moved in his direction, the man added, "They're nice and cold."

"Well, how much?" Peter asked.

"I'm a bargaining man. No one ever said I ain't." The man headed around the side of the store. His pepper-colored hair was short and arranged in matted whorls at the back. The collar of his chambray shirt was too big, and it hung down his back, exposing a creased, sun-reddened neck beaded with sweat.

Still pushing our bikes, we followed him. There was a second gravel parking lot back here and a large oil tank painted to look like a World War II submarine docked against the siding behind a fence of scraggly, leafless bushes. I relaxed a little when I noticed the six-pack of Coors tucked in the shade of some bushes.

The man stood before the beer, peering down. He had his back toward us, so I didn't see what he was doing with his hands. Counting money, I assumed. I only had a buck and a half on me.

"You two amigos wanna see something?" said the man, glancing at us from over one shoulder.

Neither Peter nor I said a word. Suddenly, the color of the world changed. Things felt instantly *wrong*.

The man turned around. The front of his shirt was tucked up under his chin, and his pants were undone. A grayish-brown penis curled over the waistband of his briefs, wreathed in wiry black hair. It jerked upward as if tied to an invisible wire.

Peter and I turned and ran.

"Hey! Amigos! Come back! I was only joking!"

Once we had enough speed, we hopped on our bikes, blasted across the front parking lot, and sped through the trees. For one bloodcurdling moment, I wondered if the pervert might give chase.

"Holy shit," said Peter. It sounded like he was struggling not to laugh or cry. "Can you believe it?" Then he did laugh, though it came out as a partially stifled squawk.

I kept seeing the pervert's dick jerk upward, the image flooding me with shame, as if I had somehow caused it to happen. I couldn't help but think my dad would be disappointed and possibly angry with me if he ever found out. I couldn't comprehend why I felt this way.

"You think that guy's the Piper?" I asked.

"I think he's just a fucking screwball pervert," Peter opined. "But that whole store looked like it could've been filled with serial killers. Those guys were monsters, man."

"Did you see that guy with the fishhook earrings?" I said as we got back on the deserted blacktop of Farrington Road. The sun was beginning its descent behind the western trees. "Even if the cops went there, those guys wouldn't have told them a single thing."

Peter looked toward the north, where Farrington Road narrowed and curved through the trees. "You wanna check out that old train depot?"

"Yeah, I guess."

We rode until the pavement turned to gravel, then dead-ended on the outskirts of town. A single-story barnlike structure that had been vacant ever since the last train ran through our city in 1950, the railway depot squatted in the center of a gravel pit overgrown with bleached weeds and discarded mounds of garbage. The entire lot was surrounded by dense woodland.

The depot's windows were veined with cracks and black with gunk, many of them boarded up like the windows of the Werewolf House. The peeling and weather-ruined façade was marred by years of neon graffiti. The sagging roof bristled with falcons' nests so massive and intricately constructed that they looked like booby traps. There was something akin to a bell tower sans bell in the center of the roof, giving the whole thing a sort of old-time Southern church look.

Even before teenagers started disappearing, I had been forbidden to come out here. Based on the stories I'd heard, there were usually bums lurking about, sometimes whole communes of them, who took great delight in chasing kids who dared to tread on their turf. But that was supposed to be in the winter when the homeless built fires in the discarded oil drums and huddled together to keep warm. Now, in the summer, the place appeared to be desolate.

Peter and I dumped our bikes in the gravel and approached the depot together. Falcons screeched and pinwheeled in the sky. We walked the circumference of the gravel pit, pausing when we reached the ancient blood-colored railroad tracks running along the western side of the depot. They were skeletal and haunted in their years of disuse, and it was nearly possible to sense tetanus radiating from them. Leafless shrubbery exploded between the ties. The tracks stretched out in a perfectly straight line, vanishing at a horizon veiled in darkening trees. As we watched, two deer trotted onto the tracks and began to feed on the sun-bleached grasses.

"The old B&A Line," Peter said.

"It looks haunted."

"It is."

The ghosts of old railway workers were said to roam the grounds. Stories of ghostly lantern lights glimpsed through the trees at night were abundant, and there were even tales of people hearing the old short line chugging along the abandoned tracks.

"We should go in there, look around," Peter said.

"I don't think so," I countered. I reflected on the morning when Adrian and I had hidden in the basement of the Werewolf House, crouching in sewage while Keener and his pals hunted us with a rifle.

"We came out all this way. We might as well." Peter stomped down the weeds on his way to the massive double doors set into the side of the depot.

Reluctantly, I followed.

I stood on the remains of a platform, and the weathered planks moaned and threatened to break apart beneath my weight. Indeed, some of the planks were busted, leaving ragged, toothy mouths in the flooring. I looked down one of the holes and saw garbage stuffed in there—McDonald's cups, dusty beer bottles, and cans of Natty Boh.

"Shit," Peter said, tugging at the massive combination lock on the double doors. "Too bad Sugarland's not here. He'd get this sucker open."

Over the side of the platform, I watched a black snake twist through the undergrowth. I hopped down into the tall grass and joined Peter. There were small square windows at either side of the double doors. I wiped an arc of grime from one of the panes. Standing on my toes, I cupped my hands around my eyes and peered inside.

After a moment, my eyes adjusted and shadows coalesced and took on definitive shapes. I made out a row of benches, the hollowed windows of the ticket booths behind a wire-mesh grate, a pyramid of crates stacked in one sun-shafted corner. The shell of an old destination board hung from one wall, though the lettering had been removed. In the center of the ceiling, a gaping black hole spewed curling electrical cables that resembled the tentacles of a giant squid.

"What's that?" Peter said. He was looking in another window and pointing to a spot on the floor. "Holy shit. It looks like a person."

I couldn't see what he was seeing. The floor was covered in debris, which, in turn, was coated in a sheet of grayish dust so thick I had originally mistaken it for carpeting. Tarpaulin was draped over what I assumed to be mounds of junk, and two-by-fours were stacked like firewood indiscriminately about the place. Holes were punched into the drywall, and powder and plaster lay in heaps on the floor beneath them.

"You're full of shit," I told him.

"Am I? Come here and look at this."

I went over and nearly pressed the side of my head against his as I peered through the window. "Where?"

"There." He pressed one finger against the filthy glass. "See it?"

I squinted, checking out the interior from a slightly different angle now. "What am I...?"

But then I saw it.

Behind the row of benches, a filthy yellow sheet was draped over the undeniable outline of a human being. The longer I stared at it the more clearly I discerned the profile of a skull and a face, the slope of a neck graduating to the rise of a chest, a torso, legs, and finally the twin tombstones of feet pointing toward the ceiling.

My breath, which had been fogging up the windowpane, suddenly seized in my throat. With the heel of my right hand, I swiped another swath of grime from the glass to get a better look. There was no denying it. The shape under the sheet was a human being.

"I'm right, aren't I?" Peter whispered.

"I think . . ." My throat clicked. "Holy shit."

"What?"

Four fingers were poking out from beneath the yellow sheet. I said as much, tapping the glass. "See 'em? There! Right there! They're fingers!"

"No fucking way," Peter said, his lips nearly pressed against the glass.

"Do you see them?"

"Yeah." There was undeniable reverence to his voice.

"They're fingers, right?"

"Yeah." He tried to open the window but it wouldn't budge. As if shocked by an electrical current, he jerked his hand away. "Damn it!"

"What is it?"

"Goddamn splinter." He opened his left palm for me to see the reddened mound of flesh speared through the center with a sliver of nasty-looking wood. He attempted to pull it out but somehow only managed to wedge it down more. "The son of a bitch hurts."

"Let me see." I grabbed his hand and examined it. "We need a pair of tweezers or a sewing needle or something."

Peter looked down at the Metallica patch pinned to his T-shirt sleeve. With his good hand he undid the safety pin that held it, stuffing the patch into his pocket and holding the pin up to his face as if to scrutinize it. Then he thrust it at me. "You do it."

I took the pin, then fished my cigarette lighter from the pocket of my shorts. After sterilizing the head of the pin, I hunched over Peter's hand and prodded the edge of the splinter to the surface of his flesh. A dollop of blood came with it.

"I'm gonna need shots," he groaned.

"Hold still," I cautioned him. It took a couple of minutes, but I managed to remove the splinter. I held the culprit up between us, pinched between my thumb and forefinger, as if we were two homicide detectives who had just located a missing shell casing. It was roughly the size and shape of a pencil point. Peter wrinkled his nose at it, and I tossed it onto the ground.

Peter stared at the depot's darkened windows. They looked like vortexes into other dimensions. "Man, we really saw that, didn't we?"

I nodded.

"Should we break in?"

"I guess we could. Though if you got a splinter that bad just from trying to open a window, I can only imagine what we might do to ourselves crawling through a busted window." *Because this place is haunted*, I thought. *Because it will do what it can to keep us out. In much the same way the Werewolf House lured us in, this place is telling us to leave. We are trespassers. We do not belong.*

I didn't necessarily believe in ghosts, but I did believe in the power a place could hold, could retain, and how the land resonated with echoes of its past.

Charles had once told me that sometimes the places where bad things happened would suck up that badness like a sponge sucks up water. The badness gets stuck and rots and becomes like a stain, even if you couldn't see anything. An invisible stain, like on cop shows on TV, and how even after blood is cleaned up you can still find it with a black light.

Admittedly, the old railway depot projected an aura of *badness*. I didn't know what evil had transpired here all those years ago when the station was in use, but it wasn't hard to imagine a horrific industrial accident or a passenger getting struck by the train. It could have been anything.

It also occurred to me that this was one of the places my father specifically told me to keep away from back in October, the night Courtney Cole's body was pulled out of the Dead Woods. *Stay away from those empty cabins along the Cape and the Shallows and the old railway station at the end of Farrington Road.*

Peter nodded, though he still stared at the depot with a determined expression. His forehead and cheeks were becoming sunburned. He winced when he looked at me, the setting sun catching his eyes. "Let's come back tomorrow with Michael. He could open that lock."

"We'll come back with everyone," I added, thinking there would be safety in numbers. *Safety from what? Ghosts?* Again, my father's voice floated through my brain: *When you go out, stay with your friends in populated areas, preferably at their houses.*

Rustling noises beyond the nearby tree line caused us to freeze. I thought it might be the deer, but when I looked toward the tracks they were already gone. As we listened, it sounded like something big moving around just beyond our line of sight. Very close. An animal?

A person?

"Let's get out of here," I said.

CHAPTER TWENTY-FOUR
THE ABANDONED RAILWAY DEPOT
(PART TWO)

The following day, after I got out of work and Michael got out of summer school, the five of us departed for the abandoned railway depot. We didn't have much time to waste if we were to make it back home before curfew.

We picked up Farrington Road by cutting through the bike trail behind St. Nonnatus, but we still had a good hour-long bike ride ahead of us. Michael had his army helmet on, and Peter had secured the dynamo-powered radio to his handlebars with bungee cords, so we enjoyed some tunes as we rode. The alternative rock station, still mourning the April suicide of Kurt Cobain, played a block of Nirvana without commercial interruptions.

On my handlebars, Adrian had assumed his rightful position—a masthead tucked into a ball, his head down to allow for better aerodynamics, his hands balled into white fists as they gripped the handlebars.

Halfway down Farrington we stopped to smoke cigarettes while Michael urinated into a thicket of holly bushes. Around us the woods had grown greener seemingly overnight, and the air smelled like sandalwood and pine sap and honeysuckle.

"Whew," Michael said, coming back out from the trees and shaking one urine-speckled leg of his shorts. "My back teeth were floating."

Everyone mounted their bikes except me.

"What?" Adrian said.

"Your turn to drive," I told him.

"Huh?"

"You know how, right?"

"Sure."

"Okay, good. Just try not to kill me."

It had been a joke, but I quickly prayed for my safety once I mounted the handlebars and Adrian started to pedal. He wove like a drunkard and jerked the handlebars back and forth so much I could have sworn he was trying to shake me loose. He seemed timid about going very fast, so he hung back from the others, content in our plodding but safer pace.

"It'll be easier to balance if you go faster," I told him.

"Okay," he said, but he didn't pick up the pace at all.

"How come you don't have a bike?"

"I used to."

"What happened to it? Was it stolen back in Chicago?"

"No. We left it in the garage when we moved away. We never took anything from the garage. Not even the car."

Because his dad killed himself in there, I thought.

When we arrived at the depot it was already late afternoon, and there was a smear of dark clouds along the horizon. Something about the way the building stood there made me think that perhaps it had been waiting for us to return since yesterday. It looked somehow . . . *anticipatory*.

"Wow," Adrian marveled. "That is one scary-looking place."

We dumped our bikes on the ground and approached the depot together. Our sneakers crushed the white gravel to powder. All around us, insects buzzed and hummed and chirruped in the tall grass, and larger animals moved around deep in the trees. The whole world seemed abuzz with life.

Except for inside, I thought, recalling the sheet draped over the form of a human being, those fingers protruding from beneath it . . .

Peter and I led them around the side of the building where the double doors stood. In the fading daylight, the building was the color of tree bark, its filthy windowpanes like pools of roofing tar. The whole thing looked like one big warning sign. I knew the others could feel it, too. It seemed no one wanted to get any closer to it, and we were all content standing here in the tall grass while crickets ricocheted off our shins.

Eventually, Peter pointed at the doors. "That's the lock, Michael."

"If it's locked," Scott said, "then how's the killer getting in and out?"

"We don't know." There was a surprising tremor in Peter's voice. "We don't know if anyone's been in there at all."

"Except for the body," I said.

"Well, yeah," Peter said. "Except for that."

"Where's the body?" Adrian said.

Peter said, "Come on," and we all went to the window on the left side of the double doors. After wiping a streak of grime away from the glass, Peter looked in for several seconds without saying a word.

Suddenly I was certain that the body would no longer be in there, that we had either imagined it or someone had reclaimed it. I thought about the noises Peter and I had heard in the surrounding woods, prompting our departure, and it seemed possible that the Piper had been watching us, and he had taken the body away with him in the night so it wouldn't be here if we returned. This notion caused a chill to ripple through me.

"There it is," Peter said after what seemed like an eternity. "Come look."

They took turns—Scott first and seemingly quite anxious; Michael next, who said he didn't see it but then cut himself off, muttering, "Holy crap"; and lastly, Adrian stood on his tiptoes and gazed through the filth-caked window. He remained there the longest, not speaking. His reflection in the muddied glass was of a terrified ghost staring out at us.

"You see it?" Peter called to him.

"Yes," Adrian said in a small voice. So perhaps he was just taking his time and letting the reality sink in.

Perhaps we all were.

This isn't really happening, is it? This can't be real.

"We need to go in there," Adrian said, climbing down from the window.

We stood in a rough circle in the gravel at the base of the building. I felt itchy, uncomfortable. "We need to pull back that sheet and see who it is."

I didn't want to. The realization struck me like lightning. Whose body was under that sheet? How long had they been there?

What would they look like?

I don't want to.

Michael tittered nervously. "This thing just became real, huh?" Then, without prompting, he went over to the double doors and began fiddling with the combination lock.

Adrian shucked off his backpack and opened it at his feet. "Looks pretty dark in there." He pulled out two flashlights and handed one to Scott.

"Quick," I told Peter. "Give me a cigarette." Then I was suddenly embarrassed by the urgency in my voice.

If Peter noticed, he didn't comment. He handed me a Camel, handed another one to Scott, then stuck one in his own mouth.

"You got another?" Adrian asked.

"For real?" Peter said, lighting his smoke. "I thought they caused cancer?"

Adrian chewed on the inside of his cheek. "They do but I guess anyone can go anytime. For any reason."

Peter handed Adrian his lit cigarette, then stuck a fresh one in his own mouth. Adrian examined the glowing red ember at its tip before sticking it between his lips where it hung crookedly like a heavy stick jammed in mud.

"You suck it," I said, "and inhale it."

"Does it burn?"

"No, not really. I mean, I guess it feels warm."

Adrian's cheeks narrowed as he inhaled. An instant later he was sputtering and gagging in the reeds.

We laughed, and Michael turned and watched us from over one shoulder while I clubbed Adrian a number of times on the back.

"You okay?" I tried to stifle my laughter.

Adrian tried to speak but only wound up coughing some more. He concluded by unleashing a trail of saliva from his mouth that spooled like spaghetti in the dirt. His face was red, and his eyes leaked tears from behind his thick glasses. "Jesus. You'd think that'd be an easy habit to quit."

Again, we laughed. It felt good. It was what we all needed.

I watched Michael messing around with the combination lock and wished that he wouldn't be able to get it open. Then we could just hop back on our bikes and maybe even leave an anonymous phone call for the police so they—

The pop was loud enough to cause a flock of nearby blackbirds to take flight. Spinning around and executing a stately bow, Michael held out the lock in one hand.

"Unbelievable," Scott said. "I'll never figure out how he does that."

Behind Michael, one of the double doors opened as if pushed by invisible hands, causing him to shriek and jump into the grass. The creaking of the door reminded me of the way the eaves of the house on Worth Street groaned during a particularly bad summer storm. When I was a young and impressionable kid, Charles said they were the sounds of the monsters Dad kept in the attic. I had believed him and imagined a platoon of grotesqueries shambling about in the dark space above my bedroom ceiling, fangs dripping and claws extending from scaly reptilian paws.

Adrian clicked on his flashlight but didn't say anything. He didn't need to: that stupid beam of light said it all.

It was now or never.

There is a dead kid in there. We've found one of the missing.

Adrian went in first. I wouldn't have guessed him to lead the charge—Scott seemed much more eager in that regard—but he was the only one of us who didn't seem bothered by the creepy goddamn building, not to mention what ultimately waited for us within.

"Come on," Peter said, shoving me forward. "You go next."

"Why me?"

"Why not?"

I staggered through the open door and was immediately overcome by the motionlessness of the place. *This must be what it's like for those explorers who enter Egyptian mausoleums.* The air tasted like the inside of a fireplace and smelled like a cross between old moldy newspapers and dog shit. I could taste the dust motes at the back of my throat, thick as sawdust. Whereas the Werewolf House had a wetness about it, this building was as dry and soulless as the inside of an urn.

The rest of the guys filed in behind me. Adrian moved on ahead, his flashlight's beam playing along the walls and the floor. Scott clicked his flashlight on, too, and blasted me right in the eyes with its beam.

I swiped at him with one hand. "Cut it out."

"Watch the floors," Peter called to Adrian, who was moving farther ahead of us still. "If they're weak, you could step right through 'em."

Adrian paused halfway to the sheet-covered body. He shined his light on the floor.

"What is it?" Peter said, crossing over to him. Scott, Michael, and I followed.

"Footprints," Adrian said.

Sure enough, the beam spotlighted a set of footprints. Adrian lifted the flashlight and followed the trail of prints across the floor. They seemed to go in a million different directions at once, leaving smudges in the thick dust.

"How many sets?" Scott asked.

Adrian shook his head. "I can't tell if it's one or twenty."

"Could they be old?" I asked.

"They don't look so old," Adrian said.

"Do you think they might be a match for the footprints the cops found down by the river?" Scott asked. This news hadn't made it to the newspapers or the TV stations, but I had told them about what I'd overheard when my father was on the phone.

"Beats me," I said.

Adrian finally settled his flashlight beam on the yellow sheet across the room. Scott brought his light up and shined it on the sheet as well. Even from this distance I could still make out the profile of a human being beneath it. I could see the vague little nubs of the protruding fingers, too.

Like someone flipping a switch, my entire demeanor changed. Suddenly I wanted nothing more than to rush over to that sheet and yank it away, revealing the prize beneath. Who was it? The Demorest boy? Bethany Frost? If it was Jason Hughes, the corpse would be a year old . . .

I felt my feet move. It was less like walking and more like the floor shifting on its own, like a conveyor belt. When I reached the sheet I realized it was nothing more than an ancient white bedsheet turned yellow with age, like the pages of an old newspaper or a paperback novel. The shape of a body beneath it was undeniable. The fingers—four of them—sticking up from beneath the death shroud were mere inches from the tip of my left sneaker. Had I wanted to, I could have tapped them with my toes.

Both Scott and Adrian had their flashlights trained on the part of the covered body that was most assuredly the head.

I took a deep breath, dropped to my knees, and grabbed a fistful of the sheet.

"Jesus Christ," someone whispered.

"Do it," said Peter.

With a magician's flourish, I whisked the sheet from the floor and quickly filled that part of the room with a cloud of ageless dust that swirled and seemed to glow a golden hue in the dual beams of light.

It was a nude person, the skin seeming to slough in places like a reptile's, gray in patches like rot, its face—

No, not a person. Not a *real* person, anyway.

The realization of what we were looking at took several moments to settle into each of us. I think Michael started to laugh first. Eventually, we all began to chuckle, though my heart was still racing, and I felt sweat rolling down my ribs and soaking my shirt.

It was a fucking mannequin.

"Holy shit," Michael said, still laughing. Sweat beaded his forehead. He pointed at us. "You should see the looks on your faces. Ha!"

"What about *your* face?" Peter scowled, still looking rattled. "Not to mention I think you shit your pants when that door swung open."

Adrian bent down beside me, and together we stared at the dummy.

"I really thought we had something here." I couldn't hide the apologetic tone to my voice. Not five minutes ago I was praying Michael wouldn't be able to get the lock open because I didn't want to face whatever hideousness was beneath the sheet, and now I felt a sinking disappointment so great it was like a lead weight dragging me beneath the surface of the sea.

Still laughing, Michael staggered backward and mopped tears from his eyes. "Holy shit, that was fun. You guys really had me going, you know that?"

"We weren't trying to trick you, idiot," Peter said.

"Well," Scott said, looking up and playing the beam of his flashlight across the rafters in the exposed ceiling, "we're in here now. We should look around."

There were two more flashlights in Adrian's backpack. Peter and I grabbed one each and joined in the search, overturning items and peeking beneath benches shrouded in cobwebs. There were many loose boards propped up against the walls, covering a vast assortment of random junk—dented metal trash cans, a basketball backboard without the hoop, dust-covered whiskey bottles that looked like they had rolled off a pirate ship, and moldering cardboard hamburger containers.

"Those don't look so old," I commented, resting my light on one of the cardboard food containers. The Quickman's faded logo—a Greek god with feathers on his shoes—stood out on the top of the container.

"Probably left here by some homeless guy," Peter said.

"Yeah, but how would he have gotten in?"

Peter shrugged.

Something creaked and both Peter and I froze, our flashlight beams criss-crossing each other like searchlights.

"Did you—?" I began as the floor underneath one of Peter's feet gave way.

He cried out and dropped his flashlight, and I instinctively snatched his arm. He sank into the floor. Letting go of my flashlight, I dropped to both knees and grabbed him around the shoulder, though he had already ceased falling. The rent in the floorboards was only big enough to accommodate one of Peter's legs; though he sank down to his thigh, he was in no danger of plummeting any farther. Unless, of course, the rest of the floor surrendered under his weight . . .

The other guys hurried over, their footfalls like the galloping of horses on an old fishing pier. Peter gripped my arm, trying to hoist himself out of the hole. I attempted to lift him out, but he was too heavy.

"What happened?" Scott said, shining a light on both of us. "Oh, wow." His voice was like the ringing of a tiny bell.

"I'm okay," Peter grunted. "Just . . . stuck . . ."

"Give me a hand," I said, beckoning to the others.

Michael and Adrian slipped their arms around Peter while Scott braced himself against me and grabbed one of Peter's hands, which he had to pry off my shirt. We extricated him from the hole, the jagged teeth of the rotten floorboards scraping the exposed flesh of his leg. Blood streaked his calf and trickled down to his sock. None of the wounds were serious, but the blood looked a little overwhelming.

"Does it hurt bad?" I asked.

"Stings," he said. He plucked splinters of wood from his leg.

"This place hates you," I told him, thinking of the splinter he'd gotten on our previous visit.

I picked up my flashlight, leaned over, and shined my light down the hole. It was deep, and I was abruptly all too conscious—and distrusting—of the floorboards beneath us.

Adrian bent down and broke some loose pieces of wood away from the hole; the pieces came away as angry-looking spears.

Beside me, Scott crawled closer to the hole on his hands and knees. He looked down into it, too. "Man, that's deep."

I realized that we were on the farthest end of Harting Farms and that beyond Farrington Road and the surrounding woods the town ended at a cliff overlooking the Chesapeake Bay. I recalled the holes and caverns I had glimpsed from the water when I was younger. The train depot had apparently been built over one of them. All of a sudden, it was as though my hearing intensified, and I was able to discern every creak and groan and tilt of not only the floorboards but the entire framework of the building.

"We should probably get out of here before this whole place comes tumbling down around us," I suggested.

"Don't be such a chickenshit," Michael commented. "If we're careful and watch where we're—"

His words were cut off as he backed into a stack of boards leaning against the wall. He lost his balance and toppled backward, splintering some of the boards through the middle and sending the rest down in a cascade on top of him where he lay slumped on the filthy floor.

Now Peter laughed. "What were you saying about being more careful?"

"Quit being a dumbass," Michael groaned, kicking the boards off him, "and help me up."

Peter took one of Michael's hands and yanked him to his feet while around them the cloud of dust continued to settle.

Scott said, "Guys?"

He shone his flashlight on the part of the wall that was revealed after Michael had knocked the boards away from it. The boards had been piled on top of a bench, some busted bits of plaster, chairs missing a few legs, and a toppled coatrack. But those items didn't catch our attention. It was the bicycle. Its chrome finish dulled beneath a layer of gray dust, its tires flattened, it looked incongruous among the rest of the detritus inside the depot.

Peter and Michael moved quickly away from the spot, as if proximity would bring about their own deaths.

Scott's flashlight beam shook as I approached the bike. It was a Mongoose, similar in style to Michael's bike, with worn blue handgrips and a narrow plastic racing seat. There were uncountable stickers on the bike's frame, mostly of rock bands and local sports teams. I bent closer to the bike, blowing the dust off one sticker in particular.

Scott came up behind me, his flashlight beam steadying on the bike.

The sticker that had attracted my attention was one I had seen countless times in the past, though now it held some sort of talismanic power over me. *Glenrock Bulldogs* was written in maroon on a gold background. Beneath the lettering was the droopy-cheeked face of an American bulldog, the mascot of Glenrock High School.

"It's Jason Hughes's bike," Scott said from over my shoulder, reading my mind.

Adrian walked up beside me, his flashlight's beam melding into Scott's and my own. He reached out to touch the bicycle—

"Are you crazy?" Peter castigated. "Don't touch it."

Adrian jerked his hand away as if burned.

"That shit's evidence," Peter continued, lowering his voice.

"That could be anyone's bike," said Michael. But the tone of his voice suggested he didn't believe his own words.

Adrian shifted his flashlight to the pile of boards and beams that Michael had knocked over. "It's like they were set up to cover the spot." Then his light locked onto a piece that looked like the unfinished leg of a wooden chair. Adrian picked it up. There were nails protruding from it. One-handed, he swung it like a mace.

"Remember the busted-up chairs at the Werewolf House?" I said to Adrian. "The ones stacked up in a pile almost to the ceiling?" I nodded at the chair leg he was wielding like a cudgel. "That's the same kind of leg."

Adrian stopped and looked down the length of the chair leg.

"Put it down," Peter said. "We shouldn't touch any of this stuff. Seriously."

Adrian dropped the wooden leg and took two steps backward to rejoin our huddle.

"Someone was killed here." It was Scott, his voice low and shaky. "I can totally feel it."

Again, I thought about Charles telling me how places soak up badness like a sponge soaks up water. Looking at the discarded bicycle with the Glenrock Bulldogs sticker on it, I wondered what horrors this old run-down railway depot had seen. Perhaps the worst of its horrors had not been so long ago after all . . .

"We need to tell the cops," Peter said.

"No way," said Scott, turning his flashlight onto Peter's face. "We found it. This is our investigation."

"You sound ridiculous. If this is Jason Hughes's bike, then the cops need to know about it."

"It's not his bike," Michael said, still trying to convince himself along with the rest of us. "It can't be."

"We've done enough," Peter went on. "We tell the police what we found and let them take it from here. I mean, what if this bike leads them to the Piper? What if there's, like, fingerprints on it or something? Do you really want to be responsible for keeping that information from them? It could save people's lives."

"But what if it leads *us* to the Piper first?" Scott countered. "Isn't that what this whole thing is about?"

Peter ran a hand through his hair. When he met my eyes, I saw his features soften. "I'll leave it up to you, Angie. Your dad's a cop. We can tell him what we found . . . or we can keep doing what we're doing while that sicko is still out there going after kids."

I looked from him to Scott, then over to Adrian, who was staring at me with Scott's matched intensity. I surprised myself when I said, "I think we should keep this to ourselves. Let's keep doing what we're doing and find the Piper on our own."

If it had been anyone else but me who had said this, Peter would have continued with his argument—and it certainly was a good argument—but he always trusted my opinions and had my back. Always.

"Okay," he said flatly, and I could tell he agreed with me against his better judgment. It made me feel as though I had just doomed all five of us. "So what do we do with the bike? Just leave it here?"

"We can write another note to your English teacher," Michael suggested, "telling him we found the bike."

"No. Mr. Mattingly didn't move into town until August. Jason Hughes disappeared in June. Mr. Mattingly's ruled out." I felt much relief at saying this.

"If we take the bike, the Piper will know we've been here," Scott said.

"He's going to know we were here, anyway." It was Adrian's small voice, and for a second I had forgotten he was with us. He let his flashlight play along the floorboards, our footprints as obvious as mortar blasts stamped into the layer of ancient dust.

"We should go," Michael said, glancing at one of the smudgy windows. "It's getting dark."

It had also grown chilly, though I didn't notice until I stopped moving and looked out one of the windows, too. And it was still an hour's bike ride home. I didn't want to be here any longer.

We headed toward the door. In that musty-smelling and awful place, my friends were suddenly nothing more than ghosts all around me in the darkness, marshaling through swirling motes of dust and accented by the occasional flashlight beam. I watched their silhouettes and was overcome by a certainty so unwavering, so undeniable, that its power nearly brought me to my knees . . .

We would end this. In our own way. *We.*

Outside, one of the falcons screamed, and we all cried out in unison.

BOOK FOUR

THE PIPER'S DEN
(JULY AND AUGUST 1994)

The peasants wanted their monster. Distrust among lifelong friends and neighbors became a palpable thing. In a display that suggested defeat, police requested random people come to the station for questioning. Rumor had it that the cops were talking to anyone who possessed a criminal record, no matter how benign. (Even Peter's stepdad was called down to speak with officers because he'd apparently amassed quite a collection of unpaid parking tickets.)

The homeless derelicts who generally loitered around Solomon's Field were also rounded up and interrogated, then finally pressured out of town. Come July, none of these grizzled, unwashed transients could be found in the cooling shade of the underpass or languishing beside the scummy water of Drunkard's Pond.

To satiate the public, the HFPD brought in an FBI profiler who cobbled together an enigmatic sketch from thin air: the Thief of Children was an adult male, most likely in his midtwenties to midthirties, and considered to be both "organized" (due to the lack of forensic evidence) and "disorganized" (due to the assumption that he operated off impulsivity and opportunity)—a nebulous assessment right out of the gate.

The profiler suggested that the discovery of Courtney Cole's body—the only body to be discovered—was deliberate, and it was the Piper's way of communicating something to the police or the general public or both. The profiler even suggested that leaving the body to be found was a cry for help, and there was a chance the Piper wanted to get caught. It's debatable whether or not anyone believed this.

In the days leading up to the town's annual Fourth of July celebration, men and women alike roved the streets, the alleyways, the woods, the beaches, the abandoned lots, the empty parks. They didn't call it a manhunt, but they could have been wielding pitchforks and torches for all its subtlety. Each night, after the streets had grown dark, tea lights would blink in the windows of many of the neighborhood houses as a sign of unity and perseverance against the faceless monster that had brought horror to our working-class bayside community.

One evening, Shelby la Cruz ran screaming from her house and pounded on her neighbor's door, exclaiming that the Harting Farms Piper was in her yard. When Shelby's neighbor, armed with a flashlight and a Louisville Slugger, went to investigate, he found the "Piper" was actually his scarecrow that had fallen over and now leaned against the fence that overlooked Shelby's yard.

On another evening, Kathy Choone spotted a swarthy-looking man hanging around the bridge off Solomon's Bend Road, and her description to a police sketch artist resulted in a sexually ambiguous figure with long, stringy hair, vacuous eyes, and a noncommittal slash for the mouth. This rudimentary scarecrow of a man appeared in every newspaper and even flashed occasionally on the nightly news as if to say, *This is me, and I look like no one and everyone at the same time. Come find me!* He appeared capable of flitting instantly out of existence while simultaneously stealing you away with him.

Come find me . . .

And summer boiled our souls.

CHAPTER TWENTY-FIVE
THE CELEBRATION

The Fourth of July celebration had been held in Market Square every year since I was a toddler. My earliest memories consisted of wending hand in hand with Charles through the labyrinth of booths, where vendors as boisterous as carnival barkers peddled their wares. The sky was always dotted with kites, the streets teeming with face-painted children, and dogs alternately barked and whimpered behind the chain-link fences on Third Avenue.

We munched on salted peanuts, guzzled fountain drinks, and got our clothes messy with soft-serve ice cream. Then we met up with our friends and spent whatever change we had remaining at the game booths. Come evening, we watched the fireworks by the waterfront with my dad and grandparents. Afterwards, Charles and I loaded our bikes into the back of my father's car, then we all climbed in together and drove home while I was rocked into a gentle sleep with my head on my grandmother's cushiony arm.

This year, the mood was different. For starters, there had been some discussion whether or not there should even *be* a celebration this year. Fireworks meant people had to stay outside in the dark, and curfew would have to be lifted. The children and teenagers of Harting Farms held their collective breaths. In the end, it was decided that the town would move forward with the celebration.

That morning, I luxuriated over a breakfast of sausage links, scrambled eggs, paprika-salted potato wedges, and a tall glass of orange juice prepared by my grandmother. Callibaugh had closed the thrift shop for the holiday, so I had nothing to do except hang out with my friends and enjoy an evening of fireworks, hot dogs, and cotton candy at Market Square.

When my father came down, he was dressed in a suit and tie. Not stopping for breakfast, he filled up his travel thermos with coffee, then dug a book of matches out of the junk drawer. His expression was grim.

"You have to work today?" I said.

"No rest for the wicked," he said.

"What does that mean?"

His grim expression turned into a weary smile. "Everyone's just on high alert, that's all." He sipped some coffee. "What are your plans for tonight?"

"Me and the guys are gonna go down to Market Square and watch the fireworks."

"I know the city curfew has been lifted for tonight, but I'd still like you in by nine."

I set my fork down. "But the fireworks don't even start until a quarter till. I'll miss the whole thing."

"There's plenty to do down there without staying for the fireworks."

It was blasphemous. "It's the Fourth of July. All my friends had their curfews lifted for tonight. Everyone else will be staying out later."

"Ah. That old 'everyone else' defense." My dad patted down his jacket pockets, presumably for cigarettes.

"At least give me till ten," I bargained.

"This isn't up for debate. I've got enough on my plate without worrying about my kid in the process."

"You won't have to worry about me. I'll be with the guys."

"No good."

"What if I'm just hanging out at someone's house? This way we—"

"Damn it, Angelo, I said no. If you don't like it, you can stay in all goddamn day."

"It's not fair," I yelled.

My father looked at me. The vertical crease between his eyebrows deepened. "That's right. The world's not fair, is it? I can give you a list of everything that's not fair about it."

My grandfather came in, a fat greenish-white cantaloupe in each hand. He set them on the table and narrowed his eyes at me. "Strange to have planted a bunch of squash only to find cantaloupes in my garden."

I kicked my chair back and stomped across the kitchen where I dumped my plate into the sink.

"Don't cop an attitude," my dad said, jabbing a finger at me.

Under my breath, I grumbled, "What do you care? You're never around."

Like a bull, his nostrils flared as he exhaled. "Yeah, I'm out there playing. I'm out there having a wonderful goddamn time."

"You just don't trust me."

"This has nothing to do with me trusting you."

"It does. You were never like this with Charles. It's only me."

My father said nothing. I could no longer read what was going on behind his eyes. Since Charles's death, we had built a wall that prohibited us from using my brother as a weapon in our battles. My words had just obliterated that wall, and there was nothing but naked vulnerability on the other side of it.

My father walked out of the room.

I was still staring at the spot he had been standing when I heard the front door slam and, a moment after that, his car start up. As he backed out of the driveway, I glanced at my grandfather, who stood beside the table, each hand resting on a cantaloupe. He looked away from the windows and at me.

I cleared the table, dumping the dirty glassware into the sink and putting the milk and orange juice containers into the refrigerator. I felt his eyes on me as I rinsed the dirty dishes, then filed them away into the dishwasher. As my face began to burn and my vision blurred, I struggled to maintain my composure. Yet when I eventually faced him, I saw that he, too, had gone.

Upstairs, I showered and dressed quickly. The game plan was to meet at Echo Base, where Scott had salted away a bag of firecrackers we intended on letting off this evening, then head over to the Quickman for a bite before footing it down to Market Square. Following the discovery of Jason Hughes's dirt bike, we had spent the past week taking turns riding out to the depot—in pairs, of course—to keep an eye on it. If it had once been one of the Piper's hangouts, there was no sign of him that week.

As for Mr. Mattingly, I felt an overwhelming embarrassment for what we had done to him. The discovery of Jason Hughes's bike pretty much solidified the fact that he had been the Piper's first victim back in June of '93. Since Mr. Mattingly and his wife hadn't moved into the neighborhood until August, that ruled him out as the killer. Even though Mr. Mattingly had no possible reason for assuming I had been involved in depositing that letter on his doorstep, I feared he would be able to read the guilt in my eyes the next time we crossed paths.

Intending to light up a cigarette, I went out the back door instead of the front but was startled by the presence of my grandfather. He was leaning back in one of the wicker chairs smoking a pipe.

"Hey," I said, realizing I had my cigarette tucked behind my ear. I snatched it and stuffed it into the pocket of my shorts.

"Gorgeous day for the parade," he commented, looking out across the backyard.

"Are you and Grandma going?"

"I think we're gonna skip it. It's too much walking, and your grandmother's knees are acting up. Not to mention I've been feeling a lazy streak coming on." He winked at me through a screen of bluish smoke. "How many war stories have I told you since you were a boy?"

"Jeez, I don't know. Hundreds?"

"At least, I'll bet. Not to mention you always made me tell your favorites over and over again."

My favorites included stories about crazy-eyed Rocko, who rode around the campground on a stolen motorcycle with no clothes on, and the aboriginals in New Guinea who electrocuted themselves when they touched a live power line that had come down in a storm. I also liked the one about the mess hall chef who dropped raisins into holes drilled in coconuts to ferment the coconut juice so he could get drunk.

"All those stories," said my grandfather, "but did I ever tell you about the day I left home for the war?"

"I don't think so."

"I was about your age. I lied about my age so I could join the National Guard. I wanted to box and they had a good program. Did I tell you I was going to be a prizefighter?"

"You said Grandma made you give it up, that she didn't want to be married to a guy with cauliflower ears."

"That's the truth of it," he said, his eyes suddenly fierce and alive. "But that was much later. Back when I was your age, I still had those dreams, and I was a pretty good fighter. I already did my time fightin' in the streets—you didn't grow up in Brooklyn, so you don't know how it is—and I thought boxing in the National Guard was maybe the next rung up the ladder.

"But then, see, one Sunday while I'm sittin' in church, the priest announces that Pearl Harbor had been bombed by the Japs. I'd never heard of Pearl Harbor in my life. Yet the next thing I know Roosevelt's got us in the war, and now they're talking about sending me and my friends overseas.

"My family didn't know I'd signed up to the Guard. But seeing how I was gonna be shipped out to Fort Dix sooner than later, I had to tell them. So I told them over dinner a few nights before I had to meet the boat at the docks."

"They must have been upset," I said.

"Upset don't quite cut it," my grandfather said. "My mother and my sisters cried, but my father, he got up from the table and sat in his room all night. And the next morning, he went straight to work and didn't say a word to me. He was furious. He was downright out of his mind with what I'd done.

"Night before I was to ship out, I went to him. After dinner, he took to sitting in the den, listening to the radio and just bein' by himself. I tried to talk to him but he wouldn't talk. He wouldn't say nothin'. So I turned around and left.

"Next morning, I got up early and grabbed my bags. I had packed a small satchel, but it wasn't much—they didn't want you taking too much with you—and my mother had wrapped me up some dried salami in wax paper. It was still dark when I left the house and went down to the corner to catch the bus.

"As you know, my father—your great-grandfather—owned a breakfast and sandwich shop in town, and he left for work before sunrise every morning. He'd already left that morning, but as I stood waiting for the bus, I see this figure coming toward me. It was my dad, wrapped in a thick wool coat and a fur hat—ah, it was ungodly cold that morning! He was a small man, my father, and very compact, and he had a bum leg that pained him in cold weather. As he came up the block, he sort of . . . well, it wasn't quite a limp. He sort of waddled." My grandfather smiled at the distant memory.

"Under his big coat he still wore his white apron from the store. I remember he had the small black nub of a hand-rolled cigar crooked in one corner of his mouth. He didn't say a word to me—just looked me over, like a butcher appraising a cut of meat. I didn't say nothin', neither. See, I'd grown a little angry at him, I guess for no other reason than he had been angry at me.

"Eventually the bus comes and those doors hiss open. I give my dad a hug, then get on the bus. I look around, and the seats, they're filled with boys just about my age. They all got their bags with 'em, and they're all on their way to Fort Dix."

"I bet they were scared," I said.

My grandfather waved a hand at me. "Scared? You would have thought we were going on vacation. What did we know? We were kids."

My grandmother's face appeared behind the screen door. She smiled at me, then wrinkled her nose at the smell of my grandfather's pipe before withdrawing into the house.

"I grabbed an empty seat on the bus," my grandfather said, "and when I looked up, there's my dad, limping down the aisle toward me. I slid over just as he sat down beside me. 'What are you doing?' I asked him.

"'Came to see my boy off,' he said."

My grandfather crossed his legs and puffed on his pipe. He stared out over the yard again. I knew he wasn't finished yet; like an ancient scribe, he was merely dipping his pen before finding the page once more, and much of what I learned about storytelling I learned from him.

"It was a few hours to Dix. We didn't say much on the trip. After a while, the other boys got quiet, too. When we finally arrived, all the boys got off the bus. My dad got off with me, his bald head beaded with sweat, his heavy winter coat damp and drooping with perspiration. 'I guess I gotta go now, Pop,' I tell him, and my dad, he just nods. He was crying . . . and he sort of smiles at me, saying we're okay . . . and . . . well . . .'"

My grandfather blinked rapidly and made a soft hitching sound way down in his chest. In all my sixteen years, I had never heard my granddad make such a sound. "It's just something to think about when you're up in arms with your father," he said, then went silent. This time, I knew he had finished.

I kissed the side of his face. His cheek was unshaven, rough, and his skin smelled like tobacco.

"Before you head out," he said, one arthritic finger pointing crookedly at the porch's awning, "tell your grandmother I saw that poor excuse for a meat loaf she's defrosting for dinner and I won't have none of it. I won't. I'm too old to eat leftover meat loaf. I'm just too damn old."

"I'll tell her," I said.

He leaned to one side and slid a hand into his pocket. "Here," he said, producing a ten-dollar bill. "Get one of them sausage and pepper dogs for yourself at the parade. But only if you promise not to smoke that cigarette you had tucked up behind your ear when you came out here."

"I promise."

"Good kid."

I thanked him, kissed the side of his face again, and fled back into the house.

Adrian was waiting for me on the curb in front of his house.

"I got bad news," I said and told him I had to be home at nine o'clock.

"But the curfew's lifted for tonight," he said.

"Not my dad's curfew."

"What about the fireworks?"

"I don't know, man."

We walked toward the highway, the day already hot and sunny. Down in the Superstore plaza, a few guys I knew from school zipped by on skateboards. One of them was Dieter Grosskopf, an Austrian exchange student and inventor of the smokeless smoke bag. It consisted of a Ziploc bag sealed shut with packaging tape and a McDonald's drinking straw poking from it. When smoking in the boys' lavatory at school, one need only to blow into the straw and fill up the bag, leaving no trace of smoke behind.

"Hey," Peter said, coming up behind us. He shook some Cracker Jacks into his mouth. "You guys hear about Mr. Van Praet?"

"No," I said. "What about him?"

"He died last night."

"No shit," I said. "How?"

"Heart attack," Peter said.

"How'd you find out?"

"Monica's piano teacher is friends with Van Praet's wife." Monica was Peter's eleven-year-old half sister. He tilted his head back and upended the box of Cracker Jacks into his mouth. Munching, he said, "Isn't that wicked?"

"Poor Mr. Van Praet."

"Who's Mr. Van Praet?" Adrian asked.

"He was our freshman geography teacher," Peter said. "Now he's worm food. Poor bastard."

Across the parking lot, Scott and Michael came out of the Quickman. Upon seeing us, Michael whooped and they both ran in our direction.

Skidding to a stop mere inches from me, Michael proceeded to juggle—quite impressively—a bunch of wrapped Quickburgers.

"Mr. Van Praet's dead," I intoned.

"Our old math teacher?" Michael said, keeping his eyes on the burgers as he juggled.

"Geography," I corrected, snatching one of the burgers out of the air. This caused the rest to fall to the ground, which Michael scooped up.

"You mean the Piper got him?" Scott said.

"No," said Peter. "Heart attack."

Scott looked momentarily crestfallen. "I guess he was a bit overweight."

"That's what you get for eating unhealthy food," Michael said and took a massive bite out of a Double Hermes Burger with extra cheese.

The five of us cut across the highway and down the embankment into the Dead Woods. More signs had been posted since our last visit—Keep Out and Park Closes at Dusk. After a fusillade of springtime thunderstorms followed by several weeks of sunny days, the woods had become a veritable jungle. The trees were big heavy things bristling with leaves. The brook flowed steadily toward some distant point on the horizon accompanied by a chorus of frogs. Little brown shrimp streaked through the water.

Just as we reached Echo Base, Scott slowed his pace.

The headless statues stood upright in a rough circle about the clearing.

We approached with caution and walked slowly around them. Only one remained lying on the ground, though it had been dragged a few feet from its usual spot beneath the chorded veins of roots and ivy and left in the center of the clearing in plain view. The other headless statues surrounded it, like witnesses at a crime scene.

"Who would do this?" Adrian asked.

No one said a word. There were other kids from school who knew about the statues, but they never really came down here, and most of what they knew had been told to them by older siblings. In the past year, we hadn't seen anyone else hanging around down here.

"Devil worshippers," said Scott.

"Cut it out," I said. I stared at the statue lying on the ground, its concrete body ribbed with weeds.

A heavy thud shook the ground as Michael knocked one of the statues over. We all looked at him, startled.

"Sorry," he muttered, stepping away from the fallen statue.

I turned back to the one on the ground, crouching beside it. It was the one that we had carved our initials into. Scott and Adrian looked down at it from over my shoulders, and I knew they saw it, too.

"Christ," Scott said. "That can't be a coincidence, could it?"

Michael and Peter came around to the other side of the statue.

"Oh, boy," Michael said.

"Maybe this one just fell over," Peter rationalized.

It looked pretty much on purpose to me, although I kept my mouth shut. I stood, swiping dirt from my knees.

"Maybe Keener did it," Scott said. "He and his friends sometimes come down here to smoke and drink, remember?" Then he spun around and raced over to a mound of upturned soil at the foot of a tree. He dropped to his knees and dug up the spot. Once he lifted out his bag of firecrackers, the relief was evident on his face.

"What about the rest of the stuff?" Peter said.

We checked our trash bags and the hidden beer cooler. As far as I could tell, everything was accounted for. It was mostly just garbage, anyway.

"The head's gone." Adrian was standing on the fallen statue, surveying the clearing. He pointed to the niche in the tree, where he usually sat. "I left it right over there."

"It's gotta be around here somewhere," Michael said.

Adrian shook his head. "Someone took it."

"That doesn't seem like something Keener would do," Peter said.

Suddenly, the woods around us seemed to obscure hidden dangers. The foliage had grown in so thick Keener and his friends could be hiding here right now, just yards away from us, and we wouldn't have been able to see them. Or perhaps someone even more dangerous than Keener . . .

"It was kids," Michael said. "Just some kids goofing off. We're getting freaked out for nothing." Yet it sounded like he was trying to convince himself of this most of all.

Again, Adrian shook his head. He stepped down from the statue. "It was the Piper. We took it from him first, and now he's taken it back."

For several seconds, no one said a word. The only sounds were of the birds in the trees and the bugs in the grass. Beyond the clearing, something splashed in the shallow brook, and we all jumped.

"Look," Scott said finally. "Are we gonna stand around here scaring ourselves all day, or are we gonna blow stuff up?"

We decided to blow stuff up. Scott slung his sack of fireworks over one shoulder, and we crossed December Park. The park was desolate this afternoon, which was unusual for such a nice summer day, but in the wake of Tori Brubaker's disappearance, it seemed the local teenagers had begun hanging out in shopping malls, movie theaters, and each other's houses. Fear had reduced our humble city to a ghost town.

We cut into the otherworldly darkness of the Solomon's Bend Road underpass, our footfalls rebounding off the black cobblestones. Michael unleashed a cry of sheer glee, and the sound seemed to crawl up the curved stone walls while simultaneously pulsing in our ears. Peter unloaded the pockets of his cargo shorts, dumping G.I. Joe figures onto the ground, and Scott rifled through the bag of firecrackers.

We wrapped one figure's arms around a small cylindrical noisemaker with a fuse curling from the top. Peter set it down on the cobblestones and Scott lit it. When the fuse caught, Peter and Scott dispersed, giggling.

It exploded, the noise so loud in the curved stone chamber that it was like being inside the barrel of a giant gun. Clutching our ears, laughing so hard that tears spilled down our cheeks, we stumbled out onto Solomon's Field, the stink of gunpowder still in our noses.

"I gotta see what's left," Michael shouted and ran back into the underpass. He returned moments later cupping pieces of the destroyed action figure in his hands, a look of utter fascination on his face.

Scott rolled some cherry bombs into the palm of one hand. One by one, we lit them and threw them into Drunkard's Pond. Each one exploded with a resounding *whumph!* and sent water geysering into the air.

With one cherry bomb left, we decided to blow up the Park Closes at Dusk sign that had been staked into the grass. It was made of aluminum, so the most we hoped for was a sizable dent.

Michael stripped off one of his shoelaces and tied the cherry bomb to the front of the sign. Scott handed his lighter to Adrian, who looked down at it hesitantly.

"Go on," I told him. "Just light it and run like hell."

He crept over to the sign, flicked the lighter—it took him several times just to arrive at a flame—then lit the cherry bomb's fuse.

"Run!" we all shouted.

Adrian dropped the lighter and sprinted toward us. His oversized glasses bounced on his face, and his mouth was peeled back from his teeth in a terrified grimace I found utterly hilarious.

The cherry bomb detonated with a boom that cracked the sky like thunder. One second the sign was a perfectly smooth aluminum rectangle; the next second, it was bent at a perfect ninety-degree angle. The shoelace whipped off into the air, and what remained of the cherry bomb's shell rained down in charred, smoking remnants to the grass.

We cheered.

Market Square was alive. The carnival barkers catcalled to us, the wondrous odors of fried foods tantalized us, and a troop of girls wearing Holy Cross polo shirts giggled and pointed at us as we strutted by.

We loitered around the game booths, scrambling for coins whenever we saw them glinting off the pavement. Once we had enough, we pooled the change into Scott's hand, and he purchased five softballs to toss at a pyramid of ceramic bottles. Scott was a crack shot—he scattered the bottles with the second pitch. His prize was a ticket for a free falafel, which the five of us tore into like vultures, then washed down with a communal bottle of Pepsi.

At five thirty, the parade started coming down Third Avenue. It was led by two women who carried a banner that read *Harting Farms Chapter of the Benevolent and Protective Order of the Elks* and wore big floppy hats adorned with bright flowers. The Stanton School marching band followed, those kids sweating in their starchy blue and gold uniforms, their trumpets and trombones and bassoons blazing like fire in the sunlight, the snare drums resonating like machine guns.

Next was a conga line of dog walkers, the owners waving to the crowd, the dogs looking hot and tired and overall miserable. A few motorcars, outfitted in red, white, and blue streamers and piloted by men in patriotic hats who grinned like they had femurs wedged into their mouths, brought up the rear.

They all banked sharply onto Center Street. The marching band diverged, claiming its final position atop the risers erected in front of the bandstand. Then they broke out into a jazzy rendition of "You're a Grand Old Flag."

There were a few older girls seated on bleachers beside the bandstand, drinking what looked like soda but was probably alcohol from clear plastic water bottles. One of the girls was Audrey MacMillan, who'd gotten drunk and driven her car off the road last October. The damage to her leg must have been extensive, since she still wore a brace.

My gaze slid along the bleachers a bit farther until I saw Rachel Lowrey seated with some friends. She had her dark hair pulled back in a ponytail and wore a purple blouse and faded pink pants. In her lap she cradled a fountain drink, and she sipped occasionally from the straw. She leaned over to Elizabeth Mosley and whispered something in her ear. Both girls laughed.

Rachel turned away and looked right at me. For a moment, she seemed surprised to see me. I wondered if she realized that I had been staring at her, and I instantly felt self-conscious. Then she smiled and waved. I smiled and waved back . . . then quickly averted my eyes as a not-so-unpleasant tingle sprung to life in the center of my stomach.

The Lambeth twins strutted over, each one sucking down a bottle of Cherry Coke. They wore Washington Bullets basketball jerseys and matching hats turned backward.

Jonathan Lambeth kicked one of Michael's sneakers. "Hey, butt cheese. You guys hear about Mr. Van Praet?"

"Sure," Michael said. "Can you believe it? A mountain lion in these parts?"

Jonathan scrunched up his face in confusion—a gesture his twin brother mimicked. "Mountain lion?"

"Yeah," Michael said. "You heard he died, right?"

"Well, yeah," Jonathan said. "It was a heart attack."

Michael casually waved him off. "That's just a rumor so people don't start freaking out. Some mountain lion came down through western Maryland and was apparently living in the woods around town, eating out of trash cans. Old Mr. Van Praet was dragging his trash to the curb and—wham! The thing jumped out from behind a Buick and tore the poor son of a bitch down the middle like an old shirt."

The Lambeth twins stared at him. In a drawn-out, somewhat squeaky voice, Jason said, "I don't think that's true."

"You're full of shit, Sugarland," Jonathan said.

"Am I?"

"It would be in the newspapers and on TV."

"Unless the local authorities don't want to incite panic."

"Oh yeah? How the hell do you know, anyway?"

Michael jerked a thumb in my direction. "Mazzone's dad is a cop, remember? Who do you think had to scoop up the body parts and put 'em in plastic bags?"

"That's not true," I said. "My dad's got an assistant who scoops up the body parts."

"There's no mountain lion," Jonathan said, looking at me.

"Yeah, that's right," I said. "No mountain lion whatsoever. It was a stroke."

"Heart attack," Jason corrected.

"Yeah," I said, "a heart attack. Or whatever. Just no mountain lion."

Both Lambeth brothers eyed all five of us. Then Jonathan grinned. "You guys are a bunch of fucking assholes, you know that?" They sat down on the curb beside Michael.

"Did you hear Sasha Tamblin's got a band?" Jason said. "They're playing later tonight on the bandstand."

"No shit?" Peter said. "What do they play?"

Jason shrugged. "Guitars and shit."

"No, I mean what kind of music."

"I don't know."

When the marching band completed its set, a local rock band took the stage. Despite the heat, the members were all grunged out in flannel and long pants with chain wallets. The lead singer looked like Michael Stipe, so predictably they opened with an R.E.M. cover.

I went with Adrian and Peter to get hot dogs while Scott, Michael, and the Lambeth twins remained on the curb, tapping their feet to the music.

"Whoa," Peter said, snagging my shirt. "Take a look."

Nathan Keener and Eric Falconette stood smoking beside a row of portable outhouses. My heart seized in my chest as Keener looked in my direction. But he hadn't seen me; he gave the finger to someone walking up the grassy incline toward the outhouses. It was Denny Sallis and Kenneth Ottawa.

"There's too many people around for them to start something," Peter said.

"Yeah, well, that doesn't mean I want to walk up and shake the fucker's hand," I said. There was another hot dog booth on the corner of Center Street. "Let's head over there."

We crossed the street and got in line. Adrian and Peter pooled their money, but they only came up with about three bucks. I took my grandfather's ten-dollar bill from my pocket and waved it in front of their faces. Peter feigned a grab for it but I yanked it away.

"If you guys buy a soda, I'll treat you to the dogs," I said.

"Deal," Peter said.

I faced the front and was absently counting the people ahead of me when a pleasant voice said, "Hey there, Hemingway. How's the writing going?"

Rachel had snuck up beside me. She wore a red, white, and blue necklace made from links of construction paper, and she had gotten fireworks done in face paint on her left cheek.

"Hi. Having fun?"

"Yeah, it's okay. How about you? I would have thought you guys were too cool for this."

"We are," Peter said from over my shoulder. "We thought we'd do the city a favor and make a guest appearance."

"So," Rachel said, locking eyes with me, "you working on any new masterpieces?"

"I've got some ideas," I said, thinking of the stack of manuscript pages currently on my desk. "How about you?"

She crossed her eyes, stuck out her tongue, then laughed. "Nothing worth mentioning."

Her smile softened and I felt that I was staring at her too hard, so I looked toward the front of the line.

"A bunch of us are going to the Shallows tonight to light some fireworks, if you're interested," Rachel said.

"Thanks, but, you know, we've got some stuff to do," I said.

"That's too bad," she said. "You guys are always doing secret stuff."

"Don't you gotta be home by nine anyway, Angie?" Adrian said.

I smiled reproachfully at him.

Adrian's eyes went wide. "Oh," he said, his voice a mere peep.

"Listen," I said, turning back to Rachel. "You probably shouldn't walk down to the Shallows. I mean, if you go, you should get a ride." I thought about how she would have to pass by the Werewolf House to get there, and I didn't like the idea.

"Kim Freeman's brother is driving us," Rachel said, then looked at me slyly. "You afraid the Piper's gonna get me?"

"You just gotta be careful," I said.

The bored-looking woman behind the counter said, "Next."

Peter shoved me forward. I ordered three hot dogs, then turned to Rachel to see if she wanted one. But she was already moving through the crowd to rejoin her friends on the bleachers.

"You got a crush now or something?" Peter muttered.

"Get bent." I peered past him to Adrian. "And thanks for blabbin' about my curfew, Benedict Arnold."

"Yeah," Peter said. "Smooth move, ex-lax."

"What's ex-lax?" Adrian asked.

"You kids want these dogs or what?" barked the woman behind the counter.

I set my money on the countertop, took the three hot dogs from her, and handed one each to Peter and Adrian. When the woman brought me my change, I stuffed it into my pocket, then carried my hot dog to the condiments table. I was pumping copious amounts of mustard onto my hot dog when a shadow fell across me.

I looked up, hoping to find Rachel again. Instead, I found myself staring into the clear gray eyes of a police officer. He was young and vaguely familiar, though I didn't know his name. I smiled timidly, then moved over to a bin of diced onions.

The police officer held a hot dog under the mustard spigot. He pressed down on it, and the spigot farted bright yellow mustard onto the dog.

"Excuse me," I said, cradling my hot dog like a football and swerving around the police office to rejoin my friends.

On the bandstand, Sasha Tamblin plugged a guitar into an amp. Some other guys from Stanton picked up their guitars, and someone else climbed behind a small drum kit. I recognized one of the other musicians as Billy Foote, a droopy-eyed kid who used to swallow rocks on the school playground to impress the older kids.

"Let's get closer," Peter suggested.

The five of us moved through the crowd and gathered around the bandstand railing.

Sasha saw us and smiled crookedly. He pulled the guitar strap over his head, then walked up to the microphone at the front of the stage. "Happy Fourth of July, everybody," he said, his voice resonating over the loudspeakers.

Applause erupted from the audience.

Sasha began strumming distorted power chords, and after two bars, the rest of the band jumped in. The song was melodic, powerful, catchy, and wholly unidentifiable. It was his; he had written it.

We cheered him on.

At 8:15, just as the county selectmen migrated toward the wall of black rocks that faced the bay in preparation for the fireworks, I told my friends I had to get home.

"Dude," Michael bleated, bouncing up on his heels. He had stolen crêpe streamers from one of the victory booths and had them taped to his arms and shoulders, three-foot-long tendrils flapping in the wind. "The fireworks, man! They're gonna start in a half hour."

"I gotta be home by curfew," I said.

"Curfew's lifted."

"Not my dad's curfew." I sucked at my lower lip and watched the people slowly migrating toward the water. Blankets were spread out in the grass. A few kids tossed around a Frisbee with their parents. "I'll see you guys tomorrow."

"Later, skater," Michael said. He flicked Scott's earlobe and said, "Let's get a spot closer to the show."

"I'll go with you," Adrian said to me.

"Thanks," I said, "but you don't have to."

"No one goes around alone," he said. "Remember?"

"Yeah," Peter said. "I'll go, too."

"Really, you guys don't have to—"

"Who wants to look at some stupid fireworks, anyway?" Peter said.

Scott looked out across the water and at the floating barge on which the fireworks display was set up. Then he looked at Peter and me. "Yeah," he said. There was a dollop of ketchup in one corner of his mouth. "It's just a bunch of bright lights flashing in the sky. Big deal."

"Are you kidding?" Michael countered. "Fireworks are the best part. Loud noises make all the babies cry."

"You're a psychopath," Peter told him.

"Let's just catch the first five minutes."

"Do what you want," I said, already heading up Third Avenue against the crowd.

My friends rushed up to flank me on either side, their footfalls falling in step with mine.

"You're right," Michael commented, holding his arms out so that the crêpe streamers flared out. "Fireworks are for pussies."

Because I felt someone watching me, I turned around and glanced over my shoulder. The crowd was headed in the opposite direction, so I glimpsed mostly the backs of people's heads. But one person stood among them, facing me, with an eerily stoic expression.

It was the police officer I'd nearly bumped into at the hot dog booth.

My pace slowed enough so that my friends paused, too.

Peter followed my gaze, then tugged at my arm. "You looking for your girlfriend?" he said in a singsong voice.

"I recognize that cop," I said . . . and just saying it aloud brought it all back to me in a rush. This was the same cop who had been at the Ransoms' house on New Year's Eve when my father and I arrived. He had been the first one on the scene.

Peter frowned. "So what? Half the cops in this town know who you are."

"That's not the same thing," I said.

"That's him," Scott said. "Michael, take a look."

"Yeah," Michael said, nodding. "Yeah, that's him, all right."

"Him who?" I said.

"The guy Michael and I saw in the woods. The guy who was going through our stuff."

"You didn't say he was a police officer," Peter said.

"He wasn't wearing a uniform," Scott said. "But that's definitely him."

"Sure is," said Michael.

Adrian swallowed audibly. "Why is he staring at us?"

"He's not," Peter said, though I didn't think he sounded too convinced himself.

At that moment, the police officer turned and blended into the crowd. A moment later, he was gone.

CHAPTER TWENTY-SIX
THE CONFRONTATION

You said yourself that the Piper could be a cop," Scott reminded me as the five of us walked home. The evening sky was full of stars, though there was still a banner of pinkish orange out in the west. The streetlights came on, the traffic lessened, and soon we heard the fireworks exploding over the water.

"Yeah, but I wasn't being serious," I said.

"So the same guy who was searching through our stuff down in the woods just happens to be first on the scene the night Aaron Ransom disappears?"

"It does sound suspicious," Peter added.

"Why would the Piper be the first on the scene to his own crime?" I said.

"To make sure he didn't leave any evidence behind," Michael said.

I shot him a glare. "You're on this bandwagon now, too?"

"Hey! I saw him down in the woods that day. This shit is real, Angie. Just because you don't want to believe cops can be serial killers—"

"What do I care if it's a cop or not?" I said.

"Well, because of your dad," Michael said.

"My dad's not the Piper, you dipshit."

Michael turned to Adrian. "What do you think? You've been pretty quiet."

After a few more moments of silence, Adrian said, "If the killer is a cop, we're in a lot of trouble."

When we reached Solomon's Bend Road, we were faced with the decision of either following the road all the way around the park to the highway or cutting across Solomon's Field. I didn't think I would make it home on time if we went the long way, so we opted for the shortcut.

Solomon's Field was dotted with lampposts at intervals along a paved running track. On the street above, arc lights cast pools of sodium light onto the grass. The mouth of the underpass looked like a train tunnel that had been bored through the base of a mountain. As we drew closer to it, the signs posted along the walkway seemed to radiate out of the dark—

Park Closes at Dusk
By Order of the Harting Farms Police Department

Just as we were about to enter the underpass, someone called out, "Holy hell! Look who's here!"

We all froze.

"Holy hell," Nathan Keener said again, materializing out of the dark. He stood spotlighted in the glow of light that spilled down from the road above, the light assigning a ghastly paleness to his complexion. He looked like a vampire.

Denny Sallis and Eric Falconette were with him, all three of them clutching a bottle of Budweiser. Sallis's face hosted a devious smirk that spoke of bad intentions, and while that was awful enough, it was no match for the psychotic wheels I saw turning behind the dead eyes of Eric Falconette. Sallis took a swig from his beer bottle, then lobbed it in our direction.

"Is that you, Mazzone?" Keener said. His body seemed to fold over into a compact missile shape, his head forward on his neck, his shoulders slightly bladed as if he were preparing to jackknife off a high dive. He dug his boots into the dirt and crunched some dry sticks. For one horrific moment, I thought he was going to charge me like a bull. "Seems you and me got some unfinished business, huh?"

"You the one who fucked up his truck?" Sallis executed two wobbly steps in our direction, and I could see that he was drunk, stoned, or possibly both. "He the piece of shit did that to your truck, Nate?"

"Get over here," Keener growled at me—actually growled. Teeth clenched, cheeks quivering. I could feel his eyes drilling into mine, and there was nothing but fiery golden hate shimmering in the depths of his pupils. "The rest of you get the fuck outta here."

No one moved.

"I said split, fuckers," Keener said.

"You split," Adrian said. His oversized glasses did little to cover up the fear on his face.

Keener's head swung in Adrian's direction. "What'd you say, you little faggot?"

"I said *you* split." Frightened or not, his voice didn't falter.

"You little queer," Keener said, his teeth still clenched. "You little cock-sucker. I'll kill you, too, you talk to me like that again."

Adrian stood his ground. "You're not welcome here."

Jesus Christ, he's going to get himself killed, I thought. *Keener will kill both of us.*

Denny Sallis bleated laughter. His teeth looked like baked beans.

Keener looked stunned. "Not welcome here? What the fuck is that?"

"This park is ours," Adrian said. "Now leave us alone. We weren't bothering you."

"Shut up," Peter muttered.

Keener lifted his beer bottle and, holding it by the neck, cracked it against the stone wall of the underpass. The bottle broke, leaving him holding a jagged weapon that glinted in the lamplight. "How 'bout this? How 'bout I cut your fucking throats? All of you. I'll carve your fucking eyes out of your skulls."

Michael made a sudden movement with his right arm, and Keener's squared head swiveled in his direction. But Falconette kept his eyes on me, sighted in his crosshairs.

Michael held up his switchblade, the one Scott had purchased for him in the spring.

Sallis broke out into fresh laughter. He was like a busted toy, unable to do anything else.

"You've gotta be fuckin' kidding me," Keener said. He sounded almost irritated. "I want to know which one of you motherfuckers messed up my truck."

"We didn't do anything to your truck," I said, finding my voice at last.

"Bullshit." He pointed the busted bottle in Scott's direction. "Spill it."

"We didn't do shit," Scott said. His fists were clenched at his side.

"Get lost," Adrian said again. This time his voice cracked. He looked like he was about to be ill.

"Let's open 'em up, Nate." Falconette's voice was disconcertingly calm. "Let's cut off some pieces."

"There's five of us," Michael said, "and three of you. And I got a knife."

"So do I," Scott said, whipping his butterfly knife out from his pocket. He twirled the blade like a pro.

"Yeah," Peter said, pulling his switchblade from his pocket. The blade sprung out with a hollow clunk. "Get the fuck outta here and leave us the hell alone."

Sallis's laughter died for good this time—it cranked to a slow and reedy whine until it wound down altogether. He shifted his bleary eyes to his discarded beer bottle, which was now lodged in the mud. He clumsily went for it, but Scott was closer, and he kicked it across the grass and into the shadows. Sallis stopped in mid-leap, a look of confusion etched onto his face.

"You little shits don't have the balls," Keener said.

"You little faggots," Sallis cried.

Adrian opened his knife and held it awkwardly at his side. I popped out the rusted blade of my knife, extended it so I was sure I had Keener's attention, then turned it upside down and let it fall to the ground. It struck the mud blade-first.

Anger gripped me. I felt a boiling heat rise through the core of my body. I was done running from these assholes.

"You want to end this," I said, "then let's do it now. Just you and me. Fair fight. With just our fists."

"I'll rip you apart," Keener sneered. Fire still danced in his eyes.

"Yeah," I said. "You probably will. But I'll hurt you, too. You won't walk away from this without hurting. I promise."

"We all promise," Adrian added, touching the tip of his nose.

"Then that'll be the end of it," I said.

"Kill him, Nate," Sallis shouted. His face was stricken, pale, trembling with anger. "Bust his fucking face in half."

I pointed at Sallis. "But it's just me and him. You try to jump in on it, and my friends will cut you up." I looked at Falconette. "Goes for you, too."

Falconette's grin was as hideous a sight as anything I had ever seen. But he didn't challenge me, and I had gone too far to back down now.

"And what about your friends?" Keener said. "They gonna shiv me in the back while I'm whooping your ass, fucker?"

"No." I looked at each of my friends. "No one steps in. No one gets involved." I held my gaze longest on Scott, who looked ready to rush over to Keener and fillet him with his butterfly knife. "It's just him and me."

Their faces were a maelstrom of varying emotions. Yet they all nodded.

"There we go," I said, turning to Keener.

The rest happened quickly but also in slow motion.

Keener dropped the busted bottle and launched himself at me. He tackled me around the waist, knocking the wind out of my lungs. When I hit the ground, my teeth shook like ball bearings in my skull, and my vision dispersed in patterns of fiery light like the fireworks at Market Square. Straddling me, the son of a bitch struck me repeatedly in the small of my back. Out of instinct I pulled myself into a fetal position, but that only exposed more of my back and spine to Keener's punches. I bucked my hips and knocked him off me.

I rolled away, my ribs and back aching, my heart thumping fervently in my throat. Just as I scrambled to my feet, Keener charged me again, swinging. I jerked backward and watched a fist roughly the size of a wrecking ball whiz past my face. As his arm then shoulder blurred by, I fired a right hook at the exposed white flesh of Keener's right cheek. The punch connected, and it felt as though my wrist collapsed like a telescope under the force.

Keener grunted. The momentum of his poorly calculated punch kept him moving forward. I threw a second punch that connected with his right shoulder blade. He whirled around, and in that instant I saw nothing but burning yellow eyes and the gnashing teeth of a bloodthirsty predator. He collided with me, all his furious weight knocking me to the ground again.

In my mind's eye, I saw my father teaching Charles and me how to defend ourselves in our backyard, the borrowed sparring gear from the police station scattered about the lawn. I saw Charles throw punch after punch, his dark hair glistening with sweat, the smooth muscles of his arms moving with each jab. There was a controlled fluidity to his movements. Then I thought of him blown apart in a foreign country, the bloody tatters of his military uniform and the pieces of his body strewn about like refuse after a storm, and the empty coffin buried next to my mother's grave on Cemetery Hill . . .

When I returned to real life, I was on top of Keener, thrashing his face in a furious barrage of punches and slaps. At one point I grabbed him by the cheekbones and drove his head down into the mud. Repeatedly. I smashed the front of his face with a fist and heard the sound of his nose breaking. A spume of blood, impossibly red, spurted up into the air and spattered in an arc across his left cheek and my knuckles. Then, in the blink of an eye, all I saw were monochromatic shades of gray—bands of gray blurring into one another and filing by like the image on a television set whose vertical hold needs adjusting.

Someone's arms looped around my waist. I howled, my eyes blurry with tears, and thrashed back and forth, clawing at the person's arms that had slid up and were now secured across my heaving chest. As I was dragged off

Keener, kicking and shouting, the color gradually seeped back into the world: beneath the sodium lights, I saw the bright red blood on my hands, my shirt, and on Keener's face as he lifted his head drunkenly off the ground.

"Stop," someone whispered very close to my ear. The command came over and over and over again, although never changing pitch. "Stop. Stop. Stop."

I ripped the person's arms off me and spun around to find Peter standing there. He held up both hands, as if offering proof that he had finally let me go.

Behind him, the rest of my friends remained standing with their knives out, expressions of utter disbelief on their faces. Even Denny Sallis looked upon the scene with incredulity. I turned and saw Eric Falconette leaning against the underpass with his hands in his pockets. There was a black streak of blood on his left cheek, and I had to wipe tears from my eyes to make sure I was actually seeing it.

Keener rolled over onto his side. Blood purled from his nose, soaking his shirt and pants. He took his time coughing and spitting onto the ground. His face was so red it looked as though it had been heated in a kiln. With great care, he propped himself up on his hands and knees and remained in that position while he caught his breath.

"Hey," Sallis squawked at Keener. It seemed like he couldn't make up his mind whether to help his friend or take off running through the underpass. "Nate, you okay?"

Keener held out one hand in Sallis's direction. He didn't lift his head to look at him.

My attention returned to Falconette. When he caught my stare, he manufactured an overlarge and humorless smile. He possessed the blank and soulless eyes of a department store mannequin.

Keener spat on the ground—a globule of reddish mucus—then climbed unsteadily to his feet.

"Nate?" Sallis queried again.

Keener faced me. A bright red banner of blood had spilled from his nose and was smeared across one half of his face. When he winced, I saw blood on his teeth. "Okay." The word sputtered out in a shaky exhalation. It was barely a whisper. "Okay." And he nodded at me. "Okay."

When I opened my mouth and tried to speak, all that came out was a thin whistling sound.

Keener stumbled toward the mouth of the underpass. Sallis, whose eyes were as large as flashbulbs, followed him.

Falconette remained leaning against the tunnel, hands in his pockets. The cut on his left cheek was leaking toward his chin now. After a moment, he slid one hand from his pocket—very slowly—and pointed at me. He jerked his finger like he was pulling the trigger of a gun and said, "Ka-pow." Then he faded into the darkness of the underpass, whistling.

As all the adrenaline was pumped from my bloodstream, pain began to blossom across my face and body. I patted my tenderized face and discovered that much of the blood on my hands and shirt had come from my own nose and mouth. "I think I'm gonna pass out," I muttered, slowly lowering myself to the ground.

I looked up and tried to focus on the Park Closes at Dusk sign to anchor myself, but it pixelated and scattered as a sickening numbness enveloped me. I closed my eyes and felt the earth tilt to one side. An instant later, I was overcome by the very real sensation that the world had opened up beneath me and I was falling, falling, falling, just as my friends and I had done in my nightmares, right down into narrow little holes in the earth . . .

Then, little by little, I felt the warm night air against my face, the trickles of sweat and blood across my skin, the numbing throb in my right hand. The world came back to me in fragments.

Scott's face appeared in front of me. "You okay?"

I couldn't speak. My throat was so dry I could have lit a match by striking it across my teeth.

"That really just happened," Peter said on a gust of pent-up breath and collapsed on the ground beside me.

Michael dropped down on the other side of me and slung an arm around my shoulders. "Your face looks like hamburger meat. It's a surprising improvement, to be honest."

"Don't make me laugh," I croaked. "Hurts."

"Should you go to a doctor?" Adrian said.

"I'm okay," I said. "Just a little banged up."

"I think you broke Keener's nose," said Scott.

"Good," I said. "What happened to Falconette's face?"

"Shit," Michael said. "Scott cut him."

"What?"

"Yeah," Scott said, a bit out of breath. He looked around nervously as if fearful he would be overheard. "He tried to jump in on the fight so I . . . well . . ."

"He just lashed out and cut him," Michael finished.

"Holy shit," I said.

Scott turned his palms up and stared at his hands. They shook.

The sky growled. Either a dump truck was bounding down the road or a storm was fast approaching. Fat drops of water pattered on my head, and I turned my hot face up to them.

* * *

Adrian let me clean up at his house before I went home. Thankfully his mother had gone to bed early, so that was one less thing I had to contend with.

In the downstairs bathroom, I scrubbed the dried blood from my face and hands while Adrian disappeared upstairs to fetch me one of his shirts. My face was a little red, and there were some nicks on my cheeks and chin and a decent horizontal gash across my forehead. But considering Keener's busted nose, I thought I had gotten off pretty easily. The worst was my right hand—it ached, and I found it next to impossible to make a proper fist.

Adrian appeared in the bathroom doorway with a Captain America T-shirt that looked about two sizes too small. "It's a little big for me, so it might fit you pretty good."

That was when I lost it. Tears sprung from my eyes, and I felt my legs threaten to collapse beneath me. My entire body burned. I sobbed—a pathetic foghorn sound.

In the mirror, Adrian's blurry reflection watched me. "Does it hurt?"

I swiped at my eyes and turned the water on. After I washed my face again, I muttered, "No. I'm not hurt."

"Then how come you're crying?"

"I'm not," I whined, feeling the anger and frustration and fear rise up in me all over again. "I'm n-n-not—"

Tears spilled down my face again. Ashamed, I hung my head and let them fall down the drain. I was thankful for the running water covering up my sobs. "Don't tell the guys," I managed, my breath hitching.

"Never," Adrian said. Then he shut the door and left me to it.

CHAPTER TWENTY-SEVEN
WHAT MICHAEL FOUND

Two weeks into July, a ringing telephone jarred me from sleep. The clock on my nightstand said it was just after four o'clock. Darkness still permeated my bedroom, and I thought the phone had been part of a dream I'd immediately forgotten the second I opened my eyes.

Then I heard the ringing again, followed by my father's gruff, groggy voice as he answered. His words were muted, but I didn't have to hear him to know it was work. When he hung up, I heard his heavy feet creaking on the floorboards in the hallway. A moment after that, I heard the pipes shudder in the walls as the shower clunked on.

I rolled out of bed, tugged an old T-shirt over my boxer shorts, then crept downstairs to the kitchen where I brewed a pot of coffee. From the window, the first glimmer of daylight could be seen between the stunted pin oaks and pine trees on the eastern side of the street.

Fifteen minutes later, my father appeared in the doorway, straightening his tie and tugging on a navy-blue blazer. "What are you doing up this early?"

"Phone woke me. What happened?"

"Did you know a girl named Jennifer Vestos?"

I felt my stomach avalanche into my bowels. "She goes to Stanton."

"She's missing."

I said nothing.

He went into the vestibule where he fished his car keys out of the ceramic bowl by the front door. From the window, I watched him drag his tired-looking body into the old sedan, then back slowly out of the driveway. I watched his car go until it hooked a right onto Haven. I could still hear the car's engine growling even after it had vanished.

I turned the coffeemaker off and went upstairs. Climbing into my bed, I found the sheets cold from my absence. My room was still dark, but I couldn't go back to sleep and enjoy the few hours remaining until I had to get up to go to work at the thrift store. My father had already referred to the girl in the past tense—*Did you know a girl named Jennifer Vestos?* That spoke volumes, I thought. My father had finally lost hope.

While I had slept, Rita Vestos had woken around four in the morning to feed the baby. As she always did, she poked her head into Jennifer's room, only to find the girl's bed empty. Panic-stricken, she'd awoken her husband, Ford, who eventually discovered that the back door was closed but unlocked. Ford Vestos swore to police that he had locked the back door earlier in the evening and checked it before going to bed.

The final conclusion by the HFPD was that Jennifer Vestos had most likely known her abductor. Jennifer had presumably gone outside to meet this individual, which would explain the pair of sneakers missing from her closet (she would have put them on before going outside) as well as the unlocked back door.

Something Scott had said to us earlier that summer returned to me upon hearing this information: "Adults don't know all the city's secrets, all the places to hide. Not like we do. We're kids and we know, and that's what we keep bringing to this thing over and over that the cops can't."

It was true: there was a secret society of children throughout the city, like an underground network of rebels in a distant and war-torn country. Adults knew nothing about Michael's penchant for stowing cantaloupes in people's gardens (just as he had done recently to my grandfather). They had never learned who'd stolen the homecoming cow or of its underwater grave in the Shallows. They weren't aware that the chain-link fence around the construction site behind the library was never locked, creating a shortcut to the Superstore plaza. Just as these grown-ups were ignorant to the hidden byways and whispered secrets concerning their town, so were they ignorant to the whims of the children who lived there.

This is what we knew about Jennifer Vestos. She hung out with a cadre of loners who smoked pot in the school bathrooms and skipped out of class more frequently than my friends and me. Though she was only a sophomore, she frequently hung out with degenerates from the local community college or the vocational school in Glenrock, guys with facial hair and shiny cars with chrome wheels and tinted windows that looked like spaceships. They would sometimes pick her up from school, their music blasting, their cars belching out clouds of black exhaust that reeked of pot. It was rumored she had gotten pregnant by one of these dirtbags and had had an abortion, though no one ever knew if it was true or not.

Jennifer also held the honor of being involved in one of only two girl fights that had ever graced the Pepto-Bismol–colored halls of Stanton School. During the fight, Jennifer had ripped out the hoop earring of the other girl, spraying blood all down the girl's cheek and across Jennifer's shirt. True to form, Jennifer wore that shirt an entire week (after returning from her suspension), the arc of blood droplets across the front like a badge of honor.

Every night after her parents had gone to bed Jennifer would sneak out onto her back porch and smoke pot. It explained the missing sneakers; it explained the unlocked back door. The rear of her house faced the side of the Lambeths' house, and the Lambeth twins frequently bemoaned their inability to sleep with their windows open in the summer because of the fat, pug-faced Vestos girl who was out there every night, smoking like a goddamn chimney.

The Lambeth twins said that the police questioned them about the night Jennifer disappeared. No, they hadn't heard anything. No, they hadn't seen anything. Did they tell the cops about Jennifer's penchant for sneaking out of the house and smoking dope? No, they did not. It never occurred to them.

A week later, the phone rang just after eight o'clock on a Wednesday morning. I was already up, having to be at Secondhand Thrift for work by nine. My father had left for the day, but he'd scribbled his beeper number on the wall pad beside the phone in case anyone called for him. I had hardly seen him since Jennifer Vestos went missing.

"Is that you, Mazzone?"

I just barely recognized the voice. "Michael? Where are you?"

"At summer school. I told the secretary I left my lunch at home and needed to call my mom."

"I'm not bringing you your lunch."

"No, man," he said, his voice urgent but hushed. I pictured the overweight school secretary who always wore too much makeup staring at him from across the office. "I don't need a lunch. Well, I mean, yeah, I could use a lunch, but that's not why I'm calling."

"What do you want?"

"Round up the guys, and meet me here after school lets out at two thirty."

"It's summer. The last thing I want to do is meet you at school."

"Dude, you have to. I found something, and you guys are gonna flip the fuck out." In his excitement his voice had risen, and in the background I heard the secretary scolding him for his language. Michael ignored her.

"I've got work all day," I reminded him. "I don't get out till five."

"You need to get here before they close the school. Can't you call in sick or something?"

Since Callibaugh was friends with my grandfather and knew my dad peripherally, any excuse I used to get out of work would eventually follow me home. I had to be careful. "I'll think of something," I said, sighing.

"Awesome. Two thirty by the smoking door." A second later, there was a dial tone in my ear.

When I arrived at Secondhand Thrift, Callibaugh was scrounging around on his hands and knees behind the front desk. He looked up, his features relaxing when he saw that it was me and not a customer.

"Morning," I said.

"The cavalry has arrived," Callibaugh intoned, locating what he'd been looking for, which turned out to be a tiny plastic sprocket no bigger than an atom.

"Can I use the phone in the back?"

"Are you planning to call China?"

"No, sir."

"Have at it, young scalawag."

The back office was no bigger than a closet, its rows of unpainted wooden shelves crowded with paperwork, three-ring binders, and a few model ships. A cheap desk was shoved against one wall, its surface frilly with curled bits of receipts and other random papers, and the telephone was buried beneath a VCR manual.

I called Peter, informed him of Michael's request, then told him to pass along the info to Scott and Adrian. "You guys may have to go without me. I'm stuck at work."

"Sneak out."

"It isn't that easy."

"That old fart wouldn't even know you were gone."

I laughed and we hung up.

I spent the morning transporting boxes from the stockroom, and to the best of my ability, organizing the shelves.

When I didn't adjourn to the back room at noon for lunch, Callibaugh said nothing yet eyed me suspiciously as if he'd just caught me doing something immoral.

At a quarter past one, the old cur shambled out from the back room, a can of Chef Boyardee in one hand. There was tomato sauce at the corners of his mouth, and he smelled of cigar smoke and modeling glue. "Your grandmother got you on some strict diet? Because you look like skin and bones to me."

"I'm sorry?"

"Food," he said, spraying flecks of Chef Boyardee into the air. "Didn't bring your lunch today?"

"I forgot it."

Callibaugh surveyed the store, which hadn't seen a customer since eleven thirty. "Why don't you skip out for your lunch hour and get some food?"

"Thanks. I'll just finish stocking this shelf first."

Thus, I was tearing across the rear parking lot of the high school on my bike by 2:25. With the exception of a solitary cheddar-yellow school bus chugging out onto the main road, the boisterous cackle and flailing arms of students spilling through the half-open bus windows, the parking lot was deserted.

I pedaled over to the set of concrete steps at the far end of the lot. Peter, Scott, and Adrian were perched on them. Behind them, the bloodred steel smoking door, which would have looked less out of place on the hull of a submarine, stood shut. We'd termed it as such because it was the door we popped out of whenever we wanted a quick smoke between classes but didn't have time to make it to one of the less populated restrooms in B Hall. It was the only door in the whole school that wouldn't automatically lock you out.

"And he arrives," Peter said. "I was wondering if you'd make it. So what's this about, anyway?"

I dumped my bike on the blacktop. "I don't have a clue. You guys know just as much as I do."

At the top of the steps, the smoking door creaked open—a sound equally befitting of a submarine—and Michael poked his head out. He beamed at us.

"Okay," I said, still a bit winded from my bike ride halfway across town, "so we're here. What's the big surprise?"

He waved us inside, and my friends hopped off the steps and filed through the doorway. I brought up the rear, thankful to be out from beneath the hot sun. It was a scorcher.

We followed Michael down B Hall, and I was overwhelmed by the sheer emptiness of the school and the sense of vacancy, of dormancy. *It's asleep*, I thought as we moved down the hall. *The large beast hibernates in summer, dreaming of the tiny children who will traipse through its innards come fall. We are insects passing through its system while it slumbers.*

Michael led us to the glass display case that held the school's trophies, pennants, ribbons, plaques, and other such paraphernalia. It hung on the wall at the end of B Hall between a janitor's closet and a water fountain that never worked.

"This?" Peter said. "What's—?"

"Check it out." Michael pointed at two framed black-and-white photos on the back wall of the display.

The photos seemed to be of the same gothic structure taken from two slightly different angles, the stone façade a confusion of various architectural motifs: medieval parapets, marble arcades, Greek pillars, obelisk posts on either side of a sweeping semicircular stairway that led to a pair of massive doors with intricate iron sigils. The windows were arched and networked with iron bars. Detailed carvings were inlaid above the entranceways. Indeed, even the date on the brass plate at the bottom of each frame was engraved with the same year—1893. Yet on closer inspection I noticed the words engraved above one set of doors said *Stanton School for Boys* while in the other picture they said *Patapsco School for Girls*.

"Wow. That's Stanton," Scott said, leaning so close to the display case that the bill of his Orioles cap touched the glass. "That must have been what it looked like when it was first built."

"It looks like Castle Dracula," said Peter.

Below those two photos were several smaller ones, which, like the Evolution of Man chart in our biology textbooks, depicted the gradual modernization of our dark and drafty Stanton School from an archaic and sprawling mausoleum to an oblong, square-windowed institution with peppermint-colored walls and black-and-blue checked tiles, surrounded by elms and fronted by a two-lane road. The final photograph was of a sepia-toned cowboy with a Ulysses S. Grant beard, circular John Lennon glasses, and a double-breasted suit. The name at the bottom of the photo read L. John Stanton.

"Yeah," Michael said, "that's Stanton. And the other one's the girls' school, the one that later became the Patapsco Institute."

"Where all those people died in that fire," Scott added.

"What's the Patapsco Institute?" Adrian asked.

"It was one of two schools built in the late 1800s at the far end of December Park," I said. "Stanton stayed but they turned the girls' school into a convalescent hospital after World War II."

"What's convalescent?"

"It's like wounded soldiers and stuff. People who can't take care of themselves."

Adrian moved in beside Scott for a better look at the photos.

"There was a fire back in the fifties that killed a bunch of people," I went on. "The place was shut down and pretty much forgotten since then."

"Creepy," Adrian said.

"It is," I agreed, "but I don't see what it has to do with—"

"Holy shit!" Scott cried. "It's—"

"I see them!" Adrian broke in. Both he and Scott leaned even closer to the glass.

Michael laughed and looked instantly proud. "Ha! You see 'em, huh? You get it?"

"Get what?" Shaking his head, Peter leaned toward the display, too.

"The statues," Scott said. "Second picture from the bottom."

"I don't believe it," Peter said. "Angie, come take a look at this."

Michael grabbed my shoulders and propelled me forward, wedging me between Peter and Scott. "I told you I found something," Michael said into my ear and not without a trace of vindication.

One of the photographs was of the east flank of Stanton School—I could tell by the rows of windows in the stonework, which, despite years of renovations, had remained unaltered (and I could even see the iron smoking door that also appeared unchanged). In the photograph, a group of construction workers removed sections of the masonry and loaded the giant blocks onto open carts. Along the foundation, in rank and file like a militia, the concrete statues that now lay scattered in broken headless heaps in the Dead Woods stood proud and tall, their heads still intact.

"Well, shit," I said. "I guess that mystery's solved."

"So they wound up tearing down those statues and just dumping them in the woods by the park?" Peter said.

"It probably wasn't a park back then," Michael said. "They could have used the woods as a landfill for all we know."

"These pictures have been here for like a billion years," said Scott, "and none of us noticed until now."

"We didn't need to until now," I said.

"Yeah," Michael said, "but that's not all. I mean, look how similar the two schools are from the front. The other photos are just of Stanton and the renovations and stuff, so we can't see for sure, but I bet Patapsco had those same statues, too." He turned and looked at us. "I'll bet that's where the statue head came from."

"Whoa," Adrian said.

"You guys think he's living there?" Scott said. "The Piper, I mean."

Hard-soled shoes squeaked behind us. We spun around in unison to see Mr. Johnson standing outside a classroom door, his short-sleeved button-down an iridescent white in the midday gloom. "Do you kids need assistance with anything?"

"No, sir," Michael said. "We were just heading home."

"The bus already left," Mr. Johnson said. He sounded distrustful. "What are you guys doing with that display case?"

"Let's split," Peter said, and we all hustled to the fire exit. Peter slammed against the arm bar, and dazzling daylight briefly blinded us.

"Hey," Mr. Johnson shouted after us, but I didn't hear his squeaking shoes following.

CHAPTER TWENTY-EIGHT
THE PURSUIT

I had glimpsed it a few times in the past, mostly in the fall and winter, when the leaves dried up and fell from the trees. And even then it was more like a mirage—the dinosaur at the edge of December Park, where the woods ended at the edge of the cliff that overlooked the bay. Perhaps at one time it had been accessible by roads, but it was now firmly hidden within the lush panhandle of Satan's Forest like a dirty secret.

The closest I had ever come to seeing it—actually looking at it, as opposed to merely glimpsing its reptilian hide through barren tree branches—had been when I was about eleven and in the midst of a short-lived fascination with model airplanes made out of balsa wood.

My journey to find the highest point in the city brought me to the cliffs that overlooked the charcoal diorama of the Chesapeake Bay. It had been a blustery fall day, and the strong winds had stripped the already withering trees bare. My balsa wood plane caught slipstream after slipstream and soared like a bird, pulling loop-the-loops in the gunmetal sky. Twice, I nearly lost it when it shot out over the cliff, carving grand arcs in the cloud-heavy sky; yet both times it boomeranged back to me, landing in a series of undisciplined cartwheels.

One final toss sent the little plane in a smooth semicircle over the cliffs yet again. The bay—whose waters were so black and turbulent they appeared ready to unleash Poseidon and all his fury—appeared to summon it. The fragile plane trembled on the slipstream and actually seemed to pause in midair, terrified. It must have caught a second current, though, because it veered left and swooped back around toward the cliff. It was suddenly no more than a crucifix-shaped pinpoint in the darkening sky, and I was amazed at the heights it reached.

When it finally descended, it did so far into the trees: it swept down and sailed through the naked, craggy arms of mummified elms before it disappeared completely. I stared through the screen of geometric branches to identify where it had landed. It was then that I realized the ruinous old building was just beyond the trees, its bone-colored façade stippled in ivy and veined in a heavy system of snakelike roots.

Before I knew what I was doing, I was halfway through the woods and heading toward the structure. I found myself in awe of this strange monstrosity that appeared both imposing yet harmless. It was tremendous and nearly absurd in its novelty; however, even with all the renovations that had taken place at Stanton School over the past century, I could still discern the skeleton of its twin in this building.

As I crept closer to the building, my sneakers snagging on brambles and thorny green spirals of flora, I recognized the remnants of the horrible fire from the fifties: it had blackened the sandstone and hollowed out parts of the structure. It was possible to peer into some of the arched windows and straight out to the woods beyond. Every ghost story I'd ever heard—no matter how outlandish or silly—resurfaced in my head, causing a chill to trace down my spine and my skin to grow tingly with gooseflesh.

The balsa wood airplane, suspended in a tangle of twiggy branches perhaps ten feet off the ground, was directly ahead of me. A vision came to me then: when I jumped up to shake the branches in an attempt to free my plane, the trees would instantly come alive and drive their twisted, skeletal protuberances through my torso, spearing me over and over again like a living voodoo doll.

I stared openmouthed at the building. Overhead, the sound of thunder was like a roller coaster. The roof of my mouth adopted all the attributes of drywall. It was at that moment nature saw fit to shuttle a river of icy wind down through the trees, rattling their bony branches like percussion instruments. I thought I saw someone flit by one of the darkened windows in the face of the building. My skin rippled like rings across the surface of a pond.

The strength of the wind increased, summoning little tornadoes of dead leaves and grit, and with it came the ghostly moan of some distant and otherworldly creature crying out in mournful regret. I vibrated like a knife stuck in a plank of wood, unable to tear my eyes from the black orifice in the masonry of the building—an orifice that was no longer a glassless window but a gargantuan eye socket.

That mournful moan rose to a pitch that resonated in my molars and liberated my balsa wood airplane from its cage of branches. The plane nose-dived to the earth, and one of its cheap wings broke at a perfect ninety-degree angle.

I snatched up the plane, anticipating those trees coming alive. Only now I believed they would lift me off the ground and carry me toward the building. The stone foundation would crack open into the ragged suggestion of a mouth, and the tree branches would feed me into it, the way a blue crab brings food to its mouth with its serrated pincers.

But nothing happened. With my airplane in tow, I turned and kicked up clods of dirt as I ran toward the slope of green lawn that trailed to the edge of the cliff.

Later around the dinner table, when my father asked what I'd done all afternoon, I told him about flying the plane over the cliffs. "Did you know there's a building back there?" I asked him.

"Stay away from it," he told me flatly. He looked at Charles, who had been listening to my story with uncharacteristic interest. "You and your friends go in there to play, you could get hurt. Or worse."

In bed that night, I thought about the shape I'd seen—or thought I'd seen—passing behind one of the eye-socket–shaped windows, and it only brought my father's voice back to me: *you could get hurt. Or worse . . .*

Back in the school's rear parking lot and still shaken by the prospect of what we'd seen in the B Hall display case, we all agreed that we needed to go to the old building and see for ourselves if there were statues up there, too.

As expected, Adrian and Scott wanted to head out right away, but I had to finish my shift at the store. Also, Michael had homework, and Peter complained that he had chores to do at home. Reluctantly, Adrian and Scott agreed to wait until seven to meet at our rendezvous point.

Back at Secondhand Thrift, I shambled through the rest of my day in a fog, my mind on things other than used clothing that needed price stickers, old Perry Como LPs, and the model of a Spanish warship Callibaugh was piecing together in the office.

It was around ten after four when someone entered. I looked up from behind the cash register, where I was stapling receipts, and felt disbelief wash over me. It was the police officer who had been watching my friends and me in Market Square on the Fourth of July. The same cop who had been first on the scene the night Aaron Ransom was taken by the Piper and had been digging through our stuff at Echo Base.

Since the disappearance of Howie Holt in June, it was common to see uniformed officers patrolling the streets and going in and out of local shops. But I found it impossible to convince myself that this was merely a coincidence. I hoped grouchy old Callibaugh would emerge from his office and help disperse the atmospheric tension.

The cop approached the counter and leveled a hard gaze at me. His face looked too young. He couldn't have been more than twenty-one. "They got you here alone tonight, kid?"

"The owner's in the back."

The cop surveyed the counter, and I could tell he was just casually taking it all in and not looking for something in particular. Eventually, he dropped a pack of cinnamon Dentyne onto the counter, along with some change. "I'll just take this."

That's not all, I thought. *You're here for a reason. I can smell it on you. You've been following us around for quite a while now, haven't you?*

I rang up the gum and gave the cop his change, anxious to be rid of him.

"Have a good night and be safe," he said, moving toward the door. He slipped the pack of gum in his pocket. "Don't forget the curfew," he added before stepping outside.

Through the storefront windows, I watched him continue down the block, roving like an alley cat at a casual, disinterested pace.

I slipped out from behind the counter and went to the front windows. It looked like the cop was heading toward the Wet Dog Pub, which already had its happy hour sign glowing in the window, but then he cut down an alley between the pub and Patty's Laundromat. I was at too much of an angle to see into the alleyway.

I went back behind the counter, grabbed a blank envelope, then paused as I listened for any indication that Callibaugh might come out of his office anytime soon. All was quiet. The old guy might have fallen asleep. He'd done it before, waking up at his desk with pieces of a model ship glued to his face.

I went outside, hurried up the block to the mailbox that stood on the corner of Second and Children Street, and dropped the envelope inside . . . then looked across the street and straight down the mouth of the alley.

I had expected the alley to be empty but it was not. There was a police car tucked away in there, its front grille facing the street. I couldn't be sure, but I thought the cop was sitting behind the wheel.

This did not make me feel better.

Trying to keep a casual pace, I walked back to the store. Once inside, I pressed my forehead against the window to see if the cop might emerge from the alley. He didn't.

"You," said Callibaugh, coming up behind me and nearly sending me straight through the roof, "are like a pathetic little puppy in the window of a pet store. Do tell. What is it you find so fascinating on the corner? Or is it just the concept that it's summer and you're in here while others are enjoying the last remaining hours of daylight?"

"That must be it," I said. "Can I use the phone again?"

"Why not? Say, would you like to borrow my car, too?"

"I'm sorry. I could use the pay phone across the street."

His face softened and he winked at me. "I'm joking with you. How's your grandpa?"

"He's great."

"Wonderful. He owes me thirty dollars from a night of poker."

"I didn't realize he still played poker."

"He doesn't. He's owed me since 1985. Go on. Use the phone."

In the office, I punched in Scott's phone number and prayed that he'd answer.

"Yeah?" It was his sister, sounding irritated and snapping gum.

"Is Scott there?"

An exasperated sigh. Kristy shouted Scott's name, then stayed on the line chewing her gum until Scott picked up the extension. Without a word, she hung up.

"It's me. Are you busy? I need your help."

"Sure," he said.

"You've got the walkie-talkies?"

"They're charging upstairs in my room."

"They've got enough juice to put 'em to work?"

"I guess so. What's up?"

I told him about the cop. "And now he's sitting in his car in the alley across the street. He's been watching us. I think he's waiting for me to leave work."

"Holy shit. Angie, this is some serious shit. You want me to get ahold of your dad?"

"That won't do any good. Can you get out here and bring those walkie-talkies?"

"Yeah. What are you thinking?"

"If he follows me home, *you* follow *him*."

"That's great. All right, I'm in."

"But don't come alone. Go get Michael or Peter."

"Michael's finishing his homework and Peter's doing chores."

"Then get Adrian."

"Adrian doesn't have a bike, and I'm not wobbling around with him on my handlebars. I'll just come by myself."

"Okay. But be careful."

"I wish I had a bazooka," he said and hung up.

* * *

Scott arrived at the store at a quarter to five. He had a backpack slung over his shoulder and his Orioles hat pulled down over his eyes.

Callibaugh, who was counting inventory on one of the shelves, glanced at him with frank suspicion. For the past twenty minutes, Callibaugh had been telling me I could go home early. I said that I wanted to finish up some work before I left, which amounted to me scrubbing the hardened gobbets of model glue off the countertop.

"I saw the police car in the alley when I rode by," Scott said, setting his backpack on the counter. "It's still there. Are you sure it's the same cop?"

"Of course."

Scott unzipped the backpack, slid out one of the walkie-talkies, and handed it to me.

"You hang out at the opposite end of the block," I told him. "When I come out and if the cop car follows, get behind him. But keep some distance, you know?"

"Yeah, I know."

"We can keep in contact with each other on these," I said, holding up the walkie-talkie.

"How are you gonna ride your bike home and talk on that thing at the same time without this cop wondering what the heck is going on?"

It was a good question. I hadn't thought of that. "Give me your hat," I said.

Scott took his hat off, his wiry brown hair popping up like mattress springs, and passed it to me.

I wrapped it around the walkie-talkie. It concealed the body of the handheld; only the antenna poked out.

"I guess that's good enough," he said.

"Just be careful and don't get caught," I warned him.

"This guy's gotta be the Piper, right?"

"I don't know."

"There's no other excuse." He peered out the window. "He's been there all day?"

"I don't know," I said again.

"You think he followed you to Stanton?"

"Maybe. Or maybe he picked me up on my way back. I was riding too fast and wasn't paying attention."

"What if he's got our statue head right there in his police car?"

"Don't go looking for trouble. Just stick to the plan."

"Yeah, yeah, yeah," Scott grumbled. As he dragged his backpack off the counter, he accidentally knocked one of Callibaugh's model ships to the floor, where it broke into half a dozen small plastic pieces.

"Oh shit," I groaned, staring across the store at Callibaugh, who stared back at me with eyes like dinner plates.

Scott bent down, picked up the pieces, and set them atop the counter. "Sorry, man," he said to me just as Callibaugh marshaled right up behind him. Scott spun around and looked at Callibaugh's incredulous face. "Sorry, sir," Scott said to him.

"After a history of noble battles," said Callibaugh, "the ill-fated USS *Monitor* is finally, sadly decommissioned."

"That's the CSS *Virginia*, sir," Scott said.

Callibaugh's gray eyebrows triggered back and forth. "You speak nonsense."

"The *Monitor* had a flat freeboard with only the turret and pilothouse sticking up." Scott pointed to the broken model. "This ship's hull is more triangular, like the *Virginia*."

Callibaugh made a sound way back in his throat that approximated a grunt of approval. "Well, then, it is the ill-fated *Virginia* that is finally, sadly decommissioned."

"The *Virginia* wasn't decommissioned. It was blown up off the coast of Craney Island during the Civil War," Scott informed him.

Callibaugh smiled sourly. "Go home." He gathered up the remnants of his poor warship and retreated to his office, presumably to resurrect the great ship with some modeling glue and tenderness.

Scott left the store, got on his bike, and pedaled down the block in the opposite direction of the alley where the police cruiser sat waiting for me.

At five o'clock, I closed down the register, then poked my head in through the half-open doorway of Callibaugh's office. I caught him in the process of excavating a particularly stubborn booger from his left nostril. I cleared my throat, and Callibaugh, startled, popped his big forefinger from his nose.

"I'm heading home now," I told him.

Callibaugh blinked and shuffled around the paperwork on top of his desk. He brushed some papers aside to reveal an open history textbook. He pointed to the reproduction of an oil painting that showed two ironclad ships firing at each other in the water. "Your friend is a smart little bugger. Clumsy . . . but smart."

I went to the stockroom, retrieved my bike, and rolled it out onto the street. Mid-July and the sun was still a blazing ball beyond the tops of the buildings even at this hour. In my right hand I had the walkie-talkie wrapped in Scott's ball cap. I turned it on, heard the brief static hum, then climbed onto my bike. I keyed the Talk button with my thumb and said, "I'm heading out. Over."

"Roger that," Scott's voice crackled over the handheld. "I've got your back. Over."

I pedaled slowly toward the intersection of Second Avenue and Children Street. The happy hour crowd had gathered outside the Wet Dog Pub, and a number of people walked home from work. As I waited for the traffic light to change, I glanced at the mouth of the alleyway. The police car was still there. No one seemed to notice it, but I sensed a strong wrongness coming off it and wafting out of that dark alley like a stink.

When the light changed, I rode across and coasted down Second Avenue, passing the library and Market Square, which looked eerily quiet. Twice I glanced over my shoulder to see if the police car had pulled out of the alley. But it wasn't pursuing me.

I cut straight through Market Square, the tires of my bike crunching over discarded Styrofoam cups and empty potato chip bags. Men in rubber waders stood in the water fishing while along the beach some kids tossed around a football. At the end of Market Square I picked up Third Avenue, which curled around the waterfront toward my side of town.

Wrapped inside Scott's ball cap, the walkie-talkie squawked. "The police car just pulled out," Scott said. "Over."

Again, I glanced behind me. I was on the curved portion of Third Avenue so I couldn't see beyond Market Square. If the cop was indeed following me, he was being awfully cautious.

I keyed the handheld and said, "Roger that. Over."

It was an uphill ride on Third Avenue, and I lifted myself off my bike seat and pedaled harder. I decided to take Solomon's Bend Road out to Counterpoint Lane and afford the cop the opportunity to keep up with me. I wanted to know if this guy was actually following me or if I was jumping to conclusions.

"He just crossed Market Square," Scott said over the walkie-talkie.

I thumbed the button on the side of the handheld and shouted, "Okay."

"And he just turned up Third Ave," Scott said. In his excitement, he had stopped saying "over" at the end of each broadcast. This was suddenly not a game anymore.

I looked over my shoulder and saw a car at the bottom of the hill.

Up ahead, the lights changed at the intersection. A few cars puttered through. I slowed down and rolled up onto the curb. I wanted to look behind me again, but I didn't want to let on that I had spotted the cop car. Instead, I spoke into the walkie-talkie. "What's he doing now?"

A few seconds passed. "He's slowing down. He's . . . wait . . . He's pulling up alongside the curb," Scott said.

"I'm stopped at the traffic light," I said into the radio.

"He must be waiting for you to go," Scott returned.

When the lights changed, I crossed the intersection and continued up the block toward the turnoff onto Solomon's Bend Road.

"He's moving again," Scott said.

This can't be happening, I thought.

Rush hour traffic backed up on Solomon's Bend Road. I couldn't see how the police car would get through the mess to keep up with me. I biked past Harting Farms Elementary, Stanton School, and the entrance to Shipley's Crossing before Scott's voice broke out over the walkie-talkie: "Whoa, man, you're like a wanted felon. He just put his lights on and is driving up the middle of the road."

"You're kidding me," I said.

"Swear to God. I mean, he's moving pretty slowly still . . . but people are getting out of his way. It's unbelievable."

I wound down Solomon's Bend Road, passing the quaint little houses with their flower gardens and picket fences. Up ahead, I saw the vast tree line that designated the woods and December Park. A part of me wanted to cut into Solomon's Field and hide in the underpass until the coast was clear. When I came to the turnoff that banked down toward the park, I resisted that urge and continued straight.

"He turned his lights off," Scott said. "Where are you?"

I gave him my location.

"What if he tries to stop you?" Scott asked.

"I don't think he will," I said. "I think he's trying to keep his distance."

Scott said something else but it was garbled.

I keyed the radio and said, "What was that? Repeat."

Silence.

I slowed as I crossed the overpass. To my left, Solomon's Field was quiet, the surface of Drunkard's Pond undisturbed. It was strange, not seeing the homeless folks around the water's edge. To my right, December Park was desolate. The woods stretched far out toward the cliffs. *The Patapsco Institute is back there,* I reminded myself.

Looking over my shoulder, I saw a vehicle approaching at a slow pace. Sunlight glinted off the chrome grille.

I brought the walkie-talkie to my mouth and said, "Scott? You still there?"

More silence. Maybe we were too far apart now.

I could lose him when I cross the highway, I thought, picturing the cop getting snared at a traffic light if I went through without waiting for the lights to change. Suddenly, I didn't want to play this game anymore.

Behind me, the police car drew nearer.

I hopped onto the curb and slowed my pace. This part of the road was a single lane that bowed over the park; there weren't many places for the cop to keep hidden. It was just him and me out here now.

I slowed nearly to a stop.

The police car eased up beside me, the windows down, the engine purring. The cop behind the wheel had on sunglasses. He didn't even glance at me—he just kept motoring down the road.

The whole thing struck me as false. Any normal cop would have looked at me, a lone kid biking over the park after five in the evening.

The police car slowed to a near stop when it reached Counterpoint Lane, right around the place where they had brought up the body of Courtney Cole. I got the impression that the cop was positioning the car to create a roadblock.

I contemplated turning around. But then I caught sight of the tunnel beneath the street—the tunnel the five of us had traversed that one fated day in April, where Adrian had recovered the broken fleur-de-lis from the Were-wolf House's fence.

Without giving it a second thought, I sped around the cop car, crossed Counterpoint Lane, and rode down the embankment on the other side of the road. The mouth of the tunnel grew wider, blacker. I pedaled faster. I could only hope that I had estimated the size of the tunnel correctly . . .

Crouching over the handlebars of my bike, I shot straight into the tunnel. The world around me went pitch-black. The sounds of summer vanished. The tunnel was so narrow that my handgrips nearly scraped the walls. I couldn't sit upright because the roof would have taken my head off. I merely kept my head down, the handlebars straight, and pedaled as fast as I could. Sweat peeled down my back.

The walkie-talkie crackled, but Scott's voice did not come on.

I focused on the pinpoint of daylight at the far end of the tunnel and con-tinued to pedal. I knew I was under the highway when the sound of roaring engines and whirring tires filled my ears.

I exited out the other side into the ravine behind the Generous Super-store. The past several days had been dry and hot, and the ravine was a steaming plate of baked mud and scorching white rocks. I bounded up the embankment, my breath whistling from my throat. When I reached the road, I stopped. My T-shirt clung to my chest.

I put on Scott's ball cap and brought the walkie-talkie to my mouth. "Hey, Scott—you there? Come in! Over!"

Nothing.

"Scott," I tried again. "Hey. Come on, man. Where are you?"

It seemed like an eternity before his voice came over the radio. "I'm here. Where'd you go?"

"I took the tunnel under the highway," I said. "I'm behind the Superstore. What happened to you?"

"I was having a hard time keeping up. I'm cutting across the park now."

"What happened to the cop?"

"Wait for me," he said. "Over."

I pressed the button again and said, "Scott? Scott?"

Once again: no answer.

I watched cars glide back and forth across the plaza's parking lot. Some kids I recognized from school leaned against the plate-glass windows outside the Quickman, smoking cigarettes and laughing. I let my heartbeat regain its normal rhythm while I waited.

Seven or eight minutes later, Scott biked across the Superstore plaza. When he saw me he waved one hand high over his head.

I waved back. My muscles still felt tense and I couldn't stop sweating.

"Jesus Christ, that was something, huh?" he said as he rolled across the street and brought his bike to a stop beside mine.

"What about the cop?" I said.

"Oh, he was following you, all right. When I got to Counterpoint Lane, he was out of his car peering down the embankment. I didn't realize why until you told me you'd taken the tunnel."

"Holy shit. I don't believe it."

"Believe it," he said. "That cop was after you."

"What do we do?"

"I don't know. I guess we'll have to see what the others think later tonight." Scott checked his wristwatch. "We're still getting together after dinner to check out that Patapsco place, right?"

"That's the plan," I said, although, decidedly, I'd had enough excitement for one afternoon.

He took the walkie-talkie from me and tucked it inside his backpack with the other one. "I'll see you then. I gotta go." He plucked the ball cap off my head and pulled it down on his. "Watch your back."

"Yeah," I said. "You, too."

CHAPTER TWENTY-NINE
THE PATAPSCO INSTITUTE (PART ONE)

My grandmother prepared oven-roasted chicken dressed with peas, a plate of sweet potato patties (extra crispy), and a salad. With my father working late, it was just my grandparents and me again. I shoveled the food down, keeping one eye on the clock. I didn't want to be late for our meeting at the park.

"Look at this kid," my grandfather commented once I'd set my fork down on my empty plate. "Keep eating like that, you'll need a new wardrobe when school starts up in the fall."

"Can I be excused?"

"*Can* you?" retorted my grandmother.

"May I?"

"Are you going somewhere?" she asked.

"Just hanging out with the guys." I tried to make my voice sound as bland as possible. "You know. Same old stuff."

My grandmother glanced at the same clock I'd been gazing at throughout dinner. "Only a couple of hours before curfew."

"I know."

"Let the kid go, for Christ's sake," my grandfather chimed in. He was trying to fish something out of his coffee with one finger.

"Go on," said my grandmother. "Just be careful, Angelo."

Three minutes later, I knocked on Adrian's front door. His mother answered, and I felt my testicles retreat up into my abdomen, as if I'd just waded into freezing water.

"Oh, hi. Can Adrian come out?"

"Adrian's not home."

"Oh." Yet I remained on the porch, stupefied. "I was supposed to pick him up after dinner. We're going to the park."

"He's not home," she repeated in that same emotionless and dilatory voice. I imagined giant grubby worms eating through her brain, indiscriminately brushing up against the cranial switches that controlled her speech.

"Oh. Do you know where he—?"

She shut the door in my face.

Confused, I rolled my bike down the Gardiners' driveway and coasted up Worth Street. The sun was beginning to set, but the evening hadn't cooled off all that much. It had been a cold winter, and now we were in the middle of a hot summer. For whatever reason, I recalled that peculiar phrase my father had muttered to me on the morning of July Fourth—*No rest for the wicked*. I thought maybe I was beginning to understand it.

As I rode to December Park it occurred to me that unlike last summer (or the summers before that), we hadn't yet engaged in any of our usual summertime activities—no stealing johnboats from the slips at the Cape (they were always chained to pilings, but Michael had no problem cracking the combination locks); no Capture the Flag or citywide tag that typically lasted all summer; no afternoons languishing beneath the sun at Shoulder Beach; no late nights listening to Andrew Dice Clay cassettes in Peter's basement.

I supposed the Piper was to blame for some of it, but it was also apparent that we had changed things, too. We. All of us. Years ago, we had outgrown the Kiss Wars and the games of tag. We had outgrown a lot.

It was exactly seven o'clock when I reached the outskirts of December

Park. The park grounds were vacant except for the scraps of trash and the swings that swayed ghostlike in the breeze. It looked like a circus had just picked up and left town. Metal glinted in the fading daylight by the cusp of the woods, and I saw Peter leaning his bike against a tree. Behind him, the ground swelled up to a vast incline studded with elms and bushy fir trees. Back there somewhere, hunkered down like a beast in waiting, was the Patapsco Institute, the ugly twin sister of Stanton School.

From the Solomon's Bend Road side of the park, I watched Michael and Scott swoop down the hill on their bikes. They joined me, and the three of us biked toward Peter, our legs pumping, my sweat-soaked T-shirt cooling in the wind.

Peter snatched a leafy branch off the ground and waved it like a checkered flag as Michael, Scott, and I blew by him. Michael raised his hands in victory, balancing the Mongoose with just his legs, even though Scott had beaten him to the finish line. We circled back around, breathing heavily, and dropped our bikes in the dirt.

"Where's Adrian?" Peter asked me.

"I have no idea. I went to his house, but his mom said he wasn't home."

As if on cue, Adrian marched out of the woods, grinning. He had his Incredible Hulk backpack strapped to his shoulders and wore a wide grin. "Hey, guys!"

"What the hell, man?" I scolded him. "I said I was gonna pick you up."

"I got anxious. I've been down here for a couple hours." He glanced over his shoulder. "But I'm not so sure there's a building back there."

"There is," Michael assured him.

"What happened to not going off into secluded places alone?" I said.

"I told you, I got anxious. No big deal."

"Tell 'em what happened," Scott said to me.

I told them about the cop coming into the thrift store and following me home. Scott added the part about the cop looking into the ravine after I'd ditched him.

"You've gotta be shittin' me," Peter said. "Are you sure this is the same cop?"

"I'm positive," I said.

"So what do we do?"

I shook my head.

"Does this mean he's the Piper?" Michael said.

"I don't know what it means," I said, "but it's definitely suspicious, right?"

"It sure would make it easier to abduct those kids if the Piper were walking around in a police uniform," Michael said.

"That's scary," said Adrian.

Michael nodded. "Heck, yeah, it's scary."

"But what do we do about it?" I asked.

Peter scratched his chin. "Could you say something to your dad?"

"What would I tell him? That a cop he obviously knows has been following us around? That Scott and Michael caught him going through our stuff in the woods—the woods where, by the way, I'm not even supposed to be hanging around?"

"Come on," Michael said, marching past Adrian. "We've only got two hours before curfew. We came here to check out the Patapsco Institute, so let's do it."

It was like stepping into a rain forest. The late afternoon was muggy, and mosquitoes dive-bombed us with keen accuracy and devilish hunger. We trampled through kudzu and passed between curtains of reddish-green palms. Black-eyed Susans scrutinized us in their Cyclopean fashion, and, far above us in the treetops, birds and squirrels announced our trespass.

Our little band continued through the woods just as the reality of what we were doing firmly seated itself in my chest like an iron spike. It had all started out as a game for us—Adrian had found a heart-shaped locket and we were going to find the Harting Farms child killer. But this was no longer a game. The Piper had continued snatching his victims, and we had continued pursuing him. Now, a heart-shaped locket, an iron fleur-de-lis, and the decapitated head of a concrete statue later, we were seeking out a half-sunken building among the cliffs at the edge of the woods. I was terribly certain that we were heading toward some ultimate showdown. The notion made me tremble.

The trees soon parted, and then there it was: the old girls' school, the abandoned institute. It looked every bit as intimidating and malignant as it had when I'd approached it as a little boy chasing after a balsa wood airplane. It still radiated that same dread and sense of premonitory danger I had gotten from it back then, too. As I stared at it, I felt my palms go clammy and my mouth go dry.

On the most basic level, it hinted at a skeletal similarity to our high school. But beyond that it was its own prehistoric creature, its limestone skin the color of rotting pistachios intersected with jungle vines and bristling with hawks' nests. Semicircular stone risers fronted the building, unruly tufts of sea grass and wildflowers burst through cracks in its foundation, and the ancient front doors—twin hubs made of cast iron and shrouded in the shade of a stone arcade—faced us. There were words engraved in the stone above the entranceway, but time and weather had dulled them to illegibility. On either side of the arcade, large holes had been punched into the masonry only to be sealed up by metal latticework and poured concrete. It took me a moment to realize these rough holes had been windows.

It was as hideous and as powerful as the face of God staring at us.

"Whoa," Scott said, stopping in his tracks.

"That's one ugly fucking building," Michael whispered.

I pressed one hand against its dinosaur hide. The stone was cold and solid. There were striations resembling black ribbon that indicated where the fire had run rampant, and even all these years later, I thought I could still smell the smoke and smoldering timber, the charred flesh.

"Guys!" Adrian shouted. He had disappeared around the side of the building. "Come look!"

We followed his voice around one corner to find him staring at a stone ledge no more than three feet off the ground. On the ledge stood replicas of the stone statues that were in the Dead Woods clearing. Most of the heads were intact, the faces as stoic and expressionless as Greek busts. Farther down the ledge, the statues had fallen to the ground where they had broken to pieces and then been covered by underbrush. Some of their heads were missing.

"This must be where that head came from," Adrian said, walking around. "The one we found in the Werewolf House."

"What I'd really like to know is where that head is now," Peter said.

Scott studied the building. "Do you think there's a way in?"

"Not through those windows, that's for sure," Peter commented, gesturing at the series of barred portholes filled with concrete that ran the length of the building.

"What about the doors?" Adrian suggested.

We all went back around to the front of the building and down the short arcade to the doors. They were massive bestial things that reminded me of a medieval drawbridge. Each metal rivet in the frame was nearly the size of my fist. An industrial chain had been wound through the handles several times and was held tightly in place by a padlock. The keyhole in the lock's faceplate looked large enough to accommodate a key roughly the size of a dinner fork.

"Shoot," Michael muttered. "If it had been a combo lock, I could have tried to pop the sucker."

The wind picked up and channeled through the rents and cavities and cracks in the frame of the building, and an eerie howl emanated around us. The sound caused the hairs on my arms to stand at attention. It was the same sonorous moan I'd heard when my airplane had gotten tangled in the trees. Back then, I had attributed the sound to a faceless ghost I had seen—or thought I had seen—flitting past a window. Older and wiser, I knew this sound was the wind fluting through the openings in the rock, yet this knowledge did little to assuage my discomfort.

"I just remembered there's an open window in the back," I said. "At least it was when I was a kid."

"Why in the world would you come out here when you were a kid?" Michael asked.

"I was flying a toy airplane." I pointed through the thicket. "The woods end up there along a cliff that overlooks the bay."

As we walked to the back of the building, I kept catching glimpses of Stanton School in its façade—but those glimpses were like seeing fleeting sanity behind a crazy person's eyes. This building was something else, something other.

The rear of the building was overgrown in ivy. It looked deliberately camouflaged, and I was overcome by the unsettling notion that the building was an ancient and living thing that purposely hid itself from the rest of Harting Farms. It didn't want to be found. It wasn't part of our world.

But yet it was.

"There," I said, pointing at a high window that was mostly overgrown with ivy. It was the black pit, the Cyclops eye I remembered from my youth.

"If the interior is anything like Stanton," Peter said, "then this would be where the gymnasium is."

Adrian came up beside him. "That window is pretty high. How are we supposed to reach it?"

"We're not," Peter said. "That's the point."

"That's the only way in that I can see," I said. "I wonder if the ivy is strong enough for handholds."

Adrian approached the building and grabbed a fistful of ivy. The leaves came away in his hand, revealing spaghetti-thin vines underneath. "Not a chance."

"That's nothing," Michael said. He juggled bits of stone that had probably come off one of the busted statues. "I can get us up there."

"Yeah?" Scott said. "How?"

"My parents are freaks. They're always worried I'm gonna get hit by a car, drown in the river, or die in a fire. I've got this fire-escape ladder in my bedroom in a box. We can hook it to the window and climb up."

Peter nodded. "That could work."

"Of course it'll work. Why wouldn't it? We can come back tomorrow when I get out of school."

"It's getting late," Peter said. "We should call it a night."

"I'm not going home," Adrian said.

"You have to," I told him.

"I don't care about the stupid curfew. I want to go in there."

"We will. Just not tonight."

"I can feel it," he said. "We're at the end of it. Whatever we've been looking for is in there. I want to go in and find it."

"We will," I said again. "Tomorrow."

"I want to find out what happened to those kids." Adrian looked at me. There was a firmness to his face that I'd never seen before. "You guys go if you want, but I'm not going with you. I'm staying here. I'm going to find a way in."

I snagged his backpack off the ground. It was heavier than I'd expected. "We're going home, man."

"No."

"We'll come back tomorrow."

"No!" Adrian dropped to his knees and hung his head. I didn't know what he was doing until I heard him release an agonized sob.

We stared at him in utter amazement.

"You guys don't understand," he bawled. "This is important! Do you think this is some kind of game?"

"Hey, man," Michael said, taking a step toward him. But he froze and said no more the second Adrian spun his head around to glare at him. His face was red, and slick tracks of tears spilled down his cheeks.

Peter put a hand on Michael's shoulder. "If the cops catch us out here after curfew, we're in big trouble," he said to Adrian. His voice was calm and reasonable. "We'll all be grounded, and we can forget about coming back here for the rest of the summer. Do you understand?"

"I won't get grounded," Adrian returned. "The cops can't do anything to me."

Just as calmly as before, Peter said, "Then you'll have to finish this on your own. But then you're breaking your promise."

"What promise?"

"The promise that we stick together, that we do this together." His words were almost visible things that got caught in the air like flecks of dust in a spider's web.

I anticipated another hysterical outburst, but Adrian remained on his knees and stared at Peter in silence, his Adam's apple jouncing each time he swallowed. He flexed his hands in the dirt and cleaved trenches in the soil.

Adrian stood and brushed the dirt off his legs. He sniffled, then wiped his nose on his arm. When he looked at us, his grin was so unexpected it frightened me.

"Okay," he said in his small birdlike voice. He could have been ten years old as he shuffled over to me and took his backpack strap out of my hand. He worked his shoulders through the straps, a runner of snot glistening across his left cheek like the trail of slime left behind by a snail. "Let's go home."

That night I dragged a folding chair out to the front porch and, with a book in my lap, kept watch over the Gardiner house. Adrian could fool the others but he didn't fool me: I knew it wasn't beyond him to sneak out and go back to the Patapsco Institute by himself.

By ten o'clock, my grandmother came out and handed me a glass of iced tea. The night was still and hot, and the mosquitoes were having a field day.

At eleven, my father's unmarked sedan pulled into the driveway. He smiled resignedly at me as he clumped up the stairs and across the porch. "Doing some reading?"

"Yeah."

"How was work?"

"The usual," I said, thinking of the cop who had followed me home. "How about you?"

He laughed but there was no humor in it. "The usual," he said, and went inside.

Since our fight on the morning of July Fourth, a space had opened up between us. I had used Charles to hurt him, and it had been a much more lethal blow than I had recognized at the time.

When midnight rolled around, my father appeared in the doorway and muttered, "Go to bed," then retreated inside.

I realized I'd been nodding off. Across the two yards, the Gardiner house looked as dark and empty as a satellite coasting through space.

CHAPTER THIRTY
THE PATAPSCO INSTITUTE (PART TWO)

At five thirty the following evening, the five of us met at the far end of December Park, where the chestnut trees flanked the footpaths and the swings moved in the warm breeze. Michael carried a large box by a plastic handle. On the box's cover was a picture of a smiling family climbing down an aluminum ladder that hung from the windowsill.

"Who smiles like that when they're escaping from a window?" Scott asked.

We had all our equipment with us—the walkie-talkies (fully charged), the flashlights, our pocketknives. Peter also had his Walkman, which he cranked up so we could listen to one of his mix tapes.

Once more we entered the woods and climbed through the underbrush. I could feel the land gradually inclining as we went. Erosion had dumped old trees into dried-out ravines, their twisted roots like petrified boa constrictors. At one point, we saw a beehive nearly the size of a football hanging from a tree limb.

As we drew closer to the Patapsco Institute, the quality of the air changed: it was possible to smell the salty, fishy scent of the Chesapeake Bay on the breeze. The day was blisteringly hot—that morning's weather report put us in the high nineties—and by the time the old building appeared through the trees, my T-shirt was soaked and my hair was dripping water into my eyes.

"Is it possible it looks even uglier today?" Michael said as he paused before the looming monstrosity.

"I say the same thing about you every time I see you," Peter said, switching off his Walkman. The sudden quiet lent an air of significance to the scene.

"Hilarious," Michael said, checking the bottoms of his shoes. "I think I stepped in something."

"I smell it, too," said Adrian. He had his backpack on, which must have been tough to carry all this way. His brow glistened, and the front of his Superman T-shirt was dark with sweat. "I think it's coming from in there."

As I walked around the building, I couldn't take my eyes from it. When we passed the ledge of crumbling statues, they all seemed to be staring down at us, judging us. Or perhaps they were trying to warn us?

Don't start freaking out, I thought. *Save it for tonight when I'm home, safe in bed.*

At the back of the building, Michael set his box on the ground and opened it.

"That's not gonna be tall enough," I said.

"It'll be tall enough," he said, unfolding the ladder out of the box.

"Are you sure?"

"It's for climbing out of two-story windows. I think it'll do the trick."

"Unless your parents lied to you, and they were hoping you'd die tragically in a house fire," Peter said.

Without looking up, Michael shot Peter the bird.

Adrian undid his backpack and let it drop to the earth. His respiration was wheezy. He took his glasses off and wiped the sweat from the lenses with his T-shirt. I saw that he still wore Courtney Cole's locket around his neck.

"This is crazy," I said.

Adrian looked at me. "You're changing your mind?"

"No. I'm just stating it for the record. I want to make it known."

"For what?"

"For when we can't get back out and we have to resort to eating each other," I said. "I just want it stated that I think this is a lousy idea."

"You've said your part," Scott said. He took a pack of peanut butter crackers from the pocket of his cargo shorts.

When the cellophane crackled, Michael looked in his direction. "I just know you brought enough to share with the rest of the class."

"There's only four crackers," Scott said.

"So who goes hungry?" Peter asked.

"It should be Scott since he was holding out on us," said Michael.

It was Scott's turn to flip the bird. "Screw you. You should have packed your own food." Then he reached into his back pocket and pulled out his deck of Uno cards. "Four highest cards get the crackers," he said, fanning the cards out.

"What about the draw cards?" I asked.

"Yeah," said Peter. "Or the reverses and skips. How many points are those worth?"

Scott considered, then said, "They're all worth zero, except for the Draw Four. If someone pulls the Draw Four, they get all four crackers."

Peter nodded. "Ground rule double. Nice."

Scott turned the fan of cards in his direction. "You pick first."

Peter picked and came up with a green seven.

Scott said, "Not bad," then stepped over to Michael.

Michael licked his fingertips, began to pull out one card, considered this, then tucked it back in. He pinched a second card between his fingers but did not slide it out from the deck.

"Will you just pick?" Scott barked.

Michael selected a red seven. He frowned at it. "What the fuck? I'm tied with Chubby Checker over here?"

"Or I could knock your teeth out and you won't have to worry about eating anything that isn't through a straw," Peter offered.

Scott turned the deck toward me.

I selected what turned out to be a green zero. "Perfect," I muttered.

"Welcome to Loserville, buddy," Michael said, throwing an arm around my shoulders.

Scott held the cards out to Adrian.

Adrian picked a yellow draw card.

"Zero points," Michael shouted, pointing at Adrian's card. "Eliminated. Ha!"

"Grow up." I shrugged his arm off my shoulders.

"My pick," Scott said, and he selected a card from the middle of the deck. He looked at it, frowned, then showed it to the rest of us: a blue zero.

"So," I said. "Three zeroes and these guys are tied with sevens. Who're the four winners?"

"I think me and Peter should get two each, since you guys didn't get any points," Michael said.

"You're a real altruist," Scott said.

"What is that, some kind of bird?"

"It means all five of us share," Peter suggested, handing his card back to Scott. "Just break 'em up into pieces."

Scott tucked the cards into his pocket, then looked down—somewhat mournfully, I imagined—at the pack of peanut butter crackers in his hands. He squeezed the crackers, reducing them to crumbs held together by stale brownish paste. Everyone held out their cupped palms, and Scott emptied a bit of the crackers into them.

We all popped our handfuls into our mouths except Adrian; he just examined the heap of crumbs on his palm the way a botanist might scrutinize new plant life. "I can't eat this," he said finally. "I'm allergic to peanut butter."

We all groaned. Scott laughed.

"I'm gonna kill him," said Michael, wiping his hands on his shirt.

"No sweat." Peter shook Adrian's crumbs into his own hand. Before popping those into his mouth, too, he looked around at the rest of us. "Unless you guys wanna pick more cards?"

"Just eat it," I said, grinning.

Scott laughed harder.

Michael went back to the ladder. When he had finished unfolding it, I could see that he had been right—it would reach the window, no problem.

I helped him carry it over to the building. There were two brackets at the top, which were meant to hook over a windowsill. The window we were preparing to climb through had no sill—just a crumbling stone ledge. And to even refer to it as a *window* was giving it more credit than that inky black hole in the stone deserved.

It took us three tries to loop the brackets over the stone ledge, but we finally managed. Michael and I let go, and the ladder hung suspended three feet off the ground.

"I just realized something," I said. "What do we do on the other side? Like, how do we get down when we're in there?"

"Jump, I guess," Michael said.

"I'd really rather not break my ankles today."

"Maybe when you get to the top you can pull the ladder up and drop it through the window on the other side."

"Me?"

"Huh?"

"You want *me* to do it?"

"Or whoever." He looked over to Scott, Peter, and Adrian. "Who's first?"

"We can draw cards again," Peter said. "That worked out really well last time."

"Shut up," Scott told him. "I'll go first."

Adrian checked the flashlights to make sure they worked, then handed one to me. His fingers were grimy, the fingernails gnawed to nubs. He gave a second one to Scott, who clicked it on and off before sticking it into the waistband of his cargo shorts.

Peter stood at the bottom of the ladder, looking up. "Should one of us stay out here in case . . . Well, in case something happens?"

"Like if the roof caves in or if we're all mercilessly butchered by the Piper?" Michael said.

"Either or," said Peter.

"No, we all go in together. It has to be that way." Adrian passed another flashlight to Peter.

Scott approached the ladder, shook it. It seemed sturdy enough. He lifted one long leg and set his foot on the first rung.

"Wait," Michael said. "We need a war song. What did Jesus sing before going into battle?"

"You're an idiot," Scott said.

Michael scowled. "I don't know that song."

Peter lifted up his baggy T-shirt to expose the Walkman clipped to his belt. He dug the headphones out from the collar of his shirt and let them hang around his neck. He opened the Walkman, flipped the mix tape over, and reinserted it. "Whatever is on when I press Play, that'll be our battle song."

We all agreed.

Peter hit Play on the Walkman. Springsteen crackled through the headphones, belting out his immortal line—"Born down in a dead man's town . . ."

"Well," Michael said with a roll of his shoulders, "that can't be a good sign, can it?"

Scott took off his Orioles hat and tossed it onto the ground. "Catch you guys on the flip side."

"See you later, alligator," Peter said.

"After a while, pedophile," Scott said, and he began to climb.

We took a few steps back and watched him go. He was athletic and moved quickly, steadily, yet I wasn't too comfortable with the way the ladder shook as he climbed. The rest of us weren't nearly as lithe.

Scott reached the top without incident. He peered into the window, shining his flashlight inside.

"What do you see?" Adrian called up at him.

"It's a mess. It looks like part of the ceiling collapsed."

"Wonderful," Peter muttered.

Scott swung one leg into the window and sat straddling it. "I don't need the ladder to get down. There's enough stuff for me to climb on."

"Just don't break your neck," I shouted.

And just like that, Scott disappeared inside the building.

Peter patted Michael on the back and said, "You're next."

Michael took his switchblade from his pocket, popped it open, then held it between clenched teeth, pirate-style, as he climbed the ladder. He paused when he reached the top, peering into the black hole in the building. He said something to Scott, but I couldn't hear Scott's reply. Then he went inside.

Peter clicked off his Walkman, unhooked it from his waistband, and wound the headphones around it before setting it on the ground. His forehead was beaded with sweat, his reddish hair damp at the temples. "Give me a boost."

I threw my shoulders against his buttocks and heaved him up so he was able to stand on the first rung. Bits of rock and broken pieces of mortar crumbled to the ground as the ladder thudded against the building. Peter ascended slowly, methodically.

"I wonder what we'll find in there," Adrian said.

"Only one way to find out," I said, lacing my hands together so Adrian could step on them. I boosted him—he was much lighter than Peter—and he proceeded to scramble up the ladder more quickly than I would have thought him capable. At the top, he stared into the darkened window for perhaps a second. Then he climbed inside.

I was alone. Before joining my friends, I surveyed all our stuff strewn about the ground: Adrian's backpack, the peanut butter crackers wrapper, Scott's Orioles baseball cap, Peter's Walkman and headphones. It struck me as a sort of portent. Like Adrian, Howie Holt had left his backpack behind. Tori Brubaker's shoe had been found by the river. And of course there was Courtney Cole's heart-shaped locket, dropped and forgotten in a culvert. Echoes of recent horrors.

I slipped the flashlight into the pocket of my shorts and climbed the ladder. It felt sturdier than it looked, which brought me some relief. When I got to the top, I gazed into the darkened aperture that had once been a window and waited for my eyes to adjust.

It was a large room with a high ceiling. There were zigzag rents in the ceiling through which daylight bled, casting zebra stripes along a floor so full of crumbled stone, heaps of grayish powder, and debris that it looked almost deliberately arranged. There were other windows around the perimeter of the ceiling, each one crisscrossed with iron bars. Vegetation nearly prehistoric in its appearance climbed the walls and looped around the ironwork over the crumbling window frames.

Flashlights moved around below. Someone shouted my name, but the echo distorted the voice, and I couldn't tell who it was. Glancing over the sill, I saw a pyramid of crumbled stone arranged almost like a staircase leading from the window's ledge straight down to the floor. I swung one leg over the ledge and stepped on the heap of stone. It was solid. I dragged my other leg in behind me and descended the sloping stairwell.

"You made it," Adrian said, clapping me on the shoulder. His pale face was a checkerboard of light and shadow from the chutes of daylight that spilled down from the high windows. The lenses of his glasses glinted blue like the light cast by a black-and-white television set in a dark room.

It was oppressively hot and stank like sewage. Even the air felt corrupted by our trespass, and I was suddenly certain that no one—not even the Piper— had set foot inside this place in a long, long time.

"I was right, wasn't I?" Peter said. "This would have been the gymnasium."

Only its size alluded to that fact; otherwise, the room was a mausoleum, an Egyptian tomb deep beneath the desert, and looked nothing like Stanton School's gymnasium.

"Check this out," Scott said, waving me over. He trained his flashlight on a giant crater in the floor, large enough to swallow a compact car.

I approached the crater and peered down. Its walls looked to be made of stone, much like the interior of the drainage tunnel that ran under the highway, and it appeared ten or fifteen feet deep.

"That's just like at the train depot," Scott said. "Remember how Peter put his foot through the floor and it was hollow underneath?"

"I hope this whole place doesn't come crumbling down while we're in it," I said.

Just then, Michael belted out, "Is anybody home?" at the top of his lungs, causing us all to jump. His voice resonated throughout the room and funneled down the adjoining corridors, loud enough to cause bits of pulverized stone to rain down from the ceiling.

I expected a tornado of bats to come flurrying out from one of the adjoining corridors, but nothing happened.

Peter slapped him on the back of the head and told him not to do that again.

The tumbling of rocks caused me to look across the ill-lit room where I saw Adrian's flashlight wavering through the smoky dust-clouded atmosphere. "Hey," I said. The enormity of the room amplified my voice and made it sound as if it were coming from many directions at once.

"The acoustics are funny in here," Scott said, reading my mind.

I held up one arm to shield my eyes. "Where do we go? There's a doorway over here." I pointed.

"This way, too," Scott said, pointing in the opposite direction.

They weren't doorways, exactly—meaning, they were not geometric rectangles inlaid in the walls—but more like hasty cavities punched in the stone walls to accommodate passage. Tendrils of leafy vines hung over some of them.

Stomping over fallen rocks and mounds of crumbling white powder, we went over to one of the doorways. Ominous black sludge was packed against the walls where they met the floor, and it reeked as it baked in the humid, motionless air.

"Careful," Peter said, gesturing to a spot on the floor directly in front of me.

I paused and, peering through the darkness and the settling dust, made out a second hole in the floor, this one a bit narrower than the one Scott had found but still wide enough to accommodate a particularly careless person.

"They're all over." He pointed out two more cracks in the foundation farther ahead.

My father's voice surfaced in my head: *Stay away from it. You and your friends go in there to play, you could get hurt. Or worse.*

A vast labyrinthine corridor stretched out before us. Windows high up in the walls on one side painted white squares of light on the opposite wall. Many of the marble tiles buckled as if something large had disturbed them while tunneling beneath the floor.

To the right of the corridor, doorways with no doors stood every twenty or so feet. A shadow moved in one of the doorways, and I held my breath. The others must have seen it, too, because I could no longer hear them breathing, either. Scott flicked off his flashlight; I hadn't even taken mine out of my pocket yet.

"Wait," Peter said, taking a few hesitant steps forward. "It's a tree moving in the breeze, that's all."

"A tree inside?" Michael said.

"Yeah. Come look. It's growing right out of the floor."

We approached the doorway, the loose and buckled tiles of the corridor shifting and sliding beneath our feet, and stared into the adjacent room. It was almost as large as the one Peter thought was the gymnasium and in similar disarray. Indeed, a spindly, unidentifiable tree sprouted through a chasm in the floor. It was leafless, and its bark was the pale whitish pink of a clam. The only sunlight that reached it came in through a fist-sized hole in the ceiling that was crisscrossed by a screen of vines.

Scott pointed his flashlight into the room. Adrian did likewise. There was nothing but forgotten emptiness in there.

I took my flashlight out of my pocket but in my nervousness dropped it. The sound it made when it struck the floor was akin to a dry branch cracking off a tree. I heard it roll away. "Shit."

Scott tried to locate it with his flashlight, but the darkness had swallowed it whole.

Back in the corridor, the five of us went slowly down it, glancing in every ancient tomb-like room we passed.

"This is C Hall," Peter said, pausing . . . then walking in a tight little circle so he could survey the corridor in its entirety. "See it? Structurally, it's set up just like Stanton."

"You're right." Scott directed his flashlight down the hall where another corridor crossed it. "That's B Hall. Turn right and you go to the display case, the janitors' closet, the classrooms that look out on the rear parking lot. Turn left, and you head toward the cafeteria, the lobby, Principal Unglesbee's office."

I turned around and looked at the opposite end of the corridor. "Then the library and the A Hall classrooms would be down there."

"It's so big," Adrian said. There was a vein of defeat in his voice. "It'll take us days to search this whole place. Weeks, maybe."

At the end of the institute's counterpart of C Hall, we crossed into a series of rooms that were joined by narrow chambers that weren't exactly hallways but almost secretive passageways. They didn't currently exist at our high school, though it was possible they had at one time but had been walled over during the renovation. If my bearings were correct, this was approximately where the science hall should be—Mr. Johnson's classroom and lab and the rest. The ceiling was ribbed with iron struts, the material behind it resembling corrugated tin. What looked like blackened bits of cloth hung from some of the rafters.

I entered the room, beckoning the others to follow because I needed their flashlights even though bands of daylight filtered in through the barred and boarded-over windows. Massive oak desks had all been pushed against the farthest wall. They were terminal with rot and riddled with termite burrows. At the center of the room, undulating stone burst up from the tile like rocky hillocks on the surface of the moon.

We passed into the adjoining room. The silvery eyes of a possum were caught in the beam of my flashlight. It was a tremendous and beastly thing with fur like a matted old carpet, and it hissed at us with such venom I could see flicks of spittle spray out of its pointy, multi-toothed maw. Unlike the one Adrian and I had come across at the Werewolf House, this one turned and trundled through bits of fallen debris until it vanished into a hole in the wall. When I looked up, I spotted more bits of dark, oily cloth hanging from the ceiling joists.

In the next room, the walls had been blackened by the historic fire of 1958. One wall had been reduced to blackened rubble, and there were moist and reeking heaps of charred wood collected into Quonset-shaped dunes. Damage to the ceiling resulted in jagged cuts in the roof through which golden sunlight, intersected by a meshwork of tree branches and vines, spilled in sporadic fashion. Birds flitted in and out of the cracks and roosted in the ceiling struts. The pungent aroma of burned wood layered with the reek of decay was all I could smell: the memory of that fire was still in the walls.

As we went deeper into the connecting rooms, the damage done by the fire became more and more apparent. As did the ghostly aroma of smoke. That the smell of charred things could still haunt this place after almost fifty years was astounding. In another room, metal bed frames had been stacked against one wall. At first, the floor appeared to be covered by heaps of grayish snow, yet on closer scrutiny, I saw that it was actually soggy clumps of mattress stuffing that had been blackened by mold and left to rot. The smell made my stomach clench.

Adrian adjusted his glasses and cast his flashlight around the room, cracking open the dark and hidden places with the light. But there was nothing here so we kept moving.

At the end of the corridor, where a second hallway crossed it like a *T*, we glanced to the right. The floor was creased down the middle as if by an earthquake, the crease filled with all the debris that had slid into it from either side of the angled floor. Wires sprung like strange tropical plants from gaping wounds in the plaster.

To the left, I made out segmented indentations in the ceiling where light fixtures had probably once been. It looked like someone went berserk with a sledgehammer on the floor, and mounds of some whitish chalky substance had been spilled on it.

"Those are bats, dude," Michael said, craning his neck.

What looked like greasy pods were hanging from the high rafters, some of them nearly a foot long. There must have been two hundred of them.

"Holy shit," Peter breathed.

Adrian tiptoed down the hallway. He aimed his flashlight on the floor, though he stared into the soupy black abyss that was the other end of the hallway. I moved to follow him.

Peter snagged a handful of my shirt. "This is stupid," he whispered. "There's no one here. We're gonna get killed jerking around in this place."

I watched Adrian disappear into one of the rooms. In an instant, the light from his flashlight was gone.

I looked at Scott and Michael. Scott appeared apprehensive; Michael was still staring at the bats hanging from the ceiling. "I don't want rabies, man," he intoned.

"There's no one here," Peter said again.

I turned and shouted down the hall, "Adrian!" My voice boomed like a cannon blast.

Adrian neither reappeared nor responded.

I shouted again, and some of the bats above our heads tittered and flexed their wings. The sound of their bodies rubbing together was like the crinkling of newspaper.

"Well, we can't just leave him here." I took the flashlight from Scott, then plodded down the hall. The fault line in the middle of the floor made walking difficult; I had to straddle the slanting tiles on either side of the crease to maintain my balance.

When I reached the room Adrian had disappeared into, it was pitch-black and, as far as I could tell, empty. For whatever stupid reason, I made a hissing sound, perhaps in an effort to call to him. I listened for movement but heard nothing.

I swiped Scott's flashlight back and forth around the room. Showers. The tiles were black and the spigots looked grotesquely phallic. Opposite the shower stalls were rows of toilets, each one filthier than the next. Rats wove between exposed pipes, and a raccoon perched on a brick partition rose on its hind legs like a bear and released a high-pitched machine gun sound. At the opposite end of the room I discerned the black-on-black rectangular impression of another doorway and figured Adrian must have gone that way.

I expected further protest from my friends as I proceeded through the room, but no one said a word. Their shuffling footfalls behind me confirmed that they were following me, though I assumed it had little to do with bravery and mostly to do with the fact that they didn't want to be left alone.

When I went through the doorway, the stink of decay slapped me across the face. I skidded to a stop, my sneakers grinding across the gravelly surface of the floor. The room was long and slender, like a closet that went on forever, and I saw Adrian's light bobbing in the smoky gloom at the other end. I called his name. The sound of my voice channeled down the passage, then ricocheted back at me.

I cast the flashlight's beam along the wall to my right. There were coffin-sized inserts inlaid in the mold-blackened drywall, hastily cut with a dull blade by the looks of them. Random items—tattered blankets, metal pails, spools of black electrical wire that at first glance looked like coiled snakes— were piled within. Rickety wooden struts bowed beneath the weight of shelves bracketed into the walls on either side. Stacked on the shelves were big square things that could have been suitcases or cinder blocks; it was impossible to tell in the dark.

Up ahead, Adrian's flashlight dipped out of view once again.

I ran my light along the floor, spotlighting his footprints in the inch-thick soot. "Adrian!"

Something moved under the floor.

My body seized up like an old lawn mower engine. I heard my friends' feet scuff to a stop behind me. I let my flashlight's cone of light hang in the air, illuminating clouds of dust that roiled slowly like the eyes of hurricanes.

"That's just the building creaking," Peter whispered. "There's no one beneath us. This place makes the noises sound like they're coming from different spots."

"Okay," I managed, though, at the moment, I wasn't sure what I believed.

Michael and Scott sidestepped ruptured potholes in the concrete floor. Michael nearly lost his balance and grabbed one of the bowing struts for support. This was followed by a dry crack as the strut snapped in half, causing Michael to fall forward. Above, the unsupported side of the shelf pitched down like a slide, and the large, square items it had been holding began tumbling down.

"Scott!" Peter cried, his voice cracking.

Scott backed up against the wall as the items crashed down. The sound was like artillery fire. Bits of masonry cracked against the concrete floor. Metal rods tumbled down after them, hammering across the floor and striking Scott, who was covering his head and face with his arms. The rods were sharp and rusted, and they drew blood from Scott's arms as they rebounded off him.

Peter and I rushed over to Scott, stepping over the metal rods as they rolled across the floor. We had to pry his arms away from his face. His eyes were squeezed shut.

"You could have been killed," Peter breathed into his face.

Scott nodded.

I turned his lacerated arm up to examine it. His injuries looked superficial, but there were enough of them to cause me to wince. In my mind's eye, I was still watching the slabs of masonry sliding down the shelf toward Scott's head.

"I'm okay," he said, gently tugging his wrist free of my grasp. "Just . . . just freaked out."

Michael was facedown on the floor beneath the canted shelf, which had turned into a makeshift lean-to over him as it broke.

"Mikey," I called, "you okay?"

"Yeah." He didn't look up and his voice was muffled.

Peter grabbed my wrist and turned me to face him. "We're gonna get killed in here."

At the far end of the room, Adrian's flashlight crossed the open doorway only to disappear again.

I opened my mouth to shout at him, but I couldn't find my voice. My tongue felt like a gym sock stuffed with sawdust. Instead, I started down the length of the room.

"Angie," Peter called.

I held up one finger and continued walking.

This time, my friends did not follow.

When I entered the adjoining room, I walked through what felt like a web of string. It caught in my eyelashes and my hair. Swatting one hand out before me, I realized it wasn't a web of string but a massive cloud of flies. They rebounded off my face and neck, thumped against the damp fabric of my T-shirt like pellets fired from a toy gun. The ones that got tangled in my hair bit my scalp. I shuddered and nearly dropped the flashlight when one blew into my mouth.

As I coughed and spat wads of phlegm onto the floor, Adrian coalesced beside me like a ghost through the murk. When I looked up, bleary-eyed and nauseated, his goofy trademark grin radiated in our flashlights' beams. "Look," he said, directing his light at an angle toward the ceiling.

I blinked and saw that we were in another large room, only this one had no windows. Stone columns ran from floor to ceiling at random intervals. Industrial chains hung from the rafters. I counted seven, and each one concluded in an angry iron hook. The chains were affixed to pulleys bolted to the beams, which would allow them to swing. They looked no different than the chains on the construction barges at the Shallows, and perhaps these had even been scavenged from them.

"They must weigh a thousand pounds each," Adrian mused.

"Why are they here?"

"You know," Adrian said, his voice adopting an overly casual tone that set me on edge. "Like at a slaughterhouse."

Adrian repositioned his flashlight to illuminate a stack of sodden mattresses, the different color fabric resembling the alternating bands of minerals in a wall of stone, on the floor beneath the chains. There was mold growing on them, and even from this distance, I noticed massive black beetles creeping along the stinking mound. More flies choked the air, so many of them I could hear their miniature chain saw buzzing.

Adrian went over to the mattresses, then immediately pulled a face. "They stink."

"No kidding."

"Like, bad."

I walked up beside him while small hard things thumped against my shins. I aimed my beam down and saw enormous striped crickets with legs like pistons catapulting off the floor. One the size of a silver dollar clung to my left kneecap. Repulsed, I swiped it off and actually heard it strike the floor.

The mattresses were stacked too high for us to see the top of the pile. The beetles scuttled away to avoid our flashlights.

Something caught Adrian's eye, for he brought his face close to one mattress corner and inhaled. Even in the poor lighting, I saw the spores of mold filtering into his nostrils. Then he pinched the bottom corner of the mattress between two fingers—

"Don't do that," I warned him.

Ignoring me, he lifted it an inch or two. I could actually *see* the weight of the thing in the way it hardly yielded, except in the very spot where he lifted. Adrian examined the section of mattress he had revealed. Wrinkling his nose, he held the flashlight right up to it. "That's blood."

I gazed over his shoulder. Coagulated brownish sludge unstuck like caramel. It felt like the back of my throat was being tickled with a feather.

"It's here, too," he said, moving around the mattresses and scrutinizing another corner.

At my feet, a two-by-four seemed to summon me. I snatched it up, those horrible crickets vaulting off the floor toward my eyes. Brandishing it like a sword, I poked the tapered tip into the mattress at eye level. With a sickening digestive gurgle, the two-by-four sank into the fabric with little resistance. Disgusted, I dropped it.

My sneakers grew wet. Looking down, I saw a puddle of rusty water spreading from beneath the mattresses and across the floor. I was standing right in it.

"It isn't blood. It looks like rusty water and sewage. Like the basement of the Werewolf House. The sewer lines are so old, they probably burst." Even as I said this, I thought I could hear the faint trickling of water somewhere in the room.

Stumbling backward, I sent a stack of wooden crates crashing to the floor. The sound couldn't have been louder had the crates been loaded with dynamite.

Adrian, who had transferred halfway across the room, afforded me only the briefest of glances. He was looking at various items bolted to a cinderblock wall.

I toed one crate over and saw that someone had tied strips of cloth to one of the slats. The strips were each a different color, though so filthy it was difficult to discern exactly what color each strip was.

"I don't know what these are for," Adrian said, pointing, "but they look dangerous."

What resembled a piece of modern art—a neurotic confusion of metal angles welded together—had been bolted to the wall.

"They come apart," he said, gripping one section of the sculpture that looked like the blunted blade of a wood chisel and removing it from the rest of the chaos. "It's heavy. It's like some kind of weapon."

"Let's stop touching this stuff," I said. I glanced at the hall and saw a single silhouette framed in the doorway.

"What the hell are you guys doing?" It was Peter.

"Come see this stuff," Adrian said.

"No." He didn't budge from the doorway.

"Go put it back," I told Adrian. I was sweating profusely, and the smell in this room was making me sick to my stomach. I suddenly wanted nothing more than to be out in the fresh summer air. "Scott was almost killed back there, man. We should get out of here."

"But we're *here*," he said.

Just then, that low creaking noise emanated up from the floor again. We all looked around.

"It's just the building settling," Peter repeated, though I could tell he was struggling to keep his voice calm.

"This building should have settled a hundred years ago," I said, then turned to Adrian. "Let's leave."

Adrian said nothing. He was busy examining some of the other strange implements hanging on the wall.

Peter wavered in the doorway, mouthing something I couldn't quite see in the darkness.

"I want to leave," I said to Adrian again.

This time, when Adrian didn't respond, I tramped across the creaking floor and joined Peter. Whether subconsciously or not, I kept my flashlight trained on the floor so as not to bring into relief any of the other insane horrors that may have been in that room.

Back in the passageway, Scott stood with his bloodied arms folded across his chest while Michael paced back and forth. At the sound of our approach, Michael looked up and said, "Are we leaving yet?"

"I think it's time we talk to your dad," Peter said to me. "Let's let the cops take over. We keep stumbling around in these condemned places, we're all gonna wind up dead."

I looked to Scott and Michael. "You guys feel this way, too?"

"No," said Michael. "I mean, I don't think we should say anything to anyone. We've had that dead girl's locket since last October. That shit's evidence. We might even go to jail."

"We won't go to jail," Peter said.

"Well, we ain't gonna get medals; that's for sure."

I looked at Scott. "And what about you?"

"I don't know," he said. "Peter and Michael both have good points. What more can we do? There's nothing here. It's a dead end. It might be time to turn the clues over to the cops and see what they can do with them."

"Don't I have a say in any of this?" Michael met my eyes. "It's my life, too. I don't want to fucking go to jail."

"Nobody's going to jail," Peter reiterated, his voice slightly raised.

"If I tell my dad what we've been up to, he's going to kill me," I said. Everyplace we had been—everything we had done—had gone against his directives. No matter if they caught the Piper or not, I was bound to be grounded until the turn of the century. And was there a chance that Michael was right? Could something worse happen to us? Had we unwittingly made ourselves criminally liable in some fashion? "Just let me think of what to do. Give me some time. In the meantime, yeah, we should get out of here."

Adrian shuffled out into the hall.

"Adrian," Peter said, "we're leaving. Are you coming?" There was a firmness in his voice I'd never heard before.

Adrian muttered, "Yeah, okay. Let's go."

Together, we backtracked through the Patapsco Institute until we returned to the expansive, crumbling room where we'd begun our tour. One by one, we ascended the pyramid of stone and climbed out the window into the bright summer sun.

CHAPTER THIRTY-ONE
THE DISBANDING

There was a noticeable change in our group the moment we were back on solid ground.

Scott collected his hat off the ground and tugged it on. The cuts on his arms had dried in brownish-red streamers along his forearms. Peter gathered his Walkman and headphones. Adrian systematically replaced the flashlights into his backpack, then zipped it shut. Michael, who was usually jovial and beaming, now looked either saddened or frightened. There were streaks of grease smeared on his face—on all our faces, really—and his eyebrows seemed permanently knitted together, as if he were doomed to contemplate a difficult mathematical equation for the rest of his life.

Dusk was creeping up from the east, so we wasted no time heading back through the woods. We walked mostly in silence. Peter wore his headphones and hummed along to his tunes. Scott examined his wounds and commented that he might need stitches. Uncharacteristically silent, Michael carried the compact ladder in the box with the oddly smiling family on the lid. Adrian just stared straight ahead, seemingly lost in his own world. It looked as if a part of him had been left behind in that old building—some vein had been tapped, some vital fluid had been drained.

Something inside that building had poisoned us. Scott had nearly died and it wasn't a game anymore. It was over; we were done searching for the Piper.

When we reached the road behind the Superstore, my friends peeled off and went their separate ways. We had walked our bikes the entire time, but now I thumped the handlebars and said, "Come on. You want a ride?"

Adrian shrugged. "Not really in the mood."

"What's wrong?"

"I'm just thinking about that place. He probably lives there."

"There was no one there."

"What about the blood on those mattresses?"

"I told you, it wasn't blood."

He slid his thumbs beneath the shoulder straps of his backpack. "What are you saying? You don't want to do this anymore?"

"Me and the guys have been thinking that maybe it's time to talk to my dad, tell the police what we know."

His pace slowed. "I thought we were gonna see this to the end?"

"There *is* no end. We're not detectives. We don't know what we're doing. That building was empty. No one's living in there."

"But you *promised*," he said. The word dripped with accusation. I had wounded him with betrayal.

"Adrian—," I began.

"You promised you wouldn't say anything to anybody, and now you're going back on your word!"

"I think we—"

Adrian took off down the street, his backpack jostling from side to side. I climbed on my bike and rode up to him, but he cut right and veered across someone's front lawn. I skidded to a stop and shouted after him, but he wouldn't stop. He kept running and eventually disappeared around the back of someone's house.

Another nightmare that evening had me running with my father through a rain forest toward the circular clearing of a grass hut village. Again, some tremendous beast pursued us, rattling the earth with its Goliath footfalls. When we reached the clearing, my father—who had now transmogrified into my grandfather, though he retained much of his youthful appearance—gave me a shove. I stumbled forward, the rucksack on my back causing me to lose my balance, and slid through a pile of bleached skulls and femurs. Phalanges scattered like dice across a craps table.

As before, I quickly ditched into the nearest hut to hide from the great beast that destroyed the rain forest in its furious campaign. This time, however, the walls of the hut were braced with confusing metal sculptures of intricate (and suspiciously deadly) design. I knew that just touching one would summon blood to the surface of my skin.

There was someone else in the hut with me. I glimpsed the figure in my peripheral vision, but each time I turned to face the intruder (or was I the intruder?), he seemed to flit just out of sight.

Then his hands fell on my shoulders. I glanced down and saw fingernails like hooked talons stained brown as if by Mercurochrome. When the figure pushed his face against mine, I smelled the sweat and anger and years of seclusion on his unwashed flesh.

—Let the world hold you down, the Piper whispered in my ear. His breath was that of an animal that subsisted solely on roadkill. Then he tightened his grip on my shoulders. It's just pretending. You can be me and I can be you.

I told him I didn't understand.

—It's just pretending.

I repeated that I didn't understand.

—Don't you? he said. Don't you, Angelo? It's easy. I become you and you become me and us become us and we become we.

I told him I wanted to wake up.

The Piper laughed. It was a sound like dragging the tines of a garden rake across pavement. When you wake up, he told me, one of us will be the other, and neither of us will be the same ever again.

But it was real-life noise that yanked me from the nightmare. I jumped out of bed and peered out one open window at the moonlit sea that was our backyard. I had made it there just in time to see a figure pass from the pin oaks at one end of the house into shadows behind the shed. I distinctly heard the figure drag something along the wooden framework of the shed while tromping down broken branches in the underbrush.

Flying away from the window, I snatched my shorts off my desk chair and climbed into them. Downstairs, I unlocked the door to the back porch and peeled it open on squealing hinges. I traced the wall, found the outdoor light switch, flipped it on. The porch lit up, but the yard beyond remained as black as the deepest parts of the Chesapeake.

Standing in the open doorway, I held my breath and willed my heart to stop beating as I surveyed the property. A vision came to me: of creeping up on the trespasser behind the shed while brandishing my grandfather's samurai sword. It was both ridiculous and wholly probable and my limbs began to tremble.

A hand fell on my shoulder, and I cried out like a little girl.

"What are you doing?" It was my father, half-asleep and wearing nothing but his threadbare briefs.

"I . . . thought I heard . . . someone . . ." And I wished I hadn't said *thought*, as it inevitably brought my certainty into question. "I mean, I heard someone. I saw someone go behind the shed."

But it was too late. My father was unconvinced. "There's no one there. Go to bed." He turned me around with the hand that was still on my shoulder.

Without protest, I reentered the house while he closed and locked the door. Then he shut off the porch light but remained lingering at the door, gazing out at the yard.

I paused in the hallway and stared at the matted hair on the back of his head.

"Go to bed," he repeated without turning to me.

Silently, I went upstairs.

CHAPTER THIRTY-TWO
ADRIAN GARDINER

Sunday morning, I awoke with a dagger of guilt in my chest. I hadn't seen Adrian since he ran off Thursday evening as we were walking home after our search of the Patapsco Institute. The day after, I had knocked on his front door. His mother's car wasn't in the driveway and no one answered, so I surmised Adrian was ignoring me.

His disappointment wasn't totally alien to me. After all this time, my preoccupation with the Piper had only strengthened. In a way, my friends and I had become a part of the Piper. And the Piper had become a part of us all.

After breakfast, I got dressed and summoned the courage to return to the Gardiner house. I knocked on the front door and waited for several minutes.

Just when I thought no one would answer, Doreen Gardiner peeked out. Her eyes were dead headlamps, and her skin was the color and texture of uncooked pie crust. When she spoke, I caught a whiff of alcohol on her breath. "Adrian isn't here."

This time, I didn't bother asking where he went. Instead, I thanked her and bounded off the porch.

During Mass at St. Nonnatus, I glanced at Michael who was bookended by his parents in one of the pews. His eyes met mine. I just shook my head. When Father Evangeline had everyone come up to receive the Eucharist, I made sure to slide into line right behind Michael.

"Still no word from Poindexter?" he whispered over his shoulder.

"No. I went to his house this morning, but his mom said he wasn't home."

"Maybe she shipped him off to see those head doctors again."

"Maybe." Yet it didn't help calm my nerves, nor did it dispel the sense of guilt I carried with me for betraying him.

"Have you thought about what you're gonna tell your dad?"

"No."

"We're gonna get in big trouble."

"I guess," I said.

"Scott wants to catch a movie at the Juniper later. You in?"

"Sure."

Behind me in line, my grandmother squeezed my shoulder, which was my cue that I needed to stop talking.

When I got home from church, I changed out of my good clothes, then retrieved my bike from the wall of ivy at the side of the house. It promised to be another scorcher. The sun was high and full in the sky, the horizon a startling red that looked as serious as an arterial wound beyond the trees and houses on Worth Street.

At the intersection, I hooked a right onto Haven, then felt my legs go rubbery as I spied a familiar pickup on the shoulder of the road. Instinct caused me to squeeze the hand brakes and let up on the pedals. Nathan Keener . . .

I slowed as I passed it. No one was in the cab, though the interior dome light was on. It was parked at a hasty angle, the passenger side tires over the curb. I surveyed the surrounding yards, not putting it past Keener to use his truck as a decoy while he sprung out at me from behind a parked car or a bristling hedgerow. The strange part was, following our fight on July Fourth, I had come to believe that all bets had been settled between us. Had I miscalculated? That seemed the most disconcerting of all.

My hackles still raised, I continued up the street. When the bells of St. Nonnatus chimed noon, I nearly rocketed out of my bike seat and blasted off into the atmosphere. Even when I made it to the highway and the Superstore plaza, I was still certain I was the unwitting fool in the middle of an elaborate trap set by Nathan Keener. Was I being followed even now?

Yet nothing happened.

At December Park, kids played baseball on the diamond, and others ran in undisciplined circles playing a game of tag. I barreled past them all. At the edge of the woods, I leaned my bike against one of the metal trash cans, then hopped the fence.

The woods were hot and buggy. I forged my way through the dense trees, fanning clouds of gnats away from my eyes. When I came upon the clearing, all that remained were the headless statues. The trash bags of stuff we had collected all year were gone. So was the beer cooler where we'd kept the fleur-de-lis, the walkie-talkies, the flashlights. Either the cop had returned and taken our stuff . . . or Adrian had come by and cleaned us out.

I climbed out of the woods and retrieved my bike. Out across the park, the ballplayers cheered.

I biked up the pathway to Solomon's Bend Road, leaning over my handlebars and racing through the Point-Counterpoint intersection. On foot, the shortest way to the Patapsco Institute was to cut through the woods. Since I had my bike, I could take the longer—and easier—way around.

At the edge of the park, I veered off the main road and followed the curve of the woods along a nameless gangway of packed dirt. The trail pitched at a gradual incline as it rose out of the residential streets and joined the cliffs at the edge of the bay. Soon I was pedaling along a narrow strip of dirt with the woods to my right and the yawning still grayness of the Chesapeake Bay far below on my left. Against the horizon, the Bay Bridge was a ghostly mirage simmering in the midsummer haze.

When I reached the plateau where years earlier I had sailed a balsa wood airplane through the air, I coasted to a stop, then dropped my bike in the tall grass. I stood at the edge of the cliff, peering down at the triangles of sailboats carving white foam on the surface of the bay. I closed my eyes and inhaled, remembering that day Charles and I had taken the johnboat out. A sepia-toned filmstrip of memories flickered across the underside of my eyelids.

I turned away from the cliff's edge and headed for the woods. This close to the water, the foliage was of a different breed. I swiped through the huge sweeping ferns, ducked the jungle-like vines garlanding the trees, and stepped over the colorful bouquets of wildflowers.

After a time, the Patapsco Institute reared out of the trees like a living giant dressed in ivy and stone.

There was the window we had gone through, only now there were two thick tree branches trailing up from the ground and leaning against the sill. They looked like rails, like handholds. The sight of them caused my body to grow cold.

Despite my mounting discomfort, I trekked up to the building and stared at its ugly, empty eye-socket window. The darkness beyond was infinite. "Adrian!"

Birds exploded from the underbrush.

I shouted his name a second time, my voice echoing over the chasm of cliffs. Things moved in the trees all around me.

A fine sweat dampening my brow, I trudged around the side of the building and repeated the call. This time, my voice shook the treetops. I moved around to the front, where the great twin doors stood like steel palates beneath the stone arcade, and repeated my call once more—"Adrian!"

. . . *rian* . . . *rian* . . . *rian*: my voice crystallized in the air.

The only response came in the form of that familiar, inhuman yowl of the wind transmitting through the stone walls and pouring out of all the broken spaces in the masonry.

When I arrived at the Juniper, my friends were already in the theater waiting for the show to start. The double bill was *Village of the Damned* and *House of Wax* with Vincent Price. I sidestepped down the aisle and sat next to Peter, who had a tub of buttered popcorn on his lap. On the other side of Scott, Michael leaned into the aisle and chucked a Jujube at me.

As the previews crackled onto the screen, I told them about finding the two tree branches propped up against the window at the institute. "I think Adrian went back in there."

Peter shook his head. "No way he went in there alone."

"But those tree branches," I said.

"And even if he did," Peter said, "he's probably home by now."

"He's probably still pissed," Michael said. I had previously told them about Adrian getting upset with me and running away. "Quit worrying about it. He'll get over it."

Someone shushed us from two rows back. Michael threw Jujubes at them.

Then the first movie started, and I attempted to lose myself for a few hours.

Keener's truck was still parked on the curb at Haven Street.

Against my better judgment, I braked, got off my bike, and went to the driver's side window. The interior light was dimming, draining the battery, but I could make out the refurbished upholstery, no doubt redone after Michael Sugarland deposited his little gift on the front seat. There was a pack of Camels on the dashboard, a container of Skoal that looked like a hockey puck wedged in the console, and a few empty Budweiser bottles on the floorboard of the passenger side. The dome light was on, because the driver's door had not been shut all the way.

It made me nervous. The whole damn thing.

I hurried home.

Midway through a meal of oven-roasted chicken, artichokes, mashed potatoes, and elbow macaroni simmering in a soup of melted butter, someone
knocked on our front door. My grandmother made an attempt to get up, but
my father rose more quickly and moved out of the kitchen and into the vestibule. My grandparents exchanged a look. It was unusual to be disturbed
during dinner.

Muffled conversation could be heard through the wall. A woman's voice—
not necessarily panicked but there was a definite note of apprehension to it.

"Angelo," my father called after a moment, "could you come here, please?"

I dropped my fork and shoved my chair away from the table. Down in the
vestibule, I was rendered speechless to find Doreen Gardiner standing in our
doorway. She looked just as she always did—a scarecrow whose eyes were
made of dull plastic buttons. She wore a sleeveless blouse and a pair of beige
slacks that were so threadbare I could see the dark outline of her underwear
through them. Her hair was a nest of snakes.

"Ms. Gardiner says Adrian never came home this afternoon," said my dad.
There was an accusatory inflection in his tone that made me feel like I was
being interrogated. "She wants to know where he is."

"I didn't see Adrian today."

"Adrian said he was going to the park in the morning, then to the movies
with you and his other friends," Doreen said, the palsied temperament of her
speech suggestive of someone under the influence of sedatives. It was the
most I'd ever heard the woman speak at once.

"Do you know where Adrian is?" my father asked me.

"No."

"Did you see him at all today?"

"No, sir." I was trembling.

"They play in the park," Doreen blurted, and it was like she was ratting
me out.

I felt paralyzed. "Sometimes. We didn't today. I haven't seen Adrian since
Thursday. Neither have my friends."

To Doreen, my father said, "I'll go out and have a look around for him.
You should stay home in case he comes back. I'm sure he's just out playing
somewhere."

She nodded as if her head were spring-loaded.

"Go get my shoes from the closet," my father instructed me.

It took me a second or two before his words made sense. Then I hurried upstairs where I dug his worn cordovan shoes from his bedroom closet.

When I returned, he was jingling his car keys and telling my grandparents that he was going out to look for the boy next door.

I set his shoes down by the front door and said, "I want to come with you."

I expected a protest but he just nodded. He looked extremely tired, and despite the tension between us for the past several weeks, I suddenly felt immense sadness for him.

After we pulled out of the driveway and turned slowly up the street, I saw Doreen Gardiner framed in one of the front windows of her house, a blue strobe of television light behind her.

When my dad took a right onto Haven Street, I noticed Keener's truck still there. The truck's interior light was nearly dead now: it gave off only a pathetic little glint in the ceiling of the cab.

"If you have any idea where he might be," said my father, looking straight out the windshield, "now's the time to tell me."

I thought of those two thick tree branches leaning against the window of the Patapsco Institute. But I couldn't tell my father. If Adrian had gone in there, it was only a matter of time before he came out. It was best I kept my mouth shut and waited for him to return.

Unless something happened to him in there, said a voice in my head. It chilled me to realize it was the voice of the Piper from my nightmares. *Unless I became him and he became me and us became us and we became we.*

"The park, maybe," I said. There was a chance that we might catch him coming out of the woods on his way home for the night.

"December Park?"

"Yes."

I felt rather than saw his gaze swivel in my direction, then dart back out through the windshield.

(we became we)

It was a Sunday evening, and the streets were almost preternaturally quiet. Only a few vehicles drove past us on our way to the highway interchange. Except for the lampposts and the twenty-four-hour pharmacy, all the lights were out in the Superstore plaza.

My dad took the Point-Counterpoint intersection, which was a desolate crucifix of blacktop, straight out to December Park. I had anticipated driving the circumference of the park, but my father hopped on the shoulder of the road and drove on the grass until he reached a break in the guardrail and spun the wheel sharply to the left. The sedan eased down the grassy slope toward the dark pool that was the park grounds below.

"I told you to stay out of this park," said my father.

I looked down at my hands that were twisting in my lap.

We coasted along the field, every bump and groove and rut amplified by the vehicle's lousy shocks, and slowed as we came to the cusp of the baseball diamond. Moonlight dripped blue honey off the metal backstop.

My father clicked on the spotlight that was fixed beside his mirror—the light that looked like a small snare drum—and directed its beam across the baseball diamond. Shadows canted as he swept the light from left to right. The swings beyond the diamond swayed minutely in the soft, warm breeze. December Park looked like the dark side of the moon.

Spinning the steering wheel, my father took the car to the perimeter of the field and motored next to the plywood fence that separated this section of December Park from the Dead Woods. He drove slowly, shining his spotlight into the trees. "Any specific place you boys play down here?"

I had been dreading the question. "Just around," I said.

My father continued along the perimeter of the park. As we approached the mouth of the underpass, he slowed down again and repositioned the spotlight to shine directly into the tunnel.

My heart thundered in my chest.

He leaned over my lap and opened the glove box. A small flashlight rolled out into his palm. When he stepped from the car, I said, "I want to come, too." He didn't respond, so I climbed across his seat and out the door.

A step or two behind him, we approached the underpass. The darkness looked tangible, like a heavy black curtain. The night around us was hot and humming with mosquitoes. I thought of the clot of flies in the institute and felt queasy.

My father stopped at the mouth of the underpass. The flashlight's beam barely cracked the black curtain. I sidled up beside him, shivering despite the humidity.

The beam of light played along the stone walls, the tufts of ivy that veined the archway, the cobblestone path that ran from December Park to Solomon's Field on the other side. One of the posted signs—Park Closes at Dusk— glowed in the flashlight's glare.

"There's nothing here," my father said. There was a clicking sound at the back of his throat. He turned and walked to the car and I followed.

We wended through the dark streets of Harting Farms, the sedan's searchlight prying into black crevices and burning down haunted brick alleyways that ran between storefronts. When we approached the turnoff onto Farrington Road, I thought I might scream if he took it and headed to the old train station. But we went past it, opting instead for circling the church parking lot, then out onto Augustine Avenue.

My father took the long way to the Cape, and we cruised along the upraised band of roadway that overlooked the Shallows. Tea lights twinkled in the windows of the houses at the far end of the beach.

"He has no bike," I said. "He wouldn't have come out this far."

Again, my dad made that odd clicking noise at the back of his throat. When he ignored me, I realized he wasn't looking for a boy who had gone out playing in the neighborhood anymore. He was looking for what he feared most—another victim of the Piper.

By the time we returned to our neighborhood, the clock on the dash read 9:09 p.m. Keener's truck was still parked on Haven Street, the interior light now completely dead. We took the turn onto Worth with particular lethargy, and I wondered if my father was dreading having to tell Doreen Gardiner that we hadn't found her son. Of course, I was hoping Adrian was already home. He couldn't still be in that horrid place, could he?

Yet as we passed the Gardiner house, it looked unchanged. Adrian was not sitting on the stoop, waving at us. His round face was not in any of the windows. That blue light still strobed in one of the first-floor windows, though Doreen Gardiner's silhouette was no longer pressed against the glass like a hideous shadow puppet.

My dad pulled the car into our driveway and shut it down yet remained behind the wheel for several seconds, unmoving and soundless. My left hand itched to touch his shoulder, but he startled me by turning and smiling wearily at me. His face looked incredibly old in the moonlight coming through the windshield, and there were purplish crescents beneath his small and tired eyes. Each individual fleck of beard stubble stood out in sharp relief against the pasty paleness of his face. Though it had undoubtedly been happening for a long time now, I noticed for the first time just how gray his hair had turned.

"Are you okay?" he asked.

The question caught me by surprise. "I guess so."

"I'm going next door. I know it's late, but why don't you give the guys a call and see if they've heard from him. All right?"

"All right."

"Put on a pot of coffee for me, too?"

"Yeah."

We got out of the car together but went our separate ways.

In the kitchen, I started up a pot of coffee, then dialed Peter's phone number. It rang and rang but no one answered. Eventually the answering machine came on, Monica Blum's cheery schoolgirl voice instructing me to leave a message. I hung up.

I called Michael's house next. His father answered in a dull monotone. He seemed irritated at having to speak with me, particularly at such a late hour, but he called for his son nonetheless.

"Adrian hasn't come back yet," I said the second Michael came on the line. "His mom came by earlier tonight. She hasn't seen him."

Michael said, "He's an idiot. He probably fell asleep in that old building and will show up tomorrow morning."

"I'm worried about him."

"He'll turn up."

Then I called Scott. His sister answered and seemed disappointed that the call wasn't for her. When Scott came on the line, I repeated what I'd told Michael.

"Shit," Scott said. "You really think he's in that building?"

"Remember how he didn't want to leave? He was so certain we were going to find something in there. Yeah, I think he went back in."

"What if he broke a leg?" Scott said. "Or fell down one of those holes and broke his neck?"

I could only exhale heavily into the receiver.

"Crap," Scott groaned, "I gotta go. Kristy needs the phone. Call me back if you hear from him."

"I will," I said, and hung up.

When my father returned home from the Gardiners' house the look on his face told me all I needed to know: Adrian hadn't yet come back. I told him none of my friends had heard from him, either. He nodded and yawned while kicking off his shoes in the front hallway. The coffee was ready and waiting for him on the counter, but my old man went straight for the liquor cabinet.

In the morning, I hoped for good news. None came. I got on my bike and rode past Keener's truck on Haven Street. It hadn't moved. I went to work at Secondhand Thrift, plodding through my day like someone who'd had a lobotomy. Yet despite my lethargy, there was a nervous tension vibrating throughout my entire body; I could feel it like live wires strumming just beneath the surface of my flesh.

Peter stopped by the store at noon and asked if I'd heard any news about Adrian. I told him I hadn't. He seemed nonplussed. We ate lunch together and played a few hands of Uno while on my break. Then he went home.

"You," growled Callibaugh at one point during the day. "You move like you've got a pant-load of bricks. What's the matter with you today?"

I told him I didn't feel very well.

He examined a gold pocket watch that he'd procured from one of the many pockets of his overalls, then consulted the wall-mounted clock above the cash register, as if his watch required corroboration. "Give it another hour, then. No more customers come in, you can head home early. I'll take care of the receipts."

I thanked him.

I stopped by December Park on my way home from work, even though it was out of my way, hoping—and almost strangely expecting—to find Adrian waving at me from the edge of the woods. But he was not there. A few police officers milled about the grounds, but there were no kids.

Nathan Keener's truck was still parked on Haven Street.

When I turned onto Worth Street, I saw police cars in front of the Gardiner house. The front door stood open, and a uniformed officer walked around the perimeter of the property with a German shepherd on a leash. I hopped off my bike at the foot of the driveway and just watched. I wondered how far beneath the crust of the earth a German shepherd could smell.

My father's unmarked sedan was not in our driveway. With a sickness coiling around my spine, I wheeled my bike into my yard, propped it against the wall of ivy, and found today's paper on the front porch. Those editors at the *Caller* had wasted no time in putting a photo of Adrian on the front page. The headline proclaimed Piper Claims Another Teen.

My grandfather opened the front door and seemed startled to find me standing there. "You're home early. Cops are talking to your friend's mother."

"Have they heard anything?"

"No."

"Where's Dad?"

"He got called in. He won't be back till late." He drew me closer to him with one of his big rough hands on the back of my head. I smelled pipe tobacco on his shirt and the old man smell of his skin.

And I thought, *Piper claims another . . .*

I had no appetite, and my grandmother didn't make me come down for dinner. I listened to my grandparents' muted conversation through the floor while I stretched out on my bed and stared absently at the ceiling. Outside, twilight had soured the sky to the color of seawater and turned the trees on the edge of our property into black pikes.

Something Scott had said to me last night on the phone still resonated in my head: *What if he broke a leg? Or fell down one of those holes and broke his neck?*

Adrian should have been home by now.

After dinner, as per their ritual, my grandparents retired to the den to watch television. My father still wasn't home. Aside from the occasional bout of canned laughter from the TV, the house had grown uncomfortably silent.

Twice, I picked up the telephone in the upstairs hallway, intending to dial Peter's number; both times I replaced the receiver to the cradle without so much as punching the first digit. From the hall windows, rapiers of bruised light speared through the leaves of maple trees. Thunder rumbled. I felt an aching nostalgia.

I took a hot shower, hoping it would make me feel better. It didn't. I put my old clothes back on, then found myself staring at the telephone in the upstairs hall again. This time, I dialed Peter's number. It rang a few times before he picked up.

"Midnight at the rendezvous point. You don't have to come if you don't want to."

There was prolonged silence on the other end of the line. I was about to hang up when Peter said, "I'll call the others."

"I'll understand if they don't want to go."

"I think they've been waiting," he said and hung up.

At eleven o'clock, the television went off. I heard my grandparents moving around downstairs. The bathroom sink came on. Their soft voices nearly lulled me to sleep as I lay listening to them on my bed.

Twenty minutes later, as I listened to their duet of snores through the floor, I changed from shorts into a pair of blue jeans, then strapped on my sneakers. I upended my JanSport backpack and emptied textbooks, papers, pens, pencils, a slide rule, and two Ronald Kelly paperbacks onto my bed. Rachel's poems were among the items. For whatever reason, I put those folded squares of lined notebook paper in my pocket.

Out in the upstairs hall, I listened to the silence for what seemed like an eternity. Then I entered my father's bedroom.

The mattress held the faint impression of him, the single sheet and coverlet balled up at the foot of the bed. The pillows looked like they had been punched. On the nightstand stood a bottle of cholesterol medication, an alarm clock, and the framed photos of Charles and my mother.

I went to the bed and knelt down. I reached underneath and felt around until my fingers brushed the edge of a cigar box. I slid it out. It was made of very thin wood, not unlike my old balsa airplane. The lid was laid with gold foil. I had expected it to be locked but it wasn't. I opened the lid and there it was: a six-shot revolver with an inlaid wooden grip, the body and barrel shiny even in the darkened bedroom. When I picked it up, it felt heavy and very real. I searched for the lever and learned how to release the cylinder. It rolled out. The six cylindrical chambers were empty.

I opened the drawer of his nightstand. It was cluttered with junk. I rooted around until I found a box of ammunition beneath some folded papers and a checkbook. I opened the box, slid out the plastic tray, and selected six rounds. They were silver with bronze heads. Like the gun, they felt solid and very real. I slid the tray back inside the box and replaced it in the drawer.

As Scott had said, there was a chance Adrian had hurt himself stumbling around inside the building. There was a chance he needed someone to find him, help him get out. I thought about how Scott had nearly been crushed by the items on that falling shelf, and I could too easily imagine Adrian lying inside that place, bleeding, hurt, possibly unconscious.

There was also a chance that something worse had befallen him.

Piper claims another, I thought, tucking the revolver into the waistband of my jeans and hurrying into the hallway, closing my father's bedroom door behind me.

Outside, summer thunder growled its disapproval.

CHAPTER THIRTY-THREE
THE PIPER

The rain held off until I reached December Park. When it hit, it came down in sheets from the black sky, instantly soaking my clothes and backpack and plastering my hair down over my eyes. It was the type of warm summer rain that tasted like the Chesapeake and felt like fresh tears on my skin.

I pedaled like mad across the park, the ground churning and swirling in a muddy miasma choked with bits of trash. Lightning cracked the sky, briefly illuminating the skeletal puzzle of the swing set and the geometry of the chain-link backstop halfway across the park.

A waterfall spilled over the mouth of the underpass from the street above. I stopped, already breathing heavily, and felt a cool stream of mud dampen the cuffs of my jeans and patter against my legs. I climbed off my bike and walked it into the underpass.

It was like passing through a vortex to another dimension. Time stood still, stars winked out of existence, cells ceased aging, blood froze in the system of veins, arteries, capillaries. Objects tossed in the air remained in the air. Raindrops crystallized into needle-thin javelins of ice.

My heart stopped, too. As I leaned my bike against the underpass wall, my chest felt like a hollow tube. I peeled the wet backpack off my shoulders. Inside were the gun and the samurai sword, its blade wrapped in a bath towel, poking out about two feet from the backpack. I sat down, my back against the wall, and fished out a pack of Marlboros from the backpack's front pocket. There were only four left plus a plastic Bic lighter. I shook out a cigarette and the lighter, lit the smoke, inhaled. My exhalation was shaky. My hands trembled on my knees.

I wasn't halfway through my smoke when I heard noise at the mouth of the underpass. I looked and saw three figures passing beneath the waterfall toward me. The light of the lampposts from the street above caused their chrome handlebars to shimmer.

I stood up as Peter, Scott, and Michael wheeled their bikes into the tunnel, then leaned them against the wall next to mine. Scott was dressed all in black, with his Orioles hat on backward. Michael wore the World War II helmet and a backpack. Peter's hair was wet and slicked back off his forehead.

With an unsteady hand, I extended the pack of cigarettes to them. "Only three left."

Peter and Scott took one each. Michael shook out the last smoke and stuck it between his lips.

"No kidding?" I said.

"Keep your comments to yourself," he said, "and light me up."

The four of us smoked awhile.

"We'll take the dirt road out to the cliffs," I said once we'd finished, pulling on my backpack. "It's quicker than going through the woods."

But I hadn't meant *quicker*. I'd meant *safer*.

We gathered up our bikes.

We were four black souls carving our way up the cliff road on the outskirts of town. The city faded to smeary lights and dark pits of shadow. It was the world as we knew it, and we were shuttling right out of orbit. The woods spread out like a vast inky stain on the face of the city. Lights lined the coast along the bay, and I made out the blurry headlights of cars traversing the Bay Bridge. When lightning split the sky, it cast eerie bluish-white light onto the cliffs. The faces of my friends were the faces of warrior ghosts.

We arrived at the top of the cliff with our clothes soaking wet. We tossed our bikes down and marched soundlessly into the trees. Each time it seemed like we might lose our way, lightning filled the sky, allowing us to glimpse the massive stone façade of the Patapsco Institute. We redirected our course and continued onward.

And then we were there.

"There were thick branches leaning up against the window the other day," I said. The branches were gone now.

"Over there," Scott said, pointing to where one of them lay at an angle over a large boulder. "They must have fallen over in the storm."

"Come help me lift them," I said.

"Wait." Michael took off his backpack and set it down in the grass. He unzipped it and hoisted out the collapsible ladder. "Use this."

Shivering, I helped him unfold the ladder. We carried it over to the side of the building where we struggled to keep it from falling over.

"You realize we're holding up an eighteen-foot aluminum ladder in the middle of a thunderstorm," Michael said.

"Don't remind me," I countered.

He smiled.

It took us three tries to get the brackets around the window's ledge. I stepped back. Lightning lit the sky behind the building, making the whole thing look superimposed.

"I'm going in after him," I said, turning to the others. I swung my backpack off my shoulders. "At least two of you should wait out here and stand guard."

"Stand guard for what?" Michael asked.

"Well, if anyone comes," I said.

"You mean the Piper," he said. It was not a question.

I nodded. "Or . . . if I don't come back out."

"You'll come back out," Scott said firmly.

"Yeah, I know. But if I don't, you guys will have to go for help."

Both Michael and Scott nodded.

"I'm going in with you," said Peter. His shock of red hair had turned brown in the rain. His eyes were fierce, determined.

"Are you sure?" I said. "You don't have to."

He grinned. "No retreat, baby, no surrender, right?"

I unzipped my backpack and withdrew the sword I'd wrapped in a bath towel at the house. The towel was drenched, but I'd secured it with rubber bands. I undid them and peeled the wet towel away, revealing the sword's moonlit blade.

"Holy shit," Scott mused.

I held it by the handle with both hands, its weight almost preternatural. Then I passed it over to Scott. "Hold on to this."

He took the sword and held it horizontally, his gaze running back and forth across the length of the blade. "This is incredible." Then he looked at me. "Maybe you should take it."

"I've got something else," I said, reaching into the backpack and taking out my father's revolver. My hand shook, rattling the barrel.

They all stared at the weapon. No one said a word.

I stuffed it back inside the backpack and secured one of the backpack's straps over my shoulder.

"Promise me you won't get killed," Scott said.

I touched my nose. "Promise."

Scott glanced at Peter. "You promise, too."

Peter touched his nose. "I promise."

Scott nodded, his jaw firm. His stoic expression didn't change even when he touched his nose. "I promise we won't get killed out here, either."

"Good," I said, and we all looked at Michael.

He winced. "Seriously? We're still doing the nose thing?"

"Do it." Peter threw a jab at his bicep.

"Okay, yeah, I promise." Michael pressed an index finger against his nose hard enough to flatten it. "See? So now no one gets killed."

"Good deal," I said, and turned to face the ladder.

Peter gave me a boost, even though I was able to grab on and pull myself up without any assistance. I proceeded to climb, the storm raging all around me. An idea for a story came to me—a story about a boy who goes into an old building looking for a killer but gets lost and spends the rest of his life wandering around, trying to find his way out. It made me sick to my stomach.

When I reached the window, I unzipped the front pocket of my backpack and took out the flashlight I'd stowed in there. I shined the beam into the window. The pyramid of rocks fell into view on the other side of the wall. I was hoping to catch sight of Adrian, but I wasn't so lucky. The smell—that rotten fecal stench—greeted me, and the reality of what I was about to do grabbed me around the throat.

Thunder shook the sky. I glanced up, wincing in anticipation of the lightning that was sure to follow. It came, breaking out far over the bay. I felt it in my back teeth.

I swung one leg over the windowsill, braced myself, and then pulled my other leg in after me. The storm was quieter inside, but the sound of running water was all around me. I made my way down the pyramid of stone.

When I reached the floor, I shined the flashlight around the room. Adrian was not here. Clutching the flashlight more tightly, I felt claustrophobia creep up and worm its long, cold fingers around my throat . . .

Peter appeared in the window. He swung his legs in and maneuvered down the pyramid of stone and joined me. "This place is filling up with water."

Rainwater spilled from the cracks in the ceiling and ran down the walls, forming small tributaries on the floor. The fissures in the stone swelled like overflowing rivers. I followed one capillary of water along a seam in the floor until it eventually emptied into the large crater in the middle of the big room.

I panned the flashlight along the walls while my eyes adjusted to the depths around us.

"God," Peter said.

I froze when the light fell on something just a few feet away from the nearest doorway. Peter sucked in his breath.

It was Adrian's backpack. The Incredible Hulk snarled at us, his big green face dusted in a fine white powder.

Peter picked the backpack up and turned it over in his hands. The zipper was busted, and all the contents must have fallen out, because it was empty. Peter's mouth narrowed to a lipless gash when he saw that one of the shoulder straps had been torn loose. When he looked at me, his eyes were terrible.

"Adrian?" I called, my voice a weak tremolo in the vast cavern of the room. "Are you here?"

"This place is enormous," Peter said in a low voice. He let Adrian's backpack fall to the floor. "He could be anywhere."

Adrian would have wanted to pick up where we'd left off Thursday evening: that horrible room past the showers, the one with the meat hooks hanging from the rafters and the stack of soggy mattresses that smelled like death. "Follow me. I think I know where he went."

We walked through the nearest door, absently stepping over Adrian's backpack, and into the corridor. The floor and walls seemed to twist like a hallway in a fun house. There were no open windows, but rain somehow found a way in, filtering down on us as we traversed the long corridor while creating swampy black pools in the dug-out hollows of the floor.

When I thought I caught movement at the opposite end of the hall, I called out, "Adrian!" in a pathetic croak.

"What did you see?" Peter whispered.

"I'm not sure. Maybe nothing."

The shadows all had false fronts and paper bottoms. Rattling noises behind some fallen boards turned out to be more water spilling through seams in the foundation. Other slithery sounds were certainly snakes; I glimpsed the tail of one as it vanished into a hole the size of a baseball in the floor.

"Scott said Adrian could have broken a leg in here," I said, partially to Peter but also to convince myself that the only dangers we might face were the broken floorboards and the falling debris.

"Yeah," Peter said, though I could tell he was thinking worse things, too.

"We don't know anything beyond that."

"His backpack. Adrian came in here and hasn't come out. Something happened. Something bad."

"Please stop," I whispered. "Please."

At the end of the corridor, we crossed into the passageway of interconnected chambers—crooked, buckling rooms that defied the constraints of construction and sanity. Pools of water spread across the floor, setting detritus afloat like garbage jettisoned from a barge. Rats piled atop the flotsam and reared up on their hind legs when I drew my flashlight upon them. Ancient hospital implements gleamed in the flashlight's beam.

Peter and I waded through the shin-high water. Leafy tongues of flora undulated in the heightening soup. Some of the vegetation looked like human hair fanning in the tributaries of running water. I froze, the beam of light angled on some particularly troubling strands that looked like longish waves of dark hair. Peter saw it, too, and stopped moving. I prodded something solid just beneath the surface of the pool with the toe of my sneaker. *A skull*, I thought.

But it wasn't a skull—it was a stone on which the black hairlike plant grew.

In the adjoining room, water the color of beef gravy poured from ventilated grates in the concrete walls. A flash of lightning exploded through the breaks in the ceiling, and countless shadows jumped out from various hiding places. My sanity balanced on a vertiginous ledge.

"I'm getting turned around," I muttered. "I'm getting lost."

"It's Stanton School. The hallways are set up the same," Peter said, his voice blessedly calm. "We're in the science rooms right now."

In yet another room, a grumbling, belching sound caused us both to freeze in midstride. The height of the water had lessened as the floor sloped toward a crater bursting through the tiles. A muddy whirlpool swirled into the crater like bathwater going down an enormous drain. As we watched, a greasy red baseball cap bobbed toward the hole, was embraced by the whirlpool, and was summarily dispatched into the opening.

"Like flushing dead goldfish down the toilet," Peter said.

"Whose hat do you think that was?"

Peter said nothing.

As we crossed into the antechamber of shower stalls and toilets, I was struck again by the putrid reek of decay. It clotted up the humid air and created a film at the back of my throat. The storm rattled the pipes, causing the ancient shower heads to squeal as they rocked in their housings. A cacophony of frogs provided the musical score to our trespass.

There was a scraping followed by what sounded like metal pipes clattering to the floor. A cloud of dust settled around a jumble of black iron bars that had apparently been leaning against the wall before being knocked to the floor. The culprit was a large black rat, its fur wet and matted. Its eyes glistened like two drops of India ink.

I took a few steps toward the fallen iron bars.

Peter came up alongside me, peering over my shoulder as I shined a light on them. "Those—"

"Yes," I said, cutting him off. "Yes."

They were the iron staves from the fence that surrounded the Werewolf House. Some of them were still capped with a decorative fleur-de-lis.

"No way," Peter murmured. "No way those things are in here."

I bent down to pick one up.

Peter kicked my hand away. "Don't touch 'em."

We kept moving. At the other end of the room we entered the narrow passage with the gouges in the walls, fire-retardant blankets, and spools of electrical wire spilling from hastily carved cavities. Opposite us, another doorway stood at a slant. I stepped over some fallen debris, the flashlight jittering in my hand, and nearly screamed when Peter snatched a fistful of my shirt.

"What?" I blurted.

"Don't move. Give me the light."

"What did—?"

He snatched the light from my hand and swung the meager beam toward one of the gouges in the wall. A shredded blanket swayed in the stormy breeze that invaded from the countless cracks in the building's façade. "I thought I saw something move."

There were a million things that moved in here: rats, mice, bats, raccoons, possums, snakes, lizards, not to mention an infinite variety of insects. Rivulets of water coursing through the cracks made it look like the entire floor was alive. Peter could have seen anything.

I motioned to the slanting doorway. "That's the room with the meat hooks and mattresses."

"Don't call them meat hooks," Peter said, handing me the flashlight.

I pressed forward down the passageway. It was more tedious now that the storm was funneling a channel of black water down the center of the creased floor. Bits of planking surfed down the hall, knocking against my shins.

"There," Peter said, pointing.

I redirected the beam of light. Even as I stared at it, I didn't fully register what it was right away.

The statue head. It sat in a corner against the wall, the rusted iron bar protruding from its neck.

"That can't be the same—"

"It's the same," Peter finished. "Fuck. This is it, isn't it?"

I just stood there, my body a frozen plank of ice, unable to move. I listened to the storm raging outside. I listened to the water dribble in through the cracks in the foundation. I listened to the hidden rodents that scurried through the muck.

"Angie," Peter whispered.

I blinked. I realized my mouth was filled with acid. I leaned over and gagged, vomiting onto the floor. Peter's hand fell on my back.

When I'd finished, I wiped my mouth with my arm, then ran fingers through my wet hair. "I'm okay," I uttered, heading toward the rectangular doorway.

Flies dive-bombed for my eyes, and I swatted them away with my free hand, keeping the tenuous finger of light trained on the doorway ahead of me. The horrid smell intensified. I held my breath and stepped through.

I saw the stack of mattresses, the flooded floor, the crates ribboned with fingers of colored cloth, the strange metal diorama bolted to the far wall. I saw the meat hooks—

(don't call them meat hooks)

—dangling from the industrial chains, too. And that was where we saw Adrian.

He's dead.

Adrian was suspended upside down by one of the hooks, his arms behind his back. His face was red and swollen, and his eyes looked fused shut. His hair was a filthy snarl of kudzu, and his face was streaked with both grease and blood. The dark spots on his shirt looked like bloodstains, but I couldn't see any wounds. Still dangling from a length of shoelace, the heart-shaped locket hung in front of his face.

My flashlight flickered but remained on.

Peter swallowed audibly. "Is he. . . ?"

"Adrian," I called, my voice a sonorous echo throughout the chamber. Adrian did not stir.

I waded through the rising water and over to the stack of wooden crates. "Help me with these."

Peter rushed to my side but seemed confused as to what I needed him to do. He kept glancing up at Adrian's lifeless body. When he saw me drag one of the crates over to the mattresses, he did the same. I grabbed his crate and placed it on top of mine. A switch seemed to go off behind his eyes, and he dashed back for another crate so we could complete our ladder.

I steadied the beam of light on Adrian. From this angle, I could see that his ankles had been taped together, and it was this ring of tape through which the meat hook had been looped. If I climbed to the top of the mattress pile, I might be able to reach up and cut him down . . .

"There's someone else in here with us," Peter breathed. He was hunched over one of the crates, looking behind him. "I can hear it . . ."

"Hurry," I told him.

When our ladder reached four crates high, Peter steadied the base while I climbed atop the heap of mattresses—a sensation that was like crawling across the carcass of a beached whale. The fabric surrendered without protest, driving my fingers into the bedding, as my knees eased down into cool sludge. The smell was so horrible it stung my eyes and nearly made me gag. I lifted one hand, then set it down into a lukewarm porridge. Turning the flashlight onto my hand, I found I had placed my palm into a chunky custard of what at first appeared to be vomit. But then I saw that the individual chunks squirmed, and I recognized it for what it was: a puddle of writhing maggots.

I vomited over the side of the mattress.

Peter asked if I was all right.

After regaining my composure, I mumbled a weak, "I'm okay."

Directly above my head, Adrian swayed almost imperceptibly from the chain. I swung my backpack around and found my switchblade in the small front pocket. I pressed the release button, but the blade jammed halfway out of the hilt. Feverishly, I continued pressing the button, but the blade would not shoot out any farther. *Fuck it, then. It'll still work.*

I managed to stand, the surface of the putrid, wet mattress surrendering further beneath my weight; my feet sank into it up to my ankles as the fabric came apart. I felt things moving against my flesh and squirming beneath the elastic bands of my socks, and my mind summoned images of leeches, fat squirming bloodworms, and wriggling night crawlers.

This close, I could tell that Adrian was still alive. His breathing was audible, though labored, and I saw the hesitant expansion and deflation of his birdlike chest. The puffiness and redness of his face suggested some sort of allergic reaction. There was a dried exclamation of blood running from both corners of his mouth like a TV show vampire. He reeked of urine.

With an unsteady hand, I began sawing through the shackle of electrical tape at Adrian's ankles.

"Hurry, man," Peter called.

I glanced down and saw him whipping his head from side to side, searching the darkness for monsters.

"I'm telling you, there's someone else in here."

"I'm hurrying."

"Hurry faster."

The tape snapped, and Adrian's limp body dropped to the mattress head-first. He bounced and threatened to roll off, but I caught him with my free hand. I drove one knee against the small of his back while I sawed through the tape that bound his wrists.

Midway through the tape, Adrian moaned and stirred.

"He's alive!" Peter cried.

Adrian rolled his head back. The flashlight, which I had propped in the crook of one armpit, brought into relief not only the ruined, patchy mask that was his face but also the unimaginable fear in his eyes. He gaped at me. Without his glasses, his eyes looked too small. His pupils were different sizes.

"Adrian, it's me. It's Angelo. Can you move?"

He just stared at me. When I shifted gradually to the left, his gaze didn't follow me.

Then he blinked, and I saw recognition filter into his eyes. His lips quivered. There was a dried crust of snot trailing from one nostril clear across the puffy terrain of his left cheek.

"We gotta get you out of here," I told him.

He gripped my forearm. "He's here."

"Come on." I rolled him on his side so he could see over the edge of the mattress.

Peter stood below, half his face masked in shadow. He reached up and grabbed Adrian by the shoulders while I pushed against the small of Adrian's back.

". . . ere . . . ," Adrian grunted as I shoved him over the side and into Peter's embrace.

I swung one leg over the mattress and felt my foot land squarely on the top crate.

Peter steadied the tower of crates with one foot while holding Adrian against him. Adrian's head was cocked awkwardly on Peter's shoulder, his eyes like the eyes of a blind man staring off into nothingness. Insanely, I wondered if he was going to get in trouble for losing his glasses.

I made my way down the tower of crates and landed in several inches of cold, scummy water. Outside, the storm slammed against the building. To help Peter support Adrian, I took one of Adrian's arms.

Adrian screamed as I touched his flesh. He recoiled, bolting fully awake, and shoved Peter away, too.

"Adrian," I said, trying hard to keep my voice calm, "it's Angelo and Peter."

"It's us," Peter said.

"Do you know?" Adrian rasped. From even a few feet away I could smell his fetid breath, as if he'd been gargling raw sewage. His gaze darted from me to Peter, then back to me.

"Do we know what?" I said.

"Found," he croaked.

I shook my head: I didn't understand.

"What . . . I . . . found," he said, his voice grating up from his throat. "Found . . . *them* . . ."

I heard shifting off to my right. I looked and saw Peter retreating slowly into the darkness. His form was nothing more than a shadow in the insubstantial glow of my flashlight. Then the form diverged into two forms, and for a second I thought my mind was breaking apart on me.

Peter continued to back away. The diverged half of him hooked in a slow and deliberate semicircle around me. I discerned the suggestion of tapered, angular shoulders, a mat of wet, stringy hair, the flicker of a pale skull face with eye sockets like tar pits. It wasn't that Peter's form had split into two but that someone else had shifted out from behind him. The shape positioned itself between us and the door across the room.

"There!" Peter shrieked, his voice splitting the silence.

The figure extended a hand toward Adrian. There was something like a hooked blade in it. Or so I imagined.

The following events happened so quickly yet with the dizzying torpor of a drug-fueled nightmare that to this day I am still uncertain as to the exact order of them. Each event occurred in a vacuum, suspended in its own bubble: Peter stumbled backward and fell, crashing through one of the crates that had floated away and splashing water into the air; Adrian shrieked and dropped to the floor in a fetal position; the shadowy figure darted to the right, that massive arm swinging what appeared to be a blade in a controlled arc; my flashlight blinked out.

Someone screamed. It could have been me. I felt warm water—or some other liquid—splash across my face and sting my eyes. Blind, I staggered backward until I slammed into the spongy tower of mattresses, the rancid cushions sucking me in. Somehow I'd managed to swing the backpack around and was fumbling with it when a second scream pierced the darkness.

When I opened my eyes, I noticed a star of yellow light. It took me what felt like an eternity to realize it was a flame. Peter stood dripping foul water, the bobbing flame of his Bic lighter shimmering like a beacon of salvation. I glimpsed Adrian's wide, sightless eyes flash before me.

Then the dark figure rushed toward Peter, kicking up torrents of water and smashing through the stack of crates that, in all the commotion, had tipped away from the mattresses and crashed to the floor.

And then the revolver was suddenly in my hands. I extended my arms until my elbows locked. Pulled the trigger. Twice.

The muzzle flashes provided horrific snapshots that would no doubt remain burned into the gray matter of my consciousness for the rest of my life: the bleak emptiness of the figure's face, a sweep of filthy wet hair, the pale crescent of the back of a hand as it blurred into motion . . .

The figure spun and faced me in the white flash of the second gunshot, loud as damnation. His face was a blazing skull whose features seemed to shift and reposition themselves. Then, in the glow of Peter's lighter, the man fell backward into the frothing miasma of water, mud, and garbage.

The gunshots still echoing in our ears, we all stood there in silence. In fact, the whole world had gone silent: I could no longer hear anything at all. Then . . . slowly . . . sounds filtered back to me. The first to return was a mechanical whooshing; it took me a moment to realize it was the sound of my own blood racing through my veins. Then my heartbeat and respiration joined in the chorus. My entire body was made of wax.

I lowered the gun, then dropped it to the floor where it splashed between my feet and was swallowed up by the dark water.

"The Piper," Adrian said. I recognized the words, but the sound of his voice could have been the bleating of a sheep or the firing of rocket engines.

White foam collected about the Piper's fallen body. In the timorous glow of Peter's lighter, I thought I glimpsed the Piper's chest shuddering up and down. I took two, three steps toward him until I could see the tiny holes in his tattered shirt. With each dying breath, blood spurted from the holes. I had made those holes in him. I had done it.

The Piper's eyes were open. He looked at me, and I could see the life slipping from him very quickly, the—

My breath caught in my throat.

For a second, I was no longer here: I was running a field day relay race in December Park. The front of my pants was soaked because I'd been so petrified that I'd urinated in them. The crowd loomed over me as I fell behind, running to keep up, my face burning, my sides burning. I wasn't fast enough, wasn't good enough, and they said—

"Angelo." It was Peter. He was closer to me now. "Angelo." He kept repeating my name. He never used my full name. To him, I was always Angie.

I exhaled with a tremendous shudder. Beside me, a younger version of my grandfather (who wasn't my grandfather at all, I now realized) shoved me toward the triangular opening in a grass hut. When I went inside, a slightly different version of my father (who wasn't my father at all) was there. This man held my shoulders and whispered horrible things in my ear. When I asked him to explain, he just said, *I become you and you become me and us become us and we become we.*

"I don't know what that means." I must have spoken aloud because Peter reached a hand out to touch me.

I shoved him aside.

—You will find, said the Piper in my head. You will find, you will find, you will find.

Shaking, I went to the Piper and dropped to my knees beside him. He turned his head slightly, his longish hair fanned out in the water, the color drained from his face. The features had stopped shifting and had come to rest, and I now understood why they had originally appeared to be shifting.

Then my hand was out, hovering in the air. I smelled nothing. I heard nothing except the rushing water filling the room. If there was still a storm outside, I knew nothing of it: we could have been submerged beneath the sea.

I placed my hand on one of his shoulders. Around me, the water grew frigid. The Piper's breath rasped, and blood spurted from the two bullet holes in his shirt. He held what I had thought was a curved blade but was in actuality a piece of the metal configuration that had been bolted to the far wall, too crude to be called a weapon even if that was its purpose.

"Go," I said to Peter and Adrian. I didn't know how many words I had left in me, so I had to make them count. "Get Dad. Tell him."

Tears spilled down my face. My entire body burned. I was aware of Peter and Adrian talking, but their language had become nonsense to me. I was only aware that they had finally left once the light from Peter's lighter was no more.

Trembling, I rested my head on the Piper's chest. After a while, I felt his hand come up to the back of my head and settle there. By the time his heart stopped beating, I was sobbing like a baby.

CHAPTER THIRTY-FOUR
OUT

And then I was on the boat again. I was seven years old, and it was a big deal being out on the boat alone with Charles. We had our shirts off, and the sun baked our shoulders and backs. There were two crab lines tied to the oarlocks, old chicken necks at the ends. A crab would follow the chicken neck all the way to the surface, gorging itself. Mere inches from the surface, you'd bring a net underneath it and scoop it up.

As Charles maneuvered in and out of the coves, my job was to keep an eye on both lines for signs of a nibble. We caught no crabs that afternoon, and Charles had grown increasingly bored, so he took the boat out to the choppier waters beneath the Bay Bridge.

"See those?" Charles said, pointing at the face of the cliffs that loomed high above us. It was the place he called the ass end of Harting Farms. "Those holes? All of 'em?"

I nodded and asked what they were.

"Places to hide," he said.

"Hide from who?" I asked.

"Bootleggers and slaves used them."

"Who made them?" I asked.

"Maybe people did. Or animals. Or maybe they were always here even before the city was built, carved out by the water when the bay was higher."

"Wow," I said.

"We can catch bigger things," Charles said, changing the subject so quickly that it took me a second to realize we were off the subject of holes in the cliff and back to crabbing.

"What things?" I said, staring up at the span of the great bridge. I had never been out this far before.

There were seagulls wheeling overhead. Charles motioned to them. His skin was freckled but smooth, the nipples on his muscular chest small and brown and ringed with sparse black hairs.

"Birds?" I said, laughing.

"Sure. Birds. Why not?"

"You can't catch birds."

He winked at me and said, "Just watch. You can catch anything. If you really wanted to, you could catch anything in the world." He opened his tackle box, dug around inside it, and came up with a rusted barbed fishing hook. "Gimme your lunch."

"It's mine! You already ate yours."

"I'm not gonna eat it, dummy. Just pass it over and watch."

I handed him the chicken cutlet sandwich wrapped in cellophane that my grandmother had made me that morning.

Charles unwrapped the cellophane, pinched a bit of bread out from the center of the slice, and carefully rolled it into a ball. Above, the gulls cawed and screeched and deposited white clumps of shit into the water. His tongue propped in the corner of his mouth, Charles threaded the barbed hook through the white marble of bread. When he was finished, only the nasty-looking barbed tip protruded.

I watched, not speaking. Far above, cars and trucks thundered across the double-span bridge.

Bracing his feet at either side of the small boat, Charles peered up and winced at the dazzling sun. He shielded his eyes with one arm. Over his head, the seagulls shrilled like squealing hinges. When he tossed the ball of bread straight up into the air, the gulls took on a deliberate pattern that reminded me of old World War II footage of fighter jets bombing battleships. The tiny white sphere was snatched up by the most aggressive of the flock and gobbled down without incident.

I continued to stare at the birds, then at Charles, then back at the birds again. My brother stayed balanced, each foot planted on either side of the boat, one arm up to block the sun from his eyes. If he was disappointed the bird had not choked on the hook and plummeted to the sea or even into our boat, he didn't show it; instead, he looked like the statue of a Greek god, his shorts rippling in the wind, the hair on his bronze and slender legs like fine brown fuzz.

When the birds saw that there would be no more food flipped into the air, they migrated across the water to where bits of debris floated into the coves.

Charles screamed, startling me. Sharp cords stood out in his neck, and his diaphragm, like a frown, jostled in his abdomen.

Because I thought this was some kind of playacting, I made the mistake of giggling. But Charles was not playacting. He leveled his gaze on me, his dark eyes cut to slits. His lips were firm, his eyebrows knitted together.

Slowly, he brought one arm up and pointed at me. He rocked the boat with such sudden ferocity that it was almost like we'd been struck from beneath by something extremely large and dangerous.

"Stop it," I told him.

With increasing zeal, he continued to rock the boat.

"Stop it!" I shouted.

Charles laughed, but there was no humor in it: the sound was a witch's shrill cackle.

With my arms splayed out for balance, I rose from my seat and attempted to negate his unbalancing of the little johnboat with a steadiness of my own. But I was seven and I was small and I was ill-prepared and—

(scared)

—growing increasingly panicked.

When I went over the side, I swallowed a lungful of cold water and got tangled in the crab lines. The world around me went instantly black. I flailed one hand, and it thunked against the hollow aluminum side of the boat like a gong. Forgetting that I was underwater, I took a deep breath and felt the water fill my lungs and permeate my entire body. Bright spangles capered before my vision. With the crab lines entwined about my ankles, I couldn't swim to the surface. The bay thundered in my ears. Panic gripped me, yet a warm blossom of serenity, like the comforting embrace of a loved one, came over me.

Then I was back on the boat, coughing up brackish water and blinking stupidly at the blurred form that hovered over me.

"I'm sorry," Charles said. He repeated it over and over like a litany, a prayer. "Angelo, I'm sorry. I'm sorry. I'm sorry. I'm sorry."

Once I regained my senses, I shoved him off me and crawled backward on my butt.

"I would never hurt you," Charles said. The intensity in his eyes frightened me even more than having him knock me in the water. "I would never let anyone else hurt you, either. If anyone ever hurt you or tried to hurt you, I would snap their neck. I would bury their corpse in the quarry at the end of our block. I would leave them there for the rats."

I just stared at him.

Then he laughed—that carefree, boyish laugh that adults found jovial and girls found charming.

High above, traffic growled across the bridge.

Somehow, I'd fallen asleep. When I woke, it was to the stricken voices of

men, their large, indistinct forms swiping tungsten lights across the darkness.
Strong hands gripped me and lifted me off the body of the Piper. It took me a
moment to recall where I was or what had happened.

I had the vague impression of being handed off, round-robin style, from
man to man. With my eyes squeezed shut, I smelled each of my handlers distinctly—their colognes, their body odors, their breath. I struggled and fought
them around the same time my eyes sprung open and a great aching wail
burst from my lungs.

Someone held me in a strong embrace and whispered over and over in
my ear—

(i'm sorry angelo i'm sorry)

—to calm down, it's okay, kid, calm down, you're okay, you're okay.

My vision was blurry. I swiped tears from my eyes with shaky hands. There
were cops everywhere. One of them held me and kept whispering in my ear.
Before me, I recognized the enormous double doors beneath the arcade at
the front of the Patapsco Institute—or rather where the doors had been: they
had been busted down and lay on the stone floor like twin drawbridges over
a moat. I heard the storm raging around us, the rain spilling down from the
arcade in torrents.

"Angelo!"

I broke free from the cop's hold and spun around in the direction of the
voice. The slope of the woods that led away from the building was a swirling, black tornado of rain. Thin trees were pressed close to the ground by the
force of the wind. More tungsten lights bobbed in the miasma, along with
figures that emerged through the trees like ghosts of Civil War soldiers coming through an early morning mist.

"Angelo," the man said again.

It was my father. He stumbled through the trees, his hair and clothes
soaked, his face a cadaverous cut of moonlight. His eyes were two colorless
stones. When he saw me, he ran toward me. I wanted to run to him, too, but
my legs would not obey.

He grabbed me, pulled me hard against his chest. My face went into
the crook of his neck while my fingers dug into his back. I sobbed again,
trembling. He squeezed the back of my neck and I said, "Don't g-g-go in
th-there . . ."

"Shhh," he said, cradling me.

"Don't g-go in," I said. It was important to say it. I didn't think the words
even passed through my lips, or if they did, they were gibberish.

"It's okay, Angelo. Calm down. You're safe now. You're safe."

I pulled away and looked hard at him. His face seemed to tremble and
threaten to disperse into nonexistence at any second, as if made of dreams.

I opened my mouth and stuttered, "Ch-Ch-Ch—," but I couldn't get the name out.

"Doesn't matter," he said, his voice calm and his words coming slowly. "It's okay now. It's okay."

But it wasn't, I knew.

It wasn't.

I sat with my legs hanging out of the open rear doors of an ambulance, a fire-retardant blanket around my shoulders, and shivered. The ambulance looked out over the promontory and at a sky that flared occasionally with lightning.

Peter stood in the rain beside the ambulance, seemingly unable to take his eyes from me. I couldn't be sure, but I thought he had seen and understood. It looked like he wanted to say something to me but couldn't find the words.

Michael and Scott came up behind him, Scott clutching the samurai sword to his chest. Rain danced across Michael's army helmet and cascaded over the brim of Scott's Orioles cap.

Briefly, I closed my eyes and willed my thoughts into their heads. But my thoughts were messy and confused beasts, and even if they managed to pierce their brains, they wouldn't have understood them. I didn't understand them myself.

My father talked to some cops near the edge of the cliff. When he finally came to me, I said, "Where's Adrian?"

"Ambulance took him. Hospital."

We said no more.

Sometime later, when they brought the Piper's body from the woods, my father dropped to his knees in the mud and hung his head. He sobbed. I watched as his shoulders hitched and the rain drenched his clothes. I watched as the dark, wet curls of his hair hung down over his eyes.

He stayed like that for a long, long time.

CHAPTER THIRTY-FIVE
AFTERMATH

The rain had stopped and sunlight was beginning to crack the distant sky by the time my father and I got home. The sedan rolled heavily into the driveway, the chassis groaning. There was a squad car parked at the curb in front of our house. The rack of lights on the roof was dark, and I couldn't see anyone behind the wheel.

"You sure you're okay?"

I nodded, staring at my hands in my lap. I had refused to be taken to the hospital. I'd just wanted to go home. "Your gun," I said, the word *gun* sticking to the roof of my mouth like peanut butter. "I'm sorry. I took it from your room. It's . . . it's b-back th-there in—"

He reached out and pulled me against him. His clothes were wet. I smelled his aftershave and the sweat and fury and confusion and sadness on him. Like a child, I sobbed uncontrollably against his chest while he held me and smoothed back my damp hair.

"Shhh," he whispered. "It's okay. Shhh."

When he finally let me go, I smeared the tears from my face and saw a figure standing on our front porch. The figure wore a police uniform.

Clearing his throat and running a thumb along the rim of his lower eyelids, my father said, "I should go inside and see to your grandparents. Do you want to come in or sit out here awhile longer?"

I couldn't face my grandparents in whatever condition they were in. What did they already know? Had someone told them what had happened? Or had this cop just been sent here to babysit until my dad got home?

"I don't want to go inside just yet."

He squeezed my shoulder. "Do you want me to stay with you?"

"No, it's okay. I'm okay." I looked at him. "I don't understand what happened, Dad."

"Neither do I," he said, and he nearly lost it and broke down again, too.

When he got out of the car, I felt the vehicle rise on its shocks. *Fathers are big, heavy things*, I thought. He closed the door gently, then walked like a man to judgment up to the front porch. He spoke briefly with the officer before going inside. Lights went on in the kitchen.

The officer came down from the porch and cut across the yard. On his way to the squad car, he glanced at me from over his shoulder, and I immediately recognized him as the suspicious-looking cop who'd been following me.

Around midmorning, two men in suits came and asked me questions while I sat with my father at the kitchen table. I told them everything we'd done that summer and all the things we'd learned, starting with the locket Adrian had discovered in the culvert beside the road last fall. I told them about finding the statue head in the Werewolf House, the railway depot where Jason Hughes's bike was hidden, and ultimately how we had arrived at the abandoned Patapsco Institute.

I thought my father would become angry when I spoke of the places I went and the things I did, but he said nothing.

"What happened to Adrian?" I asked the men. When it was clear they didn't know who Adrian was, I said, "The boy who we went in to rescue."

"Oh," said one of the men. He had a sliver of a mustache and sparkling blue eyes. "He's still at the hospital, but they say he'll be just fine."

After they left, I expected my father to lay into me for disobeying him all summer, but he never said a word. He poured himself a glass of water from the kitchen sink. Then he poured me one and set it down in front of me at the table, where I remained sitting, seemingly unable to move.

Later I met with a psychologist—a rotund bald man with wire-rimmed glasses and breath that smelled like onions. Like the men in the suits, he asked me to recount what had happened, though he seemed less interested in the details and more concerned with how I felt about what happened. I couldn't answer his questions; I didn't know how.

After a time, I asked him some questions of my own. They seemed to make him uncomfortable and succeeded in cutting our session short. Afterward, he talked for a long time with my father. I was left with the distinct impression that I wouldn't see the bald man with halitosis again.

There were other men who showed up, too—men in military uniforms and stoic expressions. They spoke to my father at the house, and twice they took him someplace else to talk. My father returned from these meetings looking like he'd had blood drawn. He never talked about them and I never asked.

When reporters from the *Caller* showed up at our door, my father said to ignore them. When reporters from the *Sun* and the *Capital* and the *Post* and the *Times* showed up, two policemen were stationed outside our house to make sure we weren't disturbed. One night, a helicopter hovered over our house for nearly half an hour, its spotlight sweeping across our backyard. When neighbors appeared outside with signs on poster boards, I asked my father if they thought we were somehow responsible.

"I can't say what's in people's heads," he replied sullenly. He noticed Tom Matherson from across the street among the mob. "We can't live here anymore, Angie. You understand that, right? We're going to have to move."

I said nothing.

Because my father didn't want us watching the news, or any TV for that matter, he unplugged the set and hauled it down to the basement. I stayed in my bedroom and listened to Pearl Jam.

Adrian suffered from dehydration, a concussion, various contusions to the head and upper chest, and a ruptured eardrum. (The eardrum thing was from the gunshots I'd fired, which had been close to his head.)

The day after I met with the men in suits and the shrink, my father took me to visit Adrian in the hospital. Doreen Gardiner was standing outside her son's room. Her dead gaze fell on me, sending a bolt of electricity surging down my spine, and I felt my body grow cold. Then something in her face softened. For one fleeting second I thought I saw a regular human being behind those sightless, taxidermy eyes.

"Thank you," she said simply. "I know what you did for him."

It felt like my mouth was full of sand. At my back, my father rested one hand on my shoulder, then urged me forward.

"Angie!" Adrian beamed as I entered the room. My father waited in the hallway for me.

"Brought you some stuff," I told him. I approached his bed and set a few comic books, some mix tapes, and my Walkman on the nightstand beneath a wall of blinking, bleeping machinery. The whole room smelled of antiseptic.

"Thanks." His face was bruised and swollen, his lips split and crusted with blood. When he reached out and pulled the comic books into his lap, I saw striated bruises running the length of his arms. He rifled through them, grinning.

"They're just some old ones I found packed away in my closet," I told him. "I don't know if they're any good."

"They're great. Thanks."

"Can you even read them without your glasses? Did you lose them in . . . uh, that place?"

"I guess so. I don't remember a whole lot." He gestured toward a small television set mounted on brackets above his bed. "Did you see me on the news?"

"No. Dad took our TV away."

"Oh. Cops came and interviewed me. A psychologist, too."

"Neat," I said.

"You killed him."

"Yeah."

His gaze hung on me. "Is it true? About . . . about who he was?"

"Yeah," I said and looked away from him. My eyes filled with tears, and I didn't want him to see.

"It's okay if you need to cry," Adrian said. On the wall behind him, machines beeped. "I won't tell anybody."

"What were you doing in there?" I said, whirling around. "If you hadn't gone in there . . ." I couldn't finish the thought.

"I'm sorry."

"I would have never had . . . had to . . ."

A tear traced down his bruised cheek. Slowly, he nodded. "I'm sorry. Don't be mad at me. I'm sorry, Angie."

"You went in there alone. It was stupid."

"I know." Adrian wiped his single tear away.

I exhaled a shuddery breath. "I'm not . . . I'm not mad . . . at you . . ."

He was still nodding.

"I'm not mad at you," I repeated, my voice steadier.

"Good. Because you're my best friend."

My anger suddenly gone, I smiled at him. I mopped tears from my eyes and regained some composure.

"You know, the guys stopped by the other day," Adrian said once I'd dragged a folding chair over and sat down.

"You've seen them?"

"Yeah." He motioned to a stainless steel table across the room where a bunch of plastic army men had been set up. There was a deck of Uno cards there, too. "They brought me some stuff and hung out awhile."

"I haven't seen them."

"Not at all?"

"No." I thought of the mob outside our house and how Mr. Matherson had been among them. My greatest fear was that my friends had backed away from me.

"Oh," Adrian said. He sounded strangely disappointed.

"Are you . . . like . . . in a lot of pain?" I asked.

"No, not really. Not now."

"Do you have to stay here much longer?"

"I'm not sure. They've been taking pictures of my brain in some big machine. They're worried about swelling."

"Michael's already got the swelled head in our group," I joked. "We don't need another."

Adrian laughed.

"What happened to you in that place?" I asked.

"I don't really remember. A lot of it's a blur. But I heard they found the bodies."

I nodded. My brother had hidden them beneath the Patapsco Institute in the network of small caves and tunnels that ran beneath it and out toward the cliffs. He had gained access to the institute via one of these tunnels, too—a narrow crawl space in the ground that came up through a broken floor. When I had heard this, I recalled those large craters in the institute's floor and the cliff face dotted with tunnels. They weren't tunnels anymore. They were catacombs.

"What do you call it when you dream about something that's gonna happen?" he asked out of nowhere.

"A prophecy?"

"Yeah, that's it. You ever have one of those dreams? A prophecy dream?"

"I don't know," I said slowly, recalling the nightmare that had me running through some rain forest while a giant prehistoric creature chased me and ultimately hiding in some grass hut only to find a whole other kind of creature waiting for me inside.

"After my dad killed himself, I used to have the same dream over and over again about an underground city. Only it really wasn't just underground but sort of hidden behind and within the other city, the real city. Every building had a secret counterpart, and every street had another street just like it but with a slightly different name, and they led to slightly different places. Even the people in the dream had twins that lived in this city."

"They're called doppelgangers," I said.

"Yeah. In the dream, this whole other city goes on existing right alongside the real one. Thing is, I'm the only person who knows the hidden city exists. I'm the only one who knows the bad things that hurt the people of the real city come from the hidden city at night. That's why no one ever knows how to stop the bad things or how to fight them or even find them.

"So I go underground and leave bits of string tied to the entrances that are like these big golden arches, which is weird, right, because you'd think everyone else would be able to see them too and figure out there's a city under the city." His eyes grew wide. "But it's not just a city. Turns out it's a whole world under there—a world beneath a world and within a world but also somehow occupying the same space as the real world."

"That's some dream," I said.

"Don't you get it? I never knew what the dream meant until all this happened. It was a prophecy."

"A prophecy for what?"

"For what we did. The five of us. We went to the world beneath the world, fought the monster, and won."

I smiled. "That would make an awesome comic book."

"Yeah," he said, returning my smile, "it would. That's a cool idea."

"Well," I said, getting up from the chair, "I should probably go. My dad's waiting for me. Let me know when you're back home, okay?"

"Okay. Thanks for coming by."

"No sweat," I said.

"Hey," he called.

I turned around. "Yeah?"

"See you later, alligator."

"After a while, pedophile," I said and closed the door on his laughter.

The next morning, I came downstairs to find Mr. Mattingly sitting at the kitchen table having coffee with my dad. Mr. Mattingly stood up. My dad got up, too, and said, "You've got a visitor, Angie." He rubbed my head on his way out of the room.

"Your dad seems like a great guy," Mr. Mattingly said.

"He's okay, I guess."

"How're you holding up?"

"I don't know. Why'd you come here?"

"Well, I wanted to see how you were doing." He came around the side of the table while sliding his hands into his pockets.

"Is this about the note?"

"The note?"

"The note we left on your door."

He furrowed his eyebrows and cocked his head. But then his features softened and he actually smiled. "Ah, the note. Yes. That prompted some interesting conversation around the Mattingly household."

"I'm sorry. It was a mistake. We thought you were . . . someone else."

"No harm done. And, no, that's not why I'm here." His smile softened even further. "Angie, I came here hoping you'd make me a promise."

"What promise is that?"

"That you continue down the path you've already begun carving out for yourself."

"I don't understand."

"Yes, you do. You know exactly what I'm talking about. That's just what I mean—you're a smart kid. Maybe you're afraid to try for something new because you think that means you have to leave everything you know and care about behind."

"Doesn't it?" I said.

"Never be afraid of who you are." Mr. Mattingly picked up a hardcover book off the table and handed it to me—*Lord of the Flies*. "When I was your age, I wanted nothing more than to be a writer. This was my favorite book. It's about a bunch of kids who get stranded on a desert island."

"What happened?"

"You'll have to read the book to find out."

"No," I said. "I mean, what happened with your writing?"

"I was afraid. I didn't think I was good enough. After a few rejection slips, I stopped sending my work out. It was easier to quit than to fight through it. And then life just got in the way. It's so much harder to try and recapture those lost years once they're behind you. So don't let them be behind you."

I nodded and looked down at the book. My vision threatened to blur, and it was all I could do to fight off tears.

Mr. Mattingly held out one hand. I shook it . . . and he drew me closer and hugged me with one arm. To my surprise, I felt myself hug him back. Hard.

"So?" he said once he let me go.

"So what?"

"Do you promise to keep fighting for it?"

"Yeah." I touched my nose. "I promise."

Mr. Mattingly laughed. He laughed so hard that tears sprung from his eyes. I felt a tear escape one of mine, though I was only chuckling along with him.

After he left, I took the book up to my room, sat Indian-style on my bed, and flipped through it. I paused when I came to the title page, where Mr. Mattingly had written me a note. I'd grown accustomed to seeing his handwriting in red ink in the margins of my papers, but the context of this note was altogether different.

To Angelo,
My life goal for you.
Your friend,
David

Your friend, I thought and began to read.

My second visitor showed up the following day, as I sat on my bed reading *Lord of the Flies*. When my father's voice boomed up the stairs, I set the book aside and moved down the hallway to the stairs with mounting agitation. I hoped to find Peter, Michael, and Scott on the front step. I hadn't spoken to them since that night at the Patapsco Institute. Their sudden and inexplicable absence from my life filled me with a fear that caused me to question who I was as a person. Not until that moment did I realize how much I had relied on my friends to define who I was.

Rachel Lowrey stood on the front porch. "Hey," she said, smiling. She had her hair swept back in a ponytail, and there was the faintest hint of rouge on her cheekbones. As I came out onto the porch, I caught the scent of her perfume—honeysuckle and warm bathwater. There was a car idling in the street, Rachel's mother behind the wheel. "I wanted to come see you."

"I'm glad you did. I haven't seen anyone. Well, Mr. Mattingly came by yesterday."

"You haven't seen your friends?" she said. "The Goon Squad?"

"No. I guess they're just . . ." I shrugged. "Busy, I guess."

"I'm sure they'll come around."

"We're gonna move," I blurted out.

"Oh. Where?"

"I don't know. We've got family in New York."

"That's far."

"Yeah," I said.

"Listen," she said. "I just wanted you to know that I was thinking of you. I'm sure this is really hard. That's all."

"That's enough," I said.

"I wish you weren't moving."

"Me, too," I said.

Rachel's mother honked the horn.

Rachel glanced at the car, then back at me. "She didn't want me coming here."

"I understand."

"It's not that. She didn't want me bothering you." She smiled softly, her cheeks dimpling. "But I wanted to."

"Thanks, Rachel." My heart was racing. "If I send you my address in New York, will you send me more poems?"

A brief sadness rippled across her otherwise happy face. Her eyes grew glassy. "Only if you send me stories."

"Deal."

Mrs. Lowrey honked the horn again.

"I gotta go," Rachel said, backing down the porch.

"Wait." When she paused, I said, "One, two, three, four, I declare a Kiss War," and I leaned in and kissed her gently on the lips. Her fingers found mine and she held my hand. When I finally pulled away, I could see my heartbroken reflection swimming in her eyes.

"Good-bye, Angie," she said and left.

CHAPTER THIRTY-SIX
THE WORLD BENEATH THE WORLD

My brother's second funeral was held on August 22 after the US Army and the FBI finally surrendered his body to us. It was a private ceremony held far from Harting Farms. Time, date, and location were kept out of the newspapers. Aside from the police officer who drove us there in a shiny black car, no one else attended, which was exactly how it had to be. Charles's body was interred in an unmarked plot far from the other graves. The day was bright and hot, and I perspired in my black suit and tie. It was a wool suit, the only one I owned.

The police officer who chauffeured us was the one who had been following me around town for the past several months. As we walked back to the car after the graveside service, he was standing beside it in full uniform, smoking a cigarette. When my grandparents approached, he opened the door for them. He caught my gaze lingering on him and nodded.

It had been my intention to mention this to my father once we arrived home, but as the policeman pulled into our driveway, I saw three familiar shapes sitting on the woodpile in the backyard. I opened the door before the car came to a complete stop, then jumped out and ran around the house.

Peter's smile was as bright as his shock of red hair, his eyes greener than I had remembered. Michael's hair was perfectly combed, and he had on a pair of Blues Brothers sunglasses. Scott had his Orioles cap on backward and was shuffling a deck of Uno cards. Leaning against the woodpile was the samurai sword.

"Will you look at this guy, all dressed up?" Michael said, peering at me over his sunglasses. "You look like a used car salesman."

"Hey," I said. I wanted to ask them where they'd been and what had kept them away for so long—I wanted to ask them a million things—but I found it impossible to organize even a single thought.

"We've been sittin' out here for over an hour," Scott said, still shuffling the cards. "We gonna play some Uno or what?"

"Or what," Peter, Michael, and I responded in unison.

Then we all broke up, laughing.

We sat on the porch and played game after game of Uno. At one point, my grandmother brought us bologna sandwiches and Cokes, and we took a break while we ate and listened to the sounds of summer winding down. When Peter started in with his elephant jokes, we all groaned and Michael threw a pinecone at him, but inside I couldn't have been more elated.

"Did you hear about Eric Falconette?" Scott said as he dealt a new hand.

I shook my head.

"Killed in a car crash in Baltimore. It was on the news. Denny Sallis was with him but he survived."

"Was Keener with them?" I thought of his truck parked on Haven.

"News didn't say anything about Keener," Scott said.

We played another round of Uno, and I thought I wouldn't ask them the question that was most on my mind. Ultimately, though, I was bested by curiosity. "What took you guys so long to come by?"

They glanced at one another, and Scott slowed down in his dealing of the cards.

When they offered no response, I provided one for them. "Did your parents not want you to come over?" I thought of Rachel and how she said her mother hadn't wanted her to bother my family and me.

"Well, no," Peter said evenly. "Not exactly."

"Then what was it?"

"We thought you might be mad at us," Michael said.

"Me? Why would I be mad at you guys?"

"Because we went along with it," Scott said.

"Because what happened in that old building would've never happened if we didn't let you go in there," Peter said.

"We thought you might blame us," Michael finished.

"I don't blame you guys at all," I said, finding myself relieved. "In fact, I thought you guys were mad at *me*."

Scott made a face. "Why would we be mad at you?"

I tried to answer but my throat had tightened up.

"Always making up stories," Michael commented. "Always creating drama."

"Yeah, Mazzone," Peter said, "you've got some imagination."

We played cards until dusk when Scott had to head home. Before leaving, he nodded toward the samurai sword I'd leaned against one of the wicker chairs. "That is a sweet fucking sword."

The three of us remained on the porch, watching the sun sink below the line of trees.

Michael announced that he might try to run for class president again this year. "I've done my time in summer school and have been on the other side of the tracks. I think that would really appeal to the working class."

Peter and I called him names, which only egged him on.

When my grandmother poked her head out onto the porch and told Michael that his mother had called and wanted him home, he saluted her, then gave me a big sloppy kiss on the cheek.

"Madonna mi," exclaimed my grandmother, who quickly withdrew into the house.

"Great to have you back, you big toolbox," Michael said to me as he hopped off the porch.

"Get bent, butt cheese," I tossed back at him.

Michael threw both middle fingers in the air. Running around the side of the house toward the street, he shouted at the top of his lungs, "Gorbachev's wife!"

Once Peter and I stopped giggling like a couple of schoolgirls, Peter said, "Did you hear Adrian's coming home from the hospital tomorrow?"

"That's great."

"We're gonna have to get that turd a new backpack. No more superheroes and shit. It's embarrassing."

I smiled and looked down at my hands.

"What's wrong?" Peter said.

"I'm moving."

"Moving where?"

"Away. Me and my family. We can't stay here."

Peter was silent for a moment. Then he said, "No. That's stupid. Who said you have to move? You didn't do anything."

"We still can't stay here. It's too much."

"But . . . when?"

"I don't know. Soon, I guess."

"Where are you going?"

"Maybe New York."

"That's like a million miles away!"

I stared down at my hands. A single teardrop fell on my left thumb.

"So this was our last summer hanging out? No way. I don't believe it. You're joshing me, right?"

I shook my head.

"Come on, Angie. Say you're only joking, okay? Just say it."

"I'm not joking."

"But we promised each other that when we left, we'd do it together."

"I guess that was a silly promise to make, huh?"

Peter hung his head as he sat there on the porch steps beside me.

I knew then that everything that had happened over the past year would not have been possible without him and without the others, too. And not just what happened at the end but all the stuff that led up to it. The good stuff. The stuff that made us stronger, better friends. The stuff that mattered most.

"Do me a favor and look after the guys," I said after a time. "Make sure Scott doesn't cut his thumbs off with that stupid butterfly knife. And make sure Michael actually graduates."

Peter laughed. There were tears in his eyes.

"And look out for Adrian," I said. "Don't forget about him when school starts."

"No way, man. He's one of us now. He always will be. Just like you are. We're brothers, man. The five of us."

"Brothers," I said, liking the way that sounded.

Grinning, he threw an arm around my shoulder, and we sat like that until it was time for him to go home.

That evening, I stood outside my father's bedroom while he reclined on his bed, staring blankly at the ceiling. When he sensed my presence, he turned and looked at me.

"That cop who drove us to the cemetery today," I said. "He's been following me around town the past few months."

Something akin to a sad smile overtook my father's features. He sat up on the bed, swinging his legs over the side. "He mentioned to me that you had finally noticed."

"You knew?"

"I asked him to keep an eye on you."

"Because you didn't trust me? Because you wanted to know what I was up to?"

"No," he said. "To make sure you were safe."

When I didn't respond, he asked me if I was okay.

"I guess so," I said, though I was unsure exactly how I felt. "I'm gonna go for a walk."

"Don't be too late," he said, reclining back on the bed.

What difference does it make now? I wondered.

While having a smoke, I walked down to the end of Worth Street where the pavement turned to crushed gravel before dead-ending into a fan of overgrown shrubs, wildflowers, and the fences that surrounded the quarry. I thought about Nathan Keener's truck, which was still parked at the curb on Haven Street. It hadn't been moved in weeks.

As I approached the fence, I found what I had expected—the padlock chaining the gates had been popped. The chain lay in a rusted coil in the gravel, the sprung lock beside it like some medieval torture device. I eased one of the gates open just wide enough to permit access and crept inside.

The quarry was no larger than a crater left behind after the demolition of a large house. When we played down here as children, Charles and I used to pretend it was the sarlacc pit from *Return of the Jedi*. I crossed over to the edge and peered down at the sludgy brown soup at the bottom of the pit. There were crevices in the stone walls, and some of them were big enough to hide in.

Or to hide someone else.

Carefully, I crawled down into the pit where a shelf of limestone extended over the drop. I peeked into the larger gaps in the rock, but the darkness made it impossible to see anything inside. I thought of the holes in the cliff face at the ass end of Harting Farms. How far did they go? Were there tunnels just below the surface of the earth crisscrossing every inch of the city?

There was nothing down here. Nothing I could see, anyway.

I climbed out of the pit, my sneakers kicking up dry white clouds of dust and rolling loose pebbles down into the pool of mud at the bottom. Crickets trilled and the sky was afire with countless stars. As I tramped through the bushes and overgrown grass, something misshapen and unnatural poking up from a patch of kudzu caught my eye.

I went to it, bent down, prodded it. It rocked.

It was a boot. Someone's Doc Marten. Scuffed clasps and worn leather. I had stared at these boots on Mischief Night as Nathan Keener approached me while his friends held my arms.

It was Keener's boot.

(If anyone ever hurt you or tried to hurt you, I would snap their neck. I would bury their corpse in the quarry at the end of our block. I would leave them there for the rats.)

I stood and surveyed the quarry and the dense woods that surrounded it. It had become fully dark in just a matter of seconds, making it difficult to see anything beyond the mere suggestion of things. All around me, a chorus of insects lit up the night.

Sucking one last time on my cigarette, I chucked the fading ember down into the quarry. It sizzled when it hit the water.

Back at the house, I pulled my bike out from the patch of ivy and wheeled it up the Gardiners' driveway. I was propping it on the kickstand on the front porch when the door opened. Startled, I looked up to see Doreen Gardiner luminescing out of the darkness.

"Hello," I said quietly.

She stood framed in the doorway, her face a colorless mask. She glanced at the bike. "What's this?" Her voice was just barely audible.

"My bike. I'm leaving it for Adrian."

"Won't you need it?"

"I'm sixteen. I'll be getting my license soon. Besides, he's gonna need it if he keeps hanging around with the guys."

"He had a bike back home, you know," she said.

I offered her a wan smile but said nothing.

"He's never had lots of friends. Maybe that's my fault. I mother him too much." She stepped out onto the porch. She wore nothing but a man's thin white T-shirt and longish shorts. "Thank you for being there for him."

"Sure," I said.

"You know why he doesn't have a bike here?" she asked.

"Yes." My voice shook.

"He told you about what his dad did," she said, and this time it wasn't a question.

"Yes," I answered nonetheless.

She fingered the horrid scar on her neck. "He did this, too. With a knife from the kitchen. But it didn't kill me. If it had, we would have all been dead."

She took another step closer to me. I was powerless to move.

"I found them in the car together, the engine running and the garage door shut. He'd carried Adrian straight out of bed and strapped him in the backseat. Then he got behind the wheel and turned the car on, reclined the seat, and closed his eyes," she said with the detachment of someone reciting a poem from memory. "I was able to get Adrian out in time. It was very lucky I found them."

One of her hands came up, and before I could flinch away, she caressed the side of my face. Her hand was cold but not ungentle. That was when I noticed tears in her eyes.

"He's very lucky to have a friend like you," she said. "Please don't forget him."

Mounting the rear porch steps at the house, I shook a cigarette from the cellophane, then froze as movement off to my right caught my attention. I jerked around to find my father's silhouette slouched in one of the wicker chairs.

"Oh." I dropped my arms in an effort to hide the cigarettes.

My father leaned forward, and the moonlight played across the left side of his face. I was shocked by how ancient he looked. "Got an extra one for me?"

"Uh, sure." I handed him the cigarette, then took out another one for myself. I'd never smoked in front of my father before. When I brought the lighter to the tip of my cigarette, it was all I could do to keep the flame steady. Then I handed the lighter to him.

He lit his cigarette and eased back in the chair with a satisfied grunt. He gestured toward the empty chair beside him. "Have a seat."

I sat.

"You doing okay?"

"I guess."

We sat there smoking together in silence for a long time. After a while, I felt my hands shake and my face grow hot.

"I spoke with a fella from the Army this evening," he said. "They still don't have a lot of information, and there are questions I know we'll never have answered, but he told me what they know so far. At least it's something."

I looked at him. The tiny red ember of his cigarette bobbed as he spoke.

"We were told Charles was killed when his unit attacked Iraq in February of '91. Turns out many soldiers were killed, and very few bodies were ever recovered. Others were injured and taken to hospitals. A soldier named Frank Belknap was one of the injured. He spent a lot of time in the hospital before being discharged and sent back to the States. Police found Belknap's dog tags and discharge papers in the Patapsco Institute, along with some of Charles's stuff. Best they can figure, Belknap was killed and Charles stole his identity.

"Army doctors said the soldier they thought was Belknap—the soldier who was really Charles—suffered from severe post-traumatic stress disorder."

My father sighed heavily. "Charles could have been living in that building in the woods ever since he came back."

"Why didn't he come home? Why did he lie about who he was in the first place?"

Even in the poor light, I could see my father grimace. "There're things about your brother you don't know. Things I hope you never learn, though maybe all that's pointless now. He didn't want to join the military. I didn't give him a choice. He had a temper. He was getting into trouble and needed to be reined in. He . . . he did a bad thing to a girl in Baltimore—an accident, I guess, but due to his own carelessness, though now I'm not so sure what it was exactly. He had to straighten up. He had . . ." His voice broke.

"I was his father. I did what I thought was best at the time. And he was your brother and he loved you," he said, quickly regaining his composure. "You didn't need to worry about the things I worried about. And you don't need to change your opinion of him. Do you understand?"

And then I heard Adrian speak up in my head: *What do you call it when you dream about something that's gonna happen?* Could there be an inverse to a prophetic dream? A dream that clued you in on the secrets of the past instead of the future, secrets that didn't belong to you and you had no right knowing?

I thought about my own recurring nightmare, being chased through the woods by an unseen beast while I ran alongside my grandfather who was not my grandfather, my father who was not my father. I realized why the soldier looked like a younger version of my grandfather and father: he had been Charles. And Charles had ushered me through the rain forest and into the village where he told me to enter the hut. Inside, I had joined the Piper, who had also been Charles, only the dark and hidden side of him. *I become you and you become me and us become us and we become we.*

He was my brother, but he had been something else, too. A man hidden within a man.

Again, Adrian's ghostly voice sang out to me: *Turns out it's a whole world under there—a world beneath a world and within a world but also somehow occupying the same space as the real world.*

"Do you hate me for it?" I said at last.

My father stared at me.

"I wouldn't have done it if I knew it was him." It was like a confession pouring out of me.

"Angelo," he said, leaning toward me, "I could never hate you. I'm proud of you. And what happened . . . what you did . . . it wasn't your brother in there with you that night. That was someone who needed to be stopped. You were man enough to do it."

Tears spilled down my face. My leg bounced uncontrollably.

"That story you had on your desk?" he said, changing the subject and shaking me back to reality. "It's very good."

"You read it?"

"After your teacher left that afternoon, I wanted to know what I'd been missing." He patted my knee and I saw that his hand shook. "You've got a good talent. I think that Mattingly fella was right about moving you to advanced English."

It won't be here, I thought morosely. *It won't be at Stanton School. Not anymore. Because we're leaving.*

"AP English is full of nerds and dweebs," I said.

"So maybe you'll teach them nerds and dweebs a thing or two about writing stories," he said.

"Yeah, maybe," I said . . . then my entire body began to tremble. I couldn't breathe. Tears spilled from my eyes, and the world lost its clarity.

"Oh, Angie. Oh, sweetheart." He came toward me just as I fell toward him, and he held me in arms that felt like great bands of steel. He rubbed my back, kissed the top of my head, and let me get it all out. Soon he was crying right along with me. And once we'd finished, we held on to each other a little bit longer.

EPILOGUE
THE LAST OF THE VANISHING CHILDREN
(SEPTEMBER 1994)

We left Harting Farms on a Sunday in September, just as the bells of St. Nonnatus tolled noon. My grandparents had left for New York days earlier, so it was just my father and me. Astride their bikes, my friends watched from the street as I climbed into the car and slammed the door. When my dad pulled out of the driveway and headed up Worth Street, they followed us.

Michael raced along on his Mongoose, sunlight gleaming off his newly polished army helmet. He had on his Blues Brothers sunglasses and was pedaling just about as fast as I had ever seen him.

Peter lifted himself off the seat of his bike, his red hair whipping back from his forehead in the wind, his green eyes blazing. He had his headphones down around his neck, and I knew he was blasting one of his mix tapes. On his face was a dazzling smile.

Scott came right up the center, his long legs pumping effortlessly, his Orioles cap turned backward. He wore a pair of black cargo shorts and his Oh Shit Shark Shirt despite the chill in the air.

Doing a fine job keeping pace, Adrian rode along with them on my bike, seemingly unsteady at first but slowly gaining confidence. Dangling from a length of shoelace around his neck was a small heart-shaped locket.

When we reached McKinsey, my dad glanced up and saw them all in the rearview mirror. He laughed, then reached over and rubbed the back of my head. I turned around in the passenger seat, watching them through the back window, my eyes brimming with tears. My dad slowed as we crossed the highway so my friends could keep up.

But they couldn't keep up forever.

As the distance between us became greater and greater, I leaned out of the window and waved at them with both hands. Tears streamed from my eyes.

They waved back at me, and one of them—I believe it was Michael—shouted my name.

And that was how I chose to remember them, with the sunlight shimmering off Michael's army helmet, with Scott fanning his Orioles cap high above his head, with Peter's hair a fiery red beneath the noonday sun, and with Adrian waving at me almost timidly as the distance between us grew. I hung on to them for as long as I could until they were nothing more than ghosts against the backdrop of December Park.

ACKNOWLEDGMENTS

Any writer worth their salt has inside them at least one good book about their childhood. This one is mine. Thanks to D.G., D.S., S.S., J.T., and C.S. for a great childhood and a lifetime of great memories.

Thanks to my gracious and dedicated editor, Lorie, and the staff at Medallion Press. Thanks to my family and friends for putting up with me during the course of writing this book; I know what a chore that can be. And thanks to my wife and daughter, who give me new memories on top of all the old great ones.

My grandfather passed away during the writing of this book. I loved him very much, which made the sections about my protagonist's grandfather particularly difficult to write. Yet I felt my grandpa's hand on my shoulder guiding me through to the end, much as he guided me in real life, and his spirit made it possible to complete this work.

—RM
9/6/2013
Arnold, MD

ABOUT THE AUTHOR

Ronald Malfi is an award-winning author of horror novels, mysteries, and thrillers. Known for his haunting literary style and memorable characters, he is the recipient of two Independent Publisher Book Awards, the Beverly Hills Book Award, the Vincent Preis International Horror Award, and the IBPA Benjamin Franklin Award, as well as a nominee for the Bram Stoker Award. Malfi was born in Brooklyn, New York, in 1977, and eventually relocated to the Chesapeake Bay area, where he currently resides with his wife and two daughters.

RONALD MALFI

FROM OPEN ROAD MEDIA

OPEN ROAD

INTEGRATED MEDIA

OPEN ROAD

INTEGRATED MEDIA

Printed in the USA
CPSIA information can be obtained
at www.ICGtesting.com
LVHW090941181123
764187LV00001B/1